MADE TO ORDER

A Naughty In Pendleton Story

BRIGHAM VAUGHN

Two Peninsulas Press

Editing by Rebecca Fairfax

Formatting by Brigham Vaughn

Cover design by Brigham Vaughn

Cover Images:

© NataKor/Shutterstock

© ArtOfPhotos/Shutterstock

Printed in the United States of America

First Printing 2021

AUTHOR'S NOTE

I have been wanting to write Donovan and Tyler's story since they appeared in *Three Shots*. I adored their antagonistic encounters and knew there was a great story lurking there.

Thank you to Helena Stone, DJ Jamison, and Allison Hickman for your excellent beta feedback. I appreciate you all so much. Thank you also to Rebecca for her fantastic edits, and Rebecca, Melissa, and Julie for their amazing proofreading. I couldn't do this without all of you!

Although I always strive to tell realistic and accurate stories to the best of my ability, BDSM is both complicated and dangerous and this is a fictional portrayal of the dynamic. If you are interested in exploring kink, do your research and reach out to knowledgeable and trusted people with experience before diving in. This is not meant to be a How To.

Thank you to DJ Jamison for coming up with the brilliant title (seriously don't know what I'd do without you), and all of WBs for the endless brainstorming and feedback. You're the best!

AUTHOR'S NOTE

As always, a big thank you to all of you readers who make this possible. I couldn't do it without you either!

I have a lot of new and exciting plans in the works after this, so if you'd liked to keep up with them, please sign up for my newsletter or join my reader group.

Happy Reading!

ONE

"Have you found any new men to tie up lately, honey?"

Donovan Ryan rubbed his forehead. "Grandma June, can we not discuss my love life? *Please.*" This was not the first time they'd had this discussion, nor would it be the last, he suspected. June Frazier was the sweetest, loveliest human being on the planet. But she had no filter whatsoever.

"I just worry about you." She took a seat at the table across from him in her sunny yellow kitchen, a gentle frown wrinkling her skin.

"You're worried your grandson isn't getting kinky enough?"

She shrugged, the bangles on her arms clanking musically. "It's nothing to be ashamed of. It's a perfectly normal part of life and sexual expression. I just want you to be happy."

"I know that. And appreciate that you've always been so supportive. But do we have to *talk* about it?"

"Pffft. Your grandfather and I—"

"And you can stop right there," Donovan said with a chagrined smile. "I am thrilled and delighted that you and Grandpa had an amazing sex life together, but I do not need to know the details."

"Fine. But my question still stands. Have you met anyone?"

"I haven't." He nibbled on a lemon shortbread, enjoying the sweet-tart hint of sugary zest in the midst of all the buttery richness. "I work all the time."

"I know you do." Her frown deepened. "I don't like that. You should get out more."

These days, Donovan's grandmother had a much more active social life than he did. She was the one out with her friends most days of the week. Despite her age of seventy-eight, she was spry and mentally sharp. She still drove, and so far, he hadn't seen any issues with her reflexes slowing, thanks to the yoga and Zumba classes she attended at the studio downtown. He was convinced that one of these days, he'd have the wrestle the car keys out of her hand. She'd probably be 103 before it happened, but for now, she was healthy, active, and a social butterfly.

"You know I love the restaurant," he protested.

"Yes." She smiled proudly at him. "And I couldn't be more pleased you're executive chef at the Hawk Point Tavern now. Not to cast aspersions on Frank, but the man only knew one technique: frying."

"They only had the bar side open then and he was a fry cook. He did his best."

The owner of the tavern, Rachael Bradford, had inherited the business from her father, David. Apparently, at the time of David's death, it had been a nice little bar. David's dreams to expand from bar food into a full sit-down restaurant had gone unfulfilled until a few years ago, when Donovan came on board.

Frank had been happy to retire, and together, Donovan and Rachael had renovated the previously vacant half of the building and opened an adjoining restaurant. David Bradford hadn't lived to see his own dreams become a reality, but Donovan was glad he'd been able to help Rachael fulfill them for her father.

Since they opened, the restaurant had quickly flourished into an upmarket place serving a seasonal menu of new-American cuisine in downtown Pendleton Bay.

Donovan had grown up in the nearby city of Fort Benton, Michigan but he'd spent most summers in Pendleton, staying with his grandparents while his parents went off to work. He hadn't minded.

Donovan had loved to run along the beach of the bay, enjoying the cool waters of Lake Michigan and collecting the shells that washed ashore. He'd loved baking with Grandma June and going fishing with Grandpa Harold.

He remembered the sizzle of butter in a pan and the sharp scent of lemon and fresh herbs, along with the aroma of roasting freshly caught rainbow trout. His grandparents' kitchen was where he'd discovered his love of cooking and they had both encouraged him to pursue a career in it, even when it meant defying his parents.

"I still appreciate you helping me get to this point," he said. He reached out and took his grandma's hand. She squeezed it, her blue eyes twinkling brightly behind her hot pink glasses.

It wasn't that Kate and Phillip Ryan were unsympathetic to the idea of their son chasing his dream of becoming a chef. They'd just worried about him. The long hours. The low pay. The career that was worlds away from their day-to-day lives as defense attorneys.

They'd struggled to understand why anyone would be willing to work under the conditions of a restaurant kitchen. They'd encouraged him to find something more stable. To go to a university instead of culinary school. It hadn't been a dramatic thing, no threats to cut him out of the will or anything like that, just a pervasive sense of concern and disappointment.

Which was also difficult. Donovan had wanted to make them proud. They'd come around eventually, particularly when he'd been hired as the sous chef at Plated, an upscale place in Fort Benton. And they certainly were proud of him now, as part owner and executive chef of the Hawk Point Tavern. But it was his grandparents who had been his staunch allies from the get-go, and Donovan would always be grateful.

June smiled at him. "Of course. You know I support you no matter what. Which is why I worry you work too hard. It's all well and good for you to love your job, but if you can't have a social life …"

Donovan groaned. "I know, I know." But he spent six days a week in the kitchen. Sunday evenings and Mondays were really his only time off. And even then, it wasn't unusual for him to stay late or come in when he was supposed to be home relaxing. The arguments against his career had been valid but Donovan had never been able to imagine doing anything else. His worst day as a chef was better than any he could ever hope to have in an office. He came alive in the sizzle and heat. In the chaos, he found peace.

"It's not like I have time to go out and meet people. And my, uh, *tastes* do limit my options," Donovan admitted.

His grandma had found out he was kinky in the most awkward fashion imaginable. Well, maybe not the *most* awkward fashion. He'd been fully dressed at the time, at least.

"Happy twenty-eighth birthday," Grandpa Harold had said, giving Donovan a hug. "Thanks again for inviting us."

Donovan had smiled warmly at his grandfather. "Of course! I wanted everyone who mattered to me to be here." His friends and family mingled in the apartment, chatting and laughing over the food he'd made, and a swell of happiness went through him. They teased him about catering his own party, but cooking was his way of letting them know he loved them. That he appreciated them in his life.

"We should probably get going. It'll be dark soon." Harold looked around. "Where has the love of my life gone off to this time?"

"I'll go find her," Donovan said, patting his grandfather on the back. Not that his grandmother could have gone very far in his condo, but she had a tendency to wander off to read the books on his shelves or poke around in his kitchen. He slipped out of the living room where everyone else was gathered, brushing his fingers against Jude Maddox's as he passed him.

His boyfriend turned to him with a smile, grabbing his hand and squeezing briefly before letting Donovan continue. He peeked into the dining room, then the guest room to find them empty, before discovering his grandmother standing in the bedroom he and Jude shared.

She had a thoughtful expression on her face as she stared at the wood and leather trunk at the foot of the bed.

"Is that a Joseph Lynch piece?"

Donovan's eyes widened. "Yes. How do you know his work?"

"Well, he sells it at the farmers market and the craft fairs around the area. He's quite well known."

Right. Joe made wooden furniture and accessories that weren't kinky. Donovan had a few of his olive wood cutting boards, spoons, and spatulas in his kitchen, but in certain circles, Joe was better known for his gorgeous paddles and spanking benches.

Or, in this case, furniture that was kinky and vanilla. A spanking bench/storage trunk that looked perfectly tame. The straps along the sides looked decorative instead of useful for restraint.

She turned and smiled at him. "I haven't seen this design before but he does brilliant work. So multifunctional."

"Yes, the storage and seating is nice."

She gave him an unamused look over her turquoise glasses. "Sweetheart, I may be old but I'm not enfeebled. I know what these are used for."

"Spare pillow storage?" he said weakly.

"Bondage."

"How do you—" He gaped at her for a moment, then shook his head. "No, scratch that. I don't want to know."

She chuckled. "Your generation thinks you invented being kinky. BDSM practices have been recorded as far back as early Mesopotamia. That's 4000 BCE. This is nothing new. There's just more information out about it."

Donovan pinched the bridge of his nose. "I know you're a former sex-ed teacher, but this is not something I want to talk about with you."

She shrugged, amused. "You always were too much like your mother."

Which meant tightly wound. Kate Frazier-Ryan was a fiery redhead with a low tolerance for bullshit—just like Donovan—but significantly less free-spirited than her mother.

"Anyway, Grandpa wants to head out. I came to fetch you."

"Yes. He does hate driving late at night now." She leaned in and gave him a kiss on the cheek. "I won't embarrass you further. But let me just say, this isn't the first time I suspected you were kinky. You think those pamphlets and books got left out for no reason?"

Donovan thought of the ones he'd surreptitiously snuck into the guest bedroom to read under the cover of darkness as a teenager, wanting to understand why he felt a pull to the things he fantasized about. His head had spun with information as he read about consent and safety, all informative and non-judgmental. It had helped guide him toward being an ethical Dom and sadist, while most people in his shoes were fumbling their way through it with a wing and a prayer. He was grateful. He'd just had no idea her providing it was intentional.

"I thought they were for school," he said weakly.

"You think Pendleton High would have let me teach high schoolers about BDSM? No. I had to fight to get as much info about AIDS and contraception into my lesson plans as I did. I battled it out with the school board more times than I could count. No, my dear, I left those out for you."

Donovan couldn't fathom what had made his grandmother realize that about him, before he'd really been sure of it himself. It had gone a long, long way toward making sure he got some good, healthy information instead of whatever he gleaned from porn. But it was still vaguely horrifying to realize.

Donovan cupped his grandmother's face. "I love you for that. But please, let's never, ever talk about this again."

Now, ten years later, she smiled at him from across the kitchen table. Clearly telling her that hadn't worked. He suspected it never would.

"No munches around?" She took a sip of her coffee.

"The closest is in Fort Benton. And on a night I have to work."

"There are apps, right?"

Jesus, she even knows about kink apps. Which was even more alarming when he thought about the fact that she'd been widowed almost a year now. She'd loved his grandfather to pieces, but Donovan also knew she was a vibrant, active woman and … No, Donovan was *not* going to let his brain go there.

"There are," he admitted. "Not as big a selection of people on the apps here as there was in Fort Benton. Smaller town, smaller dating pool."

She let out a little sigh. "I was so sorry to hear about you and Jude." She reached out her hand, resting it on his, her fingernails a vibrant shade of pink that matched her glasses.

"Me too," he said with a sigh. "But we wanted different things."

She looked at him shrewdly. "In the relationship or in the bedroom? Or were those two things intertwined for you two?"

"They were intertwined," he admitted. "We weren't meeting each other's needs anymore. And it got ugly."

She frowned. "I am so sorry. He seemed like a good man."

A lump rose in Donovan's throat. "He is. I loved him a lot. But …"

They'd just no longer worked. Jude's switchiness and desire for an open relationship chafed at Donovan's dominance and desire for monogamy. And after a while, working together at the restaurant and trying to navigate an increasingly fraught romantic relationship had spilled out into an ugly argument over a rack of lamb.

Donovan had quit his job and ended his decade-long relationship on the same night.

So ugly. So very, very ugly.

He still cringed thinking about it. His bridges in Fort Benton had been burned, accelerated by a jilted ex with an axe to grind and an executive chef suddenly short-staffed.

Donovan Ryan was persona non-grata in Fort Benton these days.

So, he'd retreated to Pendleton Bay, lured in by the soft comforts of his grandmother's understanding and the promise of a new direction for his career. It had been a good change, if a little lonely.

He covered his grandma's hand, trapping her soft fingers between his. "I'll find someone when the time is right," he said.

She smiled at him, and it was like the sun coming out from behind the clouds, or the feel of cutting into a perfectly poached egg yolk. "I know you will, sweetheart."

TWO

“Hey there, handsome.” A blonde in a low-cut dress leaned over the bar, resting her arms on its wooden surface. “Any chance you could make me a strawberry daiquiri?” She batted her lashes.

“Sure thing.” Tyler Hewitt smiled tightly.

“And make sure I can taste the alcohol in it! I’ve had a week. My girls and I are all out tonight. Looking to let loose, you know?”

Right, Tyler could read between those lines. *I want to get drunk and pick up a guy.* Which, hey, he got it. He’d done similar things on a night out. He just no longer picked up women where he worked. After one hookup had started stalking him here, he’d called it quits. She’d been nice and all at first, but he’d made it clear from the beginning he wasn’t looking for a relationship and she’d definitely crossed the line.

“It’ll be the best damn daiquiri you’ve ever had,” he promised.

Which was probably true. He was good at what he did, and the tavern made them from scratch rather than the bottled mix. That shit was more corn syrup than strawberry purée so it was icky sweet, and the owner, Rachael, had always prided herself on running a place that offered more than the average bar. Tyler did too.

He fucking hated making daquiris from scratch though.

Pulling out the blender for the sticky drink was a pain in the ass, plus making them took so much longer than mixing a martini or an old fashioned. He'd end up with sticky strawberry all over his hands and the bar top. Worst of all, once one person ordered it, at least half a dozen more customers would see it and want it too.

Tension gathered in his shoulders as he realized it was going to be one of *those* nights. Where he'd go home feeling annoyed and exhausted.

He loved his job as bar manager here at the Hawk Point Tavern, he really did, but sometimes …

People got on his last damn nerve.

His phone buzzed in his pocket, but he ignored it, reaching for the rum and simple syrup instead. There was a lineup staring him down with daggers in their eyes and he wasn't about to piss off the people stuffing tips in the tip jar.

Two hours later, Tyler had made at least a dozen daiquiris and the demand showed no sign of slowing down. And the damn freezer was empty of strawberries now. He let Lacey Martin, one of their newer hires, know he was stepping away. Thankfully, she was new to the tavern, not to bartending.

He ducked out from behind the bar and strode down the service hallway to the kitchen.

Donovan Ryan, the executive chef and part owner of the restaurant side of the tavern, looked up as Tyler stepped into his domain. He arched a reddish-blond eyebrow, large knife poised in midair. "Do you need something?" His tone was cool.

Hello to you too, Tyler thought, but the lack of warmth wasn't exactly unusual for the chef. He was … abrupt. Tyler didn't have time to make small talk anyway.

"Yeah, strawberries, if you've got any. We've had a run on daiquiris and we're out in the bar freezer."

"The Wholesome Root delivery won't be here until Thursday. You should know that."

"I do know that," Tyler snapped. "I thought maybe you had some in the freezer. I don't need fresh. Frozen is better anyway, then I don't have to add ice and water it down."

Donovan narrowed his blue eyes at Tyler. "I might. I sometimes keep it on hand for purée." He wiped his hands on a towel. "I take any that are starting to go slightly soft and freeze them, so we don't have to toss them. They're perfectly good, just not for salads or garnish. Let me look."

Tyler had made the mistake of looking in the freezer himself one time. That had *not* gone over well. The kitchen was definitely Donovan's kingdom, and no one fucked with that. Admittedly, Tyler would be annoyed if Donovan grabbed a bunch of limes from behind his bar without telling him, so he understood. He just didn't understand why the guy had to be so damn unpleasant about it.

Tyler followed the tall red-haired chef into the walk-in freezer, shivering as the icy air hit his bare arms.

After a quick scan of the freezer contents, Donovan handed over a large bag of fruit with a glare. "Here. But you need to fill out—"

"The log. Yeah, I'll do it tonight after I count the drawer and tally receipts."

The inventory log let the tavern owner, Rachael Bradford, know when something from the kitchen side of the business got used at the bar or vice versa. It was handy as hell to borrow items from the other side of the business, because the last thing they wanted was to run out of something when they were in the thick of a busy evening. But Donovan made what should have been a simple task monumentally annoying.

The expansion of the Hawk Point Tavern was definitely a good thing. They'd seen a huge increase in bar sales since the restaurant side opened. Tyler just wasn't so sure he was crazy about working with Chef Donovan.

He pushed open the door of the freezer, the heat of the kitchen welcome on his chilled skin.

"Better hope I don't need any strawberries for cheesecakes," Donovan called over the noise of sizzling pans and clanking dishes.

"I'll buy you some replacements at the farmers market," Tyler yelled back.

"You're welcome for saving your ass, by the way!"

"Thanks," Tyler muttered on his way out of the kitchen before realizing that was an asshole move on his part. He *should* have sincerely thanked the guy at least. Even if Donovan was a Grade A dick.

Thankfully, after two hours, several more trips to the kitchen to beg for strawberries, and what felt like seventy daiquiris, the line finally slowed.

Tyler sagged against the back counter with a sigh and glanced over at Lacey. "Gonna take my break now."

Lacey looked up from the drink she was shaking. "Oh, sure thing."

Tyler was hours overdue for a chance to step away, but the bar had been slammed all night. His staff had all gotten their breaks already, but he'd only stopped long enough to wolf down a dinner.

He dragged his phone out of his pocket as he walked down the hall and shouldered the exit door open.

The phone had buzzed several times tonight but there was no way he'd had time to check it with as insanely busy as they were. Besides, he liked to set a good example for the bartenders he managed and that meant no phones in sight of customers.

"Fuck." Tyler stared down at the screen. He'd missed three messages from Eddie Silva. His best friend. His ride-or-die buddy from the Army. That was never good. He'd had too many of these late-night phone calls recently. He could almost guarantee Eddie was drunk.

Tyler listened to the voicemail as he strolled to the outdoor employee break area and rested his butt against the edge of the tabletop.

"She left me, man." Eddie let out a noise like a sob had been strangled and died in his throat. "She left me. Said I was scaring her. Scaring the kids. I don't know what to do, man. She's everything. We've been together since we were fifteen, you know?"

Tyler pictured the photo Eddie had always carried with him of Andrea and, later, their babies. Tyler's heart ached. Eddie loved the shit out of his wife and kids. He was one of the guys who didn't use their R&R time to screw around. He spent it writing his family emails, letters, and Skyping when they could. He did everything he could to stay in contact with the people he loved. But when Tyler had left active duty and become a reservist, Eddie had reupped for another tour of duty.

Eddie had planned to be a lifer, a career military guy. He'd joined because he needed a stable job to support him and his family and what the fuck else could guys like them do?

Tyler's parents had been better off than Eddie's but he'd had no direction at the age of eighteen. He'd been okay at school but not great. And faced with the option of joining his father's plumbing business or enlisting in the Army, the military had seemed like the better choice.

But reality had shown him he'd have been better off choosing plumbing. He might have been elbows-deep in literal shit at times but at least he wouldn't have had to see his buddies either not make it home at all or come home like Eddie had.

Eddie's plan for career and advancement had been completely fucked by the unending months in the sand. By the shit he'd seen, the shit he'd done, by the fact that there were piss-poor safety nets. Nothing to help him when he struggled.

Oh, sure, Eddie had been honorably discharged on medical grounds because of a busted shoulder. Nothing tragic, just a repetitive stress injury aggravated by years of grueling physical exertion. But he'd been in a bad place mentally long before then. He'd just hidden it well.

It hadn't been easy for any of them to return to civilian life. Tyler had struggled for a while too, feeling out of step with the rest of the world. What had happened overseas had seemed sharp and real, whereas the "real world" had been foggy and hazy.

He'd still been enlisted of course, transitioning from active duty to being in the reserves but there had been a strange surreal feeling to being home. He'd sat at the dining room table, listening to his mom talk about the neighbors, how the girl Tyler had taken to prom had gotten married and had a baby, and been sure that at any moment, he'd jolt awake and find himself back in Iraq.

Tyler had been rudderless, distant from everyone. He'd missed the structure and discipline of military life. He missed having a purpose. It had been easier when he simply had to follow orders and do as he was told, content in the knowledge that someone else was in charge.

He'd been unable to reconnect with old friends, preferring the company of the guys from his platoon. It had been like he'd spoken a different language from the rest of the world and it had taken him far longer than he'd ever expected for that fish-out-of-water feeling to fade.

One afternoon, still waiting for word back from the Veterans Employment Center on leads for a civilian job, he'd wandered into the Hawk Point Tavern for a drink. He'd found Rachael Bradford, a friend since grade school, behind the bar, slinging drinks and looking frazzled. Between customers, she'd confessed she was in over her head, struggling to manage the bar with her parents gone and college courses drowning her in work.

Tyler had asked if he could step in. Not out of any real plan for his future or desire for a job as a bartender but a need to help a longtime friend out of a jam. The look of pure relief on Rachael's face, even after he told her he didn't know a damn thing about mixing drinks, had made him feel good. He'd felt useful for the first time since he'd been back in Pendleton.

She'd been willing to work around his reserve training schedule, just grateful for a reliable pair of hands to help bear some of the burden she carried. For a little while, he'd even wondered if something romantic might happen between them, but in the end, he'd found true friendship rather than love. And he'd been grateful.

It was Rachael's willingness to give him a chance, her faith in him, that had helped him find the first tether that tied him to the civilian world again.

But for some veterans, that anchor never appeared and for others, that wasn't always enough.

Tyler had always described that transition period as like being trapped in a thick plexiglass box. He could see the rest of the world, even interact with it, but he couldn't quite reach any of the people on the other side.

Eddie had seemed to struggle more than the rest of them after his discharge and the trouble was, no one had ever found a way to get Eddie out of the box he was in.

Neither Eddie's family nor any of his friends could quite reach him.

Tyler had done what he could but what Eddie really needed was best left to the professionals. The ones Eddie could never seem to get an appointment to see. Tyler had talked to Andrea about it a few times, worried Eddie was just blowing it off but no, she'd tearfully told him she'd tried, too. Called everyone she could, including blowing up the VA representative's phone, but no matter how much she'd tried to escalate it, they told her the same damn thing.

Eddie was on his own.

Oh, they didn't say it in so many words of course, but they talked about wait times and referrals and what it amounted to was that it only got escalated if you were a threat to yourself or others. And half the time, it was too damn late.

Unlike some of the guys Tyler and Eddie had served with, they hadn't come home hating the US military. Tyler had been proud to serve, though the people shaking his hand and calling him a hero always made him feel uncomfortable as hell.

But he'd come home sure of several things. There was no point in the military investing in billion-dollar weapons systems when the people who were supposed to run them were a fucking mess. Tyler wasn't naïve—there were always casualties in war—and he'd been more than willing to put his life on the line, but when over twelve percent of military vets came home with PTSD and nearly two dozen former soldiers killed themselves every day? Something was off.

Maybe not all of those could be prevented, but goddamn it. They needed to *do* something for these guys before it got that bad.

But they didn't. And those numbers weren't just facts and figures. Those *statistics* were Tyler's buddies. His best fucking friend. And now, Tyler got calls like this frequently. Eddie drunk off his ass and crying, reaching out for help Tyler didn't know how to give him.

Tyler's hand shook as he stared down at the screen, terrified that one day, he'd be too late. He'd fail. He'd lose Eddie too. They'd already lost Rafe Johnson and Charles French, or Frenchie, as they'd known him. They'd both died in the war but it was almost worse to imagine losing Eddie now.

Now, Tyler considered his options, his stomach clenching with worry. It was after midnight and the last thing he wanted to do was wake Andrea or the kids. Of course, from the sounds of it, they might not be living together anymore.

Tyler sent a text to Eddie first, just to be safe. ***Sorry I missed your call, man. I was behind the bar. You still up?***

He fired off another one to Andrea. ***I got a couple of calls from Eddie. Sounds like he's in rough shape. You okay?***

A response from her came in almost immediately. ***He is. I don't know what to do, Ty.***

Hope I didn't wake you up.

No. I couldn't sleep.

Eddie said you left??

Not forever. I'm at my mom's for a few days. I needed some space. What else was I supposed to do? I hate the kids seeing their dad like that. I love him, Ty, but he's in a bad spot.

I know. What can I do?

I don't know. Be there for him if you can. It's just exhausting.

I'll keep trying but I don't know what to do. I feel so fucking helpless.

Me too.

Well, if you need me to come visit and take the kids off your hands for an afternoon, let me know. I always enjoy playing Uncle Tyler.

I will.

Hope you can get some sleep. I'll check in soon. Love you guys.

Love you too. Have a good night.

Still nothing from Eddie. Which probably meant he was passed out. Tyler tried not to let the thoughts of what else could happened creep into his head.

The Silvas lived hours away in Grand Rapids so it wasn't like Tyler could swing by on his way home. Maybe he'd go up there and visit on his day off.

But his stomach churned with worry as he returned to the bar with a heavy sigh.

It had been a long-ass night and he still had hours to go.

"Got another number, huh?"

"Hmm?" Tyler looked up from the receipts he'd been sorting to see Donovan staring down at him.

The chef stepped toward him, smirking. God, his face drove Tyler *crazy*.

Donovan always looked smug. From the toes of his stupid black clogs to the top of his ridiculous red hair, he irritated Tyler. And Tyler's mood had not improved with the news that his friend's mental health was getting worse.

"The numbers you get every night." Donovan nudged a napkin with scrawled digits on it across the wooden surface of the bar. Tyler had found it in the tip jar and set it aside to toss in the trash later. He now regretted he hadn't done it immediately.

"It's not like I *ask* for them," Tyler pointed out. "Women just give them to me." Tonight, it had been the really pushy blonde. The dark-haired one with an amazing ass had scrawled hers on a receipt.

"Like you don't encourage that? The flirty little comments. The winking …"

"I don't—" Tyler forced himself to take a deep breath. "Look, yeah, it's part of the job, right? Tips are better if you're friendly and a little flirtatious. But I don't lead women on. I don't ask for their number. And I definitely don't call the ones they offer."

"Right."

"Why do you *care*, anyway?"

"I find it a bit … desperate."

Tyler crossed his arms over his chest and sat back. "Oh, like you never chat up the customers in the restaurant? You get called out there all the time."

"Because they want to compliment my *food,* not my face."

Tyler bit back a comment that maybe it was because he wasn't as good-looking as Tyler was, but that wasn't fair. Donovan was good-looking if you were into red-haired, freckled, bearded dudes. Which Tyler most certainly was not. "And you've never had someone slip *you* their number?" he said instead.

"Not often."

"Okay, whatever." Tyler waved it off. "I'm just saying, it's part of the biz. I don't encourage it and I don't take advantage of it. I don't know what you want from me, man."

"I *want* you to fill out the log." Donovan nudged a clipboard toward him.

"Seriously?"

"I don't want it to get forgotten."

"It's not gonna get forgotten," Tyler growled. "I have it right *here*. I just haven't gotten to it yet."

"I can wait." Donovan slid onto the stool next to his. "Give me a beer?"

Tyler glared at him. "Seriously?"

"IPA. Something with grapefruit. We'll call it even for all of the strawberries I gave you."

"Jesus Christ, you're a pain in my ass," Tyler grumbled. "Fucking Strawberry Police or something."

"I heard that."

"I meant for you to," he snapped. "Tap or bottle?"

"I'll trust your judgment."

Tyler stifled an eye roll and got up.

He fetched a bottle for Donovan and plunked it down on the bar in front of him. "There. I should charge you for it."

"I believe free drinks and food were part of the perks Rachael offered in her employment contracts."

"Yeah, well, drinks are at my discretion," he pointed out. "So don't push your luck, bud."

Donovan smirked. "So, what you're saying is, I need to stay in your good graces to get service here?"

"That's exactly what I'm saying."

"And to think I was so generous with the flat iron steak for staff dinner," Donovan said with an insincere smile. "Maybe I'm starting to regret that."

Tyler stifled an annoyed grunt. Damn it, the food tonight had been fucking amazing and they both knew it. Of course, all Donovan's meals were. The place wasn't super high-end fancy fine dining but the stuff that came out of Donovan's kitchen was *always* delicious.

Tonight, it had been a thin steak, perfectly grilled on the outside with a nice juicy pink center, and some kind of cherry sauce on top. With tons of roasted potatoes and vegetables.

They always got fed here if they wanted it. And it was the best damn food Tyler had ever put in his mouth. Considering how much he hated cooking, he knew he was spoiled getting to eat Donovan's food every day. When Frank had been running the kitchen and churning out bar snacks, it had been good. Tyler had been perfectly happy to chow down on burgers, fries, and appetizers, or whatever there was extra of. But being able to enjoy a *real* meal every night he worked—even if it was eaten in about ten minutes flat while standing up—was a luxury he couldn't squander.

"The sooner you fill out that log, the sooner you get rid of me," Donovan said with an infuriating smile on his face. He took a long sip of his beer, his throat working as he downed a good third of it.

"Thirsty much?" Tyler asked. He ignored the other comment.

"It's been a long night." A flicker of something crossed his face and for the first time, Tyler really looked at him.

Truth be told, he did look tired. His freckled face was paler than usual, and he was slumped on his stool like he didn't have the strength to keep himself upright.

Tyler knew the feeling. He reached for the log and filled it out without any further bitching. "That look okay?" He slid it across the wooden surface.

Donovan scanned it. "Looks right to me." He reached for the pen and signed his name elegantly, finishing with a flourish.

Show off.

Tyler scratched his own far messier signature next to it. "I'll make sure Rachael sees it. I'll tuck it in the inbox by her office door."

He expected Donovan to get up then, to head home, but he sat there, slowly sipping the rest of his beer. Even after he was done, he waited silently as Tyler continued to make sure everything tallied up properly.

Now that Tyler had an office of his own, he could have done the paperwork in there but it was easier to do it by the bar and well, he was tired.

Getting increasingly annoyed by the minute, he looked up at the chef. "Are you waiting to make sure I put it in Rachael's inbox or something?" he said with a scowl.

Donovan offered him a lazy shrug. "Just want to make sure it was done right."

"You're an asshole," Tyler said. "Seriously. Do you have to *micromanage* everything?"

"If people did as they were told, I wouldn't have to."

"You're not my boss," Tyler pointed out.

"I'm well aware."

Tyler gritted his teeth to keep himself from snapping *then why are you acting like you are?* but it took all his willpower. "Fine. You can walk me out."

With Donovan at his side like his damn shadow, Tyler doubled checked that everything was buttoned up tightly. He flicked off the lights as they walked down the hall to the employee entrance at the back, their quiet footfalls the only sound.

Donovan pushed open the back door, allowing the warm summer night air to flow in. His black shirt stretched across his shoulders and Tyler felt an odd twinge in his gut at the sight.

Those twinges were not unlike the ones he'd felt when he was overseas, when it had been so long since he'd gotten off that even other dudes had started to look good. And hey, a hand was a hand. And, a mouth was a mouth. Tyler and Frenchie had never really talked much about the fact Frenchie was into dudes but he'd offered and well … Tyler had indulged a couple of times. He'd been single, so why the hell not? But it was just a pressure release valve. A chance to blow off steam until he could find a woman. He definitely wasn't into guys when he had any other *option.*

Why the hell he was so wound up now was a mystery.

Of course, now that Tyler thought about it, it *had* been a while since he'd hooked up with anyone. Between the bar hours and trying to help his dad out around the house since his hip replacement, he was short on free time and usually too exhausted to try to meet a woman, even if it was a low-effort hookup through an app.

Still, even if Tyler ignored that Donovan was a man, he was the last fucking person Tyler wanted to be attracted to.

With a muttered, "g'night" that Donovan returned with a surly nod, Tyler made a beeline for his truck.

Maybe I should have kept the blonde's number, Tyler thought with a rueful shake of his head as he slid into his blue F150. *Clearly desperation is starting to hit.*

THREE

"Rachael." Donovan nodded at the tavern owner as he took a seat in the chair across the table from her. She preferred to keep staff meetings casual and, like always, they were at a table in the bar side of the tavern.

"Donovan." Rachael smiled brightly, tucking her dark hair over her shoulders. At times, he'd chafed at working for people younger than him, but she had more than proven herself over the past couple of years and really, it was only by about five years. They were both in their thirties. Donovan was just on the later side of it.

An introduction through a friend of a friend had put them in touch with each other, just as Rachael was searching to expand her business and Donovan was looking for a restaurant to get in on the ground floor of. Especially after the way he'd ended his last job and the shitshow of a breakup with Jude.

Donovan had been impressed by his first meeting with Rachael, even if it had been a casual chat at a backyard BBQ. She'd passionately spoken about the tavern her father had owned and the restaurant he'd always wanted to open. She talked about his death and the work she'd done to bring the restaurant up into the new century while preserving his legacy.

He'd been sold by her enthusiastic love of the place. By her passion for running a business with the kind of integrity and high standards he'd always held himself to.

She was an excellent business partner, and he hadn't once regretted his decision.

"We're just waiting on Tyler," she said, crossing her legs. She smoothed her light summer dress down over her thighs. "Help yourself if you'd like." She nodded to the pitcher and plate of cookies on the table.

A pitcher of mint lemonade—*no, lime*, he thought as he took a sip—and ginger molasses cookies. The cookies he recognized as being from the bakery downtown but the drink was probably something Rachael had made herself. He knew she used to have a bigger hand in working behind the bar before the expansion.

"This is good," he said, lifting his glass.

"Isn't it? Tyler's been making more mocktails lately. There's a trend toward them, people either cutting back on alcohol, or cutting it out completely, so we're trying to offer more options for people than soda water."

"Tyler made this?"

"Why do you sound so surprised?" Tyler said drily as he slid into the chair to Donovan's left. "I have been working here for, God, how many years, Rach?"

She frowned. "Well, my parents died in 2007 and you hired on just after you left active duty so … almost eleven years?"

"Must be. Wow."

It irked Donovan that Tyler called their boss 'Rach'. She wasn't his *buddy*. She was his employer. And if anyone had a right to be on a more level footing with her, it was Donovan. He owned half of the restaurant side of the business, for fuck's sake.

The business structure here was a little unusual and it meant the hierarchy was a bit lopsided. Donovan had some financial stake in the business, but overall, he still answered to Rachael. Tyler managed the bar side of the business, but he wasn't an investor. Tyler had no right to be all buddy-buddy with her, even if they had grown up together.

But frankly, everything about Tyler irked Donovan.

His ex-Army tough-guy attitude got on Donovan's last nerve. The first week they'd met, Donovan had come into the tavern for a meeting with the contractors about the restaurant remodel and seen Tyler lugging heavy boxes of booze. He'd offered to help but Tyler had looked him up and down and shaken his head like he thought Donovan didn't have the strength.

Fine, maybe Donovan didn't have the bulging muscles Tyler had. He ran toward wiry, lean strength. Maybe he didn't have six-pack abs either. He was a chef, for God's sake. He spent every single waking minute of his day thinking about *food* so he was a little softer around the middle than he'd like. But he tried to stay active and fit with martial arts, if for no other reason than he was often on his feet for ten or twelve hours a day and he had to be at peak physical and mental performance to run a kitchen with the precision and level of quality he expected of himself.

He could have helped lug around some boxes of alcohol, but clearly Tyler thought Donovan couldn't manage it. Fine. He hadn't offered again.

"Donovan?"

He glanced up to see Rachael and Tyler staring at him expectantly. "Ahh, sorry. I was thinking about the menu for next week." He didn't approve of dishonesty but a little white lie to avoid pissing off the bartender in front of Rachael? Yeah, that seemed forgivable.

Rachael nodded. "Well, the reason I wanted to meet with you both is because I'm going to be going out of town. Reeve and Grant have talked me into going away on vacation."

Tyler smiled. "Oh, that's great. You deserve a break. You work so hard."

She gave him a little smile back.

Rachael, Reeve, and Grant weren't the first triad Donovan had met. He'd spent some time in the poly and swinger communities and explored it a bit himself, because he'd thought opening up his relationship with Jude might save it, but in the end, the experience had left a sour taste in his mouth.

There was nothing wrong with the idea of open or poly relationships *in theory*. People like his boss and her partners made it work. He'd seen the genuine love and connection there but he'd seen it turn toxic too. No more than it did in monogamous relationships maybe, but shitty people were shitty people, and drama was drama, no matter what the relationship configuration.

He clearly wasn't wired that way and adding complication to his life was not something he had the time or energy for. Still, Donovan could see that it worked for Rachael and her partners, despite the stress of running a business that undoubtedly made the relationship even more difficult.

"I'm glad you have the opportunity to get away," he said graciously. "When will you be leaving?"

She listed a week in June that she and her partners were considering and asked if that worked for their schedules.

Donovan nodded. "That works for me."

"Me too." Tyler adjusted the baseball cap on his head.

Tyler always wore the damn thing. Donovan had never seen him without one, in fact. He idly wondered if Tyler was going bald. Ha. That would be funny.

Donovan might be a ginger but at least he had a full head of hair.

"Which leads me to my next topic." Rachael cleared her throat. "Who is in charge while I'm gone."

Donovan sat up straight and Tyler shifted in his seat as she looked between them.

"I'm going to be honest; this was a tough decision. You're both fantastic at what you do. But I think it'll be easier if there's one single person in charge. It'll be temporary. Only for a week and then you'll go back to reporting to me."

Donovan nodded. Well, that was fine. He could take on more responsibility if he needed to.

"After some careful consideration, I'm putting Tyler in charge."

White noise filled Donovan's head. "What?" he said hoarsely.

"You know I respect you, Donovan, but the truth is, you're already doing so much. You're running the kitchen and the front of the house. Kristin does a great job managing the servers but she's answering to you as it is. So, it doesn't make sense to put this on her."

"I don't *mind* taking on more while you're gone," he said stiffly.

"I know you don't. And I appreciate that. But the truth is, Tyler has been here for more than a decade. He knows this place and our vendors like the back of his hand."

"He doesn't know the kitchen vendors," Donovan argued. "I do."

"And you don't know the bar vendors," Tyler shot back. "What is your problem, man?"

"My problem is that I'm part owner in this place. I don't see why I should have to answer to a bartender."

A startled expression crossed Rachael's face and Donovan guiltily remembered his mom scolding him when he was a kid. *Just because your hair looks like it's on fire doesn't mean you have to act like it is.* Coming from a fellow hot-headed ginger, he knew it was good advice. He wasn't always good at remembering it, however.

Sorry, Mom, he thought.

"I'm sorry," he said. "That didn't come out the way I meant it."

Rachael leaned forward. "Tyler is the bar *manager*, not just some bartender. Though, for what it's worth, I'd prefer you don't talk down to my bartenders either. Yes, Donovan, you are a co-owner in the restaurant. And I respect that, I absolutely do. But Tyler currently has fewer responsibilities than you do. He has more time to take on the extra work." Her tone was kind but there was clearly no arguing with her. "And I think this is what's best for the business overall."

"Right." Donovan cleared his throat, trying not to grit his teeth as he looked over at Tyler and his stupid smug face. "I want what's best for the tavern too."

"So do I," Tyler said.

Well, he would say that, wouldn't he? He's won.

"Good," Rachael said. "We'll talk more in the next few weeks about the details, but I wanted to give you a heads-up."

"I appreciate that," Donovan said stiffly. He was definitely gritting his teeth now.

"We won't let you down, Rach," Tyler said.

She smiled at them both. "I know that."

Donovan tried to smile back as pleasantly as he could. Because while Rachael was a kind, friendly person who looked out for her staff as though they were family, she was also a businesswoman who was doing a brilliant job running the place. *She* was the one in charge here and if she didn't like Donovan's attitude, it could get ugly for him.

Maybe not ugly—she didn't seem like the vindictive type—but as of right now, he had almost full authority over the kitchen as executive chef. He decided the menus, he chose the vendors, he hired the new staff, he got to run the show. But if he wasn't a team player, that might change.

Hell, if she really thought he was a problem, she might even buy him out and go into business with someone new. Someone less hot-headed. Someone who worked better with her bartender—bar *manager*—and Donovan couldn't lose his position here. It was too important to him.

"The restaurant will be in great hands while you're gone," Donovan said, lifting his chin. "You won't have a thing to worry about."

Because I won't let you fuck this up, Tyler.

By the time the restaurant closed for the night, Donovan was bone-tired. His feet and his back ached, but there was a buzz in his head that wouldn't quit. It was always like that for him. Ever since he'd begun working in a kitchen in high school. There was an energy there unlike anything else he'd ever experienced, and a good night made his blood sing.

His ex, Jude, was the only person who'd ever understood. Jude Maddox was a chef too, a talented one, and they'd worked together for years in the kitchen of Plated, a high-end restaurant in Fort Benton.

They'd met there, in fact, both working their way up to sous chefs. They'd competed against each other, supported each other, and discovered a love of kink together.

They'd dove into that with the same ferocity they'd tackled everything else, only to discover that they weren't as perfectly matched as they'd hoped.

Jude was a switch. Which was fine. It meant he could submit to Donovan. But Donovan was never going to meet Jude's needs to top because Donovan didn't submit to anyone. He'd happily let a guy fuck him, but get ordered around? Not in a million years.

Still, they'd tried to keep their relationship going. Kink was always the way they ended good nights in the kitchen. No matter how exhausted they were, the minute they got in the door of their apartment, they were on each other like they'd die without the other's touch. It had been heady and powerful stuff, and the perfect way to wind down after a high-energy night in the kitchen.

It had quieted that buzz and let them sleep. Days off were different. Lazier, a little more loving. But those nights, high on the energy that was impossible for anyone outside the restaurant business to understand, they'd sizzled with the heat of the twenty thousand BTUs in a commercial kitchen range.

And then it had all gone sideways in a spectacular, ugly fashion, and he and Jude had barely spoken since.

Now, Donovan unlocked his apartment door, feeling the itch for that release he experienced as a dominant grow under his skin. It had been too long since he'd toyed with a willing sub. Teasing him. Tormenting him.

Donovan thought about it in the shower, washing off the sweat and kitchen smells that clung to his skin. He stroked his cock a little as he thought of binding a man. Putting him through his paces.

In bed after the shower, skin still damp and hair slicked back and darkened from water, Donovan propped himself against the headboard.

He scrolled through his kink app but found no one that pinged his radar. Almost no one on at all. Not surprising at this hour of the morning. It had been so much easier in Fort Benton. More men to choose from. More who fit his needs. But there were only a handful here.

Donovan frowned down at his phone. None appealed. He didn't know why.

Truthfully, he had no idea what he wanted anymore. He just wanted *something*.

He scrolled through the profiles again, reading their words as much as looking at the pictures.

There were the guys looking for a sweet, loving dynamic, and he could do that. He'd done it in the past.

There were guys looking for a rough, wild night and yeah, since his breakup he'd done that too.

But none of them seemed *right*.

Donovan slowed as he stared at one profile, flicking through the photos. The tattoos reminded him a bit of Tyler. Donovan looked down at his own inked skin. Yeah, so that was probably the one and only thing he and Tyler had in common.

The guy on his screen definitely wasn't Tyler. He'd posted a face shot and he was nowhere near as good-looking.

When did I decide Tyler was good-looking? Donovan wondered. But he supposed there was a certain appeal to him. His muscular frame would look great all trussed up in ropes and his dark stubble and piercing blue eyes would look gorgeous as they stared up at Donovan. But *that* was a terrible idea if he'd ever heard one.

Work conflict aside, they couldn't stand each other. And Donovan knew he was at least partly to blame. He needled Tyler, just because he could. Because he enjoyed it.

Besides, Tyler was straight, at least according to all appearances, and he certainly didn't look like the type to go down on his knees easily. Of course, that could be half the fun …

Donovan looked again at the pictures of the guy's toned abs and hard cock and closed the app. Nah, if he was going to fantasize about someone, he might as well pick the better option.

So, if Donovan tossed away his phone, shut his eyes and stroked his cock while he pictured binding Tyler's muscular arms, grabbing Tyler by his chin, and pushing him to his knees, well, no one would ever need to know.

FOUR

Tyler settled the weight back in the rack, sweat dripping from his body.

"Nice, dude."

His gaze flicked to Leo on the bench beside him. "Thanks. It was a good workout." Tyler mopped at his face with his towel and slung it over his shoulder as he stood with a groan. "Need me to spot you?"

"Nah, I'm good. I think I might have overdone it on chest presses yesterday so I'm trying to take it easy today, bro."

"Cool, man. See you tomorrow?"

"Sure thing." Leo held out a fist for him to bump.

Tyler hit the gym in the late afternoon most days, so he was a regular around here. He and Leo had never hung out any other time, but he was a good gym buddy.

Tyler sprayed disinfectant on the bench he'd been using as Leo stretched out on one nearby to do decline sit-ups. Tyler wiped the surface absently as his gaze drifted over to where Leo's shirt slid up, exposing several inches of his toned abs.

Nope, nothing.

Tyler had wondered if it was desperation that had led his wandering thoughts toward Donovan a few weeks back, but there were plenty of guys at the gym with fit bodies and none of them made him look twice.

But Donovan Ryan, who drove him absolutely insane, somehow did.

Tyler gave the bench one last aggravated scrub, then tossed the paper towel in the trash. He walked to the locker room, catching a glimpse of a woman in a crop top and leggings. His gaze slid across her as quickly as it landed, the way he'd done with Leo. The way he'd done with everyone lately.

Except the asshole he worked with.

So, maybe not desperation. Tyler still didn't know what it was though, and it was driving him nuts.

After he got home, he mentally reviewed what he had to do before he left for work. He'd gotten up early this morning to tackle chores at his parents' place, though he hadn't even come close to finishing the list he'd made. He still needed to shower and have a bite to eat before he headed into the tavern too.

He sighed as he thought more about his love life. It was pretty fucking sad that his hand was his best companion these days. It was hard to meet people, working the shifts he did. Other bartenders were a good bet but there was no way he was going to hook up with anyone on his staff at the tavern. He'd heard way too many horror stories from the women who worked for him about sleezy bosses at other bars to ever want to go there.

No, dating the people he managed was completely out of the question.

For a while, a few years back, he'd had a thing with a nurse at the local hospital. Her midnight shifts had meshed pretty well with his and they'd hooked up when her kids were at their dad's house.

They'd gotten pretty kinky too, although something had always felt a little off between them. It didn't help that she always wanted him to be in charge.

Hey, he got it. High-stress job—she just wanted a chance to unwind and not have to make a decision about anything—but damn, sometimes he just needed the same thing. He'd love to come home and not have to deal with it all too.

And the one other kinky woman he'd gotten involved with had been a little *too* far into it. The rough sex had been nice, but she'd started talking about him wearing lingerie and heels and crawling around the floor to kiss her boots while she called him a sissy and … no. Not his bag.

Tyler was pretty open-minded about trying new things, but he had a line.

And these days, he just didn't have the time to date.

The most intensely sexual thing he'd done lately was eat Donovan's wild mushroom fettuccine last night. Tyler could still feel it on his tongue, the thick creamy sauce and slippery pasta. So good he'd gotten bread to mop up every last bit of the sauce and licked his fork clean.

He'd caught Donovan eyeing him with an amused smirk and went hot under the collar. But hey, it was damn good. Donovan should take it as a compliment.

But it was still pretty fucking sad if that was the best he could manage these days.

Tyler's phone buzzed in his pocket. *Fuck.* Another one. He surreptitiously slipped it out and glanced quickly at the screen. Eddie again. *Fuck.* This was happening way too frequently.

"Phone out, boss?" Lacey eyeballed him, a twinkle in her gaze as she flipped her dirty-blonde hair over her shoulder. "Thought that wasn't allowed."

"It's not." He grimaced and stuffed it in his pocket again. "But I'm a little bit of a hypocrite sometimes."

She chuckled. "We all are."

Still, Tyler ducked out as soon as he could take a break and made a beeline for the back door. He hit dial as soon as it closed behind him.

Eddie picked up immediately. "There you are, man."

"Eddie. What's going on?" His stomach knotted with worry.

"Nothing. Just wanted to talk."

Tonight was a good night. Eddie was drunk, but it was still the early stages. Where he'd reminisce about the stupid shit they'd done together. Where he was happy and not weepy.

Tyler was no closer to knowing what to do about him. He'd gotten another drunk call from Eddie last week. Andrea and the kids were back home. For now.

Tyler had been too busy to make the trip up to Grand Rapids and guilt nagged at him. *My next day off*, he promised himself.

Oh wait, that was tomorrow. He stifled a groan. He'd promised his dad he'd mow his lawn. And he needed to catch up on sleep. *Fuuuuck.*

"I'm on my break so I can't talk long," he warned Eddie.

"I was just thinking about that time we went white water rafting, man. That was fucking awesome."

"It was," Tyler agreed, his shoulders loosening a little as he leaned against the table in the break area. "We had a great trip."

"And we did the bungee jumping off the bridge."

"I remember." Tyler smiled. Fuck, that whole trip had been wild. Tyler, Eddie, and a couple of guys from their platoon had driven down to West Virginia for a crazy weekend of adrenaline-fueled adventure. Together, their motto had always been, 'If it doesn't scare the shit out of you, it isn't worth doing.'

They'd done a lot of things that weekend that had scared the shit out of them. And they'd had a blast.

That was the last memory Tyler had of all of them together.

"I miss those days," he admitted, feeling a lump in his throat.

"We should do it again, man."

"Yeah." But it would never be the same. They weren't the same guys they'd been twelve years ago. Rafe and Frenchie were dead now and Eddie … well, Eddie was struggling.

If Tyler thought it would help, he'd ask Rachael for some time off and take Eddie down there. But as bad as he was doing, Tyler wasn't sure they'd both make it home. Eddie's mental health and drinking troubles made him too much of a wild card these days. Doing risky stunts all in the name of recapturing their youth sounded like a suicide mission.

"I'll try to make it up to GR soon," Tyler said instead. "We can talk more then."

"I'd like that."

"You hang in there, okay?" Tyler asked. "I know it's been rough but …"

"I'm trying." Eddie drew in a ragged breath. "Some days it just feels like my head is so full, man. There's just all this extra shit cluttering it up and I can't …I can't make it stop."

"Is that why you drink so much?"

There was irony there, the bartender worried about a guy drinking too much. But it was one thing to throw back a cocktail or two with friends in celebration and another to drink yourself into oblivion to numb yourself out.

He'd done a bit of numbing out when he got home too but thankfully it had never been out of control and now, he only drank occasionally.

"Yeah. It helps, you know."

"It's just a temporary fix, you know that, right?" Tyler said softly. "It isn't—"

"I know." Eddie sounded on the verge of tears now. "I know, but what else can I do? It won't *stop*."

Shit. Tyler had tipped Eddie from happy drunk to sad drunk. He should have kept his fucking mouth shut. "We'll do something wild when we get together, I promise," he said.

Eddie probably wouldn't even remember this when he woke up in the morning.

"Yeah, okay."

"You take care of yourself, okay?" Tyler said.

"Okay. You too. Thanks for being here for me." His words were beginning to slur.

"Always," Tyler promised. "Give Andrea and the kids my love."

After they said their goodbyes and Tyler hung up the phone, he typed out a message to one of the group chats. There was one conversation with all the guys and another one with everyone except Eddie. It always made Tyler feel vaguely guilty, talking about Eddie behind his back, but he didn't know what else to do.

He typed out a text and sent the message to Jackson, Hayes, and Gordo.

Hewitt: ***Hey, have you talked to Eddie much lately?***

Jackson answered almost immediately.

Jackson: ***Yeah. Rarely when he's sober. Been gettin' a lot of late-night phone calls.***

Hewitt: ***Same. It's been bad lately, hasn't it?***

Jackson: ***Yeah.***

Hewitt: ***What the fuck do we do?***

Jackson: ***If I knew, I'd already be doing it. Any of us would.***

Tyler sighed. It was true. If any of them had figured out a magic solution, they'd have done it long before now.

With a heavy sigh, Tyler set his phone on the table beside him. He needed to get back to work. As manager, he had leeway, but he knew how hard his staff busted ass and he always wanted to set a good example. He was just so goddamn tired.

Eventually, he mustered up the energy to stand. He punched in the key code on the door, but when he opened it, Donovan was on the other side, hand poised in midair.

"Oh, sorry," they both said, nearly in unison.

"Just finishing up my break," Tyler said, feeling awkward. Lately, he'd been thinking about Donovan and the way his muscles played under his shirt a hell of a lot more than he knew what to do with.

"Yeah, I was just coming out for one. Kitchen's closed so I figured it was a good time to get some air."

Tyler was aware of how close they stood. Donovan had been doing that a lot lately, or at least that was how it seemed. Any time they interacted he was close, crowding into Tyler's personal space. Or maybe Tyler was just more aware of it now.

Whatever it was, it sent a strange feeling skittering over his skin. It was like the hair on his arms rose every time Donovan stepped near or used that bossy tone. Seriously weird.

Donovan tilted his head and looked down at him. He was a few inches taller than Tyler to begin with but right now, with Tyler on the ground outside and Donovan on the step above, Tyler had to crane his neck to look up at him. It made him feel small. And he wasn't a small guy. He shrugged, trying to get rid of the strange feeling crawling across his back.

"Are you okay?" Donovan asked.

"Yeah, I'm fine," Tyler said automatically.

"Are you sure?"

"I'm sure I'm sure," he snapped.

Donovan held up his hands. “I’m sorry. I’m not trying to intrude, you just looked … upset or something.”

Tyler hesitated, staring at Donovan’s chest in his black T-shirt. He’d taken off his chef’s coat and it looked like he’d been sweating. The fabric clung to his skin, molding across it to reveal some surprisingly nice pecs. Tyler had a sudden and almost overwhelming urge to press his palm against Donovan’s chest.

“A friend’s going through some stuff and I’m worried,” Tyler admitted, gaze still glued to Donovan’s body.

“Ahh. I’m sorry about your friend.”

Tyler glanced up. The lights in the hallway were brighter than the lights outside and it was hard to see Donovan’s face. But there had been real, genuine sympathy in his voice.

“Thanks.” Tyler’s mouth felt dry all of a sudden and he licked his lips.

Donovan’s gaze flashed down to his mouth as a weird tension filled the air.

“I should, uh, get back to the bar,” Tyler said.

“Right. I should take my break.”

But they both stood there a moment, staring at each other.

Donovan cleared his throat and stepped back, letting Tyler into the building. Tyler’s shoulder brushed his chest as he passed. He jerked at the feel of Donovan’s warm hand on his arm. He looked down at it, the long, pale fingers slightly rough against his skin.

“If you ever need anything, I’m here,” Donovan said.

Tyler glanced up. “I’m fine. Thanks.” The words came out brusquer than he’d intended. “I know you don’t seem to think I can handle my job here or, apparently, my personal life, but I'm perfectly capable of managing."

Donovan looked taken aback. "I wasn't implying—"

Tyler shrugged off his hand and walked forward, feeling strangely unsettled. His heart beat too fast and the phantom heat from Donovan's hand against his skin lingered.

Weirdest of all, his cock had thickened behind the fly of his jeans. *What the fuck?*

Several hours later, Tyler gave the bar one final glance and shut off the lights. The restaurant side was dim too, though there was light in the hall, meaning someone was still here. Donovan, probably. Usually, he was gone by the time Tyler wrapped up—kitchen service ended a couple of hours before the bar closed—but Donovan never left until every last thing in the kitchen was clean and in its precise spot, ready for the following day. If nothing else, Tyler did have to admire the guy's work ethic.

Tyler just wished he understood why he found him so damn unsettling otherwise.

As he passed the door of Donovan's office, he slowed to a stop without conscious thought, his gaze drawn to the view inside. The door was open maybe a quarter of the way, and Tyler caught a glimpse of Donovan's bare back as he slipped his shirt off and tossed it into a hamper.

He has ink. And he's fit.

Tyler had no idea why it mattered. Sure, maybe Donovan was in better shape than Tyler had anticipated. He looked skinny in his chef's uniform or dressed casually. But he had lean, defined muscles. Strong, the kind that were functional, not just vanity muscles, like some of the muscle-bound dudes at the gym Tyler went to who didn't care if they could actually lift a couch without fucking up their back, just that they had an eight pack.

Freckles covered every inch of Donovan's body but they somehow worked with the mostly black ink he had scattered across his back and arms. Tyler liked ink. He liked it on himself, he liked it on the women he dated, and he'd admired it on some guys before. Not in a sexual way, just kind of a "hey man, nice ink" thing but *this* was more than an urge to check out some art.

He'd noticed the tattoos on Donovan's arms of course, but he hadn't known the ink extended to his back. Or how good they would make Donovan's shoulders look.

Red hair, freckles—they were *not* Tyler's thing, damn it—but Donovan made them look better than he had any right to. Now, Donovan hooked his thumbs into the waistband of his uniform pants and pushed them down.

I really, really should look away, Tyler thought. *But Jesus.*

Donovan had those little dimples on his lower back and his snug black underwear hugged his ass just right, showing off his full glutes. But why did Tyler care? He'd never checked out a guy's ass before. *Ever.*

Donovan turned to reach for a set of clothes draped over a nearby chair. Tyler stepped back, nearly tripping over his own feet in his haste to hide, but it was too late. Donovan made eye contact, smirking as he slipped on a pair of jeans. There was something so intense in his gaze that Tyler felt pinned in place as Donovan stalked over to the door and pulled it open wide, his jeans snug enough to stay up without being buttoned or zipped.

"Enjoying the show, Tyler?"

He forced a look of indifference onto his face. "I've seen better."

Donovan snickered, his gaze flicking up and down Tyler's body. "Your cock says otherwise."

Tyler glanced down automatically to see his dick, clearly visible through the denim of his jeans. He was hard. *Jesus. Why am I hard?*

"Shit happens when you're desperate," Tyler said coolly. "I learned that in the sandbox."

Donovan stalked toward him, still shirtless. "I could work with that. I don't like you but that *might* make it more fun. Problem is, I don't think you're into what I like."

"Excuse me?"

"I don't play nice," Donovan said.

Tyler squared his shoulders. "What's that supposed to mean?"

"It means, I play with the big boys." Donovan's smile was condescending. "And I don't think you can handle that."

Tyler crossed his arms over his chest, knowing it would make the thin material strain over his muscles. Damn it, not even a flicker in Donovan's expression. "I'm not big enough for you?"

"Oh, not like that. I enjoy a good muscle jock on his knees as much as the next guy."

"Fuck if I'd ever get on my knees for a guy. Especially *you*."

There was an answering flash of heat in Donovan's eyes.

God, why was Tyler goading him like this? He didn't even like Donovan. Or find him attractive. His stomach twisted at that little lie. Fine, he was attractive. But it wasn't like Tyler was going to drop to his knees and suck the guy off. Though *that* was a mental image that wasn't going to leave his head any time soon.

What the fuck is wrong with me?

"Well, I don't play with men who claim to be straight," Donovan replied coolly. "And I don't play with men who wouldn't know a whip from a flogger."

Tyler blinked. "You're into kink?"

"Yes." Donovan pointed to some ink on his bare hip. A black and white circle that reminded him a bit of a yin-yang symbol except with three little swirls instead of two. "The BDSM triskelion. I've been involved in the lifestyle for years."

"Huh."

Donovan's gaze flicked over him, assessing. "Do you know it?"

"The symbol? No. I'm not really in the community at all. I do know a whip from a flogger though."

Donovan nodded. "I'm guessing you're used to being on the other end of it."

"Yeah." Tyler shrugged. "Before I enlisted, I had a girlfriend who was into it. Nothing too extreme. We were barely out of high school at the time really and were only playing around, but she enjoyed some choking. Some spanking. I got a little more into it when I got out, but it's not like a regular thing. I don't go to the munchies or whatever you people call them."

"Munches," Donovan said. "Stupid name but that's beside the point."

Tyler shrugged. "I'm just saying, I do my kink thing in private. I don't need to make friends who are into the same stuff."

"Socializing notwithstanding, you've never been on the other side of it? With anyone?"

"No. An ex tried but I wasn't into wearing lingerie and licking her boots and shit. You?"

Donovan let out a little huff. "No. I don't bottom."

"Isn't something up your ass supposed to feel good?"

Not that Tyler'd ever had more than a couple of fingers in him—women's fingers at that—because he'd turned down the woman offering to peg him. But he damn well wasn't going to bring that up to Donovan.

"Not *that.*" Donovan's tone was scornful. "I enjoy ass play. I mean the kink term. Submitting to someone else."

Tyler laughed. "Yeah, no. Like I said, I don't submit to anyone." Except that one time, before the woman he was hooking up with had made it weird, he'd been kinda curious … Too bad it had felt all wrong with her.

"Shame." Donovan's gaze raked over him. "I can think of all sorts of things I'd enjoy doing to you."

"Not my scene," Tyler said automatically. But Jesus, he was still picturing Donovan feeding him his dick and that was a crazy hot mental image. He'd never sucked a cock in his life, only been on the receiving end of a blowjob, but there was something about the thought that made his mind whirl.

He suddenly wondered if Donovan was a fire crotch too. Based on the thin trail of hair that led from his navel into the top of his black pants, Tyler was sure he was. But why did he care? And why in the hell did he have a sudden desire to find out?

"Like I said, shame." Donovan shrugged. "I bet I could turn you inside out and make you feel all sorts of things you've never experienced before."

"I don't even *like* you," Tyler pointed out, trying to suppress a shudder at the mental images Donovan's words created. "Why in the fuck would I let you do anything to me?"

"Because I think you're more curious than you let on." Donovan stepped closer and smirked at him. "I think a part of you might just wonder what it would be like to have another man take total control of you."

"I'd have to respect him to let that happen," Tyler said with a sneer. "So that's out of the question."

"Shame," Donovan repeated with another shrug like he didn't care at all. "Your loss."

My loss, my ass. Tyler fumed as he turned and stalked out of the break room.

But the heavy, insistent throb of his cock made him wonder if maybe he *was* missing out.

Tyler scanned the bar, checking to make sure everything was fully supplied. He did inventory every two weeks and he'd stocked up the week prior, but Rachael was heading out of town tomorrow, so this was his last chance to make sure everything was set behind the bar before he checked on the kitchen.

And that was going to be a barrel of fun because things had been weird as hell with Donovan lately. After he'd been caught ogling Donovan, Tyler had thought about little else. He'd thought about what Donovan's cock would look like. What it would taste like. What it would feel like on his tongue.

The weird thing was, he'd pictured himself all tied up and helpless while it happened.

And just thinking about it had made him come harder than he had in a while.

It was weird as fuck.

He didn't understand it. He didn't like it.

And Donovan had *definitely* been eyeing him differently lately.

Like he was sizing Tyler up and trying to figure out what made him tick. What he'd look like on his knees.

Tyler thought about the feel of closing his hand around a woman's throat and pressing. Or slapping her upturned ass, watching it turn pink, listening to her cry out. He'd liked it a lot. But he'd also liked the feel of her fingernails digging into his back. That flash of pain had kept him in the moment, heightened everything. What would it be like to let someone else take charge of him in the bedroom?

He shuddered at the idea, but he wasn't sure if it was fear or revulsion. Or a surge of lust.

Swallowing hard, he remembered being tucked behind the insulated shipping containers that served as their home away from home, Frenchie's mouth on his cock, hot and wet as he worked Tyler over. His big rough hand, gripping the base of Tyler's dick.

Would Donovan be rough like that? Or would he take his time? He seemed like the kind of guy who would go slow, just to torture Tyler.

What if he made Tyler *beg*?

The shiver that went up Tyler's spine at that thought was one thing but the rush of blood to his dick was something else and

Tyler had to close his eyes for a moment to get himself under control.

It was a weird fantasy, that was all. Not something he was going to do anything about.

Tyler wasn't into men. Not like *that.*

He didn't date them. He didn't fuck them. What had happened overseas was one thing, but it was just a few moments of desperation a couple of times.

He wasn't going to start dating guys. He wasn't going to fantasize about Donovan. And he definitely, *definitely* wasn't going to submit to him.

Tyler was going to be Donovan's boss this week, in fact.

Tyler smiled at the thought.

Morning preparations were in full swing in the kitchen as Tyler stepped inside. Prep cooks were doing their thing, chopping vegetables, and simmering something on the stove that smelled like a little bit of heaven.

Donovan stood at his usual station, tall and imposing in his white jacket. Tyler would give him this, Donovan might be the boss of the kitchen, but he worked as hard as everyone else.

"Something I can do for you, Tyler?" Donovan asked without even looking up.

The words sounded weirdly formal and forced. Not like his usual snark.

"I just wanted to talk about plans for tonight. Make sure we're on the same page about everything since Rachael is leaving this afternoon. If you can't step away now, that's okay, but I'd like to go over it"—he glanced at the clock—"within the next hour or so."

Donovan nodded once, tightly. "Now's fine."

He set his knife down and unbuttoned his jacket. He hung it on a wall-mounted hook and stood in front of Tyler like a soldier waiting for inspection, with a ramrod straight back and closed-off expression. "Where would you like to do this?"

"Why don't you just follow me into the bar?"

The servers were busy laying out place settings in the restaurant but the bar would be private enough. Nerves built in Tyler's belly as he and Donovan walked across the space. It wasn't like Rachael was in the tavern every day, so her being gone for a week shouldn't have been such a big fucking deal, but with the entire weight of the business's success resting on his shoulders, he felt weirdly nervous.

It was one thing to run the bar for the night, knowing he could call Rachael if he needed anything. But his goal was to not have to do that. She deserved the time away and the last thing he wanted was to make her vacation anything less than relaxing.

In the bar, he turned to face Donovan. The big open space was bright with sunshine streaming in the windows. It made Donovan's hair even redder than usual. His beard was thick and full, neatly trimmed, and his hair was slicked back. *Every inch the hipster chef.*

His black T-shirt stretched over his shoulders and his eyes were especially bright blue today, like the water out in the bay probably looked, glistening under the summer sun.

"I don't have all day," Donovan said frostily, crossing his arms over his chest. "Can we move this along?"

"Yes." Tyler cleared his throat and tried not to look at Donovan's biceps, straining against the snug fabric. Jesus. How had he ever thought the guy was *skinny*? There was a solid strength to him that made Tyler's traitorous mind wander to contemplating what he'd look like wielding a whip or a flogger.

Tyler flinched. *No, stop thinking about that,* he ordered himself.

On autopilot, Tyler went through the plan for the day, hitting on all the highlights. Donovan interjected a few times, bringing up things that Tyler hadn't mentioned yet but had planned to, and the third time it happened, Tyler stepped forward and glared at him.

"Would you stop it? If you'd just let me finish what I was saying—"

"Well, it's not my fault you're leaving the most important things out!"

Tyler gritted his teeth. "I'm not leaving them out. I just hadn't gotten to them yet. I would get to them if you'd give me the damn opportunity. I know what I'm doing here!"

"I still don't understand why Rachael put you in charge," Donovan said, his tone icy as he scowled at Tyler.

"She put me in charge because I've been here for a fucking decade," Tyler said with a snarl. "And you have a shitload on your plate already. You're running the whole kitchen, and Kristin is up to her eyeballs dealing with the front of the house. We're fully staffed at the bar, so there's no reason I can't be the one overseeing everything for both sides while Rachael's on vacation."

"You don't have the experience with kitchens," Donovan said, glaring down at him.

"I've handled inventory and staff management here at the bar for years. What the fuck do you think I've been doing with my time?" Tyler protested, stepping up into Donovan's space. He tried to ignore the whiff of cologne that teased his nostrils.

"I don't care what you've been doing. I don't take orders from a bartender."

Tyler bared his teeth. "I'm the bar manager, thank you."

Donovan grabbed Tyler's chin and narrowed his eyes at Tyler. Tyler's breath growing shallow at Donovan's tight grip on his face and his intense glare. "I don't take orders from anyone. I'm accustomed to giving them."

Pissed off by his reaction to Donovan, Tyler broke free of his hold and spun him so he gripped Donovan's hands behind his back. "And I don't take orders from anyone I don't respect. You haven't earned that."

He pushed close and groaned softly at the way it pressed his cock—half-hard already—against Donovan's ass. Tension crackled between them, and Donovan growled under his breath, struggling to break free.

"Guys," someone said in a warning tone.

The sound made Tyler drop Donovan's hands, mortified that anyone had seen him acting so immaturely at work. Worst of all, it was Grant McGuire, Rachael's partner. He had a concerned look on his handsome face.

"I'm in a tricky position here. I don't want to step on your toes, or Rachael's. It probably isn't even my place to say something, but you two have got to work this shit out. We're leaving on vacation tomorrow, and she's trusting you two to run this place. This is the longest amount of time she's ever had off in one stretch, and she deserves to be able to take that time off without worrying that you two are going to kill each other instead of keeping this place running. I don't want her spending the week thinking about what's happening here and not enjoying herself and actually relaxing for the first time in more than a decade! And I don't think you want that either."

"Shit."

Tyler glanced over at Donovan, who was staring at Grant, a red flush staining his cheeks and making his hair look carrot-y orange by comparison. They stood, frozen for a second, before they stepped apart.

Tyler looked down at his feet, heat crawling up his neck as well. He was lucky to have this job. People were wary of hiring vets. And Tyler had no secondary education or ambition for anything better. At the time he was hired, he'd been desperately searching for a new direction in his life and he'd found that here.

"You're right, Grant," Donovan said, clearing his throat. Tyler glanced at him in surprise. He sounded genuinely sorry for his reaction. "I let my ego get in the way of what I was supposed to be doing."

"I get it," Grant said, stepping a little closer to both of them. "You're both used to running the show and answering to Rachael. But she wasn't trying to slight you, Donovan, when she put Tyler in charge. You're already managing so much. She was trying to keep from piling too much on. Tyler has the time to handle it and the most experience with this place. You respect Rachael as a manager, right?"

They both nodded.

"Then trust her decision. She thought long and hard over it and came to the conclusion that it was for the best. Don't undermine her authority. She's damn good at what she does here."

"She is," Donovan agreed, an apologetic expression crossing his face as he glanced over. "I … I'm sorry, Tyler. Yes, I'll do my best to work with you. I'm not saying it's going to come easy, but I don't want Rachael worrying about leaving any more than I think you do."

"Agreed," Tyler said. No way in hell was he letting Rachael down. Or making her regret her decision to take a vacation. He stuck out a hand. "Truce?"

"Truce," Donovan shook too. He looked over at Grant. "Sorry about that."

"You don't have to apologize to me." He held up his hands. "Hell, I feel like I'm overstepping here. It's not my business, and the last thing I want to do is get involved where I'm not supposed to."

"Nah, I'm glad you called me out," Tyler said. He clapped a hand on Grant's shoulder. "We'll work it out. Rachael won't get any calls from us this week about problems here, I promise."

Relief crossed Grant's face. "Good."

Grant walked back toward Rachael's office and Tyler glanced back at Donovan. "I mean it. I don't want to fuck up her vacation because we can't put our differences aside."

"Me neither. What else did you want to discuss?"

Tyler shook his head, trying to clear it as he reached for the notes he'd left on the bar.

And he tried not to remember how it had felt to have his body pressed up against Donovan's. And how, just for a second, he'd wondered what it would be like if the positions were reversed.

If he were the one helpless in Donovan's grip.

FIVE

"Good morning."

Donovan looked up from his phone. He'd been in his usual a.m. mode, shouldering the door of the restaurant open and walking down the service hallway as he caught up on news articles before the rush of his day began.

He hadn't anticipated an ambush by Tyler. Donovan eyed him skeptically, his broad frame blocking the hallway. "Morning. You're here early."

"Yeah. Well, it is Sunday and …"

Sundays meant brunch service and an earlier dinner service.

The "and" was because Rachael was on vacation and Donovan was answering to Tyler. A flash of guilt washed over him for how rude he'd been before. There was no denying he cared about the place. Donovan was feeling salty about the responsibilities being given to Tyler, but Tyler deserved respect for what he'd earned. Manager was a title like chef was. And it would be shitty of Donovan to deny Tyler that.

"Yes." Donovan cleared his throat. "We have a busy day ahead of us."

"We do," Tyler said.

Donovan noticed for the first time that Tyler wasn't dressed in his usual uniform of a black T-shirt with the tavern's logo and jeans. The bar was the more casual side of the tavern, so his typical outfit made sense, but today he was dressed more like the staff at the front of the restaurant, in black trousers and a black button-down shirt. His ever-present ball cap was gone too and with it off, Donovan could see that Tyler wasn't losing his hair at all. He was definitely starting to get some silver at the temples, but though his hair was closely cropped, it was thick and black otherwise. *Huh.*

Tyler was around Rachael's age—early thirties—so he was going gray young. He looked good like that. The more formal dress and silvery hair added a touch of seriousness to his normally casual style. He looked the part of a bar manager now.

Donovan cleared his throat. "Is there anything you need from me this morning?"

"Oh." Tyler shook his head. "Yes. I was wondering if we could sit down for a brief rundown of the plan for the morning. I'm not usually here for brunch service."

Another meeting? Jesus, that was unnecessary, but Donovan had caught the faint tremble of nerves in Tyler's voice, so he took pity on him. *Better overprepared than underprepared.*

"Sure. Just tell me when and where."

"My office. And now, if that works for you."

Donovan nodded and followed Tyler into his office. It was unremarkable. A couple of chairs and a desk that was devoid of anything but some paperwork neatly stacked on the surface. Huh. He'd have expected Tyler to be a messy guy, but no, everything was lined up perfectly. *Oh, military service. That makes sense.*

"Would you like some coffee?"

"Sure."

"I'll be back in a few."

Donovan nodded and dropped into a chair. He'd finished an article about the catastrophic effects of the declining bee population by the time Tyler arrived with a tray. Tyler poured coffee from a French press into mugs and handed one to him. "Help yourself to sugar and cream."

Donovan sipped the coffee first, surprised but pleased by the richness of the roast. Good beans, perfectly roasted and expertly brewed. Tyler had gotten the water temperature, brew time, and grounds-to-water ratio just right. There was no harsh acidity to it or weak and watery taste. Donovan added the tiniest bit of sugar and a small splash of cream, not wanting to detract too much from the enjoyment of the coffee itself.

He glanced up at Tyler, pleasantly surprised. "This is excellent. Thank you."

Tyler flashed him a faint smile. "I may not be able to cook to save my life, but if it's liquid, I've *got* it."

Donovan chuckled though he was always mildly horrified by people who couldn't cook. It was one thing to lack the time to do it—he understood people had busy, stressful lives and didn't get the kind of joy he did from fussing in the kitchen for hours on end—but damn. He'd never understand the pride they seemed to have when they said that they *couldn't* cook.

Donovan eyeballed the pastries as he set down his mug. "Are those from the bakery order?"

"Yes."

"We're not going to—"

Tyler held up a hand. "I added them onto the order. I didn't take them from the ones you'd ordered for brunch."

"Oh." Chagrined, Donovan reached for a pecan roll. "I apologize."

Tyler sighed. "I know you think I'm an idiot but—"

"I don't think you're an idiot," Donovan admitted. "I'm just … I'm used to a rigid structure in a kitchen. I went to culinary school. They teach a very formal, very classical French style. It's strict and hierarchical. I could spend at least three hours arguing why that's a good thing and make at least a dozen points about why it isn't the be all and end all of cooking, but I won't subject you to that."

"Thanks for that." Tyler smirked as he took a sip of his coffee.

"I'm just saying this is hard for me," Donovan admitted. "I don't … I don't answer to others well."

Tyler gave him a skeptical look. "Because of culinary school?"

"Because of that and because I'm a Dom," he said simply. "I see a power vacuum and I want to fill it."

"There isn't one here," Tyler said. "I've *got* this."

"I'm doing my best to trust that."

Tyler sighed and pressed his thumb to a spot between his eye and his brow bone for a moment before he lifted his head to look

Donovan in the eye. "I didn't ask you to come in here so we could argue."

"So I gathered." Donovan gestured with his pecan roll. It was perfectly done, the dough rich and buttery, tender without being underdone. The glaze was rich and buttery too, sweet but not cloying. The pecans were toasted and there was just the faintest hint of real vanilla and a sprinkle of salt to keep it all balanced. "I *do* respond well to food bribery and Aimee Lucas's pastries are sublime."

Tyler snorted. "Glad I got *something* right. And I'll keep that in mind for the future."

"To business?" Donovan asked, gesturing toward Tyler's notes on the desk.

Tyler nodded and cleared his throat. "So, I thought we'd start with discussing brunch."

To Donovan's surprise and pleasure, brunch service went well. They were busy with plenty of covers—diners—this morning but it was a good test run for how things would go tonight. Brunch was generally easier than dinner. The menu was a bit more limited, and most people chose the buffet.

There were omelet and waffle stations where people could have the chef customize their breakfast and Donovan enjoyed cooking in front of the diners, interacting with them as he flipped the omelets in the pan with a deft wrist flick that never failed to impress. It was first year culinary training stuff, but it did look impressive.

And his sous chef, Max, a nonbinary person who had quickly become his most trusted staff member in the kitchen, drew *oohs* and *ahhs* with the weekly special of flambéed Crêpes Suzette.

Donovan looked longingly at the crêpe turner as Max deftly folded the thin pancakes into fourths on the flat griddle. Donovan enjoyed crêpes, though he preferred them stuffed with ham, nutty Gruyere cheese, and chives or mushroom, goat cheese, and thyme. But the draw was more the wooden utensil than the food.

Generally about a foot or so long, crêpe turners were thin pieces of wood with flat rounded edges designed to slide under the thin pancakes and fold them, but they also made delightfully wicked paddles.

Donovan kept one in his kitchen for cooking purposes and another in his gear bag in the bedroom. It was loved by some submissives and absolutely loathed by others. It packed a hell of a wallop and a sting, if wielded correctly, and it had been ages since he'd used one.

Donovan caught a glimpse of Tyler across the room, speaking with some diners. He was in profile and Donovan felt that familiar itch in his fingers as he trailed his gaze across Tyler's muscular backside. What he wouldn't give to get Tyler all trussed up and helpless, then take the crêpe spatula to his firm ass and thighs. Donovan let out an audible sigh.

"Chef, your omelet," Max hissed.

Donovan glanced down to see his hand was still and tossed the skillet to flip the omelet, scowling when he realized it had gone from lightly browned to something too close to burned. "Oh no. Let me start a new one for you, ma'am." He made a move to toss it in the trash tucked beneath the table, but the woman in front of him laughed.

"Oh, I do that all the time myself. Looks good to me."

"If you're sure …"

"Absolutely."

Donovan reluctantly reached for a warm plate beside him, then deftly flipped the omelet onto it. He garnished the food with a sprinkle of chopped herbs, then handed it over a little reluctantly. He didn't like putting out anything less than perfection. And Tyler had distracted him.

Still, they were nearing the end of brunch service and the morning had gone off without a hitch. He'd give Tyler this; he was off to a good start.

———

"Where the hell are my servers?" Donovan bellowed. Plates were collecting on the pass and not getting taken out. Donovan had been working flat out but the servers were lagging, and his annoyance had been building all night as plates stacked up and complaints rolled in. He'd gritted his teeth for the past hour, but he'd reached his boiling point. The warming lights helped keep everything up to temp but they also dried the food out and toughened the meat and delicate seafood. Three meals had been sent back tonight and that was unacceptable. He had a reputation to maintain. His as a chef and the restaurant's as a whole.

"Sorry, Chef," Teri, one of the servers, said as she hustled toward him. She grabbed two plates, looking unusually frazzled. "We're a little short-staffed tonight and it's busier than usual out there. And with Kristin running late …"

Donovan narrowed his eyes. There had been an unusual number of covers tonight. Sunday nights were usually a time when people were either dining with family or getting ready for the week ahead, so the tavern typically had steady but not frantic business. Still, even with the increased volume, the servers should have been able to handle it. "Why?" he asked.

She stared at him wide-eyed. "Well, I mean the storm that went through earlier today knocked out power in half the town. I think a lot of people went out to eat."

"Not the increase in covers. The— Never mind. Just get the food out there. I'll worry about the rest."

"Yes, Chef," she said, grabbing plates and hustling off again.

Donovan didn't know why he'd bothered to ask. He knew *exactly* why they were short-staffed. Tyler had failed to do his job. He'd been the one responsible for making the schedule for the week. While Kristin, the front of house manager, should have had input, Tyler had probably assumed he knew better and staffed leanly. Jesus, this was exactly why someone with no restaurant experience shouldn't be running the show.

Donovan grumbled under his breath and returned his focus to the plating. He'd been doing it so long he could do it in his sleep. Some days, he felt like he *was* doing it in his sleep. But he could artfully arrange food on a plate and garnish it without his brain being too engaged. Still, he couldn't afford to be distracted.

We wouldn't be slammed like this if Tyler had just done his damn job, Donovan thought as he slipped the plate of rosemary turkey meatloaf onto the pass and grabbed the next ticket, calling out the order.

"What the hell was that?" Donovan roared as he stared down at Tyler after service ended.

He looked up from his desk. "What was what?"

"We were short *two* servers tonight," he snarled. "We had way too many plates sent back because diners weren't happy with it. You did a piss-poor job staffing tonight. I know Kristin knows how many people we need to have on hand, so I don't know what in the hell you were thinking cutting it so short tonight but—"

"I didn't cut anything short," Tyler snapped, rising to his feet. "I didn't have a choice. Sam had to go out of town for a funeral and won't be back until Tuesday. Kayleigh has a tree down from the storm and can't get out of her driveway. What the hell was I supposed to do?"

"Call someone else to come in!"

"I *tried*!" Tyler listed off half a dozen names, giving reasons why none of them had been able to pick up shifts.

Donovan rubbed his head. "And you didn't think to warn *me* about any of this?"

"I didn't want to bother you. I was trying to handle it on my own."

"Well thanks to that, you fucked over service tonight," he snapped. "And then when I went to find you, you were nowhere to be found."

"I was busting my ass filling in for the bartender who also couldn't make it because of the storm. Jesus, Donovan, tonight was a fucking fluke. A lot of shit went wrong."

"Yeah, well you know what the first rule of hospitality is?" he asked, stepping closer.

"What?"

"If something can go wrong, it will go wrong. And usually, it won't happen on its own. Multiple things will go wrong. If you can't handle—"

"I can handle it." He stepped forward too, his chest brushing Donovan's.

Tyler smelled incredible. As angry as Donovan was, the scent teased at his nostrils and distracted him from his rant. Donovan had never noticed it before, but even after a long shift of working, there was only the rich aroma of whatever cologne Tyler wore. Like warm cedar and leather with spicy hints of peppercorn, ginger, and tangerine.

Donovan's mind ran wild with thoughts of a gorgeous cedar-smoked plank of salmon with a spicy citrus glaze, the recipe already beginning to form in his head even as he leaned in and took a deeper whiff. He abruptly realized how close they stood. How few inches were between their lips and how tempted he was to see if Tyler tasted as good as he smelled.

Because this wasn't just about recipes or his food-focused brain liking the smell. It was the way the cologne mingled with Tyler's own body chemistry and drove an even more primal urge. The urge to *fuck.*

Half of Donovan wanted to reach out and choke Tyler because he was so damn frustrated with him. The other half … well, it urged him to choke Tyler too but in a far more sexual way.

God, Donovan had never been like this. Never wanted someone he didn't even *like.* Sure, he had a temper, but he'd never found himself so easily riled up by someone. So desperate to exert his authority. Tyler might be in charge here at the restaurant. Might be the one calling the shots right now. But Donovan was itching to turn the tables.

He stepped forward, watching with interest as Tyler took a step back. Then another. "You sure you didn't do it on purpose?" Donovan asked.

"Do what?"

"Piss me off."

Tyler scowled. "Me *existing* seems to piss you off."

"There's some truth to that," Donovan admitted, pressing forward until he had Tyler trapped between him and the wall.

"Why do I get under your skin so much?"

"Because I fucking *want* you," Donovan admitted with a little growl. "I don't like you being in charge because I have so many damn things I'd like to do to you."

Tyler wet his lips. "Like what?"

"Thought you weren't interested," he taunted.

Tyler narrowed his eyes. "Call me curious."

Donovan shifted closer, allowing their bodies to touch full length. Tyler let out a little shudder.

"You're curious, huh?" Donovan leaned in and braced his right hand against the wall, leaning more of his weight against Tyler's chest. "Curious about *what*?"

Tyler's gulp was audible. "What a guy like you could do to me," he whispered.

Donovan's own cock, already half-hard from the fight and proximity, thickened.

"What I'd do to you, huh?" Donovan drew in a short, sharp little breath. "I'd put one hand around your throat and the other on your cock. Make you completely helpless to do anything but take it."

Tyler licked his lips. "Try it."

Donovan's cock jerked at the thought. He wasn't sure it wasn't a trap and that Tyler wouldn't haul off and slug him for it.

Moving warily, Donovan took his left hand and settled it gently against Tyler's throat. "You want this?"

"Yes."

He squeezed a little, pushing his fingers so lightly Tyler would only feel the barest hint of pressure. He removed his hand from the wall and reached back, slipping his fingers into Tyler's back pocket to fish out his wallet.

Tyler's lips parted as if he was going to ask something, but Donovan shook his head as he pushed the leather square against Tyler's palm. "You hold on to the billfold. You want *this*"—he gripped Tyler's throat—"to stop, you drop it, okay?"

"Okay."

Tyler's breathing was ragged already, his eyes wide. Donovan had never looked at them this closely before, but they were pale, almost silvery gray with a dark ring around the pupil. Tyler dragged his tongue across his lips again, leaving a shiny trail of moisture behind.

"You want my hand on your throat? My fist wrapped around your cock?"

"Yeah." Tyler's voice turned hoarse.

Donovan slipped a hand between their bodies to find Tyler hard against his fly. It wasn't easy to work open the button and zipper one-handed, but he did it, rubbing the length of Tyler's cock. He was thick, weighty in Donovan's hand. "You hate this, don't you? You hate that I'm the one making you feel like this."

Tyler nodded, a jerky little motion of his head. Donovan squeezed his fingers more. There was an art to breath play. Any idiot could grab hard and squeeze, but it was more likely to either make the person cough or, if you went too hard, crush their windpipe. No, the secret was in applying pressure to the sides where their carotid arteries were. It wasn't about cutting off their breathing but restricting the blood flow to their brain.

Too long, you could kill a person. But properly done, it would cause a hell of a rush. A gorgeous light-headed feeling that made the whole world go dreamy. Donovan did it now, pushing in on the sides of Tyler's throat. His eyes went wide but there was something in them, a fire, a desperation. And the way he thrust into Donovan's hand told him he was very, very into this.

Donovan released his grip and brought his hand to his face, licking his palm. He returned it to Tyler's cock, stroking. Tyler groaned.

"You like that?"

Tyler nodded. Donovan tightened his grip again and kept his gaze on Tyler's face as he stroked harder, jerking his dick roughly. It had to hurt with little more than spit to slick it, but Tyler was leaking now, shivering against him. Donovan let up on his throat, just a little, then pressed back in, twisting his other hand tightly around the head of his cock. He increased pressure around Tyler's neck, then just as he felt the little tremors of his approaching orgasm, he let up, allowing all the blood to flow back into his brain.

Tyler let go with a strangled groan, spurting into Donovan's hand as he gasped, shaking, his forehead coming to rest on Donovan's shoulder.

Donovan milked Tyler through the orgasm till he let out a rough groan and pushed his hand away, straightening. Donovan stepped back and looked him over, checking in.

Tyler let his head fall back against the wall, panting. "Jesus." He sounded wrecked.

"Good Jesus?" Donovan was so fucking hard right now he could bludgeon someone to death with his dick, but a rush went through him too. The pleasure that always came with that kind of power over another person. For a few brief minutes, he'd held Tyler's life in his hands, and Tyler had gotten off on that. That was powerful as hell. But Donovan had to be sure Tyler was okay with it now that it was over.

"Yeah." Tyler shoved past him and tossed his wallet onto the desk. He reached for the nearby box of tissues and Donovan helped himself too.

"Hey, talk to me, Tyler."

Tyler turned to look at him. "It was good, okay? I came harder than I have in a long time."

Donovan frowned, concerned by his combative tone.

"Why is that hard for you to admit?" he asked, curious.

"Cause …" Tyler cleared his throat. "I mean, that was kinda new. It was hot but …" He rotated his head like he was trying to crack his neck. "Weird."

"What is it? The fact that I'm a man or that I was in control of you. Or both?"

Tyler just glared. "The fact that it was *you*."

Donovan chuckled as he tossed the wadded-up tissues in the trash. Okay, he could live with that. "I just got you off in about two minutes," he pointed out.

"Doesn't mean I have to *like* it."

"It doesn't," Donovan agreed. "You don't have to like me at all, in fact. Doesn't mean we have to stop either."

Tyler gave him a skeptical look as he tossed his own dirty tissues away. "So what? We have a bunch of kinky hate sex whenever we get horny?"

"I've heard worse ideas."

Tyler fastened his trousers. "Guess I have too. I still don't know about this …"

"Why?"

"I'm just … we *work* here."

"Hey, I'm not suggesting we keep doing this at the tavern," Donovan said firmly. Tonight had been a risky and very hot moment but he had no intention of hooking up at work regularly. "All it would take was one person seeing us for it to end very badly for both of us, and this job is incredibly important to me."

"Agreed. So where?"

"My place?"

"You here in town?"

"Yeah, the Bayview apartments. You know where they are?"

"Yeah, just north of here. They're close."

"Seems like a good choice to me then. Unless you'd rather go to yours?"

"No, your place is fine." Tyler shifted a little, tucking his hands in his pockets. "But what about working together? Isn't whatever we do going to make it awkward as hell?"

Donovan snorted. "It isn't like we've had a seamless working relationship previously."

"Yeah, okay, fair point."

"We get on each other's nerves. This seems like a good way to release that tension if you ask me." Unorthodox? Maybe. But maybe orgasms would mellow them both out a little. And God, Donovan was dizzy with the need to feel the rush of being dominant again. It always sent him flying high and when he couldn't indulge, he ached for it.

"Guess it's worth a try." Tyler turned away like he was going to leave.

"Don't you need my address?" Donovan asked, half-amused, half-annoyed.

"What for?" Tyler turned back to him with a puzzled frown.

"Oh, I don't know." Donovan gestured to the front of his pants where his cock still strained against the fabric. "Maybe *me* getting off tonight."

"Oh." Tyler licked his lips. "You didn't come?"

"Just from jerking you off, no." Donovan's tone was dry. "Look, I like choking a guy out and getting him off and all, but it's not enough to make me come."

"What is?"

"Come over to my place now. I'll show you."

"Nice place." Tyler shifted back and forth on his heels.

Donovan glanced around. "It's not bad."

He had only chosen the place because it ticked all his boxes—namely having a kitchen with a gas stove and ample work surfaces—and its proximity to the restaurant. Which, admittedly, was handy tonight.

Tyler looked spooked though.

"You want to grab a shower before we get started?" Donovan offered.

Tyler swallowed. "That would probably be good."

"I only have the one, so we can take turns. I'll show you where it is."

"Thanks."

He gave Tyler a quick tour, then stepped out into the hall. "Call out if you need anything."

"I will."

While Tyler showered, Donovan turned on a few low lights in his bedroom, changed the sheets, then checked to make sure he was fully stocked on condoms and lube. He'd need to buy some soon but they should have enough for the night.

He shut the door and glanced up to see Tyler hovering in the doorway. "All set?"

"Yeah, I think so."

He wore a towel wrapped around his waist and water glistened on his body. He was a work of art both from the time he clearly spent at the gym and the tattoos that covered both arms from his knuckles to his pecs. The ink showed off how flat and honed they were, and his shoulders and biceps were perfectly sculpted.

"I'll grab my shower. Help yourself to anything in the kitchen. I have beer and wine. I don't drink much liquor and I don't play with drunk people, so keep that in mind."

"Yeah, okay."

"You can take the edge off if you need to, but I want you in control." Donovan let a firmness creep into his tone.

"Thought that was *your* game."

"You need to be in control of yourself for me to control you."

"Okay. Got it. One drink, max."

"If you're hungry, feel free to grab whatever you want to eat. We'll be up for a while, and I won't go easy on you. You'll need your strength."

Tyler's gulp was visible in his throat. "Right. Okay. I have some questions though."

"Of course." Donovan smiled reassuringly and softened his tone. "I'll be back shortly. I'll answer them then, okay? I promise."

"Sure." But Tyler still looked a little spooked and a flicker of worry went through Donovan.

He showered as quickly as he could, scrubbing the restaurant smells from his skin and hair as fast as he was able, but he still expected to walk out of the bathroom to find Tyler gone.

Instead, Donovan found him in his living room, drinking a beer and eating leftover Chinese takeout.

So sue him. Donovan was a chef, but sometimes he was lazy and the new place just outside town was really good.

A quick glance at the food Tyler was inhaling told Donovan that was the Hunan beef, so he went into the kitchen to retrieve the lemon chicken and pork fried rice.

Juggling beer, chopsticks, and food, he took a seat on the couch adjacent to Tyler, then peeled open the carton of food. "Tell me what you like."

Tyler looked up. "Like?"

"In the bedroom. You said you're new to being on this side of things so tell me what you know you don't like or wouldn't even consider doing."

"Well, no bodily fluids. Like … no peeing on me or anything."

"Noted."

"And I'm not dressing up in lingerie or anything. Just cause I'm gonna let you do shit to me doesn't mean I want to dress like a woman."

"I don't want you to dress like a woman," Donovan assured him. "Cross-dressing or forced feminization isn't my kink."

"Good." Tyler ducked his head. "I think I told you about the woman I was seeing for a while, who wanted me to lick her boots while she called me a sissy. That just feels gross to me. I don't want any of that."

"You're not into humiliation or degradation."

"Right."

"So what *do* you like?"

"I like it rough." Tyler licked his lips.

"Do you like pain?"

"I don't know. I think so? The choking was good. I liked it in the past when girlfriends used their nails or bit me. I like pain from a workout." He stabbed at his food.

Oh yes, probably a pain slut. Well, Donovan could make that happen. Happily, in fact.

"Bondage?"

"I've been tied up a few times."

"Have you ever been tied up and had pain inflicted on you?" Donovan chewed on a bite of chicken. Most places served it battered and deep fried but this place had an option to do it stir fried, just lightly velveted with cornstarch for that perfect tender bite and he always ordered it that way. The sauce was sharp and tangy with a mild sweetness underneath, pleasantly lemony but not bitter. And the peapods were just crisp enough to crunch under his teeth.

"Ahh no," Tyler said. "No pain. She just blew me while I was tied up."

"Did you like that?"

Tyler shrugged. "Who wouldn't?"

"Some people don't like feeling helpless."

"Well, she weighed about one hundred and ten pounds soaking wet and we were using an old necktie. I was pretty sure I could get out of it if I needed to."

"What if it was something you couldn't get out of? What if it was with a man who was closer to your size and strength? What if you really were *helpless*?"

Tyler shivered, but Donovan didn't think it was from the fact he wore nothing but a towel. "I don't know."

"It's okay. We can go slow."

"I don't know that I want to go slow." Tyler set his food down and reached for his beer. "I think if we do, I'll chicken out."

"You'll be free to stop or slow down any time you'd like but I'll go no faster than *I'm* comfortable with," he said. "I won't be goaded into something that'll go sideways."

Tyler nodded though he didn't look enthusiastic about it.

"Safewords?"

"Yeah, that's probably a good idea." Tyler took another drink.

"No. You *will* pick one. It's non-negotiable for me," Donovan said firmly. "I'm asking what you want. Some people use the red-yellow-green stoplight and others pick a word."

Tyler went silent a moment. "Eddie," he finally said. "My safe-word is Eddie."

Eddie? Odd choice but fine, Donovan could work with it.

"Eddie it is. If I ever need to stop, I'll use red."

"You do that."

Donovan stifled a sigh. Half of him enjoyed this antagonistic friction they had going, half of him found it exhausting. Why was Tyler so damn combative all the time?

"Anything I need to know in terms of your former Army service?" he asked. He set down the lemon chicken and reached for the pork fried rice. It was nicely savory without being over-salted and the fatty bits of pork were a contrast to the sweetness of the vegetables they used. The perfect blend of sweet, salt, and rich, flavorful umami taste.

Tyler raised an eyebrow at him. "Like what? Scars?"

"No, though that's a valid question."

"Wasn't injured aside from a small scar on my arm," he said. "And that's a cigarette burn. A bunch of us were fucking around and this buddy of mine put his lit cigarette on the table between our arms. He was playing chicken, seeing who flinched first. It wasn't me."

And now you have a scar to prove how stupid you were, Donovan thought. Jesus, the macho posturing these guys went through killed him.

"I meant PTSD," Donovan clarified. "For a while, I played with a guy who was a Marine. He had some very specific things he couldn't do. No being tied up. No blindfolds. No sudden loud noises. We worked around it."

Tyler shook his head. "Nothing like that. I didn't really see any heavy combat during my tour. Tensions were easing while we were in Iraq, and it never got too bad while I was in Western Baghdad. There were a few dicey moments but for the most part I got lucky."

"Glad to hear it."

"Yeah, me too." Tyler let out a little laugh but there was a flicker of something in his expression that made Donovan wonder if people he knew hadn't been so lucky.

Donovan ran through a mental checklist of other questions he had. "How do you feel about penetration?"

Tyler set down the bottle and Donovan noticed a slight tremor in his hand. Hmm. He was more nervous than he let on.

"Of me or you?"

"Of you," Donovan clarified. "Tongue, fingers, toys, cock? Have any objections?"

Tyler rubbed the back of his neck. "Only really had a woman's tongue and fingers so ..."

"That doesn't answer my question. If any of those are things you don't want to try, we can take them off the list."

"Everything's on the table except for the humiliation shit we talked about," Tyler said firmly. "Look I'm ... it'll be weird but I'll give the, uh, penetration a try."

Donovan raised an eyebrow at him. "Are you sure? You seem to have gone from zero to sixty pretty fast."

Tyler let out a heavy sigh. "Look, that's kinda how I've always done shit. If I'm going to try something, I'm going to go big. Little baby steps are worse. Rip off the bandage."

"This is supposed to be fun," Donovan pointed out. "I mean, yes, you said you want pain so maybe ripping off the bandage is appropriate, but ..."

"My buddies and me, we had this motto. If it doesn't scare the shit out of you, it isn't worth doing."

"Ahh. Okay."

"If we only do a little bit, I'm gonna get spooked," Tyler said, finally meeting Donovan's gaze. "It's just ... I don't work well that way. I know that about myself." His tone was firm. "If we go slow, I'm gonna have time to freak out. I need you to make it happen and not give me a choice. Except to, you know, safeword out or whatever."

Donovan respected that Tyler knew that about himself, so he nodded. "Okay. I understand that. I can work with that."

Stomach sated, Donovan closed the lids on the containers and returned them to the refrigerator. Tyler had drained his bottle of beer but Donovan had barely drunk a third of his. That was fine. He needed a clear head tonight.

He remained standing and looked down at Tyler. "Okay, sexual health concerns?"

"Tests all came back good not too long ago and I haven't been getting any lately anyway."

"Same for me," Donovan admitted. "We should be good. Condoms for anal?"

"Jesus Christ," Tyler said. "Can we just get to the good stuff and not spend all night talking about it?"

"Condoms it is." Donovan cracked his neck and held out a hand. "Come on, let's go into the bedroom."

He wasn't a hundred percent sure he could trust Tyler was telling him everything he needed to know—as much as from ignorance and lack of experience as anything else—but he'd do his best.

As long as Tyler remembered his safeword, they should be fine.

Donovan hoped.

SIX

"Strip."

Tyler stared at Donovan. His stomach churned a little from the food he'd wolfed down and the beer he'd drunk too fast. Nerves fluttered through his belly. Things had been fine earlier, when Donovan had him backed up against the wall with his hand around his throat but this … the slow conversation had been annoying as hell. And it made him more anxious about what he'd just agreed to.

Annoyed, he ripped the damp towel off and tossed it on the chair nearby. He stood naked in front of Donovan, heart beating way too fast.

Donovan had re-dressed and he wore a snug pair of black jeans and a fitted black T-shirt. His feet were bare. He was … yeah. Hot as hell. Kind of an asshole but hot.

"I'm just doing this once," Tyler said. "This is a weird curiosity that I have to satisfy. I just want to get it out of my system."

"Okay." Donovan unzipped a black bag that sat on a padded leather bench at the end of the bed. "Guess I'll have to make it good then, hmm?"

Make it good? What did that even *mean*? And why wasn't he looking at Tyler? Tyler was standing here naked, and Donovan didn't even seem to *care*.

"Guess so," Tyler said. "Once I get this itch scratched, I can stop thinking about it."

"If you enjoy it, I guarantee you'll want it again."

"You think you know me?" Tyler asked.

"No. I don't. But I know men like you." He set something on the bed.

"What's that supposed to mean?"

Donovan sighed and kept rummaging in the bag. "Men who are attracted to other men but who are too damn afraid of what that would mean, so they call themselves straight. Men who do this in secret because they're not strong enough to admit that they find freedom kneeling for someone else." He glanced up then and raked his gaze over Tyler.

Tyler resisted the urge to tighten his abs and flex.

"That's not … I'm not afraid."

"Kneel then," Donovan said.

Tyler swallowed. He … God, he was going to start with *that*? Make Tyler go down on his knees for him? Tyler's hackles rose and he stood rooted in place.

"Tyler. Did you hear me?"

Tyler nodded.

"I said *kneel.*"

Heart hammering, Tyler crossed his arms. "Make me." He smirked, like he was just joking. But a part of him wanted it. Wanted to goad Donovan into something. It would be so much easier that way.

Maybe he was scared. But *fuck.*

Donovan's eyebrow went up. Just one. Just one, carefully controlled raise of his eyebrow and a shudder ran down Tyler's spine. Shit. How did a skinny redheaded dude manage to look so menacing? Tyler was the one with military training. He shouldn't be afraid of anyone. Yet the look in Donovan's eyes as he crossed the room made goosebumps rise on Tyler's skin and the hairs on the back of his neck prickle.

"You want me to make you, huh?" Donovan asked.

"Yeah. *Make me.*"

"If you insist."

Before Tyler could blink, the room tilted sideways. One minute he was standing in the middle of Donovan's bedroom, the next he was lying flat on his stomach on the bed, his hands bent behind his back at an uncomfortable angle.

"What the *fuck*?" he muttered against the sheets.

"Jiu jitsu. I've been training since I was a kid. My mom thought it might be good for a hot-headed little kid to have some discipline and an outlet for all that."

Tyler wriggled, attempting to throw Donovan off him. He was a hell of a lot stronger than he looked. At least he'd had some training, which made Tyler feel a little better about being taken down by a civilian. It was easier to swallow from someone with a lifetime of martial arts experience.

"Don't usually use those skills in the bedroom but … guess thirty-odd years of practice comes in handy now," Donovan said with a grunt. He reached for something, but he moved too fast for Tyler to see what it was.

Donovan's weight settled onto Tyler's upper thighs and he arched up, twisting, trying to throw Donovan off, but he merely pushed his thumb into a pressure point on Tyler's wrist that made him howl and fall flat on his face.

"Oww, Jesus fuck that hurts." Tyler wriggled, belatedly realizing the struggle—or the pain—was only making him harder. Something wrapped around his wrists, hard but not cold. Plastic maybe? And then Tyler heard a familiar zipping noise as it snugged around them.

"What the fuck? Did you just use a zip tie on me?" Outraged, Tyler struggled, which only made Donovan push his palm against the middle of his back, pressing his chest into the mattress.

"Yes. They're quick, efficient, and effective," Donovan said, sounding pleased with himself. He slid a hand up and wrapped it around the back of Tyler's neck. God, like this, Donovan could do anything to him. And oh fuck, he'd felt *that* in his cock.

"Fuck you," Tyler ground out.

"Oh no. You aren't going to be fucking anyone tonight."

Tyler let out a startled yelp as Donovan's weight disappeared from his body and he was hauled upright to stand. His head swam and his cock throbbed as he stood next to the bed, wondering what came next. And how exactly he'd gotten into this position.

"Down."

Donovan pressed Tyler downward just as he knocked his shin against the back of Tyler's knees. Too startled and off balance to do anything, Tyler dropped into a kneeling position, wincing as he thudded against the carpet.

He knelt next to the bed, glaring at Donovan as he walked around to stand in front of Tyler.

"There." Donovan smiled down at him, looking way too damn pleased with himself. "Now, you're kneeling, and I've made you do it. Happy?"

"No," Tyler muttered.

Donovan's gaze drifted to his cock. "Could've fooled me."

Fine, Tyler kinda liked being manhandled and tied up. Didn't mean he had to admit it out loud, even if his body was doing it for him. "Now what?"

"Now, you be a good boy and stay there while I finish getting things ready." Donovan disappeared from sight and Tyler stared mutinously at the headboard.

He *could* stand and headbutt Donovan, rush him, but realistically, Tyler was pretty damn helpless like this. And well, he was sort of curious about what came next. And that made him even madder.

Teeth gritted, he stared at the headboard. Donovan had a black metal bed. Tyler shuddered at the thought of being tied to that. God, what could Donovan do to him *then*?

Time seemed to stretch forever as Tyler waited. He shifted, feeling the ache in his shoulders and the dig of the carpet into his knees. Donovan moved around, doing something, but he had no idea what it was.

Tyler craned his neck, trying to see, but Donovan was just out of his sightline.

"Eyes forward."

Tyler swallowed and looked at the headboard again. Donovan walked past him, sending a wave of cool air across his skin. He wondered what Donovan had planned for him next. Wondering what was in store for him. And then wondering why the fuck Donovan wasn't *doing* anything to him.

"I'm bored," he said.

Donovan chuckled. The sound made Tyler flinch. Donovan was much closer than he'd realized.

"The thing about me, Tyler, is that I don't like to be rushed. I don't work any faster than I need to. I'm meticulous. So, you can be as bored as you want. It isn't going to speed me up."

"I could call out my safeword and you'd have to cut me free so I could just walk out of here." Tyler might not have been on this side of things much before but he'd done his share of reading about kink. He knew what it was supposed to be like.

Donovan will respect that. Right?

"You could. And I absolutely would."

A little trickle of relief went through Tyler.

But damn, Tyler didn't want to safeword. There had been a few minutes earlier, when everything had felt just right. Maybe some of it was oxygen deprivation but damn it, if a man could choke him and make him come in two minutes flat, Tyler really was curious what he could do with a little time.

"I won't," Tyler admitted, swallowing hard.

"And why is that?"

"I'm curious." Tyler licked his lips. "I just want to know what it's like."

"Have you fantasized about this before?"

"No!" He shook his head. "That's it. I haven't. I mean, maybe a little recently, since we uh, talked about it. I just ... yeah, I'm curious now."

Donovan settled a hand on Tyler's shoulder, making him flinch again. "Then trust me."

Tyler's stomach swooped. It was that feeling of being on a roller-coaster. The clack-clack-clack as he went up a hill, knowing the stomach-dropping terror was waiting on the other side. But he'd always been the kind of guy to throw himself at something crazy and worry about the consequences later. To walk away, exhilarated, blood racing through his veins.

"Get to your feet."

Grateful, Tyler rose to a standing position. He hurt from kneeling, and he wobbled a little because he'd gone a little numb.

"The thing is," Donovan said, his tone almost conversational as he steadied Tyler, speaking right in his ear. "I think this is something that's been under there a while, just waiting for the right opportunity to come out. You just had to find the right man to do it."

"And you're the right man?"

"For tonight? Yes." He turned Tyler to face him. "Now, are you ready for this?"

Tyler jutted out his jaw. "I'm ready. Are *you*?"

"I was born ready."

There was something in Donovan's eyes and wicked smile that scared the shit out of Tyler. In the *good* way.

"Over here." Donovan pointed toward the foot of the bed and Tyler saw that the bench had been pulled away from the bedframe.

He inspected it as he walked over. At first glance, it had looked like simple storage. A long wooden box with a black leather top that flipped up. But it was more than that. It had leather straps that wrapped from top to bottom. And Tyler was willing to bet that was the kind of thing someone could be bound to. *He* could be bound to.

A pillow sat at one end. Exactly where someone could kneel and be bent over it. Where *he* could kneel and be bent over it.

Tyler's heart rate picked up.

"I'm going to stretch you out over this bench and cuff you to it," Donovan said. "The only question is, do you want leather or metal?" He picked up the two kinds of cuffs from the bed and held them out for Tyler to look at. "Leather will be softer. It'll allow you to struggle without worrying about marks. Metal will leave marks if you thrash around."

"Metal."

Donovan chuckled. "I see how it is."

"How what is?"

But Donovan didn't answer.

"I'm going to cut you out of the plastic tie now." He reached for a pocketknife and opened it, the blade wickedly sharp and glinting in the overhead light. "Better hold still. You wouldn't want me to slip …"

Tyler held his breath at the cool press of the blade against his skin. With a crack as the plastic broke, the cuffs fell away, and Tyler brought his hands forward, rotating his shoulders to ease the tension.

A moment later, Donovan tossed the knife onto the mattress, closed now, bouncing harmlessly.

"Down."

Tyler went to his knees. He didn't know why. Maybe because the sharp snap of Donovan's voice was as effective as the shin to the back of his knees. Maybe because he wanted this so bad. Maybe because he was itching for *something* to happen.

He landed on the floor pillow, hands at his sides, breathing in and out, trying to calm his racing heart. But it thundered erratically, making him breathless. He glanced to the side, realizing he was eye level with Donovan's cock now. He was hard under the black jeans he wore.

"Mmm." Donovan grabbed the back of his head. "I see how it is with this too. I was going to bend you over this and inflict some pain in a minute but I think you desperately want a cock in your mouth too. Shame your hair is too short to pull."

Damn it. Tyler had always kept it short, even once he got out of the service. It was easier that way. Low effort. But the thought of his hair being pulled while Donovan shoved his cock in his mouth sent a little quiver through him.

Donovan pulled him in, pressing his nose against his dick.

"You look good like that," Donovan said, a little purr to his tone. "On your knees. Mouth watering at the thought of sucking me off."

The hardness pushing against him was unmistakable. As was Donovan's size. Tyler imagined that length pushing down his throat. Forcing its way into his ass. He went a little lightheaded. He'd only had fingers in him before. Would he love it? Hate it? The idea it might hurt should have scared him but all it did was send another shiver down his spine.

"Over the bench."

Tyler glanced up at him, confused, and Donovan smirked down at him. "Come on. I said over the bench."

Tyler hesitated but his chest was forced against the cool, smooth leather as Donovan took the choice out of his hands.

Donovan let out a little tsking noise. "Making me do extra work. Guess I'll have to take that out on your ass."

There was something so infuriatingly smug in his voice. It made Tyler grit his teeth. But the strength of the hand against his back and the insistent throb of his own cock made Tyler stop the 'fuck you' that threatened to escape from his lips as he settled against the bench.

"Get comfortable," Donovan said. "I'm going to strap you down now."

Tyler shifted, feeling the stretch across his shoulder blades as he let his arm dangle along the sides of the bench.

Donovan took his hand and cool metal circled his wrist before the cuff clicked shut, cinching snugly around him. He pulled away and was stopped short, realizing Donovan had already attached the other end of it to a metal ring on the leather strap.

Donovan reached for his other wrist.

Tyler fought, struggling to break free, but a press of Donovan's thumb to a spot on his elbow sent a shooting pain through his forearm and hand, making him go limp. *Oww.*

"Would you stop it with the pressure-point shit?" he growled.

Donovan laughed. "Is it on your hard limit list?"

With a metallic click, Tyler's right hand was secured too. "No," he muttered through gritted teeth. He fucking hated it, but it sent a little thrill through him too, knowing Donovan could so effectively take him out.

God, what the fuck am I doing, letting a guy like this manhandle me? But the throb of Tyler's cock, pressed between the bench and his body, egged him on.

"I'm going to use cuffs on your thighs now."

Tyler didn't quite know what that meant but he understood a moment later as something soft but firm wrapped around each thigh and tightened, securing him to the end of the bench.

"So," Donovan said, standing. "You're helpless."

A tremor worked its way up Tyler's spine.

"And I have some fun toys to play with." There was glee in his voice now. Goddamn it, he was loving this. "Remind me of your safeword and let's get started."

"Eddie." It was the first thing that had popped into Tyler's head when Donovan had asked before. A cock-softening reminder of what could happen when things went wrong. Thinking of what rough shape his friend was in would definitely snap him out of whatever was going on.

"And mine?"

Out of the corner of Tyler's eye, he saw Donovan kneel beside him.

"Red."

"Good." Donovan clapped and Tyler jerked, startled. "Let's begin."

Tyler wasn't surprised when he felt the first smack of Donovan's hand against his ass. Predictable, he supposed. It didn't feel like much of anything at first, those first few hits. They were loud in the otherwise quiet room. Stinging a tiny bit. But they didn't hurt.

Until they did.

The hits grew harder. Tyler's ass and thighs began to heat, warming as all the blood rushed to the surface.

At first it was a little ache. A flinch as Donovan hit a spot that was already growing tender. Tyler breathed out harshly, twisting on the bench as Donovan smacked the side of his thigh.

He pressed a hand to the middle of Tyler's back.

"You're turning a lovely color," Donovan said. "Not as nice as it'll be once I really get going but it's a good start."

"Thanks."

"You hate this, don't you?"

Tyler kind of did. Not in the "I want this to stop" way, but he did hate being restrained like this. Bent over. Helpless to do anything but take the repeated smack, smack, smack of Donovan's palm against his tender skin. It was starting to really *hurt.* Tyler shifted a little, unable to get away from the relentless pace Donovan had going.

Tyler had spanked someone before, and it hurt his own palm after a while. Donovan's hand had to be aching. But he didn't stop.

Smack, smack, smack.

Tyler shrugged his shoulders, feeling the ache begin to build as heat rose from his ass and radiated outward.

Smack, smack, smack.

He twisted again, trying to get comfortable, hearing the rattle of the cuffs, the metal digging into his skin a little.

"You didn't answer me, Tyler."

"Yeah," Tyler said. "This sucks."

Donovan let out a laugh. A genuine, delighted laugh, like he was having the time of his life. *Fucker*. He probably was.

"I'm quite enjoying myself," Donovan said.

Well, that answered that question.

"Glad one of us is."

"Oh, you're enjoying it."

The smacks stopped. Tyler let out a relieved noise, but he trembled when Donovan trailed a hand along his crack. *Oh fuck.*

The pain was one thing. It was something he could grit his teeth against and take. And maybe he didn't hate it. Maybe he did kind of like the way it filled his whole body with heat and made his head sort of fuzzy. But it wasn't enough to keep the nerves at bay about what might happen next.

"I can see the way you grind your cock into the bench." Donovan pressed in a little, the tip of his finger brushing Tyler's hole, sending an electric jolt through him. Donovan chuckled. "And oh, I think you're going to like this too."

Tyler's stomach twisted with nerves. He and Eddie and the guys had gone skydiving once, on leave. Tyler had stood in the open door of a plane ten thousand feet in the air and felt the stomach-churning anxiety that he was about to do something that he could never go back from. This was worse.

Tyler swallowed hard, expecting Donovan to push in. But he pulled away and Tyler heard the familiar sound of a lube bottle opening. He twitched.

Donovan let out a little chuckle. "You know what's coming, don't you?"

"Yes," he said through gritted teeth.

"If you relax, you'll enjoy it." Donovan teased between his cheeks. "And you know all you have to do is say the magic word and I'll stop."

"Yes."

"So, what'll it be, Tyler?" Donovan pressed in, just barely breaching his entrance. "Do you want this? Do you want to see where going down this rabbit hole leads?"

Tyler rocked his hips up as much as he could manage, forcing Donovan's finger in to the knuckle.

Donovan let out a soft laugh. "So eager." And then he started to move.

Tyler was tense, clenching around the invasion but all the little nerves there woke up, coming alive. "Oh fuck." He seemed to have run out of other words to use.

"You like that." Donovan stroked in and out, just the one finger, the slick gel easing his way. "You're gonna like it more when it's my cock. When you're filled up and marked up, helpless while I beat you and fuck you."

Tyler let out a groan. He didn't want to, but the twist of Donovan's finger just as he said those words made it slip from his lips. Tyler closed his eyes, face heating. Blood heating. Everything heating until he felt like he might spontaneously combust.

He was going to get fucked tonight. By a man. The words kept pounding in his head, stoking his desire and making it build. He almost didn't notice when Donovan switched to two fingers, except it rubbed just the right way, making his heart speed up.

His breath came faster now. He was rocking into it, encouraging it. Begging for it, if not with words then with his body.

"Oh God."

There was weight against the back of his neck, a warm palm pressing his face down against the leather. Pressure in his ass, spreading him open. He wondered what he looked like right now.

"So tight, Tyler. You're going to feel so good around my dick."

Tyler groaned again, his head swimming as he imagined it. The groan deepened as Donovan slid his fingers away.

"But as much as I love to fuck, there's one thing I love more. Do you know what that is, Tyler?"

He shook his head, eyes still closed.

"Inflicting pain. And you said you wanted pain. Is that true?"

Tyler nodded.

"I need to hear the words."

"Make it hurt."

"Delighted to."

And then agony exploded on Tyler's right butt cheek. He was moving away from it, twisting and writhing against the restraints even as the sharp thwacking sound registered.

"What the fuck was that?"

"*That* was a wooden spoon."

Tyler opened his eyes, panting, still trying to absorb the spreading heat and sting that radiated from the spot on his ass, even as he wondered if Donovan was fucking with him. But he knelt there, holding up a goddamn kitchen utensil, smirking. With his stupid bearded face and red hair and smug expression. Forget it. Tyler had changed his mind. There was nothing hot about Donovan Ryan. He was the devil incarnate.

"Of course it is," Tyler grumbled.

Donovan's smile widened. "Kitchen tools are some of my favorite items to use. Oh, I've got floggers and whips. Some canes. But finding creative uses for household items is really a whole lot more fun. I think you'll agree."

Tyler had barely registered that Donovan had raised the spoon again before it landed with a firm smack on his left ass cheek. He howled, shaking and thrashing as if to get away from the pain.

"Do you like it?" Donovan asked.

"No!"

Donovan stilled. "Do you want it to continue?"

"Yes."

"Oh, all the pieces are coming together now for sure." Donovan's voice was a little smug. "A reluctant masochist. Well, you wouldn't be my first. And I do enjoy them. A little struggle play. A little roughing up. You do know glaring at me just makes me enjoy it more, right?"

"Fucker."

Donovan laughed. God, he was just so insufferable.

And then another hit landed, lower this time, right at the crease where Tyler's ass and thighs met, and he gasped. The pain twisted inside him, but before he could even breathe, there was another, in the same spot on the other side. And then a tap to his thigh. And another. One after the other. Not fast. Not one right on top of the other. But enough to make his stomach ache a little.

His whole body felt tingly and alive and his head spun. He squirmed, not sure if he was trying to get more or pull away. Donovan stopped a moment, running a hand across his ass and thighs, palm warm, touch sure.

"Mmm, you're marking up nice." There was real pleasure in his voice. He squeezed, gripping Tyler's ass cheek, making the sore spots hurt in a different way. "You'll feel it tomorrow."

Tyler didn't answer.

A few more hits. Short and sharp. Stinging and so close together that sent a wave of something through him. A queasiness followed by something sweet and mellow.

"I knew you'd be fun. But I didn't know how fun. All that snarly annoyance at being forced to do this. But that's just it, Tyler. I'm not forcing you to do anything. You *asked* me for this."

He slid his fingers into Tyler's ass again and Tyler gasped at the pressure. And fuck, the *pleasure*. Because it was so good. So good. So thick and … oh God, another finger. A little graze against his prostate. Another hit. Tyler realized Donovan was fingering him as he tapped his ass with the spoon and it was all swirling together, pain and the throb in his cock and …

It was all gone. Tyler let out a whine and Donovan stroked his head. "I'm still here. Just hold on."

Tyler shifted, vaguely aware of the pressure against his knees and the ache in his shoulders. But then he felt a thud and white-hot fire slice through him. He couldn't contain the howl that was ripped from his throat and he thrashed, the metal biting at his wrists and the cuffs gripping tight around his thighs.

Tyler panted, eyes screwed shut.

"That was a dragon's tail whip."

Tyler could barely suck in enough breath to respond so he just grunted.

"This is one of my favorite non-kitchen tools. It's short so I have lots of control and the way the tail licks you …" It sounded like Donovan was practically purring. "So stingy."

"Asshole," Tyler muttered, and Donovan let out another delighted sounding laugh.

"Oh, you are fun to play with Tyler."

Another zing of pain sliced through him. Donovan rubbed a hand over his skin. Tyler held his breath, hoping to feel the press of Donovan's fingers but instead, his touch disappeared, and another flame of stinging heat zipped across Tyler's skin.

He closed his eyes and breathed through it. He wasn't hard anymore. But it still felt good, like waves of need crashing against his brain, pushing him forward.

More hits landed. Slowly. Randomly across his ass and thighs so he never knew where to expect it.

Tyler's breathing was short and shallow, ragged, as Donovan pressed a palm against his back.

"Slow your breathing, Tyler. Do you need a break?"

He shook his head and tried to drag in another lungful of air, slower this time. Donovan hit him again, right in that sensitive spot and he howled, back arching, yanking against his restraints.

When he calmed, there was a slick, insistent pressure at his hole. Not fingers. Not a dick either.

"The fuck?" he slurred.

"This is the dragon's tail too." Donovan chuckled, pressing it forward. "The whole thing is made of silicone. It's a whip with a handle that's also a dildo. The best of both worlds. Pain and pleasure."

Tyler gasped and he must have relaxed, because the toy slipped a little farther inside. A strangled groan ripped from his throat as it was pressed deeper, then slowly dragged out. Donovan fucked him with it, all the while using his other hand to grab and stroke Tyler's cheeks.

"That's going to be my dick inside you soon," he said. "You're going to take my cock in your ass tonight, Tyler. An ass that is gorgeously marked from my beating."

Tyler shuddered.

Another zing across his body. Not from pain but from a pleasure deep inside. "I'm not a lot thicker than this toy. But I'm *long*. You're going to feel me so far up in you." He pushed a little farther in and Tyler let out a noise he'd never heard himself make.

"Oh yeah. You're going to love having a man's cock in your ass. It feels good to fuck someone. We both know that. But I think you were made for this. Made to take pain. Take a dick." He dragged the toy out slowly again, and Tyler gurgled, his eyes rolling back in his head as the toy slipping free sent little sparks through his body. He was growing hard again.

"I'm not going to be able to wait much longer to fuck you either."

"Do it," Tyler gasped.

"Oh, you're begging me now, huh?" Donovan gripped his ass cheek, twisting the skin, and Tyler huffed. "I like hearing that." He pushed the toy in again. "Now hold this in while I get a condom on. If you let the toy slip out, I'll whip you again."

Tyler clenched, holding tight. Though part of him wouldn't mind more licks of the flame.

A minute later, Donovan knelt behind him. He ripped the straps around Tyler's thighs away, leaving his legs free.

"Do you know why I freed you?" Donovan shifted forward, rubbing his cock along Tyler's ass cheek. He jerked in surprise. "Because I want to feel your cock throb in my hand as I bury my dick inside you."

"Hnnghh." The noise Tyler made wasn't even a word. It was barely a garbled sound.

"Nice job with the toy." Donovan teased it in and out, sending more sparks zipping up Tyler's spine. "Though I'm a little sad I don't get to use the other end on you again. That was *fun.*"

"I hate you a little bit," Tyler said.

Donovan let out a throaty laugh. "Oh, I know you do. That's the best part of this for me. Making you mad. Making you all surly and resentful because you're loving this."

He slid the toy free and before Tyler could stop himself, he realized he'd ground his ass against Donovan's hips. Begging for it. Begging to be fucked.

Donovan stretched forward, laying his chest across Tyler's back. His skin was hot, a little sweaty, and he smelled like a man. He *was* a man. A tall, strong man who had Tyler tied down and helpless. Who had hit him, marked him up, teased his ass open, fucked him, and was, even now, gripping Tyler's throat.

The head of Donovan's cock rubbed against Tyler's entrance, pushing forward. Tyler sucked in a breath, every muscle tensing.

"You don't *want* to like this," Donovan said. "But you do. You need this. You need me to fuck you, so I need you to open up. Push out and let me in."

Tyler closed his eyes and gritted his teeth at the firm pressure against his throat, against his ass, against his back. Donovan all around him, taking what he wanted.

Tyler let out a strangled sound as Donovan's cock slipped inside. Tyler's body seemed to pull him in farther and for a moment, they lay there silently as Tyler adjusted to the intrusion and the idea he had a man inside his body for the first time.

And then Donovan began to move. Tyler closed his eyes as the pain-pleasure radiated from the spot where they were connected and spread out across his whole body.

The slap of Donovan's thighs against his made him ache and he arched his back, driving his hips up and back so Donovan could go deeper.

"Told you you'd love it." Donovan sounded smug.

Tyler growled in annoyance, but he did. God, he did. He hated how fucking smug Donovan was about it but his entire body hummed with pleasure. That pleasure grew when Donovan wrapped a hand around his cock. He missed the pressure against his throat but the snug grip around his dick was even better.

The touch disappeared and Donovan spat, the sound obscene and thrilling at once. The grip returned, slick and tight. Donovan's thumb grazed the head, teasing the sensitive spot at the tip. Tyler had come a few hours—or a lifetime—ago but the need was growing already. Building inside him, threatening to spill over. Concentrating in his balls, as he clenched around Donovan. He heard it in Donovan's growl as he fucked him harder.

Donovan's cock, his hand, the pain still radiating from Tyler's ass, inside and out—it all combined together—forcing him toward the edge of a cliff. Toward that airplane's door. Toward the inevitable.

His whole body flushed, going tight and hot … and he jumped.

There was that moment of stillness. Of floating. Of his heart in his throat, his body bracing for impact, for release. And then with a jerk, time sped up and he was spurting into Donovan's hand, clenching around his cock, howling out his pleasure, unable to even drag in air as he let loose.

A while later, he realized someone—Donovan—was sweeping a soft, warm cloth across him.

"Mmm?" Tyler murmured. His ass throbbed, his cock was sated and limp, and he couldn't move.

"You came hard," Donovan said. He smoothed a hand up Tyler's spine. "How do you feel."

"No bones."

Donovan's chuckle was so warm and soft-sounding Tyler wanted to burrow into it.

"I fucked you boneless, huh?"

Oh shit. He'd been fucked for the first time. By a man. He swallowed hard, not sure if he liked that thought or hated it or maybe both. And maybe it shouldn't matter but it did for some reason. And Donovan was right. Tyler was limp and boneless, wrung out like he'd gone through his first day of hell week training in bootcamp. Body aching. Too worn out to move. And that part was really fucking good.

"I know. You want to just lie there but you've been in that position a long time. Your hands are free now. Can you sit back? I'll help."

Donovan's voice was soft, his hands strong as he helped Tyler sit upright. He wobbled, the world going light and hazy, and he slumped against Donovan's chest. "Just lie back."

A few moments later, Tyler was stretched out on his back on the carpet, staring up at the ceiling. He was pretty sure it wasn't supposed to move like that. "Fuck."

He felt the brush of Donovan's fingertips against his cheek, felt more than heard Donovan's laughter when it reverberated through his chest, which was pressed tight to Tyler's arm. He twitched his fingers, realizing the backs of them had just brushed Donovan's spent cock.

"Am I dead?"

"I sincerely hope not, or I am going to have some fast talking to do to the police."

Tyler managed to roll his head to the side. Through heavy-lidded eyes he saw Donovan's smirk. The twinkle in his blue eyes. Right now, Tyler didn't hate those ridiculous freckles or the red beard. Or that mouth. Tyler licked his own suddenly dry lips.

Donovan's gaze flicked straight to his mouth. He let out a little sigh and pressed forward. He didn't kiss him, just hovered an inch or so away until Tyler growled and closed the distance.

It was different, kissing a man. The catch of facial hair against his own stubble, the firm pressure, the large hand on the back of his head. The insistent tease of Donovan's tongue against the seam of Tyler's mouth.

His head was too fuzzy to dig into it now and he opened, giving back as much as he got, pushing Donovan for more. Donovan rubbed a hand down his chest and abs, making Tyler squirm into the carpet.

"Hurts," he managed. "My ass."

"Sorry." Donovan's touch was gone immediately. "Roll over, let me see."

Tyler rolled onto his stomach, head swimming, still feeling the phantom pressure of Donovan's lips against his.

He'd taken that leap. Done something big and scary and now he was flying high, buzzed and shaky and still not sure which way was up.

The only thing he did know for sure was that there was no going back now.

SEVEN

Donovan frowned down at Tyler's ass and thighs. They were red. Welted in a few places from the dragon's tail with speckled red splotches from the spoon. He patted Tyler's muscular back. "Let me get some cream for that. Arnica should help it heal and prevent bruising."

"Nah, I'm fine." Tyler moved like he was going to sit up, but Donovan held him in place.

"I know you're a big tough guy, but this was a lot. Let me do this."

Tyler let out a little grumble, but he subsided. "Fine."

Donovan reached for the water bottle he'd set out earlier. "Drink some of this while I grab it. You'll need it."

"Okay."

Donovan stood, grimacing at the remnants of lube on his body. He'd done a rudimentary cleanup, but he needed to scrub it all off. "Actually, let's hop in the shower first. We'll wash off, then I'll apply the cream. No point in washing it away, right?"

"Yeah, okay." Tyler stood with a groan. He wobbled a little and Donovan reached out to grab his arm.

"You lightheaded? That's common. You burned through a shit-load of energy."

"I just lay there and took it," Tyler said with a grimace. "I work out all the time. This was less energy than that."

"It's different," Donovan explained. "Impact play totally fucks with your body's hormone levels. It's what makes you feel great during and after, but your body doesn't know the difference between impact play and a workout at the gym."

"Yeah, fair enough."

"C'mon, let's go shower."

The water heated quickly enough, but when Donovan stepped inside the shower, Tyler lingered in the bathroom.

"You coming in?" Donovan prompted.

"Ahh, yeah." Tyler stepped in and pulled the curtain shut.

It was a good-sized shower/tub combo but the space suddenly seemed small with a guy as big as Tyler in with him.

"You doing okay?" Donovan asked. "Still light-headed?"

"No, I think I'm fine."

"Good. Let me take a look at your marks."

Tyler turned away and Donovan took a moment to enjoy the sight of Tyler's broad back, heavily inked and covered in water. Donovan ran his hands over the expanse before sliding down to Tyler's ass.

"How's it feel?"

"Hurts like a bitch."

Donovan laughed softly. "Here?" He smoothed his hand across the firm globe of Tyler's ass. "Or here?" He slid a finger between Tyler's cheeks and gently probed his hole.

Tyler jerked like he'd been electrocuted. "Outside. Your dick isn't that damn big, you asshole."

Donovan smiled. "Bet it felt big enough when it was buried inside you." He stepped closer, letting the front of his body graze against Tyler's back.

Tyler drew in a little shaky breath. "Yeah, it did."

Donovan turned Tyler to face him. Tyler looked up at him with a quizzical glance. Donovan had only meant to look him in the eye but the sight of Tyler's lips—fuller than Donovan had remembered—made him lean in.

Tyler shied away. "Don't." He pressed a hand to Donovan's chest, shaking his head.

Donovan frowned at him. "*You* kissed *me* earlier."

Tyler looked away, staring at something over his shoulder. "Yeah. I was still pretty out of it. I didn't even realize what I was doing."

"You never mentioned it as a hard limit," Donovan said, worry and disappointment churning in his stomach. He backed up, putting a little space between their bodies.

"Well, I didn't even think about it."

"Fair enough." Donovan studied his face. "Can you tell me why you don't want to? You don't owe me an explanation. I'm just curious."

Tyler shrugged, shoulders tense again. "I dunno. I'm just not sure I'm feeling the kissing thing."

Donovan considered the idea. "Is it that because now that you're coming down from the high of the scene, you're thinking about the fact it's with a man?"

Tyler grimaced. "I don't know. Maybe."

Donovan tried to soften his voice. "Look, I get it. This is new to you. A lot of new things happened tonight. I'm not going to push you about something like this. If kissing is crossing a line, you have every right to draw that line and hold firm on it. I'll respect that. And just because something was okay once doesn't mean you don't have a right to change your mind. I want you to give it some thought. I don't want to see you get so up in your head about being with a man that it keeps you from doing things you actually do want to do. Think about *why* before you decide anything."

"Okay."

Donovan reached for a bottle of shampoo. "Can we talk about the scene in general? Did you enjoy it?"

Tyler snorted. "I mean, I fucking came until I almost passed out. Yeah, I enjoyed it."

"That's … physiology. You've got masochistic tendencies and a prostate. I hit all the buttons for both. Did you enjoy it"—he tapped the side of Tyler's head—"here?"

He shrugged. "The pain kinda pissed me off. But it felt good."

"That's not abnormal. You like the results more than the experience of it. A lot of people are like that."

"I don't know that I disliked it, exactly? It just made me mad. Like why the fuck do I like this shit?" For the first time in a long while, the corners of Tyler's mouth lifted in a little smirk.

Donovan grinned back at him. "Fair enough. You liked inflicting it on others, right?"

"I mean, I didn't do half of what we just did to anyone else but yeah. It was okay."

"Did you like this more than inflicting it?" Donovan had been wondering if Tyler was a switch.

"Yeah. But you also clearly have a way better idea of what you're doing than I ever did."

"Do you want to learn?"

Tyler's smirk widened. "Why? You offering your ass up for me to practice on?"

"Uh, no," Donovan said. "Like I said the other day, I don't bottom for impact play. I'm not a switch." He'd tried. God, for Jude, he'd *tried*. And it had been miserable for both of them. "I was just curious."

Tyler hesitated. "I guess before, I was just drawn to it in general and I assumed I would be the one in charge? Cause that's how it goes most of the time."

"There are a lot of female Dommes who might disagree with that, but yeah, you were raised to expect men to be in charge. And you were with women, so …"

"I wasn't afraid to let a woman tie me up," Tyler said, sounding a little defensive.

"No, and that's great." Donovan softened his tone. "You were open-minded. So you think maybe you were drawn to it because you wanted to be on this side of it? And just didn't realize it?"

Tyler shrugged. "Maybe. I just know this was better than anything I did before."

"What about it did you like?" Donovan knew he was pushing Tyler, but he wanted to know where his head was at. He'd gone whole hog on trying things but that made it all the more likely he'd spook.

"I guess I could just stop … thinking so much. You know I didn't have to be worrying about my buddy or work or anything else. I could just …"

"Let go."

"Yeah. Like I said, it pissed me off to be helpless and being whaled on but it was nice too. Cause I didn't have to worry about anything. All I had to do was take it."

And *that* was a very submissive mindset. But Donovan wasn't so sure Tyler wanted to hear that. Especially when he was naked and vulnerable with another guy.

"So, did it satisfy your curiosity?" Donovan settled his hands on Tyler's firm pec, sliding his hands across the snarling beasts inked there.

Tyler hesitated but he didn't pull away or shrug off Donovan's touch. "Sort of?"

"Think you might want to try it again? Just to be sure?" Donovan slid his hand down Tyler's body, wrapped it around his dick, and stroked. Tyler wasn't hard, but the slide of Donovan's wet hand would probably still feel good.

"Mmm. I might."

"Then let's do that." Donovan smiled at him. "We're going to see each other at work anyway."

Tyler's expression turned uneasy, and he stepped back under the water, dislodging Donovan's grip. "No one there will know, right?"

"No. If you're in the mood for something, just say, 'hey, do you want to hang out tonight?' and I'll know what you mean." He smirked at Tyler. "What we do can be your dirty little secret."

Tyler winced. "You don't mind?"

"I don't share much about my personal life at work anyway."

"True. Honestly, I wasn't even sure you were gay. I thought maybe, only because I never saw you checking out Jenna. And every guy checks out Jenna."

Jenna Wagner was a former bartender who now had her degree in massage therapy. She worked for a wellness center in town and did some freelance stuff on the side. She was also a tall blonde bombshell who turned heads left and right.

"I can appreciate that she's attractive. It does nothing for me," Donovan said with a shrug.

"No wiggle room?"

"Guess not." Over the years, Donovan had considered if he was into women but none had ever sparked more than a mental or aesthetic appreciation. He'd never gotten hard for one. Tyler apparently had a hell of a lot more sexual flexibility to him than Donovan had expected. Frankly, Donovan was impressed by Tyler's willingness to explore being with a guy, even if he'd been touchy about the whole thing.

Donovan pointed to the water. "Can I get under there and rinse off?"

"Oh, sure." They switched spots.

"I'm not going to be upset if you aren't ready to announce to the tavern's staff that you're reconsidering how straight you are and like to get beat by men," Donovan said, tilting his head back to thoroughly wet it.

"I'm not reconsidering how straight I am. I mean, it's not like I'm going to *date* guys. I'm just a little flexible in the bedroom, maybe." Tyler's tone was stiff.

"Right. Well, either way. I keep my dating life and my sex life fairly quiet. If someone flat out asks if I'm into kink, I won't deny it, but I won't go announcing it. And I certainly won't tell anyone you're involved. Your privacy will be respected."

"Thanks." Tyler's shoulders dropped a little. "Cause as weird as it is to be in the shower with a guy who just"—he swallowed hard—"fucked me, I have to admit it's less weird than I thought it would be. And I'd like to do it again."

"Then we're in agreement."

"Might be a first for us."

Donovan laughed. Much as Tyler had driven him crazy lately, he did feel a whole lot more mellow now. "Must be the good sex."

"You enjoyed it then?" Tyler didn't quite meet his gaze.

Donovan stepped forward, letting their wet bodies slide together. "I did. The trust you put in me tonight was sexy as hell, Tyler. There is nothing hotter to me than a strong man letting me do what I choose to him. I know that may not feel very strong to you, being a bottom for impact play or sex, but it is. It takes a lot of courage to try something that scares you. And getting to be the first person you offered that to was incredible."

"It was a lot better than I expected."

"Good." Donovan resisted the urge to lean in for a kiss. "You all done in here?"

"Yeah." Tyler reached out and turned off the water. "I should get home. I'm going to sleep like a brick."

"You gonna be okay to drive? You feeling shaky or anything? You might want something to eat. Something to get your electrolytes up."

"I have some bottles of Gatorade and protein bars in my gym bag. I think it's still in the truck." Tyler yanked open the shower curtain.

"Should I be offended you're turning down my food in favor of cheap sports drinks and mass-produced protein replacements?"

Tyler scrubbed the towel across his hair. "Only if you want to."

"Much as I enjoy our arguments, I'm getting pretty tired too." A yawn crept up on Donovan and he covered it with the back of his hand.

"I'm glad we have tomorrow off. I'm looking forward to sleeping in."

"Yeah, me too. It was worth it though," Donovan said, reaching for a towel. "Or at least it was for me. I always have a lot of energy after work."

Tyler glanced at him, surprise written all over his face. "Yeah?"

Donovan nodded. "Yeah, it's this buzz I can't shake off."

"I know what you're talking about," Tyler said slowly. "Sometimes I go for a run around my neighborhood when I can't figure out how to burn it off otherwise."

"This was always my method," Donovan said, wrapping a towel around his waist.

"Sex?"

"Kink and sex, yeah."

"Was?" Tyler reached for the clothes he'd apparently left in the bathroom after his first shower of the night. "Past tense?"

"Yeah. It's been a while. Not as many kinky men in Pendleton as there were Fort Benton. And the hours we work don't help."

"I hear that," Tyler said. He zipped up his pants.

"I think this'll be good," Donovan said. "This little arrangement." Assuming Tyler didn't get freaked out and bolt. Or slug him in the nose the next time they worked together.

"Yeah, me too." Tyler shrugged on his shirt and buttoned it. "But I think I'm out of here for tonight."

"Text me when you get home?"

Tyler raised an eyebrow at him. "Really?"

"Look, I'm a Dom," Donovan explained as they walked down the hall. "That means I'm looking out for your safety during and after a scene. It hits different people in different ways. Some crash really hard and sometimes it's a while before that happens. I just want to be sure you're all right."

"Yeah, okay. Fair enough."

They paused beside the front door and Tyler slipped on his shoes.

When he straightened again, Donovan caught his elbow. "You'll text me when you get home?"

"Yeah, I'll text." Tyler let out a sigh.

"And if you start to feel weird about things, about what we did or you just feel strange or off in any way, will you message me?"

Tyler nodded once, clearly reluctant.

"I know we started off pretty antagonistic," Donovan said, trying to soften his tone. "And this week, I'm going to have to do my best to let you lead at work. But can you let *me* lead when it comes to this? I have years of experience and I've seen it go wrong too many times. Big, tough subs get laid out because they ignore what's going on in their head. It's not weak to admit you need some help. This is …" He sighed. "This is kind of a mind-fuck at first under the best of circumstances and you're not someone who ever expected to either hook up with a guy or be on the bottom side of BDSM. Just don't shut me out if you get weirded out in the next few days, okay?"

"Yeah, okay." Tyler reached for the door and Donovan let him go. He left with a small lift of his hand in goodbye. It felt strange to part ways without a hug or a kiss but Donovan wanted to respect where Tyler was right now.

Hopefully, if Tyler didn't let his head get in the way of things, they could do this again in the future and it would get easier for him.

Donovan locked the door behind him, then turned out lights as he went through the apartment, eyelids drooping.

The sight of the messy bedroom made him groan. As tempted as he was to just crawl under the covers and worry about it in the morning, he knew himself too well. He'd lie awake, tossing and turning, thinking about it until he finally got up to deal with it. Better to do it now and save himself the hassle.

Donovan cleaned and sanitized the toys, leaving them neatly laid out on the bathroom dresser to dry. When the bench was back in place, wiped down, and the bedroom was tidy, he let out a sigh of relief. He turned out the lights, crawled under the covers, and had just reached for his phone when it buzzed with a text.

Made it home. I'm about ready to crash. Thanks for tonight.

Donovan smiled, relieved. Tyler had done as he'd asked. ***Thank you. I appreciate the trust you put in me tonight.***

G'night.

Night.

Donovan plugged in his phone and closed his eyes. He was asleep in minutes.

It was late morning by the time Donovan awoke. He had a quick breakfast and drove west about ten miles to the Wholesome Root Farm. It was a bright summer day and as he got out of his car, he squinted behind his sunglasses. The sun heated his skin and the wind teased at the hem of his white shirt as he approached the little red building with the sign Wholesome Root Fresh Market.

Donovan stepped inside, inhaling the scents of fresh produce and baked goods.

He waved at Colleen Patton, who was behind the counter helping a customer, and she waved back, her smile broadening. "Be with you shortly, Donovan."

"No rush."

The market was small with just a few aisles of goods but they were all grown and made on the farm. He inspected jars of jams, jellies, pickled vegetables, and honey. There were a few freezer and refrigerator cases of organic grass-fed beef and lamb. He'd bought some for his own use, though they didn't have enough volume to supply the restaurant. He snagged a package of fresh ground lamb for himself now, thinking about the Greek-style meatball pitas he'd make. He found some sheep's milk feta-style cheese in the refrigerator case to go with it, then picked up a bunch of mint and another of oregano.

He browsed the pies—mostly rhubarb and strawberry this time of year and there would be peach, cherry, and blueberry shortly.

Because of the farmers market schedule conflicting with his work, he rarely made it there, but he liked that Colleen and Arthur had this small farm store as well. It was open most days of the week and they held all kinds of events and education opportunities on the property, which helped lure tourists in.

From what Donovan knew, their farm had been around for a few decades and the Pattons had a son in town who owned an accounting business. Forrest was around Donovan's age, and he did the books for the tavern. Donovan had seen him and the local mechanic at the recent Memorial Day parade. They'd looked cozy, watching the floats go by with their arms wrapped around each other, but Donovan was pretty damn sure they were up to something kinky, given the glazed look in Forrest's eyes and the fact that Donovan had seen the mechanic at some munches in Fort Benton a while back.

Shame he'd never spotted either of them on the kinky dating app, though he wasn't sure if nerdy accountants were really his thing. Tyler on the other hand ... oh yes, last night had been good.

The other customer disappeared out the door with a goodbye to Colleen, and she smiled brightly at Donovan. "How are you?"

"I'm good," he said, meaning it. The kink last night had put a spring in his step, and he'd slept hard after. "How are you?"

"Oh, we're good." She pushed her shoulder-length silver hair behind her shoulder. "It's busy, of course, but it always is this time of year."

He placed his basket on the counter. "Have anything special for me this week?"

Colleen liked to set aside things for him, and since he showed up most Mondays, it was easy to predict when he'd be by.

"Oh, yes! Thank you for reminding me. I was out foraging yesterday and you're not going to believe what I found."

She triumphantly held up a small basket of nettle greens. It was the end of the season for them, so he was surprised she'd found any. "Oh, nice. These are probably the last of them, aren't they?"

"I think so. I have some dandelion greens too. They're starting to get a little big so this might be last of the really good tender ones. Oh, and I have purslane and wood sorrel too."

"Oh yes, I'd love all of those, please. Wood sorrel is one of my favorites. I'll make a salad with them."

"Don't you just love how fresh and lemony it tastes?"

"I do." His mind flashed back to Tyler's cologne. "I've been thinking about doing cedar-planked salmon with a nice spicy glaze. It'll be perfect for a salad alongside that. Not too much though, because I know it's high in oxalic acid." Not that he had kidney issues, but it could be difficult for people who were prone to kidney stones. Just to be on the safe side, Donovan used it as a garnish more than a salad base. He liked it on tacos with a squeeze of lime. It added a bright acidity like cilantro.

"Feel free to invite us to the tavern when you make the salmon." Colleen grinned at him.

"Actually, we're going to be opening the patio at the tavern later this summer. Rachael and I were talking about doing a private vendors' dinner to celebrate. Before the big opening. Maybe I'll make the salmon for that."

"Ooh. Let me know and I'll see what I can do about finding you some more wood sorrel. I'm trying to cultivate more greens like that anyway."

"Perfect." He glanced over what else she had available. "Oh, these mulberries look good too."

"It's a great year for them."

A dark glossy red-purple fruit that grew on trees and resembled a stretched-out blackberry, they had a tart-sweet taste and Donovan liked to eat them on their own or cooked down into jams or sauces. They were plentiful this time of year, but a lot of people had no idea they were edible or what to do with them.

"It would be fun to do a foraging class," he mused.

Colleen perked up. "That does sound fun."

"Maybe we could figure out a joint thing with the restaurant. I'd have to clear it with Rachael, of course, but you could teach the foraging part, and I could show people how to cook what they find …"

"Perfect. Yeah, let's discuss that. Arthur and I have also talked about some farm-to-table dinners."

"Oh God, that would be amazing. That's a huge undertaking …"

"I know. I haven't gotten to the 'how to make this work' stage yet. Still daydreaming."

Donovan smiled. He understood that. He'd been like that about opening his own restaurant for years. Of course, he still hadn't. But that was because reality had smacked him in the face about how fucking expensive it was. Sliding into the tavern's business, when they already had the clientele and the location, had been much more manageable.

Maybe someday he could have a place of his own, but for now, the Hawk Point Tavern was a godsend.

"Well, keep me updated," he said.

"Can I get you anything else?" Colleen asked as she began ringing up his purchases.

"No, I think that's good." Donovan did like to cook at home, but he often ran out of time and energy to do it when he'd just spent a day in the restaurant kitchen.

After Donovan paid for his purchases, he thanked Colleen and walked back out to his car.

As he drove away from the farm, he wondered what Tyler was up to today, then winced when he remembered he was probably going to be working at least part of the day because he'd need to handle ordering and delivery. So much for a day off.

Much as Donovan chafed at Tyler being given the responsibility, maybe it wasn't so bad. At least he'd gotten some time off. Tyler wouldn't have any.

Donovan didn't get out much these days. With the hours at the restaurant and most of his friends being back in Fort Benton, it was hard to meet up. A couple of his friends had kids too, which made it tougher.

And, truth be told, he was hesitant to spend a lot of time in Fort Benton. Things had gone so spectacularly badly with Jude, and he'd definitely burned some bridges in the restaurant industry and the kink community there.

The final weeks of their relationship had been painfully awkward. They'd worked together, lived together, and barely tolerated being in the same room together.

Donovan groaned. God, had he made the same damn error all over again with Tyler? Getting involved with someone he worked with was bound to be a mistake.

But no, Tyler didn't want a relationship. He wasn't coming out of the closet, at least not any time soon. And he might always be the kind of guy who was good with a discreet hookup but not with admitting to the world that he was into dating men.

It was a good thing Donovan was realistic about what Tyler could offer him because there was no chance Tyler was going to want to get romantically involved.

And frankly, who the hell had time for a relationship anyway? The mess with Jude had taken all the shine off thoughts of romance for Donovan. A kink outlet, some great sex … yeah, that was exactly what he needed.

After Donovan returned to his apartment, he carefully lifted the canvas tote of produce. His right arm and shoulder were a little achy. He smirked at the memories of the night before, Tyler all pissed off but loving every second of getting hit with the wooden spoon and dragon's tail.

It opened up some intriguing possibilities for future scenes, and as Donovan carried his produce up to his apartment, he sent a quick text, hoping that Tyler had enjoyed himself last night as much as he had.

Hope you're not having too much trouble sitting today …

EIGHT

"Tyler!"

He jerked in surprise, then turned to look at his dad. He turned off the weed whacker and lifted the ear protection off his right ear, giving him a quizzical glance. "What?"

"You're gettin' awful close to that peony plant."

"Shit, sorry."

Pat Hewitt peered at him from his spot on the porch. "You okay? You seem distracted this morning, son."

"Just stayed up a little too late," he admitted. Which was the truth. But not the *whole* truth.

The sun had begun to lighten the sky by the time he got home from Donovan's place. He'd crashed hard after, but he hadn't been able to sleep in. He had this yard work to do for his dad and then he had to go into the tavern.

Pat smirked at him. "What's her name?"

Tyler wiped the sweat from his forehead, trying to hide a wince. "Nah, it wasn't a woman," he said truthfully. "I was hanging out with a guy from work. We had a drink, some Chinese takeout. Nothing major."

Nothing major if Tyler ignored the fact that he'd woken up with some gnarly bruises and marks on his ass. They rubbed against the denim of his jeans now and he could still feel the phantom thickness of Donovan's cock inside him. Tyler still wasn't sure how he felt about either of those things. He'd liked them, there was no denying that. But there was a perpetual refrain of "what the actual fuck?" running through his brain at the same time.

"Ahh. Well, your mother will have my head if you take out her peonies, or your own leg, so be careful, son."

"Yeah, I will." Tyler slipped the ear protection back over his ears and restarted the weed whacker. He tried to pay closer attention as he trimmed around the flower bed in front of the house. Those beds were looking a little scraggly too, with weeds growing up through the flowers, and he'd probably have to hire a neighbor kid to do some of it, if his mother would let him. She was gone for a long weekend, visiting his brother and sister-in-law, who'd had a baby last month. After his hip surgery, his dad hadn't been up for a four-hour car ride to where they lived in Illinois, so he'd stayed home.

After a lifetime of working physically demanding jobs, neither of Tyler's parents were in great health—his mom had arthritis that was getting bad quickly—and Tyler was trying to pick up the slack around the house.

There just weren't enough hours in the day.

And now that he and Donovan were doing this thing, he'd have even less time.

Tyler still felt strange and jittery every time he remembered being helpless, his ass on fire from Donovan beating it, and Donovan's cock pushing inside him. He was also sure Donovan expected him to get spooked. To freak the fuck out and tell him he was never doing it again. A small part of Tyler flat out refused to give Donovan the satisfaction of being right about that, but an even larger part simply couldn't deny that it had been good.

That he had enjoyed every last second of it. Even the kissing. His lips still tingled with the brush of Donovan's beard and the feel of their tongues tangling together.

So, no matter how weird it was to wrap his brain around the fact he was into a lot of stuff he'd never considered before, the thing that tugged at his gut was that reminder that life was fucking short.

Not everyone had a shot at a future like he did. The friends he'd lost had taught him that. So however weird and scary discovering this new thing about himself was, he was going to do it. He wasn't going to waste his life wondering about things he could be doing instead of actually doing them.

Tyler finished weed whacking the yard and he'd just hung the machine on the garage wall when his phone vibrated in his pocket. He pulled it out, expecting a message from Eddie or one of his other buddies but the preview let him know it was from Donovan without having to check the sender.

Hope you're not having too much trouble sitting today …

Tyler smiled. ***Nah. You'll have to do better next time.***

Is that so?

Yup. Kinda weak, man.

***chuckles* I'll show you weak. Name the time and place.**

Tyler gulped, his cock rising as a shiver of anticipation went through him despite the hot summer air and the laundry list of chores he still had to finish for his dad. Damn it, this was going to take all day and he still had shit to do at the tavern.

I'll keep you updated.

"You sure there's no woman?"

His dad's voice made him jump and Tyler turned to see his suspicious glance. He walked carefully toward Tyler, the movements careful but steady. His hip wasn't quite healed yet but he was already walking a hell of a lot better than he had been before the surgery.

Tyler slipped his phone back in his pocket with a little smirk. "I'm one hundred percent sure of that."

The next time Tyler's phone lit up with a text, he knew the message wasn't from Donovan.

Would you fuckfaces actually get your shit together and make a decision already? I need to put in my time off request.

Tyler unlocked his phone to see a message from Emmett Gordon, better known as Gordo.

He typed out a message. ***I was helping my dad do yardwork and shit. What'd I miss?***

Jackson: ***Gordo being a dick.***

Hewitt: ***How's that different than usual?***

Hayes: ***It's not.***

Emmett Gordon, Sam Hayes, Eddie Silva, Lyle Jackson, and Tyler had all met when they were assigned to the 10th Mountain Division light infantry division based out of Fort Drum, New York. About a year in, Tyler and Eddie had been accepted to Ranger School. The grueling eight weeks had cemented their friendship and they'd earned their Ranger qualifications together.

Rather than request to be assigned to a Ranger unit after, they'd both chosen to return to Fort Drum and their unit. During their deployment to Iraq, the five of them, along with Rafe Johnson and Charles French, had quickly gelled.

Tyler had been through literal blood, sweat, and tears with these guys and considered them the most important people in his life.

Of course, they were also the biggest assholes he knew.

Hewitt: ***What are we supposed to be deciding?***

Gordo: ***When the fuck we're getting together. JFC. How long have we been talking about this?***

Hewitt: ***I thought we decided on August?***

Hayes: ***We did.***

Hewitt: ***So what's the problem?***

Jackson: ***Gordo's got his panties in a wad because we haven't nailed down an exact date.***

Hewitt: ***FFS, this shouldn't be so hard. We're going camping and fishing, not invading a foreign country.***

Hayes: ***Yeah. Been there, done that.***

Gordo: *Well apparently that was less fucking work than getting you pieces of shit to plan a guys' weekend.*

Tyler rolled his eyes. At this rate, they'd never get the dates nailed down and Gordo would murder them in their sleep.

Hewitt*: August 8-11 work for everyone?*

Hayes: *Works for Jackson and me.*

Gordo: *Yeah I don't care when, I just need to know. Eddie, you in?*

Jackson: *Eduardoooooooooooooooooo???*

Their phones fell silent when Eddie didn't answer.

Tyler pocketed his phone and returned to reviewing staffing schedules and dealing with payroll. He liked being in the tavern on his day off. It was quiet and still, nothing like the hustle and bustle during business hours. He got up to fetch himself water and grimaced at the soreness in his body.

His ass had been colorful this morning, though the sting from Donovan's cock had faded. Still, he couldn't forget what he'd done. What he'd allowed to have done to him. It should have felt wrong and strange. The odd part was almost how right it had felt. How quiet and still his head had been as the pain burned away every thought and left only a peaceful emptiness.

Tyler wondered what the guys would think of what he'd done. It had gotten ugly when Jackson and Hayes had come out as a couple. Tyler wanted to believe it was only the shock of discovering they were together. Everyone had suspected Hayes swung both ways, though no one had talked about it. But no one had guessed about Jackson. Tyler got it. It couldn't have been easy to come out as gay then, especially for a Black man in the Army, but Jesus, the fact that the two of them had been carrying on for years behind everyone's backs had rubbed them all wrong.

Gordo had lost his shit in spectacular fashion, though Tyler had never really known if it was a combination of combat stress after another lengthy deployment and the death of Frenchie and Rafe, or homophobia. Gordo had sworn up and down it was merely that he was pissed about the fact their friends had been lying to them but it had left some gaping wounds in the group. Gordo had been distant, barely speaking to any of them for the better part of a year. It had taken a long time for him to mend fences with Hayes and Jackson and for the group to become close again.

Tyler could only imagine what their reactions would be if they learned what he and Donovan were up to. What if they thought he'd been lying this whole time too? Tyler cringed. Nope, that was never happening.

With a cold bottle of water in hand, Tyler returned to his office, wincing again as he took a seat.

He stole a glance at his phone and saw a few more messages had come in.

Eddie: ***I'm here. Jesus, you assholes are impatient.***

Gordo: ***So, can you do that weekend or not?***

Eddie: ***Let me check with Andrea.***

The conversation devolved into stupid banter after that and Tyler pushed his phone away to concentrate on work. But his thoughts kept returning to Donovan and everything that had happened the night before.

———

The following morning, Tyler came face to face with Donovan as he arrived at the tavern. Donovan got out of his small silver car just as Tyler climbed out of his pickup. The parking lot was otherwise empty.

Donovan's gaze swept over the truck, then up and down his body. "Huh. I'd ask if you were overcompensating for something but we both know that's not true."

"Hey, what's wrong with my truck?" Tyler protested.

"It's a bit large."

"We *do* get a lot of snow here in winter," Tyler pointed out as he walked toward the back of the tavern. "I get great ground clearance and I have a plow I use to take care of half the driveways on my street."

Donovan let out a chuckle as he fell into step beside Tyler. "I see we're picking right up where we left off with the arguing. So much for what we did the other night helping us resolve the tension between us ..."

Tyler let their upper arms brush. "We both know it's just foreplay."

Donovan grinned. "There's that. Feeling okay about things still, then?"

Tyler shrugged. "Yeah."

"Really?"

"Why are you so determined to believe I'm going to freak out?"

"You did a lot of new things the other night."

"I did."

"So, it would be understandable if you were a little jittery about it." Donovan punched in the access code on the keypad.

Tyler shrugged. "I'm not saying that I'm not. But I also know I had a good time. I liked how it went. Does my brain know what it thinks about the whole thing? Nope. But my gut tells me if it's good, I want more of it."

"Ahh, gut over head. I get that." The door beeped as it unlocked and Donovan held it open for Tyler.

He paused. "What do you mean?"

"Some people are all up here." Donovan tapped the side of his skull. "All up in their head. Some people go with their heart. Some go with their gut. No approach is more right than the other. You're just a go-with-your-gut person. It makes sense."

Tyler stepped inside. "Yeah, fair enough. Which are you?"

"Heart, I guess."

"So, neither of us use our brains." Tyler let out a little huff of amusement. "That'll end well."

Donovan smirked as the door closed behind him. The hallway seemed dim after the bright summer sunshine. "We seem to be doing okay so far."

"Yeah, I guess so." Tyler swallowed. The restaurant and bar were empty and still. He realized how close he and Donovan stood now. How alone they were. How his skin prickled with awareness. And how much he wanted to grab Donovan and kiss him again. "You were right."

Donovan lifted an eyebrow at him. "Right about what?"

"About why I got weird about kissing you." His tone was a little grudging.

"Oh really?"

"Yeah. I, uh." Tyler rubbed the back of his head. He'd spent the past twenty-four hours thinking about little else. "It's pretty stupid of me to be okay with a guy's dick up my ass but not his tongue in my mouth."

Donovan let out a soft laugh. "Well, I get it. Sometimes kissing is more intimate and we did put limits on this. It's an outlet for us both. Not a relationship. If you didn't enjoy it or you just want to keep some distance, I understand."

"Yeah, but I did enjoy it," he admitted. "I want—"

Donovan yanked him forward and pressed their lips together. He took Tyler's mouth in a heated, demanding kiss that pulled a moan from deep in Tyler's chest. Donovan pushed him against the door, and Tyler slid his hand up Donovan's back, remembering the way it had felt to have Donovan toss him around like he was a small guy.

"Damn," Tyler said a minute later as he pulled away panting, already lightheaded, cock perking up to let him know he was most definitely into it. He'd relished the feel of the bare, warm skin against his palm.

"You were saying?" Donovan braced his hands on either side of Tyler's head.

"Yeah, I was saying I enjoyed it," Tyler said, a little shocked by just *how much* he'd enjoyed it.

"What can I say? I'm a good kisser."

"Hey, it wasn't *all* you," Tyler protested playfully. "It takes two to tango and all that."

“Mm-hmm.” Donovan fitted their bodies more closely together. “Well, how do you feel about another dance? Tonight. At my place.”

“I’d be up for that,” Tyler admitted. Blood flowed to his cock at the thought of it.

“Excellent. Today is going to be a long day,” Donovan said with a little sigh. He dipped his head and kissed Tyler again.

Tyler groaned against his lips. “It really is.”

Reluctantly, he slipped out from the cage of Donovan’s arms, sliding his palm across Donovan’s chest. “At least I’m in charge today.”

Donovan grabbed his wrist, spun him, and shoved him up against the door, rocking his cock against the curve of Tyler’s ass. Donovan was hard, eager, and his breath was warm against the back of Tyler’s neck, making goosebumps rise on his skin. “Today, yes. But the minute we get to my place, I’m the one in charge. Don’t you forget that.”

Donovan grazed his teeth along the side of Tyler’s neck, making him tremble. “I won’t forget,” Tyler promised, breathless as he imagined what might happen tonight.

“Good. Or there will be consequences.”

The heat of Donovan’s body disappeared, and Tyler stood there, resting his forehead against the door as he sucked in a couple of shuddering breaths.

“Better pull yourself together soon, Tyler,” Donovan said, sounding ridiculously smug. “Cause our employees are about to arrive any time …”

NINE

"Need anything before we begin?" Donovan asked as he tore his lips from Tyler's. It had been a painfully long day, and he'd spent it counting down the moments until he was back at his place with Tyler. So far, they'd only made it just inside the apartment and they'd accomplished nothing but making out. "Water? Food?"

"No." There was something heated in Tyler's eyes, a dangerous glitter of need that sent lust surging through Donovan's body.

"Good. Because I have plans for you."

"What kind of plans?"

"Well, you know what I didn't get to feel last time?" Donovan wrapped his arms around Tyler's back, pulling him closer.

"No?"

"Your mouth on my cock."

"Oh." Tyler's voice was a little breathy.

"That okay?"

"Yeah. I'm probably not going to be any good—"

Donovan stopped his apology with another wet, needy kiss. "You know what I like even better than a man who knows how to suck dick?" he asked when he drew back.

"No."

"Showing him how to become a good cocksucker."

"Oh, God."

Donovan laughed softly. "C'mon, let's go shower first."

Despite the temptation to kiss and touch Tyler's wet, naked body, Donovan resisted as they rinsed off together. A specific scene had formed in Donovan's mind that he really, really wanted to make happen.

After they'd dried off, he tugged Tyler into the bedroom and ordered him to stand facing away. Donovan tried to focus as he pulled out toys and supplies, but he had difficulty tearing his gaze from Tyler's body.

There were still some marks on his ass. *Damn it.* Donovan belatedly remembered that he'd forgotten to put arnica on Tyler after their shower last time. He'd been too wrapped up in talking and making sure Tyler wasn't freaking out.

Donovan would have to be careful tonight, but there was a lot they could still work with.

"Kneel," he said firmly.

Tyler jerked, clearly startled, but he didn't move.

"Kneel and put your hands up behind your head," Donovan barked.

Tyler rolled his shoulders.

"Am I going to have to wrestle you to get you in restraints every time?" Donovan sighed in mock annoyance as he walked forward and came to stand in front of Tyler, staring into his face.

"Maybe." Tyler's eyes were heated, burning with need.

"Oh, I see." Donovan crossed his arms over his chest. "There's a word for that in BDSM, you know?"

"What's that?"

"Struggle play. Some people get off on the adrenaline rush of it."

"I do like it," Tyler said.

"And some people need someone else to 'force' them."

Not exactly unusual in bi-curious guys who weren't quite ready to flat out admit they wanted another man.

"I guess maybe that's some of it too."

"I know. Good thing I don't mind."

Donovan made his move before Tyler could anticipate it, rushing him and bringing him down to the floor with a thud. Donovan twisted, absorbing as much of the blow as he could, because they hadn't done much of this yet. His hip smarted a little, but after years of training, he knew how to safely fall.

They wrestled on the floor for a few minutes, Tyler's damp, naked body sliding pleasantly against his as Donovan grappled with him. His heart raced as the adrenaline hit. The slick pressure of his cock sliding along the groove of Tyler's chiseled lower abs was painfully arousing. It made him want to rut against Tyler, but even more, Donovan wanted to take his time and do this scene the way he'd imagined it playing out in his head for the past few days. He gripped Tyler's shoulders and hooked a leg around his thigh, rolling to pin Tyler under him.

It took more effort than Donovan had expected to get Tyler face-down with his hands behind his back. Tyler put up a good fight, Donovan would give him that. He wasn't putting up a token bit of resistance but giving as good as he got. Tyler was bigger than Donovan and his military training had given him some skills, but he'd been out for years, and as far as Donovan knew, Tyler didn't do the kind of training he did on a regular basis. Still, it was difficult to focus on technique with the feel of a hot, naked male body sliding against his.

When Donovan had finally pinned Tyler, panting heavily, he leaned in to speak in his ear. "Are you going to behave now?"

"I suppose." Tyler squirmed under him, looking petulant, and Donovan let out a little chuckle.

"Guess we'll have to *really* restrain you then."

With some effort, Donovan got Tyler to his knees again. Thankfully, he'd managed to maneuver them close enough to the bed that Donovan could reach for his toys.

Tyler didn't struggle a lot then. Not enough to make Donovan think he was really trying to get away now. More that he was enjoying testing him. So, Donovan got a bar across Tyler's shoulders and his wrists secured with the attached cuffs.

Tyler looked at him mutinously.

"Why do you look so put out?" Donovan asked with a breathless laugh. He wiped the sweat from his forehead. "This is what you asked for."

Tyler just glowered. Donovan chuckled, knowing it was all part of the fun. Tyler got off on this and Donovan's cock was painfully hard, throbbing in time with his heartbeat.

"So, there are a lot of fun things we could do right now," Donovan said, studying Tyler. "But I have several ideas I'll start with first." He retrieved lube and a silicone butt plug.

He dangled them in front of Tyler. "We're going to start with this. Don't worry, the toy is brand new. I bought it and haven't had a chance to use it on anyone yet." He pulled it out of the packaging. "So, you sit tight while I go wash it. Don't go anywhere," he teased. "Oh … wait. You can't."

Tyler's glare grew more ferocious, and he let out a growl under his breath.

When the toy was clean, Donovan slicked it up in full view of Tyler, watching his eyes dilate and his breathing pick up. Donovan walked behind him, admiring the view of a muscular man on his knees, bar across his shoulders, wrists secured to the cuffs in a position that left his arms up in a 'W' shape. Donovan sank to his knees beside Tyler, then placed his palm against Tyler's stomach. "Lean forward until you rest on my hand." Tyler hesitated. "I won't support your weight fully, but I promise, I won't let you fall on your face."

When Tyler was bent over and his ass jutted out, Donovan brushed the slick toy against his entrance, spreading lube everywhere. Messy, but it would do. He pressed in, working the plug inside Tyler and forcing a little groan to fall from his lips when it was seated deep.

"Oh, that's just the beginning. This toy has so many nice bells and whistles." It wasn't overly large, but it had plenty of fun features.

He helped Tyler straighten, then stood and reached for the remote control. Tyler's eyes widened.

"Oh yes. I get to be in charge of this." He pressed one button and Tyler let out a strangled gasp. "Mm-hmm. Vibration. Fun, isn't it?"

Tyler gulped.

"But wait, it gets better." Donovan grinned and hit a second button. "Rotating beads."

Tyler shuddered.

"It's a bit like you're being rimmed, huh?"

"Yeah." Tyler's voice was hoarse, and his cock had grown and thickened, beginning to lift to rest flat against his abs.

"And now, you get to enjoy that while you make *me* feel good."

Donovan stepped closer, his body square with Tyler's. His own cock was hard and flushing red at the tip because there were few things that turned him on more than a helpless man on his knees. He retrieved a jingling bell, then pressed it into Tyler's hand. "And this is how you tell me to stop. If you don't like what I'm doing or if it gets to be too much, you drop it. The second it falls, I stop and check in."

"Okay." Tyler licked his lips. "Am I … am I allowed to come?"

Donovan hadn't planned on restricting Tyler's orgasms. But now that he mentioned it … "Only if you want a beating. You either come, and get your ass beat, or you don't come, and you skip the whole thing."

Which pretty much guaranteed Tyler would come. He'd liked the impact play a lot.

"Oh." His expression was both alarmed and heated.

Donovan stepped closer, dragging the tip of his cock across Tyler's pink lips. "You look gorgeous like that, you know."

Tyler blinked up at him.

"Mm-hmm. All helpless on your knees for me. You should see yourself." He let his gaze wander over Tyler like a caress. "Those inked biceps bulging, your cock so hard it looks like it might burst, and those lips … anyone ever tell you have dick-sucking lips, Tyler?"

He shuddered. "No."

"You do. And I'm going to take full advantage of them. God, you have no idea how much it turns me on knowing I'm the first man who ever got the opportunity to use your mouth the way it was made to be used."

He brushed the tip of his cock across Tyler's lips again.

"Lick it. I want you to really taste me."

He held his cock steady as Tyler tentatively reached out with his tongue, lapping at the fluid there.

"Tell me how it tastes."

"Salty." Tyler licked his lips. "A little bitter."

Donovan stroked his cock a moment, coaxing more liquid out. "Any sweetness?"

Tyler lapped at him again, this time more eagerly. "A little?" he said as he pulled away. "Right at first."

"Mmm. Well, I think you need to taste some more, don't you?"

Tyler nodded.

"And if you look good now, you're going to look even better with my cock in your mouth. Open up," Donovan said, his voice huskier than he intended.

Tyler opened and Donovan groaned at the wet heat. When Tyler grazed his tongue tentatively along the underside, Donovan trembled. "Mmm, yeah."

He cradled the back of Tyler's head in his hands. "Going to fuck your face now."

Tyler's worried gaze flicked to his, and Donovan stroked his cheek with his thumb. "I'll start slow. I won't ram my cock down your throat." He grinned. "Yet."

Now, Tyler's gaze was half-startled, half-hot and needy. Oh yes, he'd enjoy it when Donovan *did* fuck his throat. It just wasn't the right time for that yet.

Donovan rocked his hips forward, slowly, so slowly, pushing into him.

"Watch those teeth," he warned.

After a minute, they found a rhythm.

Tyler's eyes fluttered closed, and he seemed to settle, the tension leaching from his body as he let Donovan take over. Donovan pushed deeper, testing Tyler's gag reflex. He choked, letting out a rough, sputtering sound and the bell rattled a little.

Donovan glanced at it, but Tyler's fingers tightened around it, and he pushed forward, eyes still closed.

Tyler was the most intriguing mixture of reluctant and eager. Donovan enjoyed it more than he had any right to.

Certainly, more than he ever could have imagined.

Donovan relaxed, his wary watchfulness easing down a notch as he allowed himself to enjoy this. He kept up the shallow thrusts, fucking the front of Tyler's mouth, groaning when Tyler sucked harder. The tease of Tyler's tongue across the underside of the head, the dance along the bottom of Donovan's shaft made the groan turn low and long.

When Donovan was shaking, struggling to keep his release at bay, he paused. "Gonna test your throat now. Drop the bell if you need me to stop."

Tyler nodded, sucking harder, and Donovan pushed in. The tight constriction of Tyler's throat almost undid him. Tyler choked again, gagging just the way Donovan had hoped he would, but when Donovan opened his eyes long enough to check in, there was nothing but defiant heat in Tyler's gaze and his knuckles were white where he clutched the bell.

Donovan repeated that a few times, pushing deep, enjoying the sound and feel of Tyler choking around him, before pulling out. And then he couldn't take another second of it.

Donovan drew back, setting up a fast, shallow pace again. "Open your mouth, I'm going to come on your tongue," he said raggedly. "And I want you to hold it there. Don't swallow until I tell you."

Tyler obeyed, and Donovan wrapped his fingers around his slick shaft. A bare handful of strokes later and he spilled directly into Tyler's mouth, pearly white cum pooling onto his pink tongue. Donovan's head went light, the room spinning a little as his hips stuttered, and he stroked himself through the final spurts. He trembled through the last of his orgasm, still stroking, trying to squeeze out every last drop.

"Hold it there."

A flicker of a grimace crossed Tyler's face.

"Now swallow. Slowly."

Tyler made another face as he did so, his nose wrinkling in a gesture Donovan might have called cute in any other moment but he was too damn turned on for it to be anything but hot as fuck.

Donovan wiped up a little of the spilled cum that had dribbled down his chin, and held up his fingers. "You missed some."

Tyler's glare was mutinous, but he lapped at Donovan's fingers before drawing them into his mouth to suck.

Donovan dropped to his knees, pushing his tongue into Tyler's mouth, chasing the flavor of his orgasm. Tyler shivered, his hard cock pressing against Donovan's bare thigh.

"Mmm, well done," Donovan said as he drew back. "We might get you trained yet."

"Yeah, good luck with that." Tyler's voice was a little hoarse.

Donovan reached down to stroke the iron-hard shaft between Tyler's thighs. "Oh, I think there are ways of making it happen." He reached out and grabbed the remote. "Don't forget, I have *this*."

Tyler's breath hitched as Donovan upped the vibration, and the tip of his cock grew slick as Tyler oozed pre-cum.

"What did you think?" He tilted Tyler's head so he could see his eyes better. "Did you like me fucking your throat?"

"Yeah. That was fine."

"You didn't like something. What was it?" He kept stroking Tyler's cock.

"The part at the end, where you made me taste it." His nostrils flared. "I don't care what anyone says, that shit is not delicious."

Donovan chuckled. "Oh, you don't have to *like* it. You just have to do it."

Tyler let out a little growl and shifted his weight.

"How are your knees and shoulders?" Donovan asked. "Need a break?"

Tyler hesitated and Donovan grabbed his chin in his hand. He looked Tyler right in the eye. "You tell me if you need a break. You understand?"

"My knees are getting a little sore," he said.

"Okay. We'll take the strain off you for a while. Can you handle staying cuffed to the bar if you lie on your back? And remember, in this case, you don't get points for toughing it out."

"Yeah, that'll be okay." Tyler licked his lower lip.

It took some maneuvering, but Donovan helped lower Tyler to the ground on his back. When he was comfortably settled, Donovan set the remote control on the carpet beside them and swirled his tongue around Tyler's nipples, dragging his teeth across them and making him buck up against Donovan's mouth.

"Fuck."

"You want my mouth on you?" Donovan asked. "Sucking that nice thick cock of yours?"

"Oh God. *Please.*"

Donovan smirked. Oh, he was going to enjoy making Tyler beg sometime. That would be fun.

Donovan suckled the tip, staring up at Tyler. "Did the blowjobs you got before ever feel like this?" Donovan tapped a finger against the toy inside Tyler's ass.

Tyler grunted. "No."

Donovan rolled his balls in his palm, then slipped a hand underneath to stroke a finger across his soft taint. Tyler shivered.

"Are those vibrations getting to you?"

"Yeah. And the beads." He groaned.

"Did you know this is just the second-lowest setting?" he teased. "I can turn things up again, if you want."

"Hnngghh."

"So, you like the thought of that, huh? Just wait until you *feel* it." He turned up the intensity and watched as a shudder wracked Tyler's whole body. He resumed stroking and Tyler groaned. "Yeah, just like that."

But when Donovan smoothed his other palm across the sensitive head of his cock, Tyler bucked up, body bowing off the floor as he cried out.

"Oh, you like this, don't you?"

"No," Tyler spat, but Donovan just chuckled. Because he could *see* Tyler's enjoyment. *Liar.* He pressed Tyler's dick against his belly and lightly slapped Tyler's balls. The desperate sound that escaped his lips shot through Donovan like a bolt of lightning.

"Oh, and you like that too." Donovan beamed at him. "A little cock and ball torture for my big, tough Army guy, huh?"

"I'm not your anything," Tyler said between gritted teeth.

"You're not," Donovan agreed. "Except when you're helpless like this. Then you're all mine to torture." He tapped Tyler's balls again, drawing a strangled gasp from him. He did that several times. Not hard enough to hurt, but enough to send a jolt through his body every time.

He took Tyler to his root and sucked. Moments later, he spurted into Donovan's mouth with a helpless groan. Donovan kept sucking, teasing the tip of his tongue into the sensitive little hole at the tip, dipping it into the slit before withdrawing to flick it against the head.

"Fuck." Tyler jerked. "I'm …"

"Getting sensitive? I could keep playing with you this way," he said. "See if I could get you to come again. I bet I could. Ever come dry before, Tyler? I've heard it's intense." He reached for another spreader bar with cuffs. "Nearly got myself kicked in the face one time by a guy who wasn't expecting it." He secured the restraint around Tyler's left ankle. "That's why I do this now."

Once Tyler's legs were restrained, Donovan spat on his cock and continued stroking, holding one hand at the base and using his other to tease his sensitive crown. Tyler turned his head, pressing his nose against his bent arm, panting.

Donovan cradled Tyler's cock in his hand and slapped, smacking his hand against the shaft this time. Tyler let out a strangled noise, so he did it again. Working his way from the tip down to the balls, then back up again.

"*Hnnnnnnngh.*"

Donovan grinned. The noises Tyler let out were absolutely delicious. His breathing was ragged and every muscle strained with effort.

"You know your safeword," Donovan reminded him.

"I know," Tyler said with a desperate gasp.

So Donovan used one hand to rub the head of Tyler's cock, while flicking Tyler's balls with his fingertips. Tyler's entire body went tense, abs clenching, thighs tightening. Donovan did it twice more and though there was no ejaculation, the sounds and facial expression were nearly identical as Tyler shuddered and spasmed.

Barely using his fingertips, Donovan continued to toy with the head of Tyler's dick until he writhed on the floor, squirming to get away.

"Oh God, it's … FUCK!"

"Had enough, soldier?" Donovan teased, gently tapping the crown of his cock again.

Tyler let out a desperate noise. "Yeah." His forehead was sheened with sweat. "I can't …"

"It's okay." Donovan let go and when he shut off the toy, Tyler went limp like someone had cut all the strings holding him up. "You don't have to. Just breathe."

He rubbed a hand across Tyler's stomach, soothing him as he eased the toy out.

Tyler jerked once, then went still.

Donovan set the toy aside, then unshackled Tyler's ankles, massaging the blood back into his ankles and feet. He slid up his body and did the same to his wrists and hands while Tyler stared up at him, eyes dazed and unfocused, mouth curved up in a little smile.

Donovan leaned in and pressed his lips to that smile, smiling too. They made out for a long time, the movements slow and languid. Donovan licked his way into Tyler's mouth, tasting the salty remnants of his own orgasm.

"Ever tasted your own cum before?" he asked against Tyler's mouth.

"A few times."

"How was this in comparison?"

"Still don't like the taste of jizz, but the rest of it … way, way hotter." Tyler kissed him again. "Shit, Donovan. I didn't know I could come like that."

"Some time we'll push you past that. Really edge you. Just for fun."

Wide-eyed, Tyler fell silent. For a few minutes, he lay there panting, staring up into Donovan's face. Donovan smoothed his hand across Tyler's chest.

"How is this …" Donovan stayed silent, not sure what Tyler was asking. "How is it like this?" he finished.

"Like what?"

"Hotter. This is like everything turned up to eleven. How is that possible?"

Donovan shrugged as he slid a hand down Tyler's chest to his abs. "Because you're kinky as hell and only now realizing it?"

"I'm only now realizing a lot of things."

"Good things?"

Tyler smiled. "Yeah, seems pretty good from where I'm at. This is … yeah. Like this shit."

"Good." Donovan stood and held out a hand. "Let's rinse off and get some food in us."

Tyler took his hand and allowed Donovan to pull him to his feet, groaning. "Fuck."

"Sore?"

"Yeah. Like you didn't even hit me, but my muscles fucking *ache*. In a good way," he hastily added.

"Ahh, well we can play more with stress positions if you like it," Donovan said. "Predicament bondage, maybe. We have options."

Tyler scrubbed a hand across his hair. "I think I'm going to need to start doing some more reading on this shit."

"I can give you a few books that'll be helpful," Donovan said. "They'll give you some more info on terminology."

"Yeah, that would be good."

"C'mon, let's get cleaned up. I'll rub your shoulders in the shower."

Tyler jerked in surprise. "You'd do that for me?"

"Hey, this isn't all about me getting my jollies," Donovan said. "It's about taking care of your well-being in every way. I'm going to challenge you, but that doesn't mean I'm just going to take what I want without making sure you're well cared for. Some people prefer a dynamic that's that way, but it isn't my style."

He flipped on the shower. "So, when we're outside of a scene, if there's something you need, you tell me, okay?"

"Yeah, okay."

"And if you need something during a scene—something big, something that absolutely can't wait or just because your head won't stop screaming that something feels bad or wrong, not just temporarily uncomfortable—you use your safeword," he said firmly.

Tyler seemed to contemplate that idea seriously. "I can do that."

"Like today. Were your knees and shoulders starting to protest?"

"Starting to, yeah." Tyler ducked into the shower, letting out an audible sigh of contentment as he positioned himself under the showerhead. "Were they screaming at me that something was wrong? No."

"Good." Donovan slid a hand across Tyler's flank as he stepped in too. "I was trying to avoid that."

"You let me move before it got there."

"That was my goal."

"It seems like a lot of work," Tyler said. "Being a Dom I mean."

"It's funny you say that," Donovan said thoughtfully. "Because I think in the end, that's what separates Doms from subs. Which role feels like it's harder. Which feels like it's a ton of work and which feels freeing. For me, controlling you is freeing. I'm focused and while, yes, I have to be thinking about your well-being constantly, that gives me this jolt of energy that isn't matched by anything else."

"Yeah, it always felt like a lot of work to me," Tyler said. "When I—when I was with a woman, I was always worrying about her and whether or not she was into it and shit."

"Sure, that makes sense."

Tyler gave him a hesitant look. "But this is good. It still feels a little weird but I think maybe I needed it, you know?"

"Yes."

"I've got a lot of stress right now and it's nice to let that go."

"I'm glad I can help with that," Donovan said honestly.

"I still kinda like being all … combative and shit about it."

Donovan chuckled and cupped Tyler's cheek in his hand. "I enjoy it too. We don't have to stop that. Knowing you enjoy that part of it makes it easier for me to really push you that way."

"So we're going to keep doing this?"

"I'm in as long as you are, soldier."

"Sunday after the restaurant closes?" Tyler asked.

"You're on."

TEN

Somehow, Tyler made it through the rest of the week with Rachael gone. He had a new appreciation for everything she took care of on a daily basis. She definitely deserved this vacation.

He'd thought, as bar manager, he was prepared for running the tavern. It turned out there was a whole lot more to it than he'd ever anticipated. Tyler spent way less time behind the bar and way more time working in his office. And working with Donovan. Which was a good thing … and a bad thing.

Good, because he was really starting to appreciate all that Donovan did for the place. And a couple of times when something had come up that Tyler had no idea how to handle, he'd turned to Donovan and he'd offered a few good suggestions.

It was a hell of a lot nicer working together instead of being at each other's throats all the time. But it was distracting as hell. He found himself studying Donovan's freckled arms, with their swirls of black ink, and thinking about how much power was contained within them.

Thinking about the way those long fingers, with their faint burns and scars, had felt on his skin. How they'd wrapped around his dick and stroked. How they'd slapped his cock and balls until he'd felt like he was ready to turn inside out. How he'd *liked* that.

Tyler shuddered, his dick beginning to fill underneath the soft black fabric of the pants he wore. He shifted in his seat, half of him wanting to sit here and let his mind wander back to that night, the other half knowing he really, really needed to focus on work.

"Tyler Hewitt!"

Donovan's voice rang through the halls of the not-yet-open-for-the-day tavern and Tyler sat bolt upright, heart hammering.

"Oh fuck," he muttered under his breath. "What did I screw up now?"

Donovan stalked into Tyler's office, a scowl on his face. *Shit, why is that hot?*

At this point, a pissed-off Donovan Ryan was like his personal porn fantasy brought to life. Unfortunately, Tyler was pretty sure he wasn't about to get bent over his desk.

Tyler stood and squared his shoulders. "Could you not bellow at me? I'm not going deaf."

"Why do I have twelve *cases* of whole canned tomatoes in my kitchen?"

"What?" Tyler reached for the folder with the order form. "That's not right. It was supposed to be one case of twelve cans."

"I'm well aware." Donovan crossed his arms over his chest. Tyler tried not to notice how damn good he looked doing it. How hot he was with that scowl on his face and his white chef coat on. "But for some reason we have one-hundred-forty-four cans."

"Shit." Tyler skimmed the purchase order and frowned. "No, I got it right. One case." He stood and thrust the form out to Donovan. "See?"

Donovan took it from him, a furrow appearing between his brows, crinkling the freckled skin. "Huh, yeah you do have it right."

Tyler sighed.

He wished Donovan had given him the benefit of the doubt, but oh well, at least he'd admitted Tyler was right now. He would take it as a win.

"Let me call the distributor and get this straightened out. I'll get them to pick up the extras and refund the money."

"Thank you." Donovan grimaced. "I am sorry if I overreacted. I should have checked with you first."

Tyler patted Donovan's chest. "I think a couple of weeks ago you would have taken my head off and insisted it was my fault. So, I guess this is progress or something."

Donovan's stern expression softened, his eyes twinkling. "Guess so." He leaned in, speaking quietly in Tyler's ear. "I was almost looking forward to you making a mistake though. I was going to take it out on your ass tomorrow night."

"You still could," Tyler whispered.

Donovan's grin widened. "Good to know." His gaze dropped to Tyler's lips. "God, I wish I could do it right now. Bend you over that desk and smack your ass with whatever I could get my hands on."

Tyler shivered. It was so close to what he'd been thinking about earlier. "Yeah, me too." His voice was soft but hoarse.

"I can tell. You're getting hard just thinking about it." He brushed the back of his knuckles across the front of Tyler's pants.

Donovan faced away from the office door but God this was risky. There were people around, and the last thing Tyler wanted was to explain to anyone that he was involved with a man. But he was so turned on he could barely draw in a full breath.

Tyler stuffed his hands in the pockets of his trousers. "Yeah, well … I know what I like."

"So do I." Donovan's smile was slow and suggestive. "And don't worry. I'll give you that tomorrow night."

Donovan disappeared through the door of Tyler's office, leaving him with a racing pulse and a raging hard-on.

He dropped into his chair, breathing hard. *Fuck.*

When Rachael walked through the doors of the tavern the following morning, a cheer went up from the staff. Tyler was as loud as any of them.

"God, it's good to see you," he said, giving her a heartfelt hug when she approached.

Rachael laughed, hugging him back. She looked relaxed and happy, her skin lightly tan. "Realized my job is tougher than you imagined, huh?" Her eyes twinkled.

"So much harder." He let out a sigh.

"I half expected to come back and see the building flattened from the blast of your collision with Donovan."

Tyler's lips twitched as he tried to fight back a smirk. "We made it work."

Truthfully, he was a little surprised by that too. Turned out, all it took was getting kinky together. Sure, they'd sparred over the tomato delivery yesterday, but it was really just foreplay.

"I see that." Her expression grew more serious. "I was only teasing. I had faith in both of you. Especially you, Tyler. I'd be lying if I said I didn't struggle a little the first day or two to let go of thinking about work, but honestly, I knew you had this. I'd feel great turning the place over to you any time, and I don't say that lightly."

"I know you don't. But maybe give me a small break before you jet off on any more vacations," he said jokingly, though he meant it. He really, really didn't want to try managing the whole place on top of everything else he had going on in his life right now.

"Done. I've missed being here." She looked around with a fond smile.

"Did you have fun on your trip?"

"I did." Contentment radiated from every inch of her. "My guys are incredible. They spoiled me. They even booked me a spa day at an amazing place up in Traverse City. Plus, the wine and beer tasting … you'd love it, Ty. I brought home some amazing stuff to try that I want to talk to you about stocking here."

"Ooh, fun. I'm looking forward to checking it out."

"We'll definitely figure out a time for that soon," she said. "I should let you get back to brunch service." She glanced around. "Looks like it's going smoothly enough."

"So far so good." He rapped his knuckles on the bar.

"Thanks again." She squeezed his upper arm in a gesture that would have made him melt when he was about fifteen. He'd had such a crush on her then. And while she was still gorgeous now, they'd become too good of friends for him to think of her *that way* anymore.

And, he realized, as a pretty blonde in a short summer dress sauntered by, shooting an appreciative gaze at him as she passed, he just wasn't really noticing that many women these days. Of course, he did have a bit of a distraction in the form of a tall redheaded chef …

"I'd like to sit down with you and Donovan after service is over tonight," Rachael continued. "Is that okay? Just a quick debrief so you can both catch me up on things."

"Sure," Tyler said though a flicker of nerves went through him. He hoped he could maintain a poker face with Donovan sitting a few feet away.

And damn it, he'd been looking forward to heading out to Donovan's place as quickly as possible after. Goosebumps rose on his skin as he wondered what was in store for him tonight. Whatever it was, he knew it would be good.

After the last of the diners had cleared out and the restaurant was closed for the day, Tyler stepped into Rachael's office with Donovan on his heels. They both took seats in the chairs across from her desk. Tyler shot Donovan a quick, furtive glance to see how he was feeling about this, only to find him with an equally apprehensive expression on his face.

Rachael chuckled softly. "No need to look so worried, gentlemen. I've been going over everything from the week and you both did a fantastic job while I was gone."

"Tyler did the bulk of it," Donovan said. "And he did it well. There were a few issues but that's to be expected and he was able to resolve them all."

Tyler shot him a startled glance. The first few days had been a little rocky. He was surprised to find Donovan so ready to go to bat for him.

"And Donovan was more than willing to work with me on stuff," Tyler blurted out. Oh fuck, now he was suddenly thinking about Donovan's hand on his cock, working him over. *Nope, nope, I do not need an erection in front of my boss.* He shifted in his chair and caught a glimpse out of the corner of his eye of Donovan smirking at him. Apparently, he'd picked up on Tyler's predicament.

Knowing Donovan, he was probably wishing he had that vibrating plug up Tyler's ass right now. Which reminded Tyler he definitely needed to let him know that anything like *that* was one hundred percent off-limits at work.

"Well, I'm thrilled how well you two worked together this week," Rachael continued with a smile.

Tyler's cheeks warmed.

She glanced between Tyler and Donovan again. "I didn't expect you two to kiss and make up, but it really is a relief to hear that you worked together so well." She cleared her throat. "Now, there's just one more thing I'd like to mention."

"What's that?" Donovan asked with a puzzled frown.

"Did either of you remember that the back hallway has a camera in it?"

Tyler nodded, his eyes widening as he suddenly remembered the other morning when Donovan had pinned him up against the fire door and kissed the hell out of him. *Fuck.*

"I generally don't even review the footage," she said. "It's only there for security reasons in case of a break-in or other major issue but when the storm happened and the power went out for a few seconds, it interrupted the feed. I wanted to take a look to make sure everything was up and running properly. While I was in there, I skimmed all the footage from when I was gone … I'm sure you can see why I'm bringing it up."

Fuck. Fuck. Fuck. Tyler snuck a glance at Donovan, whose wide-eyed expression mirrored exactly how Tyler felt.

"Now, as I said, I'm thrilled you two kissed and made up. I just didn't expect that to be quite so … literal."

Tyler grimaced. "I'm so sorry, Rach. I …" But he really had no good excuse. He should have known the damn thing was there. He remembered the hot female technician who had installed it a few years back. He'd gone on a couple of dates with her after, in fact.

"I'm sorry too," Donovan said. His voice sounded a little strained. "That was unprofessional of us. We uh—well this is new and …" He cleared his throat. "We both got a little carried away. But I take full responsibility for it and—"

Rachael held up a hand and looked between the two of them. "I truly don't care what you get up to together in your free time. It's none of my business and I only want you both to be happy and have a good working relationship. That being said, it should *not* be happening *at* the restaurant, don't you agree?"

"Yes."

"Absolutely."

Their words of agreement overlapped, and Rachael nodded. "Good. The cameras don't cover all the building, however. Can I be assured there were no health code violations that happened after the kiss?"

Donovan blanched. "No! Never in the kitchen or the dining areas. We uh"—he cleared his throat—"everything remained in the office or hallway."

"Good. Now, I think that's enough said on the subject, don't you?"

"Yeah." Tyler fidgeted in his chair. "Um, can I ask you something? Did anyone else see the footage?"

She shook her head, a puzzled look crossing her face. "No, I was reviewing it in here on my computer. Why?"

"And no one else knows? You haven't mentioned it to anyone on staff?" He couldn't look Donovan in the eye. God, it was one thing to have Rachael realize he was hooking up with another man, but the thought of the rest of the staff knowing? Ugh. He didn't need that shit in his life. He was only starting to make sense of this in his own head. Answering people's questions about it … no way.

"No," Rachael said firmly. "It isn't my place to ever spread any gossip about my staff's private lives. You have all been more than understanding about my relationship, and I know it isn't something a lot of people are comfortable with."

"Hey, I just want you to be happy," Tyler said. He couldn't imagine wanting a poly relationship. The thought of sharing someone … no that had never felt right to him. Not someone he really loved anyway, though he hadn't had much of that in his life.

"And I want the same for both of you. Whether that's together or apart, I support you both. Just don't let it impact your work."

"It won't." Tyler licked his lips. "Thanks for not spreading my business around the restaurant. I appreciate that."

"Yeah, he's ashamed to admit he has a thing for gingers." Donovan's voice was laced with amusement, and when Tyler glanced at him, he winked.

A little of Tyler's tension eased at the knowledge Donovan wasn't offended that he didn't want their coworkers to know about them.

Tyler chuckled and shook his head. "It *is* pretty crazy. I had no idea I'd be into that."

Rachel laughed. "Sometimes we meet people who offer us something no one else can. I know that as well as anyone."

Tyler's expression sobered. He'd never thought of it that way but maybe that was why this thing with Donovan was so damn good. Why he had been eagerly looking forward to their next hookup.

Donovan had definitely given him something no one else ever had before.

A chance to just let go and stop thinking about everything going on in his life.

And damn, was that nice.

After their typical post-work shower at Donovan's place to wash off the sweat and kitchen smells, he threw Tyler a towel. "Dry off and stay naked."

"Okay." Tyler scrubbed the towel across his chest. "Then what?"

"I think you should make us something to eat."

"What?" Tyler blinked. He'd been expecting something … a whole lot kinkier than *that.*

"Yeah. Scrambled eggs and toast. Bacon."

"I, uh …" Tyler grimaced as he took a seat on the edge of the bathtub, drying between his toes. "I'm *really* bad in the kitchen."

Donovan narrowed his eyes. "How bad is bad?"

"I end up burning the toast, and eggs are always kinda … rubbery." He stared up at Donovan with a sinking feeling in his stomach. Inedible was a better word.

"Oh Jesus." Donovan finished drying himself, then ran his fingers through his hair, smoothing it down. "Well, there's only one way to fix that." He reached out and hauled Tyler up by his arm. "We're about to start some cooking lessons."

"What? How is that kinky?"

Donovan's grin was so scary it sent a shiver through Tyler's whole body. "You don't give me much credit."

"Oh fuck, what have I gotten myself into?" Tyler muttered.

Donovan pressed against him. "Come on, we both know you like the fear."

Without really thinking about it, Tyler tossed the towel onto the nearby sink, then settled his hands on Donovan's chest. There was a light sprinkling of reddish hair across his pecs, not enough to obscure the inked birds in flight.

"Yeah, I do," Tyler admitted, absently stroking his fingertips across Donovan's skin.

"Good." Donovan dipped his head and kissed him. It was brief but thorough, and Tyler panted a little when Donovan stepped away. "Go in the kitchen and get out eggs, bacon, and butter. Then wait for me. I'll be in momentarily."

"Okay." Tyler's head already felt a little fuzzy at the thought of what was about to happen. He had a sudden memory of the smack of the wooden spoon the first time they hooked up.

Donovan gave him a slow smile, full of promise, and Tyler shivered as he hung the towel on the bar. As he walked down the hall and into the kitchen, the brush of cool air against his still-damp naked skin made a chill go through him. Opening the refrigerator door made it worse. He grimaced as he stared at the orderly contents. Everything was neatly labeled—with dates—and Tyler shook his head. He was pretty neat and tidy because of his military service but this was next-level shit. He supposed it came from Donovan's chef training.

How in the hell was Tyler supposed to cook well enough to impress someone like *that*?

It made it easy to find everything he needed at least, and he'd just set it on the counter when he heard soft footfalls approaching. Tyler jerked in surprise when he heard a thump behind him, and turned to see Donovan had dropped his gear bag on a kitchen chair.

Donovan's grin was full of wicked promise.

"What's in there?" Tyler asked, nerves and anticipation beginning to build in him.

"You'll find out." Donovan plucked a black apron from a hook on the wall. "Put this on."

"Thanks," Tyler said, letting out a breath of relief. "I was getting a little concerned that there was going to be bacon grease splattering everywhere and—"

"Safety first." Donovan smiled at him, his white teeth glistening in the light. The look in his eyes made Tyler tremble.

Donovan rubbed his hands up and down Tyler's arms, warming the goosebumps all over his skin. Donovan wore a pair of jeans that sat low enough to show off that he definitely wasn't wearing anything beneath them. "Want me to turn up the heat a little?"

"Yeah, that would be good," Tyler said. He was fairly sure he was going to be sweating eventually, but in the meantime …

Donovan disappeared into the hall and a moment later, the heat kicked on. When Donovan returned, he looked Tyler up and down. "I think I'd like to put one thing on you before we begin." He unzipped the bag, fished something out, and held up a black metal chain.

Tyler gulped. "Nipple clamps?"

"Mm-hmm."

"Fuck."

"Ever tried them?"

"Not on myself," Tyler admitted. And the ones he'd used on a former girlfriend were pretty wussy ones. These looked heavy duty.

"No time like the present."

Donovan stepped toward him. He licked his thumb, then flicked it against Tyler's nipple, making him jerk in surprise. A moment later he felt the cool touch of metal and he looked down to see

Donovan turning a little screw on the clamp. He hissed as it tightened, but it sent a little jolt of pleasure through him too.

Donovan did the same to the other one. It wasn't until Donovan let go of the heavy weighted chain that Tyler cried out. He gripped the counter behind him as the clamps shifted and sent jagged little sparks of need into his belly. "Fuck!"

"Good fuck?"

Tyler gritted his teeth. "Yes."

"Apron on now."

Carefully, Tyler slipped the fabric over his head, then tied it tightly around his waist. Every movement was agony, sending a sharp jolt through his body, but when he was done, it settled to a low, dull ache.

"Wash your hands."

He soaped his skin alongside Donovan. Every movement tugged at the clamps, and Tyler's cock slowly filled, beginning to push at the fabric of the apron.

After Donovan dried his hands, he was all business.

"First things first, lay out everything you'll need. The French term for this is *mis en place*. It means prepping your ingredients before you begin cooking.

"We'll begin with the bacon. We're going to cook it in the oven on a tray. Normally for baking, we pre-heat the oven, but the bacon curls less if you start out with a cold temp."

Tyler listened as Donovan pulled out a baking sheet with a metal gridded rack on top. Tyler did as instructed, laying out the bacon on the rack and sliding it into the oven Donovan had just turned on. His head swam with the feeling of the clamps tugging at him.

"Now eggs. I keep it simple; whole eggs, a little butter, salt, and pepper." He laid everything out. "I want you to crack four eggs into that bowl." He pointed at a clear glass bowl.

Tyler flipped open the lid of the carton. They were colorful eggs, various shades of browns and greens.

"Huh." He picked up a green one, hissing as his forearm brushed his sensitive nipple. "This is cool."

"Those are from a local farmer," Donovan said. "Heritage breeds tend to have more colorful eggs."

"Does it change the flavor?" Tyler asked.

"The color of the shell? No. The way they're raised, yes. Crack one open and you can see the difference there. The shells are thicker and the yolks will be a much richer shade of yellow-orange instead of the paler yellow you're used to from cage-raised supermarket eggs. Warning, you'll be punished for every yolk you break or piece of shell that ends up in the bowl."

Nervous, Tyler tentatively tapped an egg against the edge of the bowl. Nothing happened. He tapped harder and the egg broke. He tried to peel the two halves apart but it shattered, sending several pieces of shell into the bowl along with the egg. *Shit.*

He looked at Donovan with a grimace.

"We can fish that out." Donovan retrieved chopsticks and deftly pulled out the shell pieces, counting them off as he deposited them in another bowl. He instructed Tyler to put the larger pieces in there as well. Tyler realized the way Donovan did everything made sense. He was usually trying to scoop the broken bits out with a spoon and toss the shell in the trash under the sink while smearing bits of runny egg white all over his kitchen.

"A better way to crack the egg is to hit it flat against the counter." Donovan demonstrated, deftly cracking and separating a second egg one-handed.

"Now you try." He shot a smile at Tyler.

He tried. But the tug of the clamps and the thought of the punishment that would follow made him clumsy and he hit too hard, the egg shattering and yolk and white mingling as they spread all over the counter.

Donovan handed him a paper towel. "Clean up, then try again."

It took a few tries, but Tyler eventually got the hang of it.

Donovan stepped close when he was done. "Now, time for your punishment."

Tyler gulped.

"First, take this and whisk the eggs together."

Tyler tried, clumsily slopping a bit of it out of the bowl. Donovan stepped close behind him, the fly of his jeans brushing against Tyler's ass. He wrapped his arms around Tyler's shoulders and held his hand, showing him how to hold the whisk at an angle and the motion to use. With his free hand, he toyed with the clamp on Tyler's left nipple. Tyler hissed at the sharp jolt that went through him, but it spread heat through his body that made him soften against Donovan's chest.

"Mmm." He closed his eyes for a moment, his right hand slowing the whisking motion.

"Nope, keep going."

Donovan stepped back and Tyler opened his eyes, frowning down at the eggs as he mixed them together, using the motion Donovan had taught him. Huh, they were actually starting to turn a more even yellow color.

Donovan walked away, then returned a moment later. He held up a flat wooden thing. Tyler wasn't sure if it was a paddle or something for the kitchen.

"What's that?"

"This is a crêpe turner. It's one of my favorite tools. Designed for the kitchen, though if you ask me, it works equally well for punishments."

Both then. Shit.

Donovan smacked the wooden utensil against his own palm. His expression didn't change but Tyler flinched at the loud sound.

"Now. Keep whisking. I believe I owe you a baker's dozen smacks."

The words sent a quake through Tyler's whole body but he kept whisking.

The first hit landed with a loud pop and Tyler jerked in surprise. The eggs rocked in the bowl but thankfully didn't splash out that time. The pain registered a second later and he let out a gasp. "Fuck!"

It stung. Holy fuck, did it sting. Tyler groaned, barely managing to continue to whisk as he tried to take a deep breath. Donovan smacked him a few more times, leaving stinging spots in his wake. When Tyler tensed, Donovan stepped closer, running a hand across Tyler's ass. His hand felt cool in comparison to the heat already radiating from his skin.

"How do you like that?" Donovan asked.

That was a difficult question to answer. It fucking hurt, of course. Tyler didn't like that. But shit, the way he felt after …

"I mean, it's supposed to be a punishment, right?" He kept whisking, hoping Donovan wouldn't call him out on his cagey answer.

"We'll call it *funishment.* An excuse to paddle this gorgeous ass." He rubbed Tyler's cheek, squeezing a little. "And keep you on track."

"You think my ass is gorgeous?" Tyler asked with a smirk.

"You know it is." Donovan stepped back and smacked Tyler again. Once on the meaty part of his cheek, and another on the back of his thigh that made him howl. He nearly lost his grip on the whisk that time, his fingers slippery as his body flooded with pain and heat, making his head swim. "Even better when I've marked it all up."

There was something in Donovan's voice that made Tyler's cock throb with need.

"Yeah?"

Donovan tapped his ass with the paddle. "Keep whisking."

Tyler flinched, anticipating another hit that never came. He resumed the motion with his hand.

Focus.

But Tyler wailed when the next hit came, his shudders tugging at the clamps on his nipples and making his cock even harder.

They went on like that a few more times. Donovan smacking his ass and counting off the hits. Tyler struggling to keep whisking without making an unholy mess.

Tyler's whole body was hot and sheened with sweat by the time Donovan delivered lucky number thirteen, a solid, heavy smack that landed across both cheeks and made him cry out. He shivered, head hanging low. His ass stung like hell, throbbing a little and his nipples ached. He vaguely became aware that his forearm was beginning to cramp from the whisking as well.

"Arm's cramping," he said through clenched teeth, but he continued to whisk.

Donovan laid the paddle on the counter and stepped close behind him. "You can stop."

Tyler did with a relieved sigh.

"Sorry." Donovan said. He rubbed his thumb up and down Tyler's forearm, digging it into the meat of the muscle right below his elbow where it ached. "I forget you haven't spent years building up those muscles like I have."

Who'd have thought making eggs was a good workout? Tyler thought hazily. He gasped when Donovan pressed right up against his ass. The denim of his jeans felt rough and abrasive against his tender skin.

"Great job," Donovan said in his ear. He let go of Tyler's forearm and ran his palm up Tyler's arm, then slipped under the apron to toy with the clamp. He slid his other hand under the fabric as well, but much lower, and grasped Tyler's cock. Tyler was hard.

Painfully so, he realized as Donovan slowly stroked.

"Fuck," he whispered.

"Oh, we'll get to that eventually. We're not done with your cooking lesson," Donovan said. "Turn on the front right burner."

Tyler attempted to focus as he found the right knob and turned it, hearing the click-hiss of the gas burner lighting before bright flames shot out.

"Turn the heat down," Donovan instructed. "Eggs go low and slow."

"Really? I figured you'd want a really hot pan. No wonder mine never turn out."

"Put the pan on the burner. Let it warm for a minute."

"No butter?"

"Not yet. I like the pan warm before I put it in to melt."

"Okay." Tyler gripped the edge of the counter as Donovan continued to jerk him. For a minute or so, there was nothing but the feel of Donovan toying with his cock and his nipple. Donovan rubbed against Tyler's ass, lightly abrading his sensitive skin, his hard cock pushing insistently against Tyler's crack. Tyler pushed back.

"Shit." Donovan flexed his hips. "I can't wait to fuck you again." He brushed his lips against Tyler's neck. "Do you want that?"

"Yes," Tyler said with a gasp. "Oh fuck. Yes."

"Mmm." Donovan scraped his teeth against the muscle on the side of Tyler's neck, making him groan.

"Now?" He ground against Donovan's hips, despite the pain that flared from the rough abrasion. Or maybe because of it.

"No. We need to finish—"

A beeping sound interrupted, and Tyler's head swam as Donovan stepped back. "Gotta check the bacon."

Tyler let out a frustrated groan and stepped away from the stove. The sharp smack of Donovan's hand on his ass made him jerk in surprise.

"What was that for?" He rubbed his cheek. Jesus, he had *welts*. He craned his neck to see them. Yeah, there were raised marks in the shape of the crêpe paddle. No broken skin. Huh.

"Lack of focus." Donovan opened the oven door and peered in. "Two more minutes on the bacon."

Tyler snuck a glance to see it did look almost done.

"How the fuck was I supposed to focus with you touching me like that?" Tyler grumbled.

"Butter in the pan." Donovan pointed, clearly ignoring his question.

"How much?"

Donovan held up his fingers. "That much."

"That's a lot."

"Fat equals flavor." He shrugged. "I never said these were going to be the most low-calorie eggs ever. But trust me, we'll work it off tonight."

Tyler placed the butter in the pan, hearing it quietly sizzle. A rich smell rose in the air. "Mmm, that does smell good."

"It'll taste even better, I promise." Donovan reached for the pan and lifted it, swirling the butter around. "Coat the bottom and sides evenly, let it warm for another few seconds, then pour half the egg in."

"Okay." Tyler copied the motions with far less skill, feeling the tug of the nipple clamp. Fuck, that was distracting.

Donovan turned the oven off, then watched as Tyler added the egg to the pan.

Donovan talked him through gently stirring the eggs with a spatula, softly folding them until they were creamy and just starting to come together. "Now a sprinkle of salt." He'd stepped close again, his voice a soft brush against Tyler's neck. He settled one hand on Tyler's hip while he rained salt down on the eggs.

"Now, give it one more gentle stir, then turn off the heat and set it aside."

Tyler peered into the pan. "Isn't it still kinda … wet?"

"It is. But the pan retains heat. It'll continue to cook for a minute or two and by the time it begins to cool, it'll be perfect."

That all made sense, so Tyler turned off the heat and set the pan on the cool burner nearby.

Donovan resumed his earlier motions, tugging at Tyler's cock and teasing his sensitive nipples, grinding his pelvis against Tyler's ass. "Now I'm going to enjoy you for a moment."

Tyler let his head fall back against Donovan's shoulder, his eyes drifting closed. "I think I'm starting to understand why people enjoy cooking." His words came out a little slurred. God, he was getting close. If Donovan's hand was slick and he went just a little harder and faster …

Donovan's chuckle rumbled against his back. "I am more than happy to give you more cooking lessons, if you're interested."

"Fuck yes," Tyler said, rocking shamelessly into Donovan's grip.

Donovan kept working him up for a minute before he bit Tyler's neck once, hard, then stepped back. "Okay, time to put the toast in and eat."

Tyler groaned in frustration but he somehow managed to put the eggs on plates, then sprinkle on a final dash of salt and cracked black pepper as instructed. Donovan toasted and buttered the bread, pulled the bacon out of the oven, and in no time at all, they sat at the kitchen table with delicious-looking food in front of them.

"Holy shit," Tyler said after he lifted a forkful of fluffy yellow eggs to his mouth. "These are the best scrambled eggs I've ever had." They were creamy and soft without being wet or watery.

Donovan's face glowed with pleasure. "Nothing rubbery about them."

"And the toast isn't even burned. That's probably only because I wasn't doing it. I feel like I can't keep track of it while I'm finishing the eggs."

"I didn't quite trust you with handling that part tonight since I have you all worked up and distracted. It's all about timing. If you take the eggs off the heat early, you'll have time to focus solely on the toast so you don't burn it. And everything will still be hot when you're ready to eat."

"That makes a lot of sense." Tyler shifted in his seat as he took a bite of the bacon. Perfectly crispy with just a tiny bit of chewiness. "Bacon's great too."

"Yeah, that method is perfect for doing a bunch at once or just not having to focus on it while you work on other things."

"I'm a convert," Tyler said. "Baking on a tray for me from now on."

"How's your ass?"

"Sore," Tyler admitted. "Damn, welts, huh?"

Donovan grinned around a piece of toast. "Now you see why the crêpe turner is my favorite toy."

"I do," Tyler admitted. "Damn. It's a *lot,* but it is fun."

"Think you'd be up for a little more play after we eat?"

Tyler shifted in his chair. "Fuck yeah."

Donovan took a big bite of his toast, his blue eyes dancing with amusement and promising Tyler that he was in for it.

Tyler gulped, knowing he would either love what came next, or really, really regret that he'd encouraged Donovan.

Maybe both.

Tyler's bare ass rubbed against the top of the kitchen table, the furniture rocking and sliding across the kitchen floor as Donovan thrust into him. Tyler closed his eyes and groaned as heat spread across his skin, urging him to let loose.

"Don't keep me on edge like this," he said, curling his fingers around the edge of the table to brace himself. "Fuck. I'm so close."

"Hold it," Donovan growled.

Tyler gritted his teeth, colors swimming behind his eyelids as the punch of Donovan's dick hit that perfect spot inside him. His own cock bobbed, throbbing with the heavy rush of blood.

A sharp tug on the chain between his nipples made Tyler howl, bowing up, abs clenching as all that sensation shot from his chest down to his groin. "*Fuck*!"

"You like that, don't you?" Donovan growled.

Tyler couldn't manage more than a few pants as Donovan continued to thrust into him, his forearm pressing the backs of Tyler's thighs against Donovan's sweaty chest. He did something to the nipple clamp on the left and blood rushed back into it, a sharp sting shooting through it and making his cock throb even more insistently. His head swam as Donovan did the same thing to the other one.

He was vaguely aware of a metallic clink as the clamps slid to the tabletop and Donovan's fingers toyed with his nipples that were a thousand times more sensitive now that the blood had returned.

Tyler groaned, low and long, the desperate need growing with every second. "Please, please ..."

"Are you begging for it, Tyler?" Donovan asked.

"Yes! Let me come," he pleaded. "Please, Donovan."

Donovan spat, then wrapped his warm spit-slicked palm around Tyler's cock and stroked. Another thrust and stroke and Tyler was gone, his cock spurting as he clenched around Donovan.

"Oh fuck," Donovan said roughly. He pushed in with a final, savage thrust, his hips shuddering against Tyler's ass, his grip tight as Tyler came in gasping waves, his chest heaving and his head so light he saw stars.

Donovan bit his thigh as they both trembled their way through the aftershocks, his groan muffled by Tyler's skin.

"Fuck," Donovan said after a minute or so, running his hand up and down Tyler's quads.

"You just did," he slurred. "Fucked me stupid."

"How is that a change from normal?" Donovan teased.

Tyler cracked an eye open to glare at him. "I hate you."

"No, you don't." Donovan grinned and Tyler couldn't stop himself from grinning back.

That smile of Donovan's was irresistible.

Donovan eased out of him, and Tyler winced. Damn, he was sensitive. He sat up, every inch of his body protesting. "No, I don't hate you," he admitted.

Donovan stepped between his thighs, wrapping a hand around Tyler's cock, smoothing the fluid across the tip, and making Tyler jerk. "You might even be starting to like me a little bit," Donovan teased.

"I might." Tyler was a little breathless as he curled his hand around the back of Donovan's neck and pulled him in for a kiss. "I might. Just a little bit."

Donovan laughed against his mouth. "Shower?"

"Mmm, probably a good idea." Tyler didn't pull back, and they resumed making out for a while.

"What do you think about staying after?" Donovan said as he drew back. "It's getting late."

Tyler snuck a glance at the clock on the stove. Not that late. Since there was no dinner service on Sunday nights, they'd gotten out of the tavern much earlier than usual. After a shower, he'd be fine to drive home, but he found himself nodding instead of saying no.

"Yeah, I could stay."

ELEVEN

"This town has more festivals than any place I've ever been to," Donovan said with a groan. The line of customers had slowed enough for him to take a breather for two seconds while Teri, one of the tavern's servers, took over for him. Donovan dug his fists into his lower back and arched, trying to stretch the tight muscles.

Tyler flashed him a sympathetic look, then glanced at the bartender on his other side. "Can you manage the bar stuff for a bit, Lacey?"

"Pfftt. Course I can."

"C'mere. You need a break." Tyler took Donovan's arm and drew him toward the back of the rectangular booth the tavern had set up. Donovan was too tired to argue about Tyler telling him what to do.

"I hear you on the festivals," Tyler said. "I mean, I like apples as much as the next guy, but a whole festival for them? What the fuck?"

"Rachael's going to be thrilled with how well we're doing, though," Donovan said with a sigh. He was tired, but the day had gone well. The tavern was one of the big festival sponsors and they had a huge area set up in a food and drink tent.

People wandered from booth to booth, buying whatever food or drinks struck their fancy. The center of the tent held long tables where they could enjoy their meal or relax with friends while they drank. Great smells came from every direction and the air was filled with the sound of people laughing and talking, and music playing in the background. A band was setting up now, and he and Tyler had a few more hours to go before they wrapped all of this up.

"People seem to be going crazy for your apple butter BBQ chicken sandwiches," Tyler said, leaning against one of the prep tables.

"That's cause they're fucking *good.*"

"I'll have to take your word for it. I've been smelling them all day, but I haven't gotten a thing to eat."

Donovan turned to face him, horrified. "What? No, you need to eat."

"How much have *you* eaten today?" Tyler teased, though his smile was tired too.

Donovan thought back. "Fuck."

"A chef who doesn't even know how to feed himself." Tyler let out a little tsking noise. "Pretty sad."

"Watch it," Donovan said, narrowing his eyes at Tyler.

"Or what?" Tyler licked his lips.

As always, their banter sent a little jolt of energy through Donovan. "Or you'll find out later what the consequences are."

Didn't matter that they'd both be dead from exhaustion after being on their feet all night. Didn't matter that Donovan's back hurt like a bitch or that Tyler had dark circles under his eyes. In the three months since things had started with Tyler, Donovan had always managed to find the energy for their encounters.

They were on a pretty good schedule these days, in fact. A couple of times a week, Tyler came to his place after work, they got kinky, then passed out in Donovan's bed.

Donovan had been a little surprised that Tyler felt comfortable enough with him to fall asleep in his bed on a regular basis, but he had no complaints. Tyler was an up-and-out-of-bed guy, who didn't like to linger in the mornings, but that was okay too. There were still the occasional slick handjobs in the shower, and more than once, Donovan had bent him over the kitchen table before they headed their separate ways for the day.

It was a good routine, and Donovan was enjoying it, even if Tyler was currently berating him for not eating.

"Fine. I'll fix two plates and we'll take a break together," Donovan suggested. "Lacey and Teri have this covered."

"Want me to grab some ciders?"

"Yeah, that would be great."

"I'll snag us a table over there," Tyler said, pointing.

"Meet you there."

As Donovan spoke quietly to Teri, he loaded two plates with food. When he approached the table where Tyler sat, he was greeted with a grateful smile. He felt an urge to lean in and press his lips to Tyler's but stopped himself just in time. No, that definitely wasn't something Tyler would be cool with.

In general, Donovan didn't mind that they were keeping things under wraps, but recently, he'd begun to feel that nagging sense that he was getting more attached to what they were doing than he should be.

In private, things were great but Donovan knew Tyler had no intention of this ever becoming more open and that was beginning to chafe.

"Mmm, this is good." Tyler shot Donovan a little smile before he took a second bite of the sandwich.

"Don't sound so surprised," Donovan teased.

"Fuck, you need to make this again." Tyler wiped the apple BBQ sauce from his chin. "Seriously. This is amazing."

"Thanks." The pork tenderloin and apple skewers with a maple balsamic glaze weren't too terrible either. Nor were the apple and sausage stuffing bites. The restaurant had been prepping for days to get ready for this event and Donovan was damn proud of what they'd put together.

"I could teach you to make the pulled chicken, you know?" He grabbed another cube of pork from the skewer and popped it into his mouth.

"You could."

They'd done a handful of cooking lessons at this point and Tyler had become a willing and eager student. The combination of cooking and kink was a heady mix for Donovan. It took all the things he enjoyed and wrapped them up into one amazing package.

Though the romantic relationship aspect was missing from what they did, in the bedroom, things with Tyler were substantially better than they'd been with his ex, Jude. Sure, Tyler still enjoyed a good rough play session where Donovan tackled him and restrained him, but Tyler was actually far more submissive than Jude had ever been.

Not that Tyler would admit that. He still got prickly if Donovan suggested that. But he seemed to have no desire to switch. Tyler *wanted* to submit, he just had to be convinced to do it sometimes.

Jude had *constantly* chafed at the idea of never being the one in charge. Intellectually, Donovan understood the idea of being a switch. It was as innate as his dominance was.

He'd tried to explain that to Jude, to make him understand it was like being gay. Yet Jude had stubbornly clung to the idea that if Donovan would just try harder, he'd get there. That Donovan could somehow make himself become something he wasn't. That was what had set off their last ugly fight.

Now, Donovan sighed and took a long pull from his cider, enjoying the dry crisp tartness after the richness of the food. To hell with the past. To hell with the future. What he was doing *now* was good. That was all that mattered.

Donovan glanced over at Tyler to see he'd demolished half his plate of food already. A combination of military service and constantly being on the run in the restaurant meant Tyler wolfed his food down.

Donovan idly wondered if he could train that out of Tyler. Force him to eat slowly and either reward him for obeying or punish him for not. Tie him up maybe and hand feed him.

Donovan smiled at that thought. Oh, that could be fun. Being forced to allow Donovan to feed him would be a huge struggle for Tyler. Maybe Donovan could blindfold him. Restrain him. Donovan brought another cider-glazed meatball to his lips. He'd have to plan that for a day they both had off.

"What are you smirking about?" Tyler asked, narrowing his eyes.

Donovan's grin widened. "Oh, just making some plans."

"For?"

"Something we don't discuss in public."

Tyler blinked. "Oh."

Donovan hid a wince behind another sip of cider. That had come out a little more barbed than he'd intended. He'd meant it as a joke, but it hadn't really come out that way at all.

Tyler straightened, squaring his shoulders. "Something good though, right?"

"I'll enjoy it." Donovan smirk widened. "We'll see if you do."

"Oh." Tyler's cheeks turned a little pink. "That sounds interesting."

"It should be."

Donovan reached out to touch Tyler's arm, then disguised it by grabbing his napkin. He felt another little stab of frustration. Outside of the safety of Donovan's apartment, he missed the casual touches he'd grown used to in private.

But Tyler was pretty stubbornly sure that what they were doing was just an aberration. And maybe it was. Maybe Tyler was flexible sexually but not at all romantically. There *was* a difference.

The problem with that was Donovan wasn't sure that Tyler's upbringing—especially his military background—didn't play into that. What if Tyler were hardwired to be interested in dating men but had blocked himself from the idea of a relationship with a man because he'd been socially conditioned to think women were his only option?

Donovan knew Tyler was still friends with a lot of the guys he'd served with. What if he were too afraid of what they—or his family—would say about him dating a guy to ever consider the idea?

Then I'm going to be hugely disappointed. Possibly even heartbroken. The thought was grim, but Donovan had to be realistic. What they had now was good, but would he be content with that forever? He'd gone into this thinking he didn't need romance—why bother with the hassle after the mess with Jude?—but sometimes he got flashes of what it could be like with Tyler if he were willing to give it a chance. And the thought was beginning to become more seductive than he could have imagined.

And *damn it*, there he went again. Worrying about the past and the future instead of enjoying the present.

"Donovan!" His name rang out over the murmur of the crowd enjoying their meals and listening to music play. He raised his head, glancing around.

He spotted the bright red glasses first and rose to his feet. "Grandma June."

She beamed at him as she strode toward him, no hesitation in her step. He would swear the woman had sold her soul to the devil to be as healthy and active as she was at her age. Or, knowing her, she'd charmed the devil into it free of charge. "I'm so glad I caught you. I hardly see you anymore."

"I know." He hugged her, breathing in the familiar warm, spicy-sweet floral scent of her perfume. It was the same one she'd worn all her life, the one his grandfather had bought her for their first anniversary. "I'm sorry. I've been busy."

Her gaze darted toward Tyler. "Can't say as I blame you."

"Ahh, no." Donovan rubbed the back of his neck. "Gram, Tyler and I work together at the tavern. He's the bar manager there."

"Oh." Grandma June smiled over at him. "Nice to meet you, young man."

Tyler scrambled to his feet. "Tyler Hewitt. Nice to meet you too, ma'am."

"Ma'am?" She let out a peel of laughter. "Oh no. Call me Grandma June. Everyone does. Or just June, if you'd prefer."

"Sorry, m—June. I'll do my best to remember. You can take the man out of the military, but you can't always take the military out of the man."

She eyed him up and down. "I'll bet you looked nice in uniform. Which branch?"

"Army. Staff sergeant. Light infantry."

"My husband was in the army as well. Talk about handsome in a uniform." June fanned herself.

"He was," Donovan agreed.

She scoffed. "Of course, you say that. Other than the red hair and freckles, you're the spitting image of him."

Tyler chuckled. "I can't quite picture Donovan in the military. I don't think he'd much like being told what to do."

"I *am* used to being in charge," Donovan agreed.

He caught the moment that thought processed in his grandmother's head. She glanced between him and Tyler, then nodded as if confirming something.

Crap.

She wasn't known for her filter either.

"So, what are you doing here, Grandma?" he asked hastily, desperately trying to change the subject.

"Oh, I was at the speed dating event."

"The what now?"

"Speed dating." She rested her hand on Donovan's arm. "I know it's hard to see me moving on from your grandfather and you know I loved him to bits, but I can't see myself missing out on love out of some misguided sense of loyalty. He'd have been the first one to encourage me. 'You gotta get out there again, Junie,' he would have said. 'And you better find someone young and hung. You only live once.'"

Tyler went wide-eyed, and Donovan stifled a snort, turning it into a cough. Yeah, those were his grandparents. They weren't shy about any of that. Donovan and his family were more or less used to it. People who didn't know them were always taken by surprise.

"Well, Grandma," Donovan said as seriously as he could manage, "I do hope you're able to find a new suitor."

"New suitor?" She grinned. "I'd settle for a good lay."

Tyler's eyes widened even farther.

"Well, I wish you everything you desire," Donovan said, no longer able to contain his amusement. He kissed her cheek. "I hate to run, Grams, but we need to finish our food and get back to the booth." He gestured toward the banner advertising the Hawk Point Tavern. His chest filled with pride at the sight. Damn, he was proud of the work they'd done, here and at the restaurant.

"Oh yes," his grandma said, "I'll let you get back to your date."

Tyler's eyes widened again. At this rate, he was going to wind up permanently bug-eyed.

"It's not a date!" Donovan protested. "Just a working dinner with a friend."

She glanced between them over the top of her glasses. "Mm-hmm. Well, enjoy. Have good sex. And don't forget to wrap it up!"

Donovan facepalmed. "Grandma …"

She pecked his cheek, glowing with amusement. "Love you, muffin."

"Love you too." He gave her a hug.

"Nice to meet you, Tyler Hewitt."

"Nice to meet you too, June," he said with a smile. He was still grinning as she walked off.

"Well. She's uh …" Tyler took a seat at the table when she was gone, amusement lighting up his face and making his gray eyes dance.

"That's my grandmother." Donovan shook his head as he joined him. "No one else like her."

"She's fun." Tyler took a sip of cider. "Muffin, huh?"

"She's equal parts horrifying and wonderful," Donovan said with a sigh. He loved her to bits but there was no containing her. He leaned in, dropping his voice. "And you better forget you ever heard her call me muffin. There *will* be consequences if you repeat my childhood nickname."

Tyler snickered.

Donovan sobered, thinking about the earlier conversation. "Sorry about what I said. I think she probably figured out we're … uh … involved."

"Yeah." Tyler swallowed. "I mean, she doesn't *know* anything about us, right?"

"Oh no. I've never said anything to her about us." Donovan dug his fork into the apple slaw. "But she's smart. She knows *I'm* kinky and your comment about taking orders kinda tipped her off. I can ask her to be discreet. She never blabbed about me to anyone outside of the family, so as much as she is a bit of a wild card, I'm confident she's not going to out you to anyone."

Tyler's eyes widened. "Your family knows you're—"

"Yeah." Donovan glanced around, but there was no one within immediate earshot. "They do. Not the specifics but that I'm involved in the community."

"And they don't give you shit for it?"

"No."

"Probably helps that you're"—Tyler lowered his voice—"a Dom."

Donovan winced. Tyler wasn't wrong. People seemed to be more understanding of men being in charge. "Probably. But if I were submissive, I wouldn't hide it either. It's nothing to be ashamed of. And they wouldn't think so either."

"No. I know." Tyler grimaced. "It's just …"

"I know. Society is fucked up." Donovan echoed his expression. "Masculinity has one narrow box that we're allowed to fit in."

"Yeah, try joining the military." Tyler snorted.

Donovan did some quick math. Tyler was thirty-four and if he'd joined the military right out of high school …

"You were in before the DADT repeal, weren't you?" he asked, unable to hide the surprise in his voice. Damn, it seemed like a long time ago. Then again, Tyler had been out of the military a while too.

"Yeah. I enlisted in 2005." He stabbed at a stuffing ball.

"How long was your enlistment?"

"Four years active duty, four reserves."

"So, you were still in the reserves when it was repealed. It was what … 2011, I think?"

"That sounds about right. And yeah, I was in the reserves at the time. It was interesting."

"I'd imagine so."

Tyler grimaced. "It's weird. It's a really touchy thing."

"How so?"

"Well, there was one or two guys in my platoon who we all knew were into guys. They didn't advertise it but you could just kinda tell, you know? And they'd talk around it without being too blatant. No one really got too wound up about what they did in their free time and it's not like it impacted their job. But after the repeal? Two came out and announced they'd been together for years and people were *pissed*."

"Because it had been a secret?"

"Yeah." Tyler set down his fork. "Because these guys you're serving with, you're as close as brothers, you know? You know *everything* about them. The name of their dog, their high school mascot, when they got laid for the first time. What scares them shitless. You know all this stuff, but when you find out they've left half their life out of conversations or whatever, it causes a shit-load of mistrust. Even guys who aren't homophobic feel kinda betrayed. Hell, *I* felt betrayed."

"I can see that."

"And you've gotta trust that your buddies have your back. Without that, people get killed."

"Sure. That makes sense."

"And like … it's kinda fucking intimate living like that. You see one another in the showers. You spoon at night because the desert gets so goddamn cold. You don't think about the fact that you're lying nut to butt with a man because you're freezing your fucking balls off. It's just body heat you want. And it's lonely as hell, so you kinda want that touch anyway, you know? No one talks about that part but it's true. And no one gave a shit about Hayes and Frenchie being gay or bi or whatever. Long as they didn't grope you while you spooned, who gave a fuck? But knowing Jackson and Hayes had fucking lied about the fact they were together and none of us had suspected it? That felt like betrayal."

Donovan nodded. "I wouldn't have considered it that way, but it makes perfect sense."

"Like I said, it's weird."

"And complicated."

"Yeah. For sure. I get why they lied. I get why they felt like they had no other choice. But I'll be honest, I was pissed."

"Did it ever cross your mind then that you"—Donovan dropped his voice—"might be anything but straight?"

Tyler shook his head. "Never once. Even when I got a couple of blowjobs it never made me think I ever wanted anything more than that with a guy."

"And now?"

Tyler shot him a quizzical look.

"I mean, I'm not trying to push you to label yourself, but if you did, would you say you're still straight?"

Tyler shrugged. "Less than I thought."

"And what about a relationship? Can you ever see having that with a man or would that be totally out of the question?"

Tyler hesitated. "Honestly? I don't know. It feels weird to even think about."

"I get that." But Donovan's heart sank. Because there was a little part of him that had begun to wonder if this could be more but he'd just gotten confirmation that Tyler hadn't even considered the idea. *Fuck.*

"We should get back to the booth." Tyler glanced at his phone. "We've been gone awhile."

"Yeah, you're right." Donovan crumpled up his napkin and set it on his empty plate along with his fork. Clearly Tyler wanted a change of subject as well. "Ugh, I'm fucking tired."

"Same." Tyler stood with a groan. "I'm fucking old."

"You're younger than I am," Donovan teased. Though only by a few years.

"Yeah, but I've got a lot of miles on me." Tyler's sigh was weary.

Donovan rose to his feet, but as he turned to leave the table, he spotted something out of the corner of his eye that made him pause. He swiveled to get a better look at the tall man with golden blond hair walking toward the exit of the tent.

Donovan frowned. *Is that …?*

But no, it couldn't be Jude. Donovan's ex never ventured into Pendleton. He'd called it a town with no culture.

Besides, there were plenty of guys who looked like Jude. Tall, fit white men with thick sun-streaked light brown hair weren't really that rare. Sure, the guy carried himself like Jude too, with an innate confidence that bordered on arrogance, but it couldn't possibly be him. Donovan had to have imagined it.

Probably because his thoughts had drifted to Jude earlier.

Though why Donovan was thinking about his ex so much tonight was beyond him. Maybe it was because Jude's birthday was coming up in a few weeks. Late September. Weird either way.

Tyler touched his arm. "Hey, you okay? You just got the strangest look on your face."

Donovan glanced at him. "Yeah. Just thought I saw someone I knew."

"Ahh, okay."

Donovan glanced back at the exit, but the head of golden hair was gone. He had to have imagined it. Right?

TWELVE

Donovan seems off tonight. Tyler carried their discarded plates and bottles to the trash, thinking about the conversation they'd just had. Usually one hundred percent focused, Donovan seemed like he was in another world. Tyler didn't think it was just him being quiet either. Donovan had stared off into the crowd for the longest time, like his mind was a million miles away.

And his questions for Tyler had been a lot more intense than usual. Tyler didn't have a problem talking about his sexuality, but it wasn't something they usually discussed and he had no idea why Donovan was so curious now.

Unless …

No, Donovan couldn't possibly be thinking about them dating or something. Tyler knew he'd been clear from the very beginning. Hadn't he?

"Tyler?"

Lacey's voice broke Tyler from his trance and he lifted his head to see her looking at him with a concerned frown. He'd stopped in front of the booth. Now he was the one staring into space.

"You okay?" she asked.

"Ahh yeah, just in a coma now," he joked. "All that delicious food of Donovan's."

He stole a glance at Donovan, who was back behind the tavern's booth in his white coat, chatting with a couple of good-looking customers. One of the guys was tall and brown-haired, the other broader, with dark hair and glasses. They were laughing at something Donovan had said and Tyler felt a weird little stab of … something.

But whether it was the way Donovan was smiling at them or the fact that the guy in the brown suede jacket and neatly pressed khakis had his arm around the guy with the glasses, Tyler wasn't sure.

Logically, he knew Donovan was just being friendly. He was good with customers, sociable, charming. It wasn't as if he flirted any more than Tyler did. And Tyler had no claim on Donovan. He'd never wanted one before.

But something twisted up his insides and made him wonder if he wanted to be the one making Donovan smile, or wanted to be like the couple talking to him. Cozy and loving.

Damn. Why the fuck was his brain suddenly going there?

Because this is the first time you've been out in public with Donovan, he reminded himself. The realization sent a jolt through him, and he hustled around the corner of the booth, slipping behind the tables.

It was true though. He reached for his apron with a frown. They had kept their encounters strictly to Donovan's place in the past few months. And the only time they saw each other outside that was at the tavern.

Which was normal for fuck buddies. But—and this was the part that made Tyler hesitate—this didn't feel like a normal fuck-buddy situation anymore. They spent the night together at least three times a week. Which, hey, given how fucking late they were hooking up, made a lot of sense.

But Tyler was growing used to the feel of Donovan's arm slung over his waist, his palm warm against Tyler's chest. He liked the feel of his back pressed against a firm chest. It felt … peaceful. He wasn't like Eddie, plagued by nightmares of what had happened in Afghanistan, and he'd never had any trouble falling asleep. But he did sleep longer and more deeply when Donovan was there. It was like his brain could let go and not worry.

Sometimes Tyler felt like military service had made him perpetually wary. Not in the way Eddie was, where a backfiring car would have him ducking for the ground. But it had trained Tyler to be vigilant of his surroundings. To take notice of everything. To be on alert. He'd never quite let go of that. But around Donovan, he could. He could simply let himself be.

And that was pretty damn seductive.

So, if it felt like more than a fuck-buddy situation … well, that made sense.

"You sure you're okay, Ty?" Lacey asked. "You've been so quiet tonight."

"I know." He let out a little laugh. "Honestly, my mind has been wandering. I'm sorry. I know I've left you and Jake to deal with most of the customers."

"No, no, it's fine," she said. "I just wanted to be sure you were okay."

"Absolutely," he assured her. "You need a break? We've got a couple of hours left and from the look of it, business will be picking up soon."

They had entered that weird in-between hour. Too late for dinner, a little too early for partying. It was growing cool outside, and a live band had just begun playing. People were slowly returning to the tent to listen or dance to the cover band on the small dance floor where a few people bobbed to the music.

Soon, those people would come over for a drink and a snack to refuel, and once the dancing really increased, they'd probably grab a few more.

Lacey hesitated. "You sure? I wouldn't mind taking a few minutes to walk around and text my mom to make sure everything's okay at home with the kids ..."

Tyler nodded. "Of course. Go for it."

Her husband worked nights as a paramedic, so Lacey's mom did most of the childcare. It wasn't usually an issue, but one of the kids had been sick last week. Tyler gave her a reassuring smile. "Check on your family. I've got this handled."

"Thanks." She stepped back, already pulling off her apron.

Tyler slid into her spot and greeted the next customer. "Good evening. What can I get you?"

It did pick up after that and he worked his way through several dozen customers before a gorgeous blonde sashayed up.

"Well, I'm debating." She responded to his question about what she wanted to drink with a smile. "Which is better? The apple mojito? Or the apple pie Moscow mule?"

"Well, do you prefer apple vodka or white rum?"

"Oh, I don't know." She tapped a manicured nail against her lip. "Which do *you* think I'd like?

Tyler suppressed a groan. Great. One of *those* customers. He talked her through it and she finally picked out the Moscow mule.

"Oh my God, this is so good," she gushed after she took a sip. "Could I, um, get your number too?" She took another sip of the drink through the straw and looked at him through her lashes.

"I'm flattered," he said sincerely. She was just his type. Pre-Donovan, Tyler would have been seriously tempted, despite his "don't date the customers" rule. "But I'm seeing someone."

"Aww. Bummer."

"Have a good evening?" Tyler said, feeling a bit awkward.

"You too." She slid a scrap of paper at him. "But, you know, if you change your mind …"

She sauntered off with a flirty smile and a swing of her hips.

Lacey, who had just reappeared, blinked at Tyler. "I didn't know you were seeing someone!"

Out of the corner of his eye, Tyler saw Donovan falter as he carried a stack of plates to the table nearby. Damn it, he must have heard that.

"Yeah," Tyer said quietly. "I don't really talk about my personal life at work but …"

"Excuse me?"

A man approached the makeshift bar and Tyler gratefully returned his attention to their customers. "How can I help you, sir?"

Thankfully, after that, they got too busy for Lacey to question him, and he hoped she'd forget all about it soon.

———

"Well, I think that's it," Tyler said with a groan several hours later. The band had packed up and the festival was officially shutting down until next year. "Donovan, you ready to pack up?"

He glanced up. "Yes. We're just about out of food anyway." He let out a tired little laugh.

"Yeah, I hear you. We ran out of the fresh apple cider half an hour ago. And we've got about two shots of rum left." He turned back to the bar area. "Okay guys, we can pack up now."

After that, it was a blur of stacking dirty dishes in crates, folding tablecloths, and tearing down their booth setup after. Things were just wrapping up when Tyler's phone began to buzz impatiently in his pocket.

He slipped his phone out to see several texts from Andrea. The last one sent his heart rate through the roof.

Call me, Ty. Urgent.

"Fuck." He raked a hand through his hair, heart galloping in his chest.

"What's wrong?" Donovan strode over and grabbed his elbow.

Tyler grimaced. "Eddie's wife. I *have* to get this. Can you …?"

"Go," Donovan said firmly. "I'll take care of closing this up."

"Thanks." Tyler ripped off his apron with one hand and thrust it in Donovan's direction. He strode away, already lifting his phone to his ear, too worried to think twice about what his staff would think of him turning everything over to Donovan. Tyler knew he'd handle it.

Eddie had seemed okay the past few months. He'd finally gotten in to see a therapist and just last month they'd done their camping and fishing trip. He'd seemed so much more like his usual self that weekend that Tyler had begun to hope that things were improving. Apparently, he'd been wrong.

"Andrea? What is it?" he asked when the call connected. He slipped out the exit of the tent and into the cool September air.

"He locked himself in the bathroom, Ty." Andrea let out a hiccupping sob. "I'm scared for him."

Shit, shit shit. "Can you take a few deep breaths for me?"

He heard a shaky breath or two on the other end.

"What did Eddie say?" Tyler coaxed.

She sniffled, her voice thick with tears. "He's just ranting. Talking about how he's letting us down. How he's always let everyone down. About how we'd be better off without him."

"Fuck." Tyler crossed the park, a cool breeze off the bay teasing at his arms—bare in his T-shirt—as he thought fast. "Does he have access to a gun, Andrea?"

She drew in a sharp breath. "No. No, I asked him to get rid of it before Antonio was born. I watched Eddie give it to his father."

"Do you think there's any way Mr. Silva would have given it back to him?" He approached the edge of the park, stopping when he reached the metal railing that overlooked the bay. The moon glimmered off the waves, the sight too peaceful for the fears filling his head.

"No. He told me he was going to surrender it to the police. Said the fewer guns out there the better."

Mr. Silva was a pacifist and had opposed his son's plan to join the military from the very beginning. Eddie returning home worse for wear hadn't exactly made his father more supportive of gun ownership or the endless wars in the Middle East.

"Good." The little knot in Tyler's chest loosened a fraction. There were other ways Eddie might hurt himself, if he was feeling so inclined. But a gun was easy. And Eddie's aim had always been deadly accurate. Of course, if he put it to his temple or in his mouth, accuracy wouldn't matter. "Can do you do something for me, Andrea?"

"Of course." She gulped. "Whatever will help him."

"If you can get him out of the house for a little while, check it over. Top to bottom. Basement, garage … make sure he doesn't have a backup weapon. A lot of guys do." Tyler did. He kept his two firearms in separate, secure lockboxes and cleaned them regularly because he was a responsible gun owner and he'd never risk his niece and nephew or Eddie and Andrea's kids accidentally getting into them. But he had them. One in his nightstand, the other in the bedroom closet. Just in case.

She drew in a sharp breath. "You think he'd lie to me?"

"No." Tyler leaned his elbows on the metal railing, the sharp, cold bite of it anchoring him. "I think he could have convinced himself it was for your own good. That he was protecting you. He'd have it in a lockbox so the kids couldn't get to it, but he'd keep it because he'd think it would help him keep you safe."

She let out a frustrated noise.

"I know," he said soothingly. "And we're thinking worst-case scenarios. I may be totally wrong about this. He may feel better tomorrow and it won't be an issue. I just want to be cautious. Can I talk to him now? Can you get him to get on the phone with me?

"No." She sniffled. "I tried earlier. I told him to call you. I know it's asking a lot but—"

"Hey, I'll do whatever it takes to help him," Tyler said firmly. "You don't have to apologize for it. He's my brother. Of course, I'll do whatever I can." His voice was rough by the end.

They were both silent a moment.

"Do you need me to come up tonight? I'm working a booth at apple fest but I can ask my boss—"

"No, no, I don't need you to do that. Maybe tomorrow? I know your schedule is crazy ..."

"Yeah, of course." He did have to work but fuck it, Rachael would understand. He'd beg if he had to. "I'll make it happen. I promise."

"Thanks." Andrea let out a relieved-sounding sigh. "I'm just so scared I'm going to lose him, Ty."

He swallowed hard. "Me too."

He said goodbye to Andrea, then promised he'd text to let her know what time he'd be there the next day.

After he hung up, he called Rachael. She picked up immediately.

"Tyler? Is something wrong?"

"Not with the festival," he assured her. Worry made his voice tight and strained. "But I've got a personal emergency."

"Oh no! Not your parents, I hope."

"No, they're fine," Tyler assured her. "I've got a buddy from the service. He's … he's in a bad spot, Rach. And he really needs me. I want to go visit him tomorrow. It's a drive, though. He's up in Grand Rapids and I—"

"You need the day off?"

"Yeah." He sighed. "I'm sorry. I know this is short notice, especially for a Sunday shift, but I don't know what time I'll be back and frankly I think my head will be kind of a mess once I do and—"

"Don't even think about it," Rachael said firmly. "You need the time off; we'll make it happen. I'll come in and work myself."

He grimaced. "Hope you didn't have plans with the guys."

"Nope, they're up north with some friends. I'd planned a quiet night in, so I have no obligations."

"Sorry to interrupt that."

"Please don't apologize," Rachael said firmly. "Honestly, Tyler, I refuse to run my business like I have robots working for me. You're a person with a whole life outside of work. I want you to be able to call me and say you need the day off without worrying about it."

"Thanks." He rubbed his chest. "That means a lot to me, Rach."

"Of course. Now, you go have a relaxing night once you're done there at the festival and take care of your friend tomorrow. I'll see you Tuesday, okay?"

"Yes," he said firmly. "Thanks again."

"Happy to help. I hope your friend will be okay."

Tyler stood there, leaning against the railing, staring out at the dark bay for a few minutes. He knew he needed to get back. Needed to focus on work, but he was too damn tired to do anything.

He swallowed, a weird little ache forming in the back of his throat as he wished he could just walk into the tent and wrap his arms around Donovan. He wanted that. Needed it. But … but he wasn't ready for the questions that would follow about who he was. *What* he was. How the hell could he explain it to everyone else when he didn't know himself. Ugh. He hated this. Hated even having to think about it. Why couldn't it just be *easy*?

But no, everyone had to give it a label. Things would change if he told his friends and family he was involved with a guy. It would become A THING that people felt the need to comment on. And Tyler hated the thought of that. He hated having to wonder what Eddie would say. What the other guys would say. What his mom and dad would say. He didn't think any one of them would have a major issue with it but what if they did? And he dreaded the questions. People wondering if he had been hiding all along.

He'd have to explain that no, apparently it was just Donovan. Or, at least, he hadn't really looked twice at other guys since. Well, maybe twice. He'd looked at Rachael's partners—Reeve and Grant—knowing they were bi. And he thought that yeah, they were attractive. But they didn't make him hard the way Donovan did. Even if they weren't with his boss, he wouldn't want to kiss them. Couldn't imagine letting himself be vulnerable with them the way he was with Donovan.

Couldn't imagine falling asleep in a bed next to them, sex-drunk and high on endorphins. He couldn't imagine waking up and staring at them next to him in the bed and wondering how the fuck he'd ended up in that position but praying fervently that it wouldn't end.

When Donovan had asked him about his feelings on relationships earlier, he'd given him his knee-jerk response. But the truth was, questions had been nibbling at the edges of his subconscious lately. It was more than the smack of the wooden paddle he liked. More than the feel of a dick in his mouth. It was Donovan and the way they meshed.

It was the way his life made sense with Donovan in it. He felt a sense of purpose that had been missing for years. With Donovan around, the pieces of his life seemed to make more sense.

Tyler swallowed hard. He wished he could just walk up to Donovan now, kiss him, and that would be the end of that. No questions. No coming out. None of that bullshit. But he couldn't. So, he sighed and tucked his phone in his pocket and trudged back to the tent.

THIRTEEN

"Everything okay with him?" Lacey asked, nodding toward Tyler's retreating back. Tension and worry radiated from every inch of his body, and Donovan wanted nothing more than to go after him. Comfort him.

"Just a friend he's worried about," Donovan said quietly. Truthfully, Donovan was concerned too. Tyler hadn't said a lot about Eddie, but he'd said enough to reveal his friend was in real pain.

It was criminal how difficult it was for military people to reintegrate into civilian society. After being thrown into the worst of situations, there simply weren't enough resources for them once they were home. Paul—the Marine he and Jude had played with periodically—was a prime example. From what Donovan had gleaned from Tyler, he hadn't seen anything too terrible. Not that going to war was ever good, but it sounded like Tyler had stayed out of the worst of it. Paul, however, had been in the thick of it. And he'd had the scars to prove it.

Unfortunately, it sounded like Tyler's friend was in equally rough shape.

Tyler's safeword made a hell of a lot of sense now.

For a bit, Donovan had idly wondered if Eddie was the guy who'd sucked Tyler off when they were stationed overseas, but one night, after a call from Eddie had pulled Tyler from bed, Donovan had broached the subject. He hadn't listened to Tyler's conversation, but he'd been able to hear the rise and fall of his voice in the other room. When that had fallen silent and Tyler didn't return to the bedroom, Donovan had gone out to find him.

He'd found him in front of the living room window, staring out at a dim parking lot.

"You okay?" he'd asked. He settled a hand on Tyler's shoulder. He startled, but after a moment, he let out a sigh and leaned back against Donovan.

Swallowing hard at the gesture of need, Donovan wrapped his arms around Tyler's shoulders and pulled him close. He hooked his chin on Tyler's shoulder.

"How's Eddie?"

"Drunk. Struggling." Tyler let out a rough little sound. "Like usual. I hate not being able to help him."

"I know." The raw note in Tyler's voice made Donovan's chest ache. "I wish I could help you."

"You are."

Donovan squeezed a little tighter. "Good."

They stood there in silence for a few minutes.

"Was Eddie one of the guys who blew you?" Donovan asked. He'd been wondering for a while now.

"Eddie?" Tyler laughed, his body shaking in Donovan's arms. "Oh, God no. He's straight as hell."

"Well, you thought you were too, and clearly there's *some* wiggle room."

"Sure but … he has a wife. They were together then and he doesn't fuck around on Andrea."

He'd pronounced it with a little lilt. *Ahn-dreyah*, not the nasal, Midwestern *Ann-dree-a*.

"Eddie never cheated on her, never will," Tyler said firmly.

Despite his firm tone, there was a softness to Tyler's voice when he spoke of her. Of Eddie. Of the guys he'd known in the service. That part of his life was clearly important to him.

"Who was it? The guy you hooked up with, I mean."

Tyler hesitated.

"I'm sorry. You don't have to tell me if you're concerned about outing him. I was just curious."

"Oh, no, Frenchie was out. It's just … it's hard to talk about him." Tyler swallowed. "Now that he's gone. He died in Afghanistan."

"Oh." Donovan got it then. Understood Tyler's hesitation. He'd lost his friend, and Eddie was on the edge now. That was a lot. "You don't need to talk about it."

"Thanks. I'll tell you someday, maybe. But not right now."

"You want to head back to bed?" Donovan asked. It was late—or early, based on the pink tinge of the sky along the horizon.

"I don't know if I can sleep."

"Want me to wear you out?"

Tyler turned in his arms and looked up at him, expression hurting in a way that made Donovan's chest ache. "Would you do that?"

"Give you what you need?" Donovan asked. "Of course. All you ever have to do is ask."

And now, Donovan was pretty sure this was going to be another night like that. He didn't mind; it just concerned him. Tyler could handle it. He knew that. It just hurt to see Tyler so worried about his friend.

And while sex and a good scene would give Tyler a break from the anxiety, it would do nothing to fix the situation.

After they unloaded everything from the event and returned it to where it belonged at the tavern to be dealt with tomorrow, Tyler sagged against the bed of his pickup. "I'm not sure I'm gonna be up to anything big tonight. I know we planned to do a pretty intense scene but …"

Even in the light from the streetlamp, Donovan could see his exhaustion.

"Okay," Donovan said. "Well, it's up to you. If you want to just come back to my place to shower and crash, that's an option too."

Tyler tugged at his baseball cap. "I called Rach earlier to see if I could get the day off tomorrow. She was cool with it so I'm heading up to GR to see Eddie."

"That'll be good. This is just an offer, but would you like me to go with you?"

Tyler blinked. "Why would you?"

"Moral support?"

"Oh."

"You're welcome to say no," Donovan said carefully. "I just thought I'd throw it out there." Not that Rachael would be thrilled about both of them being gone the same day, especially since he was supposed to be in extra early to supervise cleanup after the event and make sure everything was prepped for brunch. Max could take over for him if need be. If Tyler wanted him there, Donovan would figure out a way to make it work.

Tyler stepped forward, sliding a hand against Donovan's hip as he fit their bodies closer together. "That's nice. I don't think I'm going to take you up on it, but I appreciate it."

"I want to be a good … *friend* to you." The word felt awkward and clumsy in Donovan's mouth because he didn't feel particularly friendly at the moment. He felt *protective*. A Dom wanting to wrap up his sub and shelter him from the shit that was raining down on him. And he couldn't. Because Tyler wasn't his submissive.

Oh, he bottomed. He even grudgingly submitted at times. More easily these days. But he wasn't out. He was fine embracing in a dark, deserted parking lot because no one would ever see them where they were tucked behind the building. But Tyler wasn't ready to take Donovan's hand in a public park and maybe he never would be.

Donovan hadn't pushed for Tyler to call him Sir during a scene because he knew it was one step too far. He'd erred on the side of caution, and now it hit him how much he wanted that. How much he wanted to see Tyler in that role. Right now, he wanted nothing more than to wrap Tyler up and keep him safe. Feel him soft and yielding in his arms. And yes, he loved the combativeness that still filled some of their scenes, but he was starting to ache for the tenderness of a full, deep D/s dynamic too, and that was about to get him in real fucking trouble.

"I won't push," Donovan said, swallowing back his own desires in favor of doing what was best for Tyler. "You said you aren't up to something big. If you don't want to come over tonight, that's fine. If you don't want me to go with you tomorrow, that's fine too." And he meant that. It ached, but he understood. "Just know that if you want anything from me, I will do whatever I can to make it happen."

"Thanks." Tyler squeezed his hip and settled a little closer. He pressed his nose—cold at the tip—to Donovan's cheek. "That means a lot to me."

"Of course." Donovan slid his hand up Tyler's neck to cup the back of his head, the recently trimmed hair prickly-soft against his palm. "I'm here for you, Tyler. However you need me. Or want me."

"Actually, now that I think about it, do you know what I really want?" Tyler asked.

"No. Tell me?"

Tyler sighed, a big heaving breath. "I just want to let go. Like I said, not … not a big scene or anything, but I want you to make everything in my head go quiet. I'm too tired to fight and wrestle and struggle and take a shitload of pain but if you can make things quiet without that, I'd really like it."

"I can do that," Donovan promised. "If you have the energy for a smaller scene, I'd be happy to give it to you." Ideas were already whirling through his mind and he considered them and dismissed them. Nothing too strenuous. Something Tyler could just sink into and relax. Nothing that would require him making any effort tonight …

"Yeah, that sounds good." Tyler drew back, licking his lips. "Can we do it at my place tonight? I don't know why, it just …"

"Sure," Donovan said, surprised. Because of Donovan's stash of toys, they'd never played at Tyler's place before, but he didn't mind that at all. He was creative enough to figure out something on the fly.

"Thanks." Tyler shot him a tentative smile.

"Anytime." Donovan pulled Tyler close and pressed his lips to his forehead. When Tyler let out a shuddering sigh and softened even more, the warmth in Donovan's chest felt suspiciously like something he'd experienced in the past.

Something that he knew Tyler might never return.

Oh, you are in for a world of heartbreak, you idiot, Donovan thought to himself. But he couldn't find it in himself to stop it.

FOURTEEN

"Over my lap."

Tyler stared at Donovan. He sat on the edge of Tyler's bed, naked, his hair damp from the shower they'd taken together. He looked tired and a little stern. But he'd been almost tender in the shower, running his hands across Tyler's body, massaging his shoulders, even washing Tyler's hair.

At any other time, Tyler would have fought him, snapped he could take care of himself. But the truth was, he was too exhausted and worried to do anything but mutely accept the help.

"Tyler? If you're too tired for a spanking, we can just sleep. But if you want this, lie down over my lap and let me take care of you." Donovan's tone was gentle enough, but there was a firm edge that reminded Tyler he *would* take charge if Tyler let him.

The words jolted him into action, and he knelt on the bed beside Donovan's hip. It was awkward, draping himself over Donovan's lap, but when he was settled, the feel of their skin pressed together made tension begin to seep from his body.

"Mmm, well done." Donovan rubbed his ass.

Normally, the words might have made Tyler bristle but tonight, he simply let out a sigh and rested his forehead on the back of his hand.

"I only need you to do one thing for me tonight," Donovan said. His voice sounded particularly deep and mellow. It washed over Tyler in a warm, soothing wave. "Do you know what that is?"

"No."

"Let go." Donovan said. He settled a hand on the back of Tyler's neck, applying a little pressure. "I'm going to spank you now. All you have to do is close your eyes and let me take care of you. Can you do that for me?"

"Yes," Tyler whispered.

"Good." A stinging slap landed on Tyler's ass. He jerked, in surprise as much as anything else, then closed his eyes as warmth spread outward from that spot. When he got comfortable again, another slap landed beside the first. Tyler let out a groan. Then another. And another. Donovan started slowly, but he worked his way up to a steady pace.

After the first dozen or so hits, Tyler felt himself slip, his head beginning to go hazy as all his muscles softened. His ass was hot and sore, but the warmth covered his whole body now. His cock grew hard as Donovan continued, moving down to slap the crease where his ass met his legs.

Tyler groaned, rocking against Donovan's firm thigh.

"Yeah?" Donovan let out a pleased little noise. "You like that, huh?"

"Mmm." Tyler let out a sound of agreement.

"Keep it up," Donovan said encouragingly. "Grind your cock against me while I spank you."

So, Tyler did. His world faded to the thwacks against his ass and the pressure against his dick. There was nothing but that and the hazy, swirling pleasure in his head. The worry, the fear, they melted away like smoke, leaving his mind quiet and still.

It went on and on, and Tyler ached by the time Donovan's hits slowed to a stop. But he was so fuzzy and relaxed he could barely respond when Donovan manhandled him, shifting and rolling him until he lay flat on his back on the bed.

His head swam as he stared up at Donovan who smiled down at him. "I'm going to take care of you now, Tyler. Just lie there and enjoy it, sweetheart."

"Whaa?" he slurred.

Donovan ducked his head, taking Tyler's cock into his mouth. Tyler groaned at the sudden wet heat and pressure around the head. He reached out blindly, cradling Donovan's head in his hands, not taking control, just enjoying the feel of Donovan's hair sliding between his fingers, fine and silky.

Everything was a hazy blur of pleasure as he let Donovan take care of him, allowing himself to simply lie there and enjoy it rather than trying to fight him. The pleasure built, sweet heat settling low in his belly and urging him onward. Donovan's mouth seemed to be everywhere at once, licking up the shaft, swirling around the head, teasing the slit, before plunging back down again until Tyler sank into the soft, wet grip of his throat.

Donovan toyed with Tyler's nuts, hefting them in his hand and tugging just the way Tyler loved. And then he moved his mouth lower, lapping and sucking, gently mouthing at Tyler's balls while his spit-slicked hand stroked the shaft and his thumb teased at the crown.

Tyler let out a desperate sound, hips arching as he sought more, so close, right there on the edge and …

It was gone.

Tyler let out a disappointed groan when Donovan sat up. "Nooo," he whined, reaching for him.

"Shh, I've got you." Donovan settled a hand on his stomach. "You can come soon, I promise."

Tyler rocked against the bed, his sheets softly abrading his sore ass and the air cool on the wet tip of his cock. He reached down and stroked his dick. For once, Donovan didn't stop him. "Need you, Donovan."

"I know. Hang on." Donovan sat up, and a moment later, Tyler heard the sound of lube, then a tearing condom wrapper and he spread his legs, but instead, Donovan wrapped a hand around his cock again.

The familiar sensation of latex being rolled over his dick made his hips jerk in surprise. He was still too fuzzy-headed to protest, and it wasn't until Donovan settled on his knees, straddling Tyler's torso, that it occurred to him what was happening.

He groaned when Donovan sank down over him. He hissed at the tightness, Donovan's body gripping every aroused inch of his dick. "Fuck," he whispered when Donovan's ass brushed his hips.

"Tell me about it." Donovan sounded breathless.

Tyler ran his hands up Donovan's thighs, loving the firm muscle and soft hair. So different than anyone he'd been with in the past. So good though. So, so good.

Donovan rose over him, then lowered down, tearing a strangled groan from Tyler's throat.

Blindly, Tyler reached for Donovan's cock. He found it half-hard and he spit in his hand to stroke it as Donovan fucked him. Because while Donovan was the one taking a dick inside him, he was still the one in charge. He was the one controlling the pace and depth. He was the one pulling sounds Tyler had never heard himself make out of his throat. He was the one who made Tyler writhe and grind his tender ass against the bed.

He was the one making Tyler's head swim even more.

Tyler's strokes slowed when he felt the pressure of Donovan's hand against his throat. "Slap my thigh three times if you need me to stop," Donovan whispered.

And then the pressure increased, and the world faded away again until there was nothing but Donovan's body around his cock and the tight grip around his neck. Loosening. Tightening. Tyler had no idea how long they went on like that, but the pleasure built and built, settling low in his groin and making his balls boil with a desperate need to orgasm. Donovan pressed in hard again, then released, and Tyler came with a gasp, hips shoving desperately upward into Donovan's body as he turned inside out and filled the condom.

He could do nothing but shake and cry out, body curling up, dimly aware of the slick sound of Donovan jerking off over him.

"Tyler!"

His name was a broken moan on Donovan's lips, and the rhythmic contractions of Donovan's body around his dick pushed his orgasm further, until it was so good it hurt. Tyler sagged back against the bed, a wash of white sweeping through his head in a warm, haze.

Donovan lifted off him, then settled on the bed beside him, stroking his abs.

"Tell me you're okay, Tyler."

"I'm okay," he gasped. His voice was a little hoarse. He peeled his eyes open to see Donovan looming over him, a concerned frown on his face. "More than okay. So good."

Donovan smiled then and dragged his fingers through the wetness on Tyler's chest. He lifted them to Tyler's mouth, and he opened obediently, licking and sucking Donovan's cum from his fingers.

Tyler shuddered at the strange pleasure of the act, and his arm felt clumsy and awkward as he reached out to touch Donovan's face. "Thank you," he whispered.

Donovan smiled faintly. "What are you thanking me for?"

"Everything." He couldn't manage anything else, just pulled Donovan in for a kiss, not caring that they were making a mess of themselves. Only desperate to feel Donovan's touch again.

Eventually, their kisses slowed, and Donovan rolled him onto his back. "Let me get a cloth," he whispered.

Tyler floated in a contented haze as Donovan washed him clean. His eyes were heavy-lidded by the time Donovan slipped into bed beside him, pulling the covers up over their bodies.

Sleep swept him away as soon as the lights were out.

FIFTEEN

Donovan awoke to Tyler slipping out of bed. "Where're you going?" His voice sounded rusty and unused. It was early still, and it felt like he'd barely closed his eyes.

Tyler froze and turned back to face him. "Heading to Grand Rapids, remember?"

"Right. Of course." Donovan sat up, dragging a hand through his hair, knowing it would do little to tame the unruly strands.

Tyler lifted a hand, a faint smile on his face, as he brushed some of it off Donovan's forehead. Last night had been unusually tender for them. There was a pang in Donovan's chest as he wondered if Tyler would freak out and bolt. Of course, they were at Tyler's place. He wasn't likely to go far.

Still, he didn't seem to be pulling away so Donovan would take it as a good sign.

Donovan cleared his throat and reached out, pulling Tyler in toward him until he straddled Donovan's thighs. "How'd you sleep?"

Tyler's smile was soft, his eyes sleepy. "Like the dead. Thank you."

"Of course." Donovan swallowed past the lump in his throat. "Whatever you need."

"I had this thing wrong, didn't I?" Tyler asked.

"Hmm?" Donovan cupped Tyler's cheek in his hand, running his hand up Tyler's broad back. "Had what wrong?"

"How this kink thing worked. I thought it was all me giving you what you need."

"It should be both," Donovan said honestly. "It should be the two of us meeting each other's needs. Last night you needed me to take care of you. I gave you what you needed and let you get out of your head. You gave to me by allowing me to take care of you. Trust me, we both got everything we wanted."

The lump in Donovan's throat grew bigger. That had been the problem with Jude. Donovan couldn't switch, so Jude had never had the outlet he truly wanted.

Oh, they'd tried. They'd brought in other men, switches or submissives who could take Donovan's orders and submit to Jude as well. But neither random, casual encounters nor regular play partners had solved the issue. Because what Donovan had wanted—truly wanted—was a sense of ownership. He'd wanted Jude to belong to him. Not in a selfish, toxic way, but in the truest, deepest sense of dominance and submission.

Donovan knew there were people out there who could have made what they did work. Who could have found happiness in open relationships or in triads, but that had never been him.

"Why do you look sad?" Tyler asked.

Donovan smiled faintly. "Just thinking about my past." He shook his head. "Doesn't matter. I'm glad last night helped you."

"It did." Tyler's relaxed expression grew troubled. "I'm nervous about seeing Eddie today."

"Why is that?"

Tyler licked his lips. He sighed and settled a little more heavily against Donovan's thighs. Donovan made slow, sweeping passes up and down Tyler's back, his skin cool against the warmth of Donovan's palms.

"I'm afraid I'm failing him."

Donovan took a deep breath. "It isn't your job to hold your friend together, Tyler."

"There's this motto in the military. 'No man left behind.' It feels like the government has done that to Eddie. I can't do it too."

The ache in his eyes and his voice made tears prick at Donovan's eyes. *This* was love. Not Donovan's for Tyler, but Tyler's for Eddie.

Tyler loved his friend with the kind of fervor that made Donovan's chest feel tight. It wasn't romantic, but it was powerful and deep, and Donovan hated how much Tyler hurt right now.

"Then you do your best," Donovan said simply. "You go there and talk to him. You let him see how much you love him."

"Is that enough?"

"I don't know," Donovan admitted. He brought his hand to Tyler's face and cupped his cheek. "But you'll do what you can for him."

Tyler let out a deep trembling breath and rested his forehead against Donovan's. "Thank you."

"For what?" Donovan brushed his thumb against Tyler's lips. He pursed them, brushing them against the tip in an almost-kiss that made Donovan pull him even closer.

"For this." Tyler drew back and looked him in the eye, expression conflicted. "What we're doing now sure doesn't feel like what we started out doing but …"

"It isn't," Donovan agreed. "But I'm okay with that if you are."

Tyler hesitated, then nodded once. "I'm okay with that."

"Good." Donovan snuck a kiss and smacked Tyler's ass. "Now, go get ready. I'll make you coffee and breakfast before you head out."

"I was going to say you could stay here if you wanted. I trust you to lock up when you're done. I know you have to work tonight, and we didn't get a lot of sleep. If you want to go back to bed, I totally understand."

"I'd rather cook breakfast for you," Donovan said.

"Okay." Tyler got up with a reluctant-sounding groan. "Dunno how hungry I am. My stomach is in knots."

Donovan stood too, smiling a little. "Good thing I'm very skilled at untangling rope."

The rhythm of the restaurant kitchen soothed Donovan's frayed nerves as he waited to hear from Tyler how the day with Eddie went. He found himself checking his phone far more than usual and Max teased him about it.

"You seeing someone or what, Chef?"

Donovan hesitated. "It's complicated."

"Hmm. Isn't it always?" His sous chef rolled their eyes.

"True enough." Donovan deftly plated three seared pork medallions on top of the mushroom sauce, then sprinkled them with fresh herbs.

"I'm sure whatever you're worried about will be fine," Max said.

"I hope so," Donovan said with a sigh as he slid the plate along the pass for the server.

They were nearing the end of the lunch service, and he was looking forward to heading out for the day. It had been a long, exhausting morning on top of a long, exhausting day before it.

"Chef?"

Donovan looked up to see Teri with a hesitant expression on her face. "Yes?"

"There's a guest at table eight who'd like to see you when you're available. I don't think he's upset or anything. He seemed to enjoy the appetizer he ordered. He just wants to speak to you about something."

Donovan stifled a sigh. "Okay."

He didn't usually mind chatting with diners. It was nice to connect with the people enjoying his meals. Today he wasn't sure he had it in him to schmooze with anyone, but it was part of his job, so he'd have to do his best.

He surveyed his appearance, then slipped his coat off. He prided himself on keeping himself tidy, but he'd been distracted plating a seared salmon salad earlier and a rogue piece of arugula had landed on his sleeve, leaving a smear of vinaigrette.

"I'll be out in a minute," he said. "I'm going to make sure I'm fit for the public first."

Max grinned at him. "You're never fit for the public, Chef."

Donovan managed a smile back. "Watch it there, Max."

They just smirked as they resumed assembling a meatloaf sandwich and plating it next to some parmesan herb fries.

Donovan ducked out of the kitchen and into the service hallway. He slipped on a clean coat, then neatly folded back the sleeves. He caught a glimpse of himself in the mirror and grimaced. He smoothed his hair down and tidied his beard but it did nothing to fix the tiredness in his eyes. It wasn't the lack of sleep either. He was used to that.

Worry for Tyler churned in his belly as he walked toward the front of the house.

His steps slowed as he approached table eight. The diner there sat alone and the tall, straight back, golden hair, and taut forearm made Donovan swallow hard.

God, please tell me it's not …

But it was. Donovan came around the side of the table and his worst fears were confirmed. *Fuck.* The guy's head was tilted down but Donovan would know the shape of his face and those eyebrows anywhere.

"Jude?" he forced out.

Jude Maddox lifted his head from his phone and smiled broadly. "Donovan. So good to see you."

"What are you doing here?"

"Aww, that's not a very friendly greeting. No 'I've missed you'?"

Donovan swallowed hard. "Well, you know how I feel about lying …"

Jude winced. "Ouch."

"Shit, I'm sorry." Donovan let out a sigh. "That was unkind. I'm just surprised. I don't remember you being very impressed by Pendleton before, so I never expected to see you here."

They'd visited the town a number of times in their ten-year relationship, going to dinner at Grandma June and Grandpa Harold's place for holidays and other visits. Jude had always preferred to go farther afield for vacation though. Indianapolis or Chicago. Ann Arbor. Detroit.

"Well, things change."

"They sure do."

They stared at each other for a long time. Jude was as fit as ever, body perfectly sculpted through long hours at the gym. He had a movie-star-handsome square jaw dusted with golden stubble and eyes the color of the worn blue denim shirt he wore.

He was still handsome too. Sure, there were a few more lines on his forehead and around his eyes, but he wore his thirty-six years well. But his looks did nothing for Donovan anymore. There was only a pervasive feeling of guilt and melancholy.

"This place is great," Jude said, finally breaking the tense silence.

"Thank you," Donovan said stiffly. "I'm quite proud of it."

"You should be." Jude reached for a pint glass and took a sip of the pale ale. "You own it?"

"Half share," Donovan said. "The entire tavern is owned by Rachael Bradford. I bought in on half of the restaurant side."

"Interesting arrangement."

"It was what I could afford at the time." He'd taken a loss on the condo he and Jude had owned together. When they'd broken up, he'd just wanted it gone so he'd agreed to the first offer that came through. Jude hadn't been happy about it but he'd gone along with it.

"Menu's all you." Jude looked down at his nearly empty plate. It contained the husk of a head of roasted garlic. He'd dug out most of the cloves, smearing them over slices of toasted ciabatta along with the soft herbed goat cheese and roasted red pepper. "I remember testing this recipe with you."

Donovan felt a sting of nostalgia. Cooking this dish in the condo's kitchen. Jude sliding his hands across Donovan's body as he tried to slice bread, so distracted he'd nearly cut his thumb.

"I remember that too." Donovan cleared his throat. "I still don't know why you're here. And why you wanted to see me."

Teri arrived with a plate. Her gaze darted to Donovan before she set it down in front of Jude.

"Here's your rosemary turkey meatloaf sandwich with parmesan herb fries."

"Thank you." Jude shot her a charming smile. "It looks delicious."

"Can I get you anything else? Another drink?"

"No, I'm set. Why don't you get Donovan something. A cider, perhaps? I saw several Michigan ones on the menu."

"I don't drink while I'm on shift," he said stiffly.

Jude shot him an unimpressed look. "That's not the way I remember it."

Jude wasn't wrong. Sometimes they'd had a few drinks with the staff at the end of a long day. The executive chef at Plated hadn't minded. Hell, he'd *encouraged* it. But that wasn't how Donovan ran things here.

"Things change," he said firmly.

Jude gave him a pained smile. "Seriously, Donovan, I'd like a few minutes of your time if you can manage it. Have a drink with me."

"I am still working," he pointed out.

Teri's gaze darted between them. "We are closing in about twenty minutes. We only have a few tables that haven't been served yet. I'm sure Max can handle things in the kitchen if you want."

"I'm sure Max can," Donovan said with a sigh. Clearly Teri was not picking up on his desire to avoid this conversation. She was just trying to be helpful, so she didn't deserve to have him take it out on her. "Fine. Let them know I'll be back as soon as possible, please. But no drink for me, thanks."

"Sure, no problem, Chef." She gave the two of them one last curious look, then turned and left.

Donovan pulled out a chair and took a seat. He interlaced his hands. "So, what is it you'd like from me, Jude?"

"Just to talk."

Frustration rose in Donovan, and he had to take a deep breath to tamp it down. "Why are you in Pendleton, exactly? Are you on vacation?"

"Not exactly. I'm opening up a restaurant here in town."

A roaring sound filled Donovan's ears. "You *what*?"

"You know that empty storefront off 1st Street? I own it. I'm opening a restaurant."

"How the fuck did you swing that?"

Jude's mouth turned down at the corners. "Well, my grandpa died. I inherited a good chunk."

The Maddox family had money. Donovan's family was well-off, but on a significantly smaller scale. Joseph Maddox had been a real estate developer with properties all over the west side of Michigan. Hell, he'd probably owned half of Pendleton. Jude's father was in the business too, and Jude had royally pissed off his family by becoming a chef. That was one of the first things that had drawn Donovan and Jude together, in fact.

"I'm sorry about your grandfather."

Jude snorted and took another sip of his drink. "Joe Maddox was an asshole and we both know it."

He had been, but that didn't mean it didn't sting for Jude. But that wasn't something that was Donovan's concern anymore. He changed the subject. "So, you're opening a restaurant?"

"That was always *our* dream. You got to it first but …"

Donovan's nostrils flared. "So, you came here to Pendleton just to rub it in my face—"

"No!" The word exploded from Jude's lips, and he looked around as if belatedly realizing how loud he had been. He ducked his head and spoke more quietly. "I looked around at a ton of places in the area, and Pendleton is booming."

"I'm well aware," Donovan said drily.

"It was the smartest choice for an investment," Jude said. "The space, the market … it's perfect for what I have in mind."

"I wish you the best of luck with it," Donovan said. "It just feels a bit weird that you'd show up *here at my restaurant* to brag."

Jude looked taken aback. "I wasn't trying to rub it in your face *or* brag. I didn't want you to be blindsided is all. I figured it was the mature, adult thing to do."

"Oh." Donovan rubbed his forehead. "Look, you're probably right. It's just … it's been a weird couple of days. I'm not trying to start another fight with you. I'm sorry if I've been rude."

Jude licked his lips. "There's another reason I came here too. I know things got … weird between us at the end. And I really regret that."

Donovan sat back in his chair. "So, you're here to mend fences?"

"In a manner of speaking. We'll be in the same town again and I just wanted to make sure there was no bad blood between us."

Donovan sighed. "Truthfully, I'm the one who should apologize. I said some things I regret when I left Plated." After that final big fight, they'd hardly spoken and only then about dividing up their belongings and selling the condo.

Cold and bloodless, but exceedingly painful.

Jude winced. "Well, I've tried to forget that. I don't hold any grudges."

He probably didn't. Jude wasn't that kind of person.

"Then let's leave the past where it belongs," Donovan said firmly. "I see no reason we can't be cordial moving forward." That didn't mean they were going to become friends. There was way too much water under the bridge for that, but they could coexist peacefully.

Jude leaned forward and rested his hand on Donovan's forearm. "What if I said I was interested in doing more than mending fences?"

"What?" Donovan's voice came out hoarse as he blinked at his ex-boyfriend.

"I've missed you, Donovan. Seeing you again, tasting your food … God, we were *so good*."

"Until we weren't," he said shortly.

"What if we could fix it?"

"How?" Donovan shook his head. "No, it doesn't even matter now. Even if we could fix it, I don't want to try."

"Why not?"

"I'm seeing someone," he said stiffly. "And it's not something I'm willing to jeopardize."

"Ahh, you've found the submissive of your dreams." There was a bitter little twist to Jude's lips. "I was afraid of that."

Donovan considered the idea. Was Tyler the submissive of his dreams? Tyler probably could be, if he could admit it. But that was a long shot. Last night … it had been so good. "That I don't know," Donovan said honestly. "It's complicated. He was a Top with women in the past, and he's fairly new to this side of things. We're still feeling out our dynamic."

"You care about him." It wasn't a question.

Donovan nodded. "I do." He swallowed past the thickness in his throat. "I care about him a lot." He leaned in. "And you and I are over. Please let this go."

"But what if we found someone—"

"No," Donovan said firmly. "That isn't what I want. It never was."

A flicker of hurt crossed Jude's face. "What?"

Donovan sighed. "I never wanted to open our relationship. I did it for you so you could get your needs met but it wasn't me. It just wasn't. I figured that out pretty early on but I saw how happy you were when you could have that outlet."

"I never asked you—"

"I know," Donovan said, lowering his voice. "I know you didn't. And I should have been honest with you about how it was making me feel. That resentment built until I lashed out at you and that wasn't fair." He swallowed past the shame as he remembered that last ugly fight in Plated's kitchen. "I apologize for my lack of honesty."

"You damn well should," Jude said furiously. "I thought you wanted it. That we just hadn't found the right person."

"*We* weren't right for each other, Jude." Donovan tried to make his voice gentle but Jude still flinched. "We weren't. And that's okay. It's possible to love someone and have them be terrible for you. I loved you, Jude, *I did.* But we were a disaster together. If you can take a step back and really think about it, you'll know it's true."

Emotions flickered across Jude's face before his expression settled into one of sadness. "I don't want it to be true."

Donovan smiled sadly. "I know that. But it doesn't change a thing. This is where we are. And it's time we both admit that and move on."

"It sounds like you already have," Jude said bitterly.

"I'm trying."

Whether or not Tyler could ever give him what he wanted remained to be seen.

SIXTEEN

When Eddie opened the cheerful yellow door of his house, Tyler tried not to wince. He looked like he'd aged at least five years since Tyler had seen him in August. Deep, dark circles ringed his brown eyes, and he looked haggard in a way he never had before.

The eight weeks of Ranger School had tested both of them to their limits. Half of the men there had failed out, and it had been one of the most physically, mentally, and emotionally taxing things Tyler had ever experienced. The exhaustion and strain had worn him nearly to the breaking point. Eddie had been the same.

Today, he looked worse than when they'd returned from Swamp Phase in Florida.

"Hey, man," Tyler said, his voice sounding like he'd swallowed gravel. "Good to see you."

Eddie managed a half-hearted smile, but his hug was hard and tight, his body as thin and wiry as Tyler had ever seen. He seemed to be wasting away, yet his face was puffy. And there was a gray tone to Eddie's normally rich brown skin. The heavy drinking, Tyler presumed. It made his heart ache.

"Come in." There was a glimmer of the old Eddie in the smile he gave Tyler.

Tyler stepped inside the post-war bungalow. It was snug for a family of five, but between the family photos on the wall and the living room strewn with kids' toys, it felt cozy and warm.

Andrea walked in from the kitchen. Her narrow shoulders were tense but her face softened when she saw him. "Hey, Ty."

"Hey, gorgeous." He kissed her cheek. She looked beautiful as ever with her long wavy hair and wide smile. But that smile was strained, and it didn't quite reach her warm brown eyes.

"Hey yourself," she said. "I've missed you."

"I know." He winced. "I had a crazy busy summer. The tavern opened a new patio area and …"

"I know," she said with a little laugh. "You told me all about the plans for it when we stopped by there last spring, remember?"

He grimaced. "Yes. God, sorry. Everything's been kind of a blur lately."

"How's your dad doing?"

"Better," Tyler said with a relieved sigh. "His mobility is way improved, and he's in a hell of a lot less pain than he was before the surgery. I'm still trying to fill in the blanks and help out with some chores. I'll take care of the leaves in their backyard this fall, but I'm hopeful that by next spring he'll be back to taking care of the mowing and stuff. If he can't handle it, I think I'll hire someone."

"Aww. You're so sweet, always looking out for the people you care about," she said. "Make sure you take time to take care of yourself. And let someone else do something for you for a change!"

"I'm trying," he said. He thought about the night before. About the worried look in Donovan's eyes this morning. His offer to drive with Tyler to Grand Rapids. Tyler hadn't wanted to drag Donovan away from the restaurant for anything less than a true emergency, but he'd appreciated the offer.

He'd thought a lot on the drive up about what was happening with Donovan, wondering what it all meant. There was no denying things were changing between them. He knew their scenes weren't just a way for them to blow off steam anymore.

Tyler knew it deep down to his bones, but it scared the shit out of him.

He wasn't ready for his life to change.

"Uncle Ty!" The thunder of feet filled the air, and a moment later Antonio bounded toward him. He was getting so big, his face beginning to take on the look of a teenager instead of a young boy. "I have to tell you all about the goal I scored at soccer."

"I'd love to hear about that—"

"Uncle Ty!" Isabella and Daniela came hurtling toward him, grabbing him around the waist and hugging him.

He squeezed the seven-year-old twins tight. "Hey, guys. It's good to see you."

All three kids talked a mile a minute, trying to cram in as many words as possible as their mother gave him a look that was both a little helpless and probably slightly relieved that for once she wasn't the one trying to wrangle them.

Tyler stood there a while, catching up with the kids, letting their torrent of words flow over him as he listened intently, nodding and trying to get a word in edgewise. Half the time he had no idea what they were talking about. Kids TV shows? Friends from school? No clue. But he gave them his undivided attention until Andrea stepped forward.

"Okay, guys. It's time to leave for Grandma's."

"I don't want to go to Grandma's! I wanna stay here with Uncle Ty." Isabella tugged at Tyler's hand.

"Hey, come here." He kissed the top of her head. "I'll come visit again soon, I promise. But your dad and I have some stuff we're gonna talk about today. Grownup stuff."

"Okay." She sighed heavily. "But you have to promise to play dolls with me next time, okay?"

"I promise."

It wouldn't be the first time, that was for sure. Hell, probably half the dolls and toys she had, he'd given her. And the same for Daniela's ponies and art kits. He was never shy about sitting on the floor of their bedroom and playing with them.

Tyler didn't have kids of his own, so he figured he might as well spoil the ones belonging to his friends.

He hugged the kids goodbye, then kissed Andrea on the cheek. She hugged and kissed her husband as well, but Tyler could see the strain between them, a far cry from the easy, loving affection that had been there before.

When Andrea and the kids were gone and the house was quiet, Tyler turned to Eddie. "I'm sorry. It really has been too long since I've come to see you."

"Hey, it's okay." Eddie draped an arm over Tyler's shoulder. "You're here now. You want some coffee?"

"Sure. Mind if I use your bathroom first? Had some on the way up and ..."

"Go for it." Eddie gave a vague wave in the general direction of the hall. "I'll be in the kitchen."

It didn't take Tyler long to empty his bladder and wash his hands, but he checked his phone before he went out again, hoping for a message from Donovan. There wasn't one. It didn't *mean* anything; he knew that. They didn't text a lot. Just shot the shit occasionally. Sent each other random crap like funny videos or tweets or whatever. The usual stuff he did with a lot of his friends.

Of course, Donovan also checked in with him periodically. Asked him about the scenes they'd done. Made sure he was doing okay. Sometimes they talked about their families or about more personal things.

Truth was, this thing with Donovan was starting to feel concrete in a way Tyler had never expected. He hadn't thought that being with a guy would ever feel like it had with his female exes, but it felt more real than it had with any of them. His military service had made relationships difficult, and he hadn't wanted to settle down while there was a real chance of him being deployed. The possibility of it when he was in the reserves had made him hesitate. But here he was, out of the military. He had a great civilian job, he owned a house, he had his shit together as much as he was probably ever going to. If there was ever a time for him to have a relationship, now was it.

Yeah, he was busy with the bar and helping out his family, but he and Donovan had managed to make this thing work. This thing that had started out casual but now felt like it could be something real.

But Tyler would have to upend his life to do it.

And that was assuming Donovan even wanted it. What if he didn't?

"What did you do, fall in there?"

The pounding on the door startled Tyler from his thoughts and he realized he'd been staring at his reflection in the mirror.

"Fuck off," Tyler called back. He grabbed his phone off the counter and stuffed it in his pocket.

He pulled the door open and glared at Eddie, who stood there holding two cups of coffee, a mischievous look on his face that Tyler hadn't seen in a long damn time.

"C'mon, get your ass in gear. It's a gorgeous day. Let's go sit in the backyard with our coffee. I want to enjoy this weather while it lasts."

Tyler took the mug and followed Eddie through the house, then out through the sliding back door. He hated that his first thought had been to wonder if Eddie had added a little something extra to his own cup.

Eddie took a seat on top of the picnic table and Tyler settled beside him, breathing in the fresh air. "It really is gorgeous."

It had been cool the night before but now that the sun was up, it was one of those perfect early fall days. The hot cup of coffee warmed his hands, and the breeze was soft against his cheek. The sounds of suburban life drifted through the air. The hum of the distant highway. The sound of garage doors opening and closing. The rumble and beep of a garbage truck.

"So, what's new with you?" Eddie asked.

Tyler made a noncommittal noise. "Like I said earlier, mostly work. Taking care of stuff at my parents' place. That's all keeping me pretty busy. Oh, my brother and his wife had a baby," he added. So far, he'd only seen the kid in pictures or sleeping on a video chat, but he was looking forward to when they came up to visit around Thanksgiving.

"Tell Gary and Kourtney I said congrats."

"I definitely will," Tyler promised.

"So that's it?" Eddie craned his neck to look at Tyler. "Nothing else new?"

"Not really." He'd dodged questions about his personal life when they were camping but now he was tempted to talk to Eddie about Donovan. It was scary as fuck though.

"Aww come on. You're not getting any action in the bedroom?" Eddie gave him a little wink. "That's not like you."

"Well …" Tyler said. His gut twisted, and he licked his lips. He didn't want to lie. And maybe if he opened up to Eddie about this, Eddie would open up to him. "I've been, uh, hooking up with someone for a while."

"Yeah? Tell me about her."

Tyler huffed out a laugh and closed his eyes. "Well, uh, that's the thing. It's, uh, it's a guy."

"Oh." Eddie nudged Tyler's knee with his. "So, tell me about *him*."

God, Tyler fucking loved Eddie more than ever for that. No big fuss. No dramatic gasp of shock. Tyler's eyes stung for a moment, and he took a big sip of his coffee to cover it.

"He's the executive chef at the tavern actually."

"The red-haired dude? Total hipster type, right? With the beard and the tatts and stuff."

Tyler let out another laugh, this time more genuine. "Yeah, that's Donovan."

Tyler had given Eddie and Andrea and the kids a tour of the place when they'd come to visit last spring, and he'd briefly introduced them to Donovan. He'd forgotten they'd met.

"He seemed cool," Eddie said. "His food was fucking amazing."

"He's not bad."

Eddie smirked at him. "So how long have you been seeing him?"

"A few months? Yeah, it was early June, I guess, when we started. So yeah, three months or so."

"And what, you just decided you were into him out of the blue?"

"Sort of. We argued at work a lot and it was kinda … foreplay, I guess? One day we both sort of snapped and … Let's just say we did something at work we shouldn't have."

"Oh shit." Eddie chuckled, clearly more amused than horrified. "Well, hey, that's good, right? I mean, you're having fun?"

"I am," Tyler said absently. He stared at the swing set across the neatly mown grass, the bikes he'd given the kids last year all parked next to it. "Donovan's … he's not like anyone I've ever been with and it's not because he's a guy."

"This more than a hookup?" There was surprise in Eddie's voice. "I mean, I know you got off with Frenchie while we were deployed, but I always figured it was … desperation or whatever. And you never talked about it."

Tyler turned to face Eddie, not trying to hide his surprise. He'd had no idea Eddie had realized what they were up to. *Talk about don't ask, don't tell.*

Eddie continued. "I mean, it just kinda sounds like it might be more for you with this guy, and I figure you probably aren't going to talk to me about it a lot unless it's pretty important to you. Not that you shouldn't. I just know you and the way you operate."

"It's … I don't know what it is," Tyler admitted. "I … we spend at least three nights a week together most weeks and … I don't know." It was so hard to put into words.

"Do you miss him when you aren't together?"

Tyler thought of the times he rolled over onto his side, hand reaching out for Donovan's side of the bed and the disappointment he felt at it being empty. He thought of how his mind wandered to Donovan every time he cooked eggs, how he was starting to be able to tell what foods would taste good together without looking up a recipe. He thought of the times they weren't together, but he wanted to tell Donovan something. About how often he started to type out a text, then deleted it, worrying it was too much. That he was demanding too much of Donovan's free time.

"Yeah. I do."

"Do you think he thinks about you when you're not together?"

"Yeah." His voice was hoarse. "Maybe? I don't know. I think so. Probably."

"That's a lot of qualifications in there, dude, but getting together a few days a week? That sounds like he's pretty into you."

"It's hard to meet people when you work the hours we do. I'm convenient." That was the argument that popped into Tyler's head any time he thought about it.

Eddie shot him a look. "Hookup apps, dude. He could find someone."

Donovan probably could. Tyler didn't want him to, though. And that was the kicker.

"I guess."

"Do you ever suggest getting together and he's too busy for you?"

"No," Tyler said slowly. "Any time I've wanted it, he's been on board for it."

"There you go. And you're holding back why?"

"I don't know," he admitted. "Guess I'm worried about what people will say. How things will change if I talk about it. What the guys would say, you know?"

"Why would the guys care?"

"They cared when Jackson and Hayes came out."

"Yeah, I know but …" Eddie shook his head. "It was different then. We were pissed about them lying about their relationship, you know that. You were pissed too. No one gives a fuck now though. Were you lying then? That you were into women?"

"No!"

"Then there's no problem. Tell 'em that. Might be a little weird at first but they'll get it. None of us are exactly the same as we were before." There was a bitter little twist to Eddie's lips. "Besides, Hayes and Jackson are married to each other. They're not going to give a fuck. I don't care. Johnson and Frenchie are gone. So that leaves Gordo and if he's a dick to you, I'll punch him in the fucking face."

"I guess it's the questions that make me squirm. People getting all up in my business about it. Asking when and why and—"

"Anyone asking those questions is being a dick," Eddie said. "And I'll tell 'em that."

"Thanks, man." Tyler smiled faintly.

"I love you, dude." Eddie draped an arm around his shoulder and Tyler pressed close. They'd sat like that a lot in Iraq. Tired and missing home. Missing touch. Tyler didn't feel the tiniest spark of attraction to Eddie, not like he did when Donovan was beside him. This was like sitting by a warm fireplace. Comforting. Homey.

"I love you too," Tyler said, his throat feeling thick.

"You love your chef?"

Tyler froze. "I … I don't know." He sucked in a deep breath. "Maybe I could." It didn't feel impossible the way it had when they'd first started fooling around.

"Does a future with him sound awesome or scary as fuck?"

"Both," Tyler admitted.

"That's how you know it's right, dude. Remember the day I married Andrea?"

"Yeah." Tyler laughed. "God, you were a fuckin' mess."

"I was. And I *knew* I wanted to spend the rest of my life with that woman, but I was scared shitless. We were so young."

"None of us are young anymore."

"Nope." Eddie gave him a rueful smile. "But I think we're still allowed to be fucking scared."

"The weird thing is, it all makes sense when we're together," Tyler admitted. "You know that restless feeling we've all had since we've gotten out? Like something's missing?"

"Yeah."

"Donovan makes it go away. When I'm with him, my mind goes quiet. I don't have to think about all the shit stressing me out."

"Think you'd be willing to loan him out to me?" Eddie's tone was joking, but it was clear there was real pain in his voice. "'Cause that sounds fucking amazing."

"I don't think you're into the kind of shit he's into," Tyler said automatically.

"Oh yeah?" Eddie raised an eyebrow. "What's that?"

Tyler froze. "Uhh. We're kinda … kinky."

Eddie snickered. "Yeah? You smack his ass and shit?"

Heart beating fast, Tyler ducked his head. "Other way around, man," he muttered.

"Oh." Eddie cleared his throat. "Well, cool. You do you. You think your man could smack my ass and shut this mess up?"

"Not sure it works that way," Tyler said, tension easing at Eddie's acceptance. At the way he made even heavy subjects feel lighter. "But yeah, if it would help, I'd be happy to loan him to you."

Not that the thought of Donovan's hands on anyone else sat well with Tyler—and that clearly meant he had something he'd have to think more about later—but for Eddie, he'd do it. He'd do anything for Eddie.

"Maybe talk to Andrea about that shit first," Tyler said. He drained the rest of his coffee and sat the mug on the table beside him.

"Fuck, if it would help, she'd hand him a paddle herself."

Tyler snorted. She probably would. "You think it would work?"

"Nah." Eddie's voice was sad. "Don't think I'm wired that way."

"Didn't think I was either," Tyler admitted.

"I dunno. You were always into weird shit. I know we all wrestled and stuff, just to burn off steam, but you were *into* it, man. You were always the instigator."

Tyler nodded. "True." He really had been. It had made him feel alive to square off with someone and get the shit kicked out of him. He'd never hesitated to go after guys with four inches and forty pounds of muscle on him that he knew he had no hope of winning against.

Had he only been trying to prove himself? To get stronger? Or had he enjoyed the sensation of being wrestled to the ground and subdued? Had he *liked* the feeling of helplessness and pain? Shit, that was something he was going to have to think more about too.

"And you always went harder at Ranger School than anyone. Even when your feet had blisters the size of a fucking half-dollar after fifteen-mile marches, you kept going."

"I didn't like *that* shit," Tyler protested. "I just refused to fucking fail out because my feet hurt."

"I'm just saying … you never shied away from pain. You remember that time you and Hayes played chicken with the cigarette."

He looked down and traced the scar on his arm, remembering. "Yeah. I do."

"Maybe you liked it."

"Always just thought I was being stupid and macho," Tyler said with a little laugh.

Eddie nudged his thigh with his knee. "Well, maybe that too."

But it did put some things in perspective. There'd been this sergeant who'd loved to get up in his face and order him around. Which, hey, that was kind of his job as an instructor. But Tyler had really liked Quinn. He'd respected him. He'd snapped to attention and dug deep to keep going when Quinn pushed him. Maybe that had been a clue he'd never put together until now.

"It isn't weird for you?" Tyler asked. "Thinking about me doing stuff like that?"

Eddie shrugged. "I want you to be happy, man. If being with a hipster chef who smacks your ass is your thing, go for it."

"Don't—" Tyler licked his lips. "Don't tell anyone else, okay? Not Andrea or the guys. Not yet. Not until I know what the fuck I'm doing."

"Sure. Your secret is my secret."

That was the way it had always been.

He leaned harder against Eddie's shoulder. "Wish I could help *you* more."

Eddie sighed. It was heavy and sad sounding. "Me too, man. Me too."

"Talk to me about it?"

"I don't know what to say." Eddie's expression turned grim. "I don't sleep much. When I do sleep, the nightmares have me thrashing around. I fucking hit Andrea a few months ago."

Tyler grimaced. "Oh shit."

"Not intentionally, of course. I'd never—"

"No, I know that," Tyler assured him.

"She caught me on the tail end of a nightmare, and I woke up swinging. I caught her shoulder instead of her face, but God." Eddie closed his eyes. "She swore up and down she was fine. That she didn't blame me. Tried to say it was her fault for startling me but … Every time I saw that bruise, man … it made me sick."

"I get it."

It was one thing to play the way he and Donovan did. Tyler had developed quite a collection of bruises since they'd been together. They felt like a little reminder of the fun they'd had.

But hitting someone you loved who hadn't agreed to it? Yeah, that was a whole different thing. Tyler couldn't imagine it.

"I've been sleeping on the floor. I don't want the kids to see we're sleeping apart, but I don't trust myself anymore."

"Oh, Eddie." Tyler leaned harder against him.

"I snap at the kids all the damn time too." Eddie's voice was weary. "And I feel like shit after, but I can't control it. You know. My head's just full of all this chatter and sometimes they're loud and giggling and … Fuck! They're just being kids. They don't mean to make me crazy." His laugh was hollow. "But I fucking *am* crazy. My head's a mess and I …" He let out a noise of aggravation. "I just want it to stop."

"I know." Tyler's heart ached. "Seems like you've been drinking a lot."

"It helps. At least for a little bit. Makes the shit in my head go a little quieter."

"I get that," Tyler said. "But don't you think it's doing more harm than good?"

"Probably." His laugh was bitter now. "I don't know what else to do. The VA isn't doing crap. I keep telling them I need help and they've done fuck all."

"You were doing some outpatient therapy stuff here in Grand Rapids, right?"

"Yeah." Eddie sighed. "The woman I was talking to at first was okay. It felt like we were getting somewhere, but at the end of August they switched me to someone else who is fucking useless. He's never served. He has no idea what the fuck we've gone through."

Sometimes, Tyler felt like he shouldn't be lumped in with Eddie. What Tyler had seen had been minimal. He'd spent a lot of time clearing the way for supply convoys and guarding other strategic points, but their interactions with insurgents had been rare. He'd seen the aftermath of the destruction but had faced little of it himself. It was a lot of time being on alert, waiting for all hell to break loose, but that moment had thankfully never come.

He wasn't the kind of guy who'd gone to war hoping to shoot someone. He'd discharged his weapon, but he'd never knowingly killed another human being, for which he was eternally grateful. He'd known he could do it, if he'd had to, but he was glad he'd never been forced to live with it after. To carry that weight for the rest of his life.

Eddie had. After Tyler had finished his four years and transitioned from active duty to reserves, Eddie had kept going. He'd been deployed to Afghanistan for a thirteen-month tour. The 87th Infantry Regiment, 1st Battalion had deployed to establish remote combat outposts against the Taliban after they had taken control of the provinces. During their tour of duty there were numerous large-scale engagements. They had been ordered to protect a critical juncture, a village at the crossroads of two main roads that were major supply lines of weapons, water, and gasoline.

Tyler didn't know all the details, but he did know that Eddie and his company had worked alongside Afghan soldiers there to secure the area. They'd lost a solider and had more than a dozen others injured when a suicide bomber had blown himself up. There had been roadside bombs, a convoy ambushed by a rocket-propelled grenade, and American soldiers had shot a teenage Afghani boy at one point.

It had been hellish and ugly, and Tyler knew Eddie still felt responsible for the loss of lives. How much Eddie had been involved in directly, Tyler wasn't sure. Eddie and Hayes had never spoken of their time there and it had left mental scars on them both. Hayes had struggled his way through but Eddie's never seemed to heal.

Tyler thought back to Eddie's comment about how the therapist didn't understand what he'd been through. "I'm sorry the counselor isn't helping."

Eddie sighed. He leaned back, resting on his hands, tilting his face toward the sun. "Me too."

"What about an inpatient rehab program? You know you need to get a handle on the drinking, man."

"I feel so fucking guilty for how much I was gone while the kids were little. I don't want to leave them again."

"I get that," Tyler said.

"It feels like I would be abandoning them, you know? I promised them I would never leave again for more than a night or two. I don't want to break that promise to them."

"In the long run, isn't it better to go away for ninety days and come back as the father and husband your family deserves?" Tyler pointed out.

"Ugh." Eddie sat up and scrubbed his hands over his face. "It is. But …"

"Eddie, you're abandoning them now. The way things are, you can't be the father they need." His tone was a little sharper than he'd intended.

Eddie's face crumpled. "I know. I know that. God, I'm trying, Ty. But the VA is no help there either. I'm on another fucking wait-list. I get it, they're underfunded, and they don't have enough spots but …"

"It's shitty," Tyler said.

"It is."

"What about a civilian place?"

"I'm on a six-month waitlist to get into a civilian inpatient rehab and even if I fucking get it, I don't know how I'll afford it. The VA will cover it partially but …" He shook his head. "The one place that could get me in sooner is so fucking pricey it would bankrupt us."

"Fuck. You know if I had the money, I'd help you out."

"I know that." Eddie sighed and pressed closer. "But you've got your mortgage payments and all that."

Tyler had considered just selling the damn place, finding a cheap rental or something. But real estate costs had only gone up in Pendleton in the past five years since he'd bought it. He could probably get a good price for his place but finding an inexpensive apartment to live was unlikely.

Not without him having to commute from somewhere in the middle of nowhere Michigan, and with his work hours, he'd be asking to crash on the way home from the bar at three in the morning.

"None of the private places would do a sliding scale for payment?" he asked.

"No," Eddie said. "Andrea looked into it. My VA insurance fucks it all up. There's all these gaps in coverage and it all amounts to the same thing: I'm fucked."

This bitterness in Eddie's voice was new. Tyler remembered Eddie being the prankster of their platoon. The one laughing and joking. The one who always kept up everyone's spirits. Seeing him so unlike himself made Tyler's chest ache.

Tyler sighed. "God, I wish Frenchie was here. He'd have busted everyone's balls until he got you in somewhere."

Eddie managed a half-smile. "Yeah, he would have."

Charles French had been a half-French-Canadian medic and the only guy until Donovan who had ever blown Tyler. The memories of Frenchie's mouth on Tyler's dick, wet and soft, a sharp contrast to the feel of the cold, gritty wind against his face as he'd closed his eyes lingered. Even now, Tyler could still hear the thwap of Frenchie jerking off as he took Tyler's dick into his throat, all business, quick and fast and rough. It had left Tyler gasping after, and Frenchie had merely stood, given him a wink as he zipped up, and disappeared behind the shipping containers, leaving Tyler to scuff out the evidence of Frenchie's enjoyment in the dirt.

After that, Frenchie had been the same guy as always, a high-energy, ball-busting medic with a quick wit and even quicker temper. He'd died several years after Tyler left the service, when a roadside bomb went off. Frenchie had pulled half a dozen men to safety and tended their wounds but had been taken out by a Taliban sniper. Rafe Johnson had died that day too.

When they served together, Frenchie had been the guy everyone went to when they needed something done. If anyone could have gotten Eddie squared away, it would have been him, thanks to his medic connections. But he was gone, and Tyler was helpless to do anything.

All he could do was sit there on the picnic table in the Silvas' back yard, leaning against Eddie like it would somehow be enough to hold his fragmented pieces together.

SEVENTEEN

By the time Donovan left the restaurant at the end of the day he felt like he'd been through the wringer. Between the conversation with Jude and the worry he felt over Tyler, he was a mess. A headache pounded behind his eyes and his shoulders were tight.

He swung by his apartment, tempted to head straight for the shower and collapse into bed for a late-afternoon nap, but there was something thrumming under the surface of his skin that warned him he was far too wound up to sleep. Instead, he changed into workout clothes and headed for the jiu-jitsu gym. It was on the outskirts of the town in a strip mall. The gym was huge, with training for adults and kids. They held regular classes and open mat sessions. People could also do cardio or weight training and spar if they could find a partner. That was what Donovan was hoping for today.

By the time he walked out of the gym an hour later, he was drenched in sweat, and he was weak and a little shaky. His right shoulder ached—he'd have to take it easy on any impact play for a few days—but his churning thoughts had settled a little and he felt calmer and more centered.

He fished his phone out of his pocket as he walked to his car, and his heart leaped when he saw a text message from Tyler that had just come through a few minutes before. ***Heading back to Pendleton.***

Rather than text back, he called.

"How'd it go?" Donovan asked softly when Tyler answered.

Tyler let out a sigh. "It was okay. He's … better than I expected, I guess. I don't know. I'm still worried."

Donovan slid into his car and closed the door. "Talk to me, Tyler. Tell me how I can help."

"I don't know that you can." His voice thickened.

"Can you let me try? Even if I can't help Eddie, I want to help you."

"Yeah." The words came out like they were being forced through gravel. "Okay."

Donovan let out his breath in a whoosh. "Good. How about this? You go to your place. Earlier, I packed up a couple of meals from the restaurant in the hopes you'd want to get together tonight. At worst, I figured I could drop yours off to you. But, if you want company, I'd like to see you."

There was silence for a moment. "That sounds nice."

"Text me when you're about twenty minutes out?"

"I will."

"You're not alone, Tyler. You know that, right?"

"Yeah, I do."

The rough appreciation in Tyler's voice didn't necessarily surprise Donovan but the way it filled up his chest did.

"Drive safe and I'll see you soon."

"Is that an order?" Tyler let out a weak laugh.

"It is if you want it to be."

There was silence for a moment. "Yeah, I do."

"Then it is."

"See you soon."

There was a heavy weight at the end of that sentence. Like there was a missing word. Donovan wondered if Tyler ever wanted to call him 'Sir.'

Then he wondered what Tyler would say if he ordered him to.

The haggard expression on Tyler's face when he opened the door to his small brick house a few hours later made Donovan's chest ache.

"Come in." Tyler pulled the door open and stepped back.

"Thanks." Donovan set his overnight bag and the bag with food down just inside the entrance. He held out his arms.

Tyler just stared at him with a blank expression.

Donovan pushed the door shut behind him with his foot as he wrapped his arms around Tyler, pulling him against his body. "How are you doing?"

"Not so good." Tyler's voice cracked as he sank against Donovan's chest. "It's … it's been a lot lately. Today was—"

He didn't seem to have any more words, so Donovan just breathed with him, feeling the little tremors in Tyler's body. "You can let go," he whispered. "You're safe."

Tyler tucked his head against Donovan's neck and clung to him. "Fuck." His words were muffled by Donovan's skin but there was no mistaking the wetness he felt.

Donovan held him close, murmuring senseless little things meant to soothe. They stood there for the longest time until Tyler's shaking subsided, and he pulled back.

"I'm sorry about that," Tyler said. He looked at the floor, swiping at his eyes.

"Hey." Donovan gently lifted Tyler's chin so he could look him in the eye. "You never have to apologize for being honest with me. Your emotions? Those are honest. I get it, okay? I get that it's hard for you to be vulnerable because of your training, but you never have to hide what you feel from me. I don't want you to. It goes against everything I believe this thing between us should be."

Tyler nodded, exhaustion radiating from every inch of his body.

"C'mon, you'll feel better once you sit down and eat something."

Donovan slipped an arm around Tyler's waist and led him to the couch. He dropped onto it with a heavy sigh.

"Want anything to drink?"

"Just some water." Tyler shifted like he was going to stand, and Donovan gave him a stern look.

"Sit. I'll get it."

"Okay, okay," Tyler grumbled.

But by the time Donovan made it back with two tall glasses, ice clinking gently in them, Tyler's eyes were closed. He had his head back against the cushion of the brown leather sofa and his lips were slightly parted. Asleep already.

Donovan set down the glasses as quietly as he could manage, then retrieved the bag of food. He warmed it carefully, then plated it. Tyler was still asleep, and Donovan was torn between waking him to eat and letting him get some rest.

Tyler solved that for him by waking when Donovan gingerly took a seat beside him.

He lifted his head, his eyes opening sluggishly.

"You passing out on me already?" Donovan asked with a little smile. He handed the plate over. "There. Your favorite."

Tyler took the food, then tilted his head at him. "My favorite?"

Donovan frowned at him. "You *do* like the steak with Michigan cherry sauce, right?"

"Yeah. How did you know that?"

"Because I pay attention to you, Tyler."

"Oh." He picked up his fork. "Thank you then."

Donovan rested a hand on Tyler's thigh. "I knew you were going to have a rough day. I thought … well if any part of it could be better, that was the least I could do."

"That was really thoughtful."

"I … I care about you, Tyler." That felt wholly inadequate, but what more could he say? Now wasn't the time. "I want to look out for you. As a friend, and as … well as the Dom who you're involved with."

He tried to hide a grimace. That sounded painfully clunky but he wasn't sure it was right to refer to himself as Tyler's Dom. He hadn't claimed him. Hadn't collared him. Wasn't even sure if that was something Tyler would ever be okay with.

Tyler nodded. He lifted a forkful of steak to his mouth and chewed slowly, the tension slipping from his shoulders. Tyler nudged Donovan's thigh with his knee. "You planning to eat or just watch me? Is that a kink of yours?"

Donovan laughed. "No, not really. I do get pleasure out of people enjoying my food. It isn't a sexual thing. More service, oddly enough."

"Hmm." Tyler poked at some roasted Brussels sprouts. "You sort of said the same thing the other day. Other night? I'm losing track of time. Whenever you said you wanted to help me. I expected you to be all … demanding, I guess. Ordering me around all the time."

"I enjoy that part of it," Donovan said with a smile. "I really do. But, at least for me, someone making themselves vulnerable to me means it's my job to look after them. They're giving me a certain responsibility and that means looking after their well-being in every way. Don't get me wrong, I get plenty of sadistic pleasure ordering you around. Putting you in bondage. Making you struggle. Hell, you know I love when I have to take you down before a scene. But to me that's only part of it. You can't fully give yourself to me if you're not in peak condition. Does that make any sense?"

"Sure, I think so," Tyler said. "You can't make a truly great drink with shitty alcohol and mixers."

"Apt analogy."

"I mean, it's probably the same for food, right? You cheap out on the quality of ingredients, you don't get as good of a result."

"Yes."

"So, you're saying if I'm a mess, you can't expect the scene to go well."

"Yes …" Donovan considered the idea. "I suppose that's partly what I'm getting at. But it's more than that. I like to take a holistic approach. As much as you give me in a scene, I need to make sure I give back. Which means meeting all your needs. At least, that's my ideal situation."

God, this was hard. Donovan was being vague, hinting at things, not really saying what he meant. And he disliked that. But he also knew this was the worst possible time to push Tyler. He was vulnerable, and any conversation about what their dynamic was would have to wait. Donovan wanted more but he didn't want to discuss it until he was sure Tyler was in the right frame of mind for it.

Exhausted, sleep-deprived, and emotionally wrung out was the opposite of that.

"Just eat your fucking food, Tyler," Donovan said with a grin to offset the harshness of the words. "Let me take care of you in the way I know best."

Tyler smiled back, a little of the sadness lifting from his eyes. "For what it's worth, I wasn't complaining."

"Good."

Tyler scooped up another forkful of mashed potatoes and shoved it into his mouth. Half his plate was already cleaned, and Donovan had barely made it a quarter of the way through his. Yes, someday, if Tyler let him, he was definitely going to train him to eat more slowly. To savor.

They ate in silence for a while, and Tyler let out a contented sigh as he licked his fork clean. "You do know your way around a steak."

"I know my way around a lot of things," Donovan said teasingly.

"Does that include dessert?" There was a hopeful note in his voice.

Donovan chuckled. "It does. I did pastry courses at the culinary academy as well. Not my specialty but I can hold my own."

"You don't do them for the restaurant, right?"

"No. We get some from the bakery downtown. A few are made in house by Laura." They didn't have a dedicated team of pastry chefs the way Plated had, but she did a good job with what they did offer, unfussy, comforting desserts like skillet brownies and bread pudding. "I might have brought something with me tonight actually," Donovan admitted.

Tyler's eyes lit up. "You have no idea how glad I am to hear that."

"Hmm, you have more of a sweet tooth than I realized."

"After a day like today …"

"I hear you." There was comfort in food. "I brought a brownie. It's warming in the oven as we speak." He'd actually filched one of the small iron skillets from the restaurant, but he didn't figure Rachael would care unless he forgot to return it.

A short while later, Donovan returned with the brownie resting on an oven mitt, and one spoon.

"I want to try something," Donovan said. He shifted so his back was to the arm of the couch, and he spread his legs. "Sit here. Your back to me. Lean your head against my shoulder."

Tyler hesitated.

"If you don't want to, you don't have to," Donovan said softly. "We're not in a scene. I won't be upset."

"But you want me to."

It wasn't really a question, but Donovan nodded anyway. "I do."

"Okay." Tyler got into position and craned his neck to look at him. "Now what?"

"Now, I feed you."

Tyler grimaced. "That's …"

Donovan raised an eyebrow.

"I'll try."

Donovan scooped up a bite of the soft and gooey brownie, rich with chocolate and drenched with melting ice cream.

He lifted it, carefully guiding it to Tyler's mouth. There was something incredibly sensual about watching Tyler open his mouth and allow Donovan to guide the spoon in. And the soft pink lap of his tongue was enough to distract Donovan for a moment as he leaned in to taste the dessert off Tyler's lips.

Donovan managed a few bites, feeding Tyler, and then himself, but after a bit Tyler pulled away, stiffening as he shook his head.

"This is weird." Tyler grimaced. "I'm sorry. I can't …"

"It's okay." Donovan swallowed down his disappointment, not entirely surprised, just regretting that he'd attempted it in the first place. Scene or not, it was the type of thing that pushed at Tyler's limits of being passive and submissive and that wasn't what Donovan was supposed to be doing now. He handed over the skillet. "Feel free to finish it."

A worried little frown flickered over Tyler's face, but he took the pan without a word.

When the last bite was gone, Donovan took the skillet and rose to his feet. "I'll go clean up."

"You sure you don't want help? I feel …"

"I want you to rest," Donovan said firmly, and Tyler subsided.

Cleaning distracted Donovan enough to find his equilibrium again, and when he returned, Tyler looked up from his phone.

"Are you staying the night? We didn't talk about it."

"Only if you want me to," Donovan said. "I packed a bag, but maybe that was presumptuous of me."

"No, I assumed you would. I just wasn't sure what you wanted."

They were tiptoeing around something here, clearly uncomfortable with each other, but Donovan wasn't quite sure why. Perhaps it was everything that lay under the surface with no resolution. The unspoken question of where they were going with this relationship. Or maybe Tyler was just feeling unsettled by his worry over his friend.

"If you want me here, I'd like to stay," Donovan said firmly.

"Yeah, definitely. Honestly, I sleep better when you're with me." Tyler chewed at his lip. "Why is this weird all of a sudden?"

"Probably in part because we've never done this," Donovan said with a little sigh. "Just hung out, I mean. We're usually at my place. We're fresh off work. We do a scene and head to bed."

Sure, there was breakfast sometimes. More sex in the morning. Showering together. But they'd never simply spent time together as friends or vanilla partners.

Tyler seemed to consider the idea. "True."

"How about a movie?" Donovan suggested.

"Yeah, great idea." Tyler reached for the remote control.

"Anything you've been wanting to watch?"

"Ehh, probably, but I can never remember off the top of my head. You can go through my watchlist and see if there's anything that interests you."

"Sounds good."

Donovan scrolled through the options before settling on a horror movie he thought looked interesting. "How's this?"

"Perfect."

Ten minutes into the movie, Donovan glanced over at Tyler who sat ramrod straight on the far side of the couch.

"You're pretty far over there," he teased.

"Guess I am." Tyler slid a little closer.

Donovan shifted so Tyler's heavily muscled arm lay draped over his shoulders, slouching so his head could lean against Tyler's chest, his hand on his thigh. It would be uncomfortable eventually but Donovan could manage it for a while.

Donovan stroked Tyler's thigh and tried to focus on the movie as he debated if he should mention the conversation he'd had with Jude. Today had been such an exhausting day for both of them. And really, what was the point? Donovan had turned down Jude's offer flat out, so it wasn't like it was going to impact his and Tyler's relationship. Whatever it was.

Tyler's hand was warm against his upper arm, the tips of his fingers stroking Donovan's bicep as he absently dragged them back and forth. It was a ticklish, shivery sort of pleasure but nice too.

Donovan had missed this part of his relationship with Jude. The quiet moments in front of a TV. The comfort in silence and physical touch.

Donovan was more certain with every moment that passed that he and Tyler were slowly transitioning into a deeper relationship. They'd need to talk about it at some point, but for now, Donovan was content to let Tyler go slow, ease his way in. There was no reason to bring it up when Tyler was raw from visiting his friend.

They'd watch the movie, get ready for bed, and after some rest, they'd see what tomorrow would bring.

"I told Eddie about us." Tyler's voice floated up out of the darkness, and Donovan jolted out of his dozing state.

"Hmm?" he managed. He had an arm draped over Tyler's midsection, spooning their bodies together.

"I talked to Eddie about what we've been doing. That I've been hooking up with a guy and that we're into some kinky stuff. Even that I was the one, uh, bottoming."

In the dark bedroom, Donovan blinked. "How'd he take it?"

"He was a little surprised, but he was great."

Donovan released a sigh of relief, pressing his lips to the back of Tyler's neck. "I'm glad to hear that."

"Yeah, it wasn't as big of a deal as I expected. I mean, Eddie's always been cool with stuff but …"

"It's a big step anyway," Donovan said. He tried not to hope that it was a sign of something more. That it was Tyler dipping a toe out of the closet. Testing the waters, so to speak.

But hope rose anyway, filling his chest like a helium balloon.

He bit back the urge to ask if it meant Tyler had plans to tell anyone else. God, he'd kill for some clarification about what their future held, but he had to let Tyler do it at his own pace.

"I'm glad it went well," he said instead. "I'm glad you have a friend like that."

"I just wish I knew how to help him." Tyler sounded frustrated.

"I know." Donovan kissed Tyler's shoulder. "If there is anything I can do, I mean *anything*, let me know."

"Have a spare fifty thousand lying around for inpatient rehab?" Tyler asked. His tone was bleak.

"I'm afraid not." Donovan sighed. "I put all my money into the restaurant and …"

"Even if you did, I wouldn't ask—"

"I know you wouldn't." *I'd offer it if I had it though.* Not just for Tyler's sake, but because it was criminal that someone like Eddie was suffering when he should be able to access assistance.

Paul, the Marine who Donovan and Jude had played with from time to time, had been bitter about his time in the service. Bitter about the scars it had left, outside and in, a thankless job for a cause he no longer believed in.

Donovan didn't know if the wars this country was in were justified or not, but even if they were, the cost seemed so very high for the men and women who served.

Tyler let out a little grumbling noise. "God, I'm exhausted, but I can't fall asleep. My mind's going a million miles an hour. I'm usually good at sleeping anywhere at any time but I must have gotten used to getting kinky with you before bed or something."

"I get it. If you need it tonight, I will do my best. Full disclosure, I'm pretty exhausted and my shoulder's hurting from the workout I had at the jiu-jitsu gym this afternoon. I'm not in a great state to top you. If we kept it simple and low impact, I could definitely do it but—"

"No, that's fine. Honestly, I don't even know if I could focus enough to make it worth your while."

Donovan smirked, pulling Tyler closer. "Oh, I bet the humbler I own would keep you focused."

"Oh God, I don't even know what that is and it scares the shit out of me."

Donovan chuckled and dragged his fingertips across the ridges of Tyler's abs. "It's a wooden bar that clamps around the base of the scrotum. It hooks behind your thighs at the base of your ass. You have to keep your legs folded forward, because if you straighten your legs, it pulls hard on your balls. How much it hurts depends on how much you pull."

Tyler shuddered, pressing back against Donovan's cock. "The sound of that shouldn't turn me on."

Exhausted as Donovan was, he was growing hard too, especially with the feel of Tyler's ass gently grinding against him.

"And yet ..." Donovan slipped his hand down to circle Tyler's dick and gently stroke up and down it. He craned his head to kiss Tyler, a dirty promise of what would come later.

"Yeah." Tyler sounded breathless. "You too though. You love the thought of torturing me that way."

"Oh, most definitely. Not tonight though. That's the kind of scene that should be savored. I vote for either jerking or sucking each other off now, then sleep."

"I like the sound of that."

Donovan shoved back the covers. "Roll over." He shifted to face Tyler's body, head toward his feet, and reached for Tyler's cock. "Think you can figure out what comes next?"

"Yeah, I think I can work it out."

"Good." With that, he licked a stripe up the underside of Tyler's cock and took him in his mouth. A moment later, Tyler did the same to him and he hummed his approval.

Two messy blowjobs later, Donovan settled his head on the pillow again, cradling the back of Tyler's neck as he licked his way into his mouth, their sweaty bodies intertwined. "Will that help you sleep?"

"Think so." Tyler's voice was soft and lazy. "Thank you, by the way. I … you've done a lot for me lately and I don't know how to thank you for that."

"No need," Donovan said lightly. "I'm here for you, however you need me."

In the morning after a lazy shower and breakfast, Donovan looked intently at Tyler. He looked better rested but there was still something weary in his expression.

"I want to take you to the beach today."

"You do?" Tyler tilted his head. His ever-present baseball cap was off, the silver at his temples gleaming in the morning sunlight that streamed through the window by the kitchen table.

Tyler's house was nice. Not fancy. Not flashy or new, but solid and warm. Much like Tyler himself.

"Yes, I do." Donovan cleared his throat. "I think you could use a day off without any responsibilities."

Tyler scrubbed his hands over his face. "God, I can't remember the last time I went to the beach. Probably last summer when I went up to Sleeping Bear Dunes with Eddie and Andrea and the kids."

"Well, it's obviously not swimming weather now," Donovan said, gesturing to the view outside Tyler's window where a few colorful leaves drifted to the ground from the big old maples that ringed the small lot. "But I thought maybe a walk would be nice. I don't know about you, but I find being by the water calming. You've had a lot on your plate lately, I thought it might be nice to take a day off and relax. Assuming you have the day free, that is."

"That does sound nice." There was something wistful in Tyler's expression. "I have some things I could do, but honestly, you're right. I need a day off that isn't stressful."

"Excellent. I'll pick up a picnic lunch on the way."

"Where are we going?"

Donovan stood, grabbing his empty coffee mug and plate. "You'll see when we get there. I promise, I know the perfect place. It's quiet and pretty private."

"Sounds great."

An hour later, Donovan pulled up to the house where he'd spent the majority of his summers.

"Is this someone's private home?"

"Not just someone's," Donovan said. "My grandmother's."

"Oh, cool." Tyler gave it a curious glance.

"The good news is, she happens to be out of town with some friends, so we won't even have her bugging us." Donovan smiled.

"Nah, she was funny," Tyler said. "Muffin."

Donovan glared. "Watch it."

Tyler just grinned.

They skirted around the large mid-century house and into the yard. A series of steps took them down to a sandy beach.

"This *is* pretty private." Tyler's gaze darted around the area. It was a tiny sheltered cove. It was just north of the headland that made up Hawk Point, where the Lighthouse B&B was situated. Most tourists headed south to the public beach, and it was rare that any of them made the more arduous and rocky trip north and down to the beach below. To the north of the cove were other houses, but the owners mainly kept to themselves, and it was rare to see anyone strolling along this section of shore.

"Yup. It is." Donovan set down his picnic basket and blanket. "This should be safe enough here while we walk for a few."

"Okay." Tyler fell into step beside him, and there was only the crash of the waves and the cry of birds as they walked for a few minutes. "So, your family has money, huh? I mean, that's a nice house and a place on Lake Michigan … that's …"

"Yes. Although my grandparents bought the place long, long before property values went through the roof," Donovan explained. "My grandfather worked as a lineman for the local electrical company when he bought this property. He fixed up the vacation cottage on it and as he took a management position, he became more well off. He built this current house for my grandmother when they were in their thirties. It was their dream home and they lived in it together for almost forty years."

"I get it," Tyler said. "What do your parents do?"

"They're both lawyers."

Tyler gave him a surprised glance. "You didn't want to go that route?"

Donovan let out a quiet snort. "No, much as I like to argue, that was never my thing. I was always fascinated with food." He went on to tell Tyler about his years growing up. His summers there on the beach. He gestured to the pale brown sand that lay between the scrubby plants and blue water, the waves slowly rolling in, the sound a soothing rhythm. "I spent so many hours out here it was like my second home."

"No wonder you're so freckled."

"Watch it. You're really begging to be punished later." His tone was teasing.

Tyler glanced at him out of the corner of his eye, smirking a little. "Maybe I am."

"Noted."

Their fingers brushed and Donovan resisted the urge to take Tyler's hand. "As a kid, I never left the house without SPF 50 and a sun hat on. But I really did spend most days out here. Picking up shells and pebbles. Building sandcastles. Swimming, of course. Grandma would set up in the shade and read a book while I swam until I could hardly walk."

"Sounds pretty idyllic."

"It was," he agreed.

"Are you …" Tyler frowned. "Never mind."

"No, what is it?"

“Are you not close to your parents or something?”

“We’re …” Donovan hesitated. “They love me. They support me. They’re wonderful people but honestly, I’m closer to my grandmother. My parents and I just have very different lives. Their jobs put them in a social circle I don’t have any interest in joining. There’s nothing wrong with it at all. Hell, they both volunteer with Legal Aid. They’re not shallow, frivolous people. We just don’t have a lot in common.”

“I get that. My dad was pretty bummed when I enlisted in the military rather than joining his plumbing business. It drove a wedge between us for a while. We’re closer now, but I know what it’s like to have some distance there.”

“You enjoy bartending, right? You seem to.”

“I do. And the manager position has been great. It’s a little more challenging. I guess I’ve always felt a little more aimless than a lot of people I know. Could’ve gone to school with the GI bill once I was in the reserves, but I didn’t have a plan for what I wanted to study anyway so it seemed like a waste.”

“I get that.”

“It sort of feels like I’ve been searching for something, and I don’t know what that is.”

“Some kinky people feel that way until they discover BDSM.”

Tyler nodded. “Yeah, I can see that. I definitely feel like it’s a piece that’s slotted into place for me. This feels good. It feels right.”

Donovan wondered if Tyler had begun to feel the pull toward deeper submission. To more than just a scene here and there. To the kind of dynamic Donovan dreamed of. Was that something Tyler longed for too without even realizing it?

"This thing with you is so much better than anything I've had in the past," Tyler continued.

Donovan smiled, feeling hope for the future kindle within him. "That's good to know."

Tyler smiled. "You just like me stroking your ego."

"I like you stroking anything of mine," he teased.

Tyler's joyful laugh made Donovan feel good. It was nice to see the weight of worry lifting from his shoulders.

They walked in silence for a little while, passing homes that were easily in the tens of millions of dollars. They made his grandparents' house look small and cheap.

Donovan's thoughts worked their way back to Tyler's earlier comment about his feelings of aimlessness and what he'd been searching for.

"Do you feel differently about who you are than you did before we met?"

Tyler let out a little hum. "I think so. You've definitely made me think about things differently."

"In a good way, I hope."

He nodded. "What we do feels right. Both the kink and … and being with you."

Donovan let their knuckles brush again, desperately wishing he could take Tyler's hand. "Good. It does to me too."

Tyler slowed to a stop and lifted a hand to brush his fingertips against Donovan's cheek. "Thank you."

Donovan went still, looking at Tyler for a long, serious moment, surprised by the public gesture of affection, even if the beach was deserted. "For what?"

"For … for showing me this side of myself, I guess. Six months ago, I would never have imagined this would be a part of my life."

"I know." Donovan stepped a little closer, enjoying the feel of Tyler's sun-warmed T-shirt against his chest. "Give yourself some credit though."

"Credit for what?" Tyler slid his sunglasses onto the top of his baseball cap and Donovan took his off as well.

"For being willing to explore it when you had the opportunity."

Tyler hummed, brushing his thumb against Donovan's lower lip. "I don't think I would have with anyone else."

There was something intent in Tyler's eyes, the usual gray shade tinted blue in the bright sunlight.

"Tyler, I …" But he couldn't finish the thought, could only stare into Tyler's eyes. Could only hope and pray.

Tyler licked his lips and leaned in a little.

The sound of a speedboat broke through their quiet bubble and Tyler stepped away, putting space between their bodies again. "You want to keep going or turn back?"

That's the question, isn't it? Donovan thought, even as he turned back to face where they'd come from. *Do I quit now or keep going, knowing you might break my heart?*

EIGHTEEN

"Hey, Tyler, do you have a minute?" Rachael called from inside her office as he passed.

He paused outside her door. "Sure. What's up?"

"Come in and close the door behind you, please."

"Uh, okay." He blinked at her. *Shit, what did I fuck up?*

"I see that look on your face. You're not in trouble." She laughed softly. "I just want to tell you about something new we're doing at the tavern."

"Jesus, woman," Tyler said, relaxing as he took a seat across the desk from her. "First it was the open mic nights, then the restaurant, and then the new patio space. Do you know how to relax?"

"No." She grinned at him. "But this is fairly small. We just have a new group that's interested in renting our event space on a monthly basis."

"Oh, sure." Tyler said, relieved. "That sounds manageable." It was usually families renting the space for birthdays or retirement parties, bridal or baby showers, the occasional community meeting or get together.

"Well, I wanted to run it by you first before I made a decision." She hesitated. "It's an alternative lifestyle group."

"Oh? What's the big deal? There's the poly meetups here already."

"It's a BDSM group."

"Oh. I see."

"They have a regular munch in Fort Benton but would like to expand to Pendleton. They said they've had some interest lately for mixers and munches in this area and wanted to see if we'd be a good fit for their needs."

Tyler scrambled to think of how to word his response like someone who wasn't involved in that kind of thing. Not that he was part of the community even now, but he'd spent enough time reading about stuff that he knew the lingo pretty well and he didn't want to tip his boss off that he was into it. "That's just … um, people talking, having drinks or dinner or whatever, right? Not like …"

"Oh, no," Rachael said. "They assured us it would be quite family friendly, other than some of the discussions. That's why they requested the private space. Everyone will be expected to show up in street clothes and behave as they would in a family restaurant. Nothing … kinky other than the topics of conversation."

"Right. That seems okay to me." Agreeing to this wouldn't tell people he was kinky too. Just that he was open-minded, right?

"I just wanted to run it by you," she said. "Donovan said he was fine with it."

Tyler suppressed a snort. Yeah, he bet Donovan would be.

"But I'd also like you to bartend for the mixer they want to hold next month. If you're not comfortable, I'll talk to Lacey, but I trust you more than anyone else here. The organizers stressed that privacy was of the utmost importance. They're not advertising it to the general community, just trying to hold an event that will be word of mouth within their own community, and I assured them any of the staff they encountered would be respectful and discreet. I trust Lacey, but I'd prefer if you were the one there."

"Yeah, of course," Tyler assured her. "I have no problem with that." But his heart beat a little faster, imagining going to a kink event. Even if it was low-key and he'd basically be there undercover.

She smiled. "I had a feeling you would understand."

He gave her a quizzical look. "Why did they choose the tavern? Are you …" Oh God, maybe he shouldn't have asked that.

She chuckled. "Kinky? No. Or at least no more than your average person, I don't think. Reeve and Grant and I certainly don't have a boring sex life, but we're not in that community. The organizers just knew we held the poly meetups and thought the tavern might be a good fit. Open-minded and non-judgmental, you know?"

"Makes sense. Yeah, I'm happy to help out."

"Well, great," Rachael said with a smile. "That's settled then."

That next month passed in a blur. Eddie had pushed and was now seeing a new therapist. Tyler got fewer drunken phone calls from him, and Andrea assured him she'd checked the house top to bottom for any weapons but there were none in sight. That allowed Tyler to let go of some of the tension he had been carrying, and he felt like he could breathe a little easier.

Nothing drastic had changed between him and Donovan. They still saw each other three or four nights a week, sometimes at his place, sometimes at Donovan's, and they occasionally watched movies or did something not kinky. There was no shortage of kinky sex either though, and those nights Donovan paddled Tyler or choked him as he fucked him were what made everything in his life feel right.

Neither of them had talked about what it meant or where they were going in the future, and it was too good for Tyler to risk changing anything.

But nerves built in him the closer they got to the date of the kink event.

The morning of the mixer, Tyler stood in front of his closet wondering what to wear, then shook his head at himself.

"Wear your work clothes, you idiot," he muttered under his breath. "You're going to be there bartending."

Donovan, who had just stepped out of the bathroom and wore nothing but a towel around his waist, gave him a quizzical look. "What are you muttering about?"

"Nothing. Just being an idiot." He reached for one of the many black button-downs he owned. He'd worn one when Rachael was out of town, and he'd continued since then. He thought it gave him a little more of an air of authority if he were dressed up. Plus, he liked the way Donovan looked at him when he rolled up his cuffs, exposing some of the ink on his forearms.

"Are you nervous about the event tonight?" Donovan asked with a concerned frown. He warmed a tiny bit of pomade in his hands, then smoothed it over his beard, making sure it was neat and tidy.

Tyler frowned. "I guess? It's stupid, right?"

"It's not stupid. You don't have to be nervous though. No one there will know you're kinky too. They'll assume you're there to help with the event."

"I know that." Oddly enough, that wasn't what made Tyler nervous actually. Part of him wanted them to know. Wanted them to realize he was one of them too.

"It's not like you're collared or anything." Donovan reached out and touched his throat.

The light touch made Tyler shiver. "Is that something you'd want? I mean, obviously not with *me,* but … do you want to collar someone someday?"

A weird expression crossed Donovan's face as he stroked Tyler's skin with his fingers. "Someday, yes."

Tyler knew what that meant. That it was an enormous commitment to some people. As important as marriage. There were people who wore it as an accessory or used it as a tool that didn't hold any more meaning than a paddle but Tyler knew Donovan well enough to be sure that for him, it would mean something. It would be a promise.

"Did your ex have a collar?"

"No." Donovan stiffened and dropped his hand. "He … he was too much of a switch. He said it didn't feel right. That it felt too restrictive. Too submissive for who he was."

"Oh." Tyler swallowed hard. "Do you miss him?"

"Sometimes." Donovan's smile was tight. "But I wanted him to be something he wasn't."

"And what was that?"

"Mine and mine alone."

"So, do you come here often?" A tall blond guy braced a hand on the bar and leaned toward Tyler. His bright grin and the twinkle in his blue eyes said he was fully aware of what a cliché his question was.

Tyler laughed. "I do. I work here, so I'm here nearly *every day*, in fact."

"Oh, for the tavern? I thought maybe the organizers hired someone in the community, but I guess that makes sense."

"Ahh, nope, I've worked here at the Hawk Point Tavern for about a decade," Tyler said, deliberately being vague about it. "What would you like to drink?"

"Another one of these." He held up a bottle of a Traverse City IPA Tyler had recently added to the bar menu.

"Oh, that's a great beer, isn't it?

The guy nodded. "I've never had it before, but I'm a convert."

"It goes so well with the Brussels sprouts and bacon flatbread. Donovan and I planned out the menu and drinks together."

They had talked to Rachael about it as well and ultimately decided they wanted to avoid servers running in and out of the private room in the back of the restaurant. Max was openly part of the kink community, so they'd offered to serve the food, though most of it was set up the way they did it at the bigger town events, with food prepped ahead of time and kept warm. Easy for Max to serve without having to make many trips to the kitchen.

"Donovan?" the guy asked.

"The executive chef here." Tyler tried not to smile, thinking about the way Donovan had sensed his earlier nerves and bent him over the bed this morning before they'd left for work. He'd shaken off his odd mood to fuck Tyler into the mattress. They'd both had to take a second shower and were a little late this morning, but it had been worth it. Rachael had only given them an amused look as if she understood. "We try to coordinate drinks and the food for special events."

"That's a lot of work to put toward a small kinky mixer." The guy gestured to the crowd. It wasn't huge. Maybe three dozen people. There was a good blend of couples. Gay, straight, lesbian … Tyler recognized a few from around town too. One was a woman who owned one of the art galleries on Main Street. She was flirting with another woman he didn't know. And he'd spotted the gay couple he'd seen at the Apple Festival again. They were deep in conversation with a few other people he didn't recognize.

Surprisingly, there were several guys who'd caught Tyler's eye tonight, in fact. Including the one who was leaning against his temporary bar, looking at Tyler with an expectant expression.

"Oh," Tyler cleared his throat. "Well, we try to offer the same service to anyone who books space here."

"And that includes making sure the best-looking bartender here is doing the service, apparently."

The back of Tyler's neck warmed. "Well, I'm the bar manager actually. And yes, when it's an important event that the owner wants to make sure goes well, especially when discretion is important, I am the one who works it." He'd done the poly meetups in the past and those had always gone off without a hitch.

"So modest."

"I don't know about that."

"Oh, I do." His look was assessing. "I was in here a while back, and you are *definitely* the best-looking of the bunch, Tyler."

"Well, thank you," he managed. Several things occurred to him then. One, that this guy was *flirting* with him, and two, that Tyler probably came across like he was flirting back. Which he hadn't intended. Also, how did this man know Tyler's name?

Tyler shot him a quizzical look and asked the question aloud.

He reached out, flicking his fingertip at Tyler's nametag. "This clued me in."

"Ahh." Tyler's neck heated again but he wasn't sure if it was the flirtatious tone or the memory of Donovan flicking his nipples like that a few nights ago before torturing them with ice and his warm, wet tongue.

Tyler suppressed a shudder and cleared his throat. "And you are?"

"Jude." His smile widened. "Jude Maddox." He held out a hand.

"Nice to meet you, Jude." Tyler wiped his damp palm on a bar towel and shook. "Aren't you supposed to be here to mingle?" he asked with a quizzical glance. "I mean, that's the purpose of this, right? So you can talk to people."

"I am talking to people," Jude said with another grin. "Or one person in particular."

Jude was really kind of ridiculously good-looking. Charming. A little part of Tyler responded to that, but the bigger part suddenly wished Donovan were there. That they were out in the crowd, mingling with people and talking kink and … *Huh.* Tyler had no idea he'd even wanted that, but now he definitely did.

"Yeah, but I'm not your target demographic," Tyler pointed out.

"No?"

"Well, you're here looking to meet someone kinky, right?"

Jude shrugged and took a long pull on his beer. "I suppose. Although this isn't strictly a dating thing. Just a chance for people in the community to chat and mingle. But if you were interested, I am always open to the idea of meeting someone kinky to get involved with." He leaned in. "Or someone who is new to it but curious. Are you sure your interest in this event is only for work? Because you were listening pretty intently earlier when the people over there were discussing stress postures in bondage."

"It's interesting," Tyler admitted. "But someone doesn't have to be actively involved in any of this to find it fascinating."

"True." Jude licked his lips. "I guess you could just be an open-minded guy who enjoys learning new things. But there was something in your expression that made me think it was a little more than intellectual curiosity."

Damn, he was good. Donovan was like that too. He could read Tyler's expression scary-well. Maybe it was a Dom thing. Of course, Tyler didn't even know if this guy was a Dom. He certainly hadn't been shy about approaching Tyler though.

"Excuse me?"

Tyler gratefully turned toward the sound of the woman's voice. He really had no idea how to answer Jude's question. Drinks were much easier. "Yes. What can I get you?" he asked her.

"Could I get a glass of the chardonnay, please?"

"Of course." Tyler smiled at her as he reached for the bottle of white that had been chilling in a tub of ice. He noticed the thin metal band around her neck and wondered if that meant she was someone's collared submissive.

He shivered at the thought of Donovan putting a collar around his throat, but he wasn't sure if it was excitement or fear. Maybe both. Or maybe just the strangeness that he'd even consider allowing someone to do that. To *own* him.

Not that the Army hadn't owned his ass for eight years, but this was different.

A moment later, Tyler handed her the glass of white wine, wishing she'd ordered something more complicated. Jude had stepped back, but he hadn't left. Which meant Tyler was going to have to figure out how to respond once she was gone.

She paid him, then slipped some money into the tip jar. "Thank you."

"You're welcome. Enjoy your evening." The words left his lips automatically, even as he scrambled to figure out how he was going to reply to Jude.

Jude, who stepped close again with a charming smile. "So, you were going to tell me what your curiosity earlier was about."

"I didn't say that," Tyler protested. "I never said I was curious at all."

Jude frowned. "I'm sorry, I shouldn't be pushy. There was just something so undeniably gorgeous about the way you looked as you listened. Your lips parted, your gaze curious as you leaned in … I thought maybe you were someone who was curious about kink but hadn't ever had the opportunity to explore it. Maybe I misjudged." His expression sobered even more. "And I never meant to force you out of your comfort zone." At that, his expression lightened, his moods as quickly changing as the water in the bay outside. "I only do that when I'm given permission to."

Tyler chuckled a little, then chewed at his lip, trying to figure out how to word this. A part of him wanted to admit that Jude had been right. A part of him wanted to take another tiny little baby step out of the kink closet. Partly because he'd seen the look in Donovan's eyes earlier and knew how much he wanted a collared submissive. And while Tyler had no idea if he could ever manage to be what Donovan wanted, what he needed, Tyler knew that staying in the closet in either sense definitely wasn't going to cut it. Plus, Tyler wanted Jude to know he wasn't on the market.

Maybe things wouldn't work out with Donovan. But he wanted a shot at it, and Jude didn't stand a chance, no matter how charming and good looking he was.

Tyler took a deep breath and glanced around. No one was paying any attention to them right now. "Look, you guys are trusting me to be discreet so if I can trust you to do the same …"

"Of course. Discretion is my middle name."

"I am involved with … with a Dom." Tyler's face went a little hot. "It's new-ish."

Not so new, really. They'd been seeing each other since June. Five months now. His longest relationship.

"Ahh." Jude gave him a slow smile. "So, you *are* gay?"

That was what he'd latched on to?

"Nope," Tyler said. "Bi, I guess. I'd only really been with women before but …"

"He was too tempting to resist?"

Tyler smiled. "Something like that."

"Were you involved in kink before you met him?"

"Sort of," Tyler admitted. "I topped a few women in the past. Nothing… not like I've been doing lately but …"

"Hmm." Jude gave him a long speculative glance. "Interesting."

"Yeah?"

"Mm-hmm. I'm a switch myself." Tyler opened his mouth to correct Jude but he continued. "I love that chance to experience both sides of it. Get all my needs met. I've been … well I've been looking for someone who wants that too. You caught my eye earlier and I'd love to see if we click."

"Look, I'm flattered," Tyler said hastily. "And I'm not saying you aren't attractive, but like I said, I'm seeing someone and it's really good and …"

He just couldn't see himself getting involved with Jude. Not when his head was full of Donovan. The other night they'd finally done that scene with the humbler that they'd talked about a while ago. Donovan had taken him down, wrestled him into submission, tied him up and used that on him.

Tyler would swear he could still feel Donovan's fingers sliding into his ass, opening him up as he struggled not to thrust into it, every movement torture as the humbler tugged at his balls. And the feel of Donovan's arms around him, the look in his eyes after … no, there was no way he was going to give that up. Not for anyone.

"Ahh. That's a shame." Jude gave him an assessing look. "I mean, good for you that you found someone but … too bad for me."

"Look, I mean it. I'm flattered but …"

"I get it." Jude's tone was light. "Seems to be the story of my life. I'm open to something with both of you if that's something you'd be into. Just throwing that out there."

"Ahh, well, I think it's complicated enough with just the two of us."

It felt sort of nice to have a guy that attractive hitting on him though.

It wasn't like Tyler had never been hit on by guys before either. Working the bar for ten years, he'd had more than his share of men flirt with him. But Jude was hotter than most and it was flattering to have a sexy, kinky guy interested in him. He was no Donovan though. And the thought of this guy and Donovan together made Tyler's hackles rise.

"I don't know what the future holds for me with this guy, but …" Tyler swallowed hard. "I can't see sharing him."

"Even if that's what he wanted?"

Tyler considered the idea and shook his head. "I can't see him wanting that."

"Hmm."

Someone else appeared at the bar then, asking for a drink, and Tyler hustled to mix the cocktail.

With a smile and nod to Tyler, Jude wandered off then, and Tyler let out a sigh of relief. It had been sort of fun flirting, but when it came down to it, he'd meant what he'd said. He wanted to see where this would go with Donovan. Without anyone else getting in the way.

After Tyler served a few more people, he stepped back to lean against the wall, watching the crowd talk as they mingled. Laughing, flirting, hugging. There was a real sense of community there, which he liked.

But could he imagine being as open as these people were? Throughout the night, he'd spotted several subs in collars, some discreet metal that looked like jewelry, others in thick black leather with obvious D-rings that left no doubt as to what they were for. There was a decent number of LGBTQ people there too. They were all open. Maybe not open in all aspects of their lives with their kink, but they had the courage to be themselves, at least here with people they trusted.

So why was it so hard for him? Why was he so damn worried?

Tyler could come out to his parents as being bi without telling them he was kinky. Donovan sure as hell was discreet. No one would know he was Donovan's submissive just because they were involved.

Was he submissive? That word made him feel anxious for some reason. He was though, wasn't he? Tyler might have topped those women in the past, but he couldn't imagine ever doing that with Donovan. Jude had implied Tyler was a switch but that didn't feel right. Now that he'd had this with Donovan, Tyler couldn't see going back to what he'd done before.

He considered Jude's offer and swallowed hard.

It felt all wrong. Even if they got involved with someone like Jude who switched, Tyler couldn't imagine topping anyone.

The appeal was both the dynamic he had with Donovan and the way Donovan knew just how to push until his mind went quiet and his worries faded.

The appeal was Donovan himself.

With those thoughts whirling in his head, Tyler spent the remainder of the mixer filling drinks and briefly chatting with the people who approached his bar. And the whole time, Tyler thought of Donovan and what the future could be like if only he had the courage to reach for it.

NINETEEN

"How'd it go?" Donovan asked in a low tone as he stood up from his desk.

The restaurant had closed several hours ago, and the bar was about to shut down. The mixer had just ended too. People were leaving in small groups, talking and hugging as they said their goodbyes. He'd texted Tyler, asking him to stop by his office once he was done cleaning up after the event.

The sight of him put Donovan at ease.

"Pretty well," Tyler said, leaning in the doorway with his hands braced on either side of it and a small smile on his face. Seeing him kicked Donovan's heartbeat into overdrive. God, Tyler was sexy in the well-fitted black trousers and shirt. As always, his sleeves were rolled up and Donovan was starting to think he had a serious forearm kink. It was even hotter when it showed off the heavy black ink that covered them and the back of Tyler's hands.

Donovan stood and walked toward him. "I'm glad to hear that. You seemed nervous this morning." He'd hoped it would go well and that Tyler would see that the kink community was filled with a broad range of decent people. There were always a handful of assholes who gave it a bad name but for the most part he'd found it welcoming and friendly, filled with people who built a real sense of community and looked out for one another. He hadn't been active in it in a few years but he respected it a lot.

Maybe if Tyler could see the good in it, he'd feel more comfortable embracing that side of himself.

Tyler nodded and dropped his arms. "Yeah, I guess I was nervous. But everyone seemed nice. Weirdest thing happened—"

Donovan frowned and stepped forward, wondering what on earth Tyler meant. Soft footfalls caught their attention, and Tyler paused midsentence to peer over his shoulder.

Donovan let out a curse under his breath as Jude sauntered into view, a smile on his face.

"I think you must have gotten turned around," Tyler said. "This area is employees only."

"I know. I came in search of your executive chef."

"Jude." Donovan pushed past Tyler to square off with his ex. "What are you doing here?"

Tyler looked between them. "You two know each other?"

Donovan let out a quiet snort, though he didn't feel an ounce of amusement. "Yeah, you could say that."

"Oh, from the kink community. I guess that makes sense," Tyler said quietly.

"No." Donovan's tone was short. "This is Jude Maddox."

"Yeah, we met earlier at the mixer."

There was no hint that Tyler had a clue who Jude was to him. Apparently, he'd never mentioned him by name. "My ex-boyfriend," he clarified.

Tyler went still, his eyes widening. "Oh. You never told me his name—"

"It's fine. You couldn't have known." But Donovan felt a grim sense of certainty that this was about to get messy and awkward.

Jude stepped forward, closing the distance between them. "So, *this* is the guy you told me about?"

"You told him about me?" Tyler hissed.

"Not by name." Donovan said quietly, wanting to reassure him. "Only that I was seeing someone and that you were new to kink and being with a man."

Tyler turned to face him. "And you didn't bother to mention to me that you'd seen your ex?" The hurt in his voice was clear.

Donovan frowned at him. Shit, shit, shit, this was what he'd been afraid of. "He came into the restaurant a while back and we talked briefly. There was really nothing to tell you about." He tried to make his voice as soothing as possible.

"Ouch." Jude clutched a hand to his chest.

"Oh, don't make it out to be more than it was," Donovan snapped. God, there Jude went, always trying to make it about *him*. Donovan was so tired of it.

"We *did* talk about getting back together." Jude's tone was flippant.

Tyler winced, and Donovan resisted the urge to hustle Jude out the door before he caused an even bigger mess. The last thing he wanted was for Tyler to think that Donovan had even considered it for a moment.

"*You* were the one who talked about that," Donovan said, his tone short and irritated. "I told you I wasn't interested. As I said before, I'm seeing someone." He put a protective hand on Tyler's shoulder. "Plus, we had problems that were unfixable."

Jude stepped forward again, closing the distance between them. "Are you sure they're unfixable? I'm starting to wonder if our problem was that we had casual partners before. I think we should have tried to find a permanent third. I know you and Tyler are involved now but what if all three of us gave something a shot?"

Donovan stared open-mouthed at his ex-boyfriend for a moment before he glanced at Tyler. The look on his face was filled with hurt and fear as if he thought Donovan would actually consider that. Donovan rubbed his shoulder, trying to reassure him he wanted no part of what Jude was proposing. Whether or not he and Jude could have fixed their relationship with a third wasn't the point. Donovan had moved on and he had no desire to share Tyler with anyone. He opened his mouth to say so but once again, Jude spoke first.

"I talked to Tyler earlier, and I totally see the appeal, Donovan. He could top me and submit to you. Or submit to both of us. We could figure out the logistics of that as we went." Jude shot them both a hopeful smile. "I think it was the chaos of things that didn't work before. Having new play partners and hookups muddied everything. We were constantly in flux, trying to figure out the right dynamic." Jude beamed, like he'd come up with the solution to all the problems that had existed between them. "This would be perfect. We'd all have an equal part in the relationship, and it would be so much more balanced that way."

“Do I get any say in this?” Tyler snapped, looking between them. “Look, Donovan, I thought *we* had something. I know I haven’t been ready to come out, but I honestly thought we were getting … somewhere.”

Donovan pulled him closer. “We *are*.”

Tyler looked straight at Jude. “And I told you earlier that I wasn’t interested in you, Jude.”

Jude rolled his eyes. “Come on, I’m not trying to be pushy here but—”

“Well, you are,” Donovan said.

He felt ferociously protective of Tyler right now. Tired of Jude talking about this like it was *fait accompli*, like they’d already discussed it and had a plan to move forward when Donovan had told him he wasn’t interested. It was infuriating. Then again, that was what their relationship had always been like. Jude getting these brilliant ideas and Donovan trying to rein him in. He didn’t know why he’d ever thought Jude could be the kind of submissive he wanted. Tyler was plenty strong, but he didn’t seem to have the same urge to push and push at every boundary Donovan had.

“I have told you this before, and I’ll say it again if that’s what it takes to sink through your thick skull, Jude. We. Are. Over.”

“You won’t even hear me out?” Jude scowled. “What the fuck, Donovan? You used to at least *listen* to me. You owe me that at least.”

“I owe you nothing.” Donovan let go of Tyler, then stepped forward until his chest nearly brushed Jude’s, glaring straight into his eyes. “I tried. For years. I made myself miserable for you. I loved you with all my heart for a long time, and you’re a decent guy, Jude—or at least you used to be—but we were fucking miserable together by the end. Nothing can fix that. We are *over*. Done. This relationship has been dead for years and there's no resuscitating it even if I wanted to. Which I don't. Tyler and I have some things to figure out but that's *between us*. I'm not sharing Tyler with *anyone*. Not you or anyone else. Look, if you want a triad with a Dom, go find it. But it isn't going to be with *me*."

Donovan turned to look at Tyler. He was ninety-nine percent sure that Tyler wanted the same thing he did, but he had to be completely certain. He had to offer him this out if he wanted it. At least then Donovan would know. "Tyler, if you're interested in being with Jude, you and Jude can discuss it, but I want no part of it. I can't share you."

There, he'd laid it all out on the line.

"No!" Tyler grabbed his arm. "I don't want Jude. I want what we already have." He glanced over at Jude. "Look, you seem like an interesting guy. You're good-looking and I'm flattered but I'm not interested in what you're proposing either. I care about Donovan. I have shit to figure out, but I do know for sure that I don't want what you are offering."

Donovan felt nothing but relief.

Jude winced, however. "Jesus, you two really know how to hit a guy when he's down, and I didn't even consent to it."

"Don't you dare say that," Donovan said in a low, furious tone. "*You* asked for this. *You* pushed for it, in fact. This isn't *kink*. This is you pouting because you aren't getting what you wanted. I'm sorry, Jude. You know I loved you, but I've moved on. It's time you do the same."

Donovan brushed past Tyler, heading for the back door. If he stayed, he was likely to try to shake some sense into Jude or say something he'd regret. As he walked through the door, he glanced back and saw Jude standing with his hands in his pockets, head bowed.

Donovan winced at the dejected posture, almost feeling bad for his ex. *Almost.* He truly hadn't wanted to hurt him, but Jude just didn't seem to know when to quit.

More important, Donovan was relieved to see Tyler. When the door closed behind them, Donovan felt a wave of exhaustion wash over him. He staggered back and leaned against the table with a heavy sigh.

"Hey, you okay?" Tyler asked softly, his forehead wrinkling with concern.

Donovan rubbed his temple. "I … don't even know. Jude really threw me for a loop there. I did not see that coming."

"Neither did I. I mean, he hit on me at the mixer but …"

Donovan lifted his head, voicing the one little nagging worry that just wouldn't go away. "You *are* switchy to some degree. If that's the kind of thing you want …"

"It's not. Honestly." Tyler stepped toward him, his gaze earnest.

"If we go forward, I can't … I'm not wired to switch," Donovan warned him.

"I know that. I've never once felt the urge to top you, Donovan. I don't want to be a Dom."

"Not even to a woman?"

Tyler shrugged. "I don't know how to explain it. What I did in the past was good. I liked it. But this is something else. This feels right in a way the other things never did. Maybe I'm bisexual.

Maybe I am a little switchy. But at the end of the day, I just want what we have. I just want *you*."

Donovan swallowed audibly. "Then you've got me."

Tyler rested his hands on Donovan's splayed thighs. "I know I have stuff to figure out. That we're … still trying to feel our way through this, and I don't know that I'm ready to be collared and come out and all that yet … I want to try, but it's going to take me a while."

"It's okay." Donovan grasped Tyler's hips and pulled him forward, so he stood between his knees. "This is enough for now. We can work up to that. I just had to be sure of where you stood."

"I'm sure I want to be with you," Tyler said firmly. He slid his hands up Donovan's thighs and leaned in for a kiss.

"Someone on the staff could walk out at any minute," Donovan warned him before their lips made contact. "Hell, someone could have heard our earlier argument."

"I don't care," Tyler whispered. "I just need to be close to you."

Donovan took a deep breath, closed his eyes, and kissed the ever-loving hell out of Tyler. The last tendril of fear unfurled in Donovan's chest as he relaxed into the kiss, trusting that while they weren't where he wanted to be yet, they were getting there. In time, they'd figure it out.

Donovan trapped Tyler between his knees, delving his tongue between Tyler's lips to show him who was in charge, and Tyler softened, leaning in, letting him lead.

TWENTY

The Sunday before Thanksgiving, the tavern was a hub of activity. Rachael had closed early to host a big dinner for friends and staff. Tables had been pushed together to create large family-style seating and stations had been set up where people could help themselves to drinks and appetizers. She'd also given out holiday bonuses that afternoon as a thank-you for all their hard work. She'd been generous, though she'd brushed it off when Tyler had told her as much.

"You all work so hard to make this place a success. The least I can do is give that back."

The smells that had been coming from the kitchen all day were amazing and Tyler's stomach rumbled happily as he took a seat across from Donovan, who smiled as he surveyed the table with a look of pride. The décor was simple, which was just as well because the table was laden with food.

Tyler knew most of the guests, including Rachael's partners, Reeve and Grant, and Reeve's parents. Jenna Wagner and her husband Karl. Tyler spotted the town mayor and her husband as well, along with some other faces he recognized from around town. He'd met a handful of new people too, some from the poly community, and some others from the kink one. Thankfully Jude was nowhere in sight.

The weeks since their encounter with him had been good. Tyler and Donovan had spent more nights together than apart. Oddly enough, clearing the air about Donovan's ex had brought them closer. The only thing hanging over them was the fact that Tyler still hadn't come out. God, he needed to just bite the bullet. Maybe one of these days when he went to his parents' house he'd just blurt it out. Or maybe he should just shoot the guys a text letting them know. Then he wouldn't have to see the shocked looks on their faces.

"Nice ink, man."

Tyler looked up from the mashed potatoes he'd been spooning onto his plate to glance at the guy sitting next to him. "I'm sorry?"

"I said I like your ink."

"Oh." Tyler's gaze drifted to the guy's forearms, the swirling colors of his tattoos visible with his white shirt folded up to his elbows. "Thank you. I like yours too."

"Where do you go?"

"Nick's place. Here in town. Ink About It."

"Me too. The name caught my eye, and I took a look at his work. It's top notch. I've gotten a few pieces from him since."

"It is top notch," Tyler agreed. "I've been going to him for years. Long before he opened his own place."

Tyler took a longer look at the guy. He was broad-shouldered with a rugged handsomeness. His warm blond hair was swept back, and he had a short, neat beard. Tyler's fingers flexed, remembering the softness of Donovan's red beard against his fingertips, brushing against his skin.

He swallowed and shot a glance at Donovan who was immersed in conversation with an older couple next to him.

"Jarod."

"Hmm?" Tyler turned back to look at the guy.

He held out a hand. "Jarod Keener. Thought I should introduce myself."

"Tyler Hewitt. I'm the bar manager here."

"I've seen you when I've been in. Nice to meet you."

The quick, firm handshake was friendly, and Tyler gave Jarod a curious glance as he reached for the bowl of roasted Brussels sprouts with orange and walnuts. He'd been sure he hated the vegetables until Donovan made him try them.

"How'd you get an invite?" Tyler asked. "Do you know Rachael?"

"She's more or less my sister-in-law."

"Oh?" Tyler shot him a quizzical glance, trying to figure out that one.

Jarod laughed. "It's complicated."

He had a hint of a southern drawl, and the pieces came together in Tyler's mind. "You're related to Grant?" Tyler guessed. He glanced over at one of Rachael's partners. He could definitely see a resemblance and the Tennessee accent was a dead give-away. Tyler had a vague memory of seeing them in the tavern together in the past.

"I am. We're half-brothers. And while Grant, Rachael, and Reeve may not be legally married, they're family, you know?"

"I get it," Tyler said. Eddie wasn't related to him by blood or marriage, but he was every bit as much family as Tyler's sister. Maybe more when it came down to it. He loved Kourtney, but she wasn't the one who'd been by Tyler's side during the most difficult moments of his life. "You were at their commitment ceremony last year?" Tyler guessed.

He had a vague memory of seeing Jarod there now that he thought about it. Funny they'd never officially met until tonight.

"Yeah. I got there late because of work so I didn't have a lot of time to meet people, but I was there."

"I knew you looked familiar. What do you do for a living, if you don't mind me asking?"

"I'm a mechanic. I opened Keener's Auto Body a few years ago."

"Oh, right." Tyler usually went to the dealership to get his truck serviced but he'd have to keep Jarod's place in mind. He'd heard great things about it. And, if he remembered right, there had been rumors about the guy who owned it being kinky. He snuck another glance at Jarod. *Huh.*

The rumor mill in small towns was one of the reasons Tyler dreaded the thought of coming out. The constant gossip and scrutiny made him uncomfortable. The thought of his parents' neighbors speculating about his relationship with Donovan made Tyler cringe. But he knew how important being open was to Donovan. And it felt like he was stuck between a rock and a hard place.

Jarod sat back and gestured to the man by his side. "And this is my boyfriend, Forrest."

A tall, thin man with wavy brown hair shot a look at Jarod through his lashes. "Boyfriend?"

"You want me to call you somethin' else?"

There was a little edge to Jarod's voice that sounded a bit like Donovan when he was in Dom mode. *Interesting.*

"No, boyfriend is good." The guy leaned in and smiled brightly at Tyler. "Forrest Patton. I do the accounting for the tavern."

Tyler nodded and smiled back. "Nice to officially meet you, Forrest."

"You too."

Forrest returned his attention to his meal and Jarod glanced at Tyler's arms again. "So, did Nick do all of your ink then?"

"Close to it," Tyler said. "Though I got some pieces when I lived outside of Michigan."

There had been a good place just outside of Fort Drum. Tyler, Eddie, Jackson, and Frenchie had all gotten matching tattoos with the crossed swords of the 10th Mountain Division logo. Hayes and Rafe had wussed out on them. It had been a fun night. Tyler smiled faintly as he took a bite of the stuffing with cranberries and mushrooms.

As they ate, Tyler and Jarod fell into easy conversation about tattoos, talking about Nick's talent and what pieces they'd like to get next.

At one point, Forrest asked Jarod something, and he turned away for a few minutes, so Tyler smiled at Max who sat diagonally across from him, next to Donovan. "You didn't bring your wife tonight?"

Rachael had invited the staff to bring a plus one but most of them had declined.

Max shook their head. "Nah. Della's traveling for work."

Max was nonbinary and married to a woman. Tyler wasn't quite sure how they navigated all that, but it did kinda put things in perspective. It wasn't like Tyler was the only person with a complicated personal life. There were a lot of people who figured out how to come out in all sorts of situations. If all these people he knew could do it, why couldn't he?

Tyler glanced at Donovan to find his chair empty.

"He went to finish dessert," Max said. "If you're wondering."

Tyler gave them a puzzled frown. "Donovan made dessert? I thought he usually left that to Laura?"

"He does." Max gave him an odd look. "Said something about wanting to try new things. He made a pumpkin tart with a crème brulée topping."

"Huh. I didn't know that was a thing," Tyler said.

Max shrugged. "He seemed weirdly determined to make it a thing. Laura made a few other desserts, but he was insistent he'd make that one."

It wasn't a coincidence that those were two of Tyler's favorite desserts. Donovan was too deliberate to do that accidentally. Tyler smiled to himself.

After dinner, Rachael got up and made a nice speech about how well the tavern was doing and how she was grateful to all of them for everything they did in her life. Warmth settled in Tyler's chest. He had a great job at an amazing place. Great friends. A great boss. And … a great guy. Maybe he needed to start being thankful for everything he had instead of worrying about how other people would feel about it.

Once they'd all clinked glasses, Donovan helped serve the pie. He saved Tyler's piece for last.

"So, pumpkin crème brulée, huh?" Tyler said with a small smile.

"Two very popular desserts combined into one," Donovan said as he handed Tyler a slice, their fingers brushing.

"I'm sure everyone will appreciate it."

Donovan leaned in. "There's only one person whose opinion really matters in this case." He spoke quietly, but his words were a warm caress.

Tyler took a bite, his gaze never leaving Donovan's, and he caught the hitch in Donovan's breathing as he licked his fork clean.

There was a promise in his gaze, and Tyler's belly tightened in anticipation of what they had planned for that night. Donovan had been teasing him with ideas for it for days.

When Donovan turned away, the rest of the world came into focus again. Tyler glanced around, wondering if anyone had seen their interaction. Grant gave him a smile and nodded as if he'd worked something out for himself. Tyler took another forkful of pie, the back of his neck heating. Maybe he should talk to someone like Grant. He'd understand what kind of position Tyler was in.

Tyler watched Donovan lift a drink to his lips, laughing and talking to Max and Laura, but Tyler would swear as he reached for a second slice of tart that he could feel Donovan there with him.

Showing him how much he cared.

It was past time for Tyler to prove to Donovan he felt the same.

"Oh." Tyler stepped into Donovan's office and froze at the sight of Donovan partially dressed. "Sorry. I didn't realize …"

Donovan tugged on a T-shirt. "I had a run-in with some pie. Besides, you know I never mind you seeing me this way."

He reached for his chef's coat again, shrugging it on over the shirt.

Tyler gave him a quizzical look. "Aren't you done cooking for the day?"

"Yes, but I'm trying to avoid getting anything else on me before the night is over." Donovan buttoned the coat, still smiling at Tyler. He was off by one, and the sides hung unevenly.

"Here let me …" Tyler brushed Donovan's hands away and unbuttoned the button Donovan had been fussing with, fixing it. "There."

Donovan leaned in. "How service submissive of you."

Tyler shook his head in mock annoyance. "You just can't resist, can you?"

Donovan shrugged with an unrepentant little smirk. "Just trying to get you used to the idea. Like I said, I have plans for tonight. There's lots and lots of training in your future."

"Training, huh?" He settled his hand against Donovan's chest.

"Mm-hmm. It's time I really start putting you through your paces."

Tyler swallowed hard. "Why does that scare me more than the thought of being back in Ranger School?"

The wicked light in Donovan's eyes made Tyler's blood heat. "Because it should." He leaned in. "By the time I'm done with you, you'll be begging to serve me. I'll even have you calling me 'Sir.'"

Tyler crossed his arms across his chest. "Oh, I see what this is all about you. You just want the ego boost."

Donovan let out a rumbling little laugh. "Oh, not even close. What I want is you on your knees, submissive and hungry for everything I'll give you. I want you to know in your bones you belong to me."

"Fuck." That thought made Tyler's blood heat.

"You'll get there. Trust me."

"Is that a promise or a threat?"

"Which do you want it to be?"

Tyler considered it. "I don't know."

"Both?"

"Yes, Sir. Is that what you want to hear?" Tyler snarked.

Donovan smirked at Tyler, amusement lighting up his eyes. "Why yes, it is. Nice of you to finally acknowledge my authority."

Tyler made an outraged noise. "If you think for one minute—"

"I have things to attend to in the kitchen," Donovan said, his lips turning up at the corners. "I'll speak to you again when you've calmed down."

Half-laughing, half-annoyed, Tyler opened his mouth to tell Donovan where he could shove it after that comment when Donovan pushed his way past him and out the door. He paused and Tyler saw a glimpse of Jarod in the hall. Tyler grimaced as he realized they'd been overheard.

"Feisty sub you've got there," Jarod said, clearly amused.

Tyler felt his heart speed up as panic set in. Damn it, the guy clearly knew what he'd seen. He stared wide-eyed at Donovan, begging him to fix this.

"He's not my submissive." Donovan's tone was cool.

Those words sent a strange wash of emotions over Tyler. Relief that Donovan was clearly trying to protect Tyler's identity. Fear that it wouldn't be enough. That Jarod would still know about their involvement. Then shame because it felt incredibly wrong to have Donovan dismiss him like that.

Donovan continued, an odd, uncomfortable expression crossing his face. "To be my submissive, you have to actually *be* submissive, and he's not capable of that."

"I'm not his fucking submissive. I'm not anyone's submissive, damn it." Tyler pushed past Donovan and Jarod with a scowl. The words had been instinctive, an attempt to hide the truth, but the moment they left his lips they felt wrong.

"My mistake. I apologize," Jarod said.

"Nothing to apologize for," Donovan said. He sounded distant. "Now if you'll excuse me."

Tyler strode away, a sick feeling of dread beginning to build inside him. Sure, he was in the closet, but Donovan didn't have to imply he was incapable of submission. Unless … maybe he believed it. Maybe he was afraid Tyler would never get there.

His stomach sank.

Tyler turned the corner, his mind whirling. Donovan's denial of him as a submissive had stung more than he'd expected it to. Donovan had never been intentionally cruel. Had he just done it to protect Tyler? Or did he mean it?

Tyler's eyes stung and his chest felt tight, and he suddenly wondered where it had all gone wrong. They'd been flirting earlier, playfully teasing each other. But what if him denying who they were to each other was hurtful to Donovan? How long would he wait? Earlier, Tyler had been so sure he was ready to come out but given the opportunity, he'd panicked.

Tyler spotted two abandoned mugs of cider on the table and snatched them up, carrying them to the kitchen to dump in the sink. Trevor, the dishwasher, shot him a confused look, opening his mouth to say something, but Tyler plunked the dirty dishes down onto the stainless-steel counter nearby, then kept walking, out through the back door and into the parking lot behind the restaurant.

The night was cold, and his harsh breaths created clouds of fog as he jammed his hands in his pockets and wondered how much longer Donovan would be patient with him.

With a sick certainty, Tyler realized that if he hadn't already created a rift between them that couldn't be fixed, he needed to get his shit together fast or he would lose Donovan.

TWENTY-ONE

The Thanksgiving event had wrapped up for the evening and Donovan was going through the last of his shutdown checklist to make sure the kitchen was all buttoned up for the evening. Rachael was long gone. She'd left with a glow of happiness on her face and the two people she loved most in the world on either side of her. It had made Donovan ache for that. For that with Tyler.

And he wondered if he'd made a monumental mistake earlier when he'd reacted to Jarod outside his office. He'd been trying to protect Tyler, urged on by the terrified look in his eyes at being outed, but had Donovan gone too far?

Had he permanently damaged something that was already fragile and tenuous?

Once the kitchen was closed up for the night, Donovan went in search of Tyler, intent on fixing whatever damage he'd done. Tyler hadn't responded to Donovan's text, and he was starting to wonder if he had left without even saying goodnight when he heard Tyler's voice behind him.

"Can we talk?" His words came out tight and strained.

Donovan slowed to a stop and turned to look at him. Even in the dim glow, with more than half the lights off, he could see how worried Tyler looked.

"Of course. I didn't even realize you were standing there. I'd texted you to see if you were ready to head out, but you didn't respond. I thought maybe you were on your way home already or something."

"I didn't leave," Tyler said. He patted his pockets. "Just wasn't paying attention to my phone, I guess."

"Okay." Donovan was silent a moment. "What did you want to talk about?"

Tyler stepped around the end of the bar. "I want to say I'm sorry. I think I fucked up earlier. You know I care about you."

"I do know that." Donovan frowned. "I also know that isn't always enough. Caring for someone. Loving them. It doesn't fix incompatibility."

"You think we're incompatible?" Tyler blinked. The hurt in his gaze made Donovan's chest ache.

"No." Donovan closed his eyes. "This worries me though, that I'm doing the same thing I did with Jude. Wanting someone to be something they aren't."

"Oh." Tyler swallowed past the sudden lump in his throat. "So, you meant it then."

"Meant what?"

"That you didn't think I'm capable of being submissive."

Donovan winced. "That came out wrong."

"Did it? Or do you believe that?"

"I absolutely believe you have that potential in you. I'm concerned you don't want to take that step forward."

Tyler let out a frustrated grunt. "It's not that I don't want to, Donovan. I just … I don't know *how* to be."

"I could teach you, if you'd let me." Donovan reached out and cradled Tyler's face in his hands. Just touching him was a relief. "You just have to trust me to show you how."

"But what if I can't?"

"I've seen it," Donovan said, frustrated. "I've *seen* you submit to me, Tyler. You are capable of it."

"But a scene or two is different than it being a full-time thing, right?"

"It was more than a scene or two. We've been seeing each other for almost six months, Tyler. That's not insignificant."

"It's not," Tyler agreed. "But I'm struggling with this. It's a big step. You want me to come out of the closet. You want to collar me. That's no small thing."

"I know that." Donovan closed his eyes briefly to try to collect himself. "I know that. And maybe I've pushed too hard. Too fast. If you need to go slower, we can do that. I'll let you take your time to get there. I just need to know you're going to *try*."

"I *am* trying," Tyler argued. "I just panicked earlier. I saw that someone had overheard us and … I freaked out."

"I know that. That's why I said what I did. I was trying to protect you. I could see how upset you looked."

"I know why you did it. And that means a lot to me," Tyler said.

"But?"

Tyler hesitated. "It hurt."

Donovan groaned. "I can't win! You'd be pissed at me if I'd outed you."

"I know." Tyler scrubbed his hands over his face. "I'm fucking this up left and right."

Donovan took several slow, deep breaths. "Tyler, you're struggling. That's okay. I understand that. I'd be lying if I said I was the most patient person ever. I'm not. But I will *try*, for you. I just want to be sure you're going to give this a fair chance. Give *us* a fair chance."

Tyler shook his head. "No, you want me to undo my whole life. You want me to shift my brain from being sure I was a straight dude who liked to smack my girlfriend's ass to being a submissive to another man. You have no idea what that's like."

Donovan's chest ached, because Tyler wasn't wrong. "Maybe I don't. So tell me."

"I don't know how to explain it. It's like who I thought I was is suddenly upside down and nothing makes sense anymore."

"I can help you make sense of it if you'll let me."

"Tell me what you need, Donovan." Tyler glanced up at him, and the beseeching desperation in his gaze made Donovan's chest hurt. "I guess … I guess I don't even know what you're looking for. You tell me you want me to be submissive but I don't know what that actually *means*."

Donovan winced. "That's fair. Maybe we've gone about this all wrong."

"What does *that* mean?" The words came out with a little bit of an edge. "Are you ending this?"

Donovan reached for him but Tyler shook him off.

"Hey, no, not at all," Donovan said soothingly. "I just mean I need to take responsibility for the fact that maybe I haven't been a very good Dom to you. We started off so casually, and well, combative, for lack of a better word, that we haven't really sat down and talked about expectations of what those words mean to each of us. What that dynamic would look like for us."

"Oh." Tyler leaned back against the nearby table. "That's true."

"So how about we do *that*?" Donovan said. "We'll take a day or two to think about it. Then we can sit down and discuss it. See if maybe our definitions are closer than we think."

"And if they aren't?"

"Then we'll figure out a way to compromise."

"What if we can't?" Tyler grimaced. "Not that I don't want to. I do, I just …"

"We won't know until we actually talk," Donovan admitted. "But I don't think we're that far apart. I think maybe we just need to adjust our expectations."

"When you say take a few days, do you mean … do you want a break?"

"Not unless you do. I just meant maybe set the kink aside until we figure this out. I don't want to muddy the waters and have a scene go bad. I think we're both feeling a little on edge. So let's spend the night together. We can talk more in the morning." Donovan stepped closer, sliding his hand across Tyler's pecs and leaning in. "And sex is definitely not off the table unless you want it to be."

“I’d rather have sex on the table,” Tyler admitted.

Donovan chuckled, his mouth so close to Tyler’s it would hardly take any effort to touch their lips together. “Not *this* table. Unless you know how to break into Rachael’s computer and delete video files. Or you have an exhibitionist streak I don’t know about.”

“Nope.” Tyler looped his arms around Donovan’s neck. “Don’t need my boss to see you balls-deep in me.”

Heat flared in Donovan’s gaze. “Oh yeah?”

“And that has *nothing* to do with being ashamed of being with you or being the one getting fucked,” Tyler said. He slipped his fingers into Donovan’s hair, sending a little tremor down his spine. “It’s just … there’s some lines you don’t want to cross with your boss, even if you are close.”

“I get it.” Donovan reassured him. “And I don’t want you to think I’m constantly second-guessing you. Doubting you or your feelings for me.”

Tyler ran his hands up and down Donovan’s back, warming him through and through. “I know that.”

“So, I’m going to put it all out there and tell you how I feel.” Donovan smoothed the side of his index finger down Tyler’s cheek, feeling the rasp of his whiskers. “I love you, Tyler.”

It had hit Donovan like a bolt of lightning earlier as he’d watched Tyler walk away after the conversation with Jarod. He’d been gripped by fear that he would lose Tyler for good.

Tyler’s lips parted and Donovan pressed his index finger against them, feeling the warm puffs of air against his skin.

“You don’t need to say it back. I have no expectations that you’re there yet. But I want you to know. This isn’t … this isn’t something I say lightly, Tyler. You're the second man I've ever said I love you to."

Tyler smiled and Donovan dropped his finger.

"Well, you're the *first* I'm going to say it to."

Donovan blinked. "You …"

"Yeah." Tyler's voice was husky. "I love you, Donovan. I'm still not sure how to get over this block in my head about coming out, about being your submissive, but I do love you. I …" He let out a helpless little laugh. "I sure as hell wouldn't be trying to figure this out if I didn't."

Donovan pulled him closer, wrapping him tightly in his arms. "Oh, Tyler. God … you have no idea what that means to me."

"So, we're okay?" There was genuine worry in Tyler's eyes.

"We're going to be," Donovan promised. "Let's just take it slow. We'll go home tonight and have a quiet night in. And if you're ready tomorrow we can talk more about our expectations. We've both got the day off."

"That sounds good to me."

"We don't have to have it all figured out right away," Donovan said. "I've been trying to rush things, I think, without taking all the proper steps to get where I want to be. We'll get there in time, but it doesn't have to be immediately. We started fast and messy and maybe it's time to try slow and methodical."

Tyler licked his lips. "Could I maybe take you to my favorite place tomorrow?"

"Sure." Donovan grinned. "I thought that was my bed though."

Tyler's smile matched his. "Okay, second favorite place."

"Yes. I—" Donovan froze as he felt the vibration of Tyler's phone against his thigh. "You need to get that?"

"Yeah, I'll check it real quick, then we can head out."

"Sounds good."

But when Tyler glanced at his phone screen, his face went white. "Andrea's calling. That can't be good. Not at this hour."

"Answer it," Donovan said firmly.

Tyler's fingers were shaking but he did it. "Andrea?"

He walked away to pace as he listened, a frown furrowing his brow as he nodded. He let out a pained sound and closed his eyes. "Yeah, yeah of course. We'll be there."

He looked drained as he hung up the phone and turned to Donovan, a stricken expression on his face. "It's Eddie. He's been in a car accident. He was driving drunk."

TWENTY-TWO

"I'm driving." After the call, Donovan had plucked Tyler's keys from his nerveless fingers and gently but firmly pushed him into the passenger seat of Tyler's truck. And now, as they sped up Blue Star Highway toward I-196, Tyler's heart was still lodged in his throat where it had been since he'd heard Andrea's tear-filled voice.

Eddie. Accident. Car hit a tree. Drunk. The words echoed in Tyler's head. He reached out blindly, seeking Donovan's hand for reassurance. He switched hands, gripping the wheel with the left while he threaded their fingers together with the right.

"It's going to be okay," he said.

"Is it?" Tyler's voice was hollow.

"Yes."

"You sound so sure."

"Then trust me."

Tyler took a deep breath, about to tell him it wasn't that easy, and he realized it kind of was. The firm, sure steadiness of Donovan's voice made him believe it could be okay. Because he did trust that Donovan wouldn't lie to him. That if Donovan had it in his power to fix it, he'd do it. But what could he do for Eddie?

"I can't lose him, Donovan."

"You won't." Donovan gripped Tyler's fingers harder, and the little flash of pain sent a wave of calm over him. "Andrea told you he had some broken bones but was stable. It could have been a lot worse."

"It could have." Tyler's voice caught. "God, he could have killed someone. Or himself."

"Do you think …"

"I don't know. I … I don't know." Had Eddie tried to kill himself? Or had he merely made bad choices and lost control? Made a mistake that could have cost him his life.

"You'll be there for him no matter what. And I'll be here for you." Donovan's tone was firm.

Tyler glanced over at Donovan. In the dim light from the dashboard, he could see the focused determination on Donovan's face. He really would do whatever it took to help Tyler through this. It sent a wave of relief over him. He was more grateful to Donovan than ever.

Earlier, Tyler had been terrified that Donovan would end things and he was now doubly grateful he hadn't. It was horrible to deal with in the first place but the thought of having to do this alone was daunting. With Donovan at his side, it all felt more manageable.

Tyler was terrified for his friend. But he wasn't alone.

"I could ask my parents for money," Donovan said after a few minutes of nothing but the humming the truck's tires on the road. "I could get fifty thousand from them. They'd do it if I told them it was important."

Tyler swallowed. "For Eddie's rehab?"

"Yes. If you think he'd accept it. Or, hell, if you want to just give it to him and don't tell him where you got it, I'd be fine with that."

"That's really kind of you," Tyler said thickly. "And God, you have no idea how much I appreciate that. It means so much to me."

"But …"

"It's not my pride," Tyler assured him. "Or even that Eddie would put up a fuss. I'm just not sure he's going to need it." His voice caught. "He may have to go to something court-ordered."

"True." Donovan glanced over at him briefly. "I could ask my parents if they'd take his case if he needs a good lawyer. That's also an option."

"That's really generous too. Maybe? We can talk about that later."

"Sure. Just know the offer stands. Either of them."

Tyler licked his lips. "Thank you. Honestly, I think even if the court doesn't order it, this may be the escalation the VA needs to get him bumped up the waiting list. They do work faster if they think you're a danger to yourself or others …"

"Do you think Eddie did it for that reason?"

"God." Tyler sighed and leaned his head against the headrest, watching the lights of the cars blur by in a wash of white and red, distorted by the wetness in his eyes. "Maybe. I don't know."

"I shouldn't speculate."

"No, it's okay." Tyler squeezed his fingers reassuringly. "I know you're just trying to help."

"I am."

"You want what's best for me."

"Yes, I do." Donovan squeezed again.

"Like today wasn't exhausting enough already," Tyler said with a sigh.

"I know. You can take a nap if you want. I have the map to the hospital up on my phone."

"I don't think I could sleep now."

"Okay."

But Tyler closed his eyes anyway and tried to breathe deeply, hoping it would make the fear and worry go away.

"We're here, sweetheart." A brush of lips on his forehead pulled him from sleep. He didn't have to open his eyes to know it was Donovan. He sat up, the mental fog clearing immediately as he remembered what had happened.

"Eddie." Tyler glanced around to see they were in a large parking ramp. Signs pointed to the emergency room. "Fuck."

"Yeah." Donovan rested a hand on his thigh and squeezed.

Tyler glanced at the clock, cracking his neck to relieve the stiffness of sleeping in a vehicle with his neck at a weird angle. His time in the military had made him really fucking good at passing out the second his eyes closed and being alert the moment they popped open.

Funny that he'd felt comfortable enough to close his eyes at all. Usually in a stressful situation, he was on high alert—also part of the legacy of his service—but he'd been able to relax tonight. It must have been because of Donovan.

Tyler glanced over at him and felt something in his head settle into place as everything came together. That final missing puzzle piece that somehow unlocked the entire picture. He'd spent years searching for something. Aching to find the sense of purpose in his life that had been missing since he left the Army.

Wanting that sense of belonging. Of structure. Of relief at being a part of something larger, of having someone he trusted and respected to answer to.

Tyler smiled with a sudden certainty that what he'd been searching for was right in front of him. His fears that he wasn't up for the task of being Donovan's submissive faded away as the truth settled over him.

He already knew how to do this.

For all practical purposes, Donovan was Tyler's commanding officer.

He'd had a difficult time wrapping his head around the idea of having a Dom, but it wasn't such a stretch at all. Tyler had spent eight years of his life training for this relationship. What on earth was he so afraid of?

"Thank you, Sir," Tyler said aloud as a sudden peace and stillness settled over him.

"For what?" Donovan blinked at him. "And did I just hear you right?"

"Thank you for taking care of me. For getting me here in one piece."

A large part of Tyler was dying to rush out of the truck, bolt through the doors of the ER, and beg someone to tell him how Eddie was doing. But something in his gut told him that he needed a moment with Donovan first. That taking that time would do more good for him than anything else. He needed to be calm for Eddie and Andrea and to do that he had to be sure that things were settled with Donovan first. He could be the guy he'd always been before. The one who was there for his friends. But now he had someone to lean on too.

"I'll always look out for you," Donovan said, smiling softly. "You know that."

"I do," Tyler said, and he did. He knew it deep down in an unquestionable way. "And yes, you heard me right. I just had a realization."

"What's that?"

Tyler leaned over, grabbed the front of Donovan's jacket, and dragged him closer, almost giddy with the rightness of the moment. "I just need to think of this thing between us like my time in the Army."

Donovan's look was skeptical. "How's that?"

"You're my commanding officer," Tyler said, his tone sure and steady.

"You always manhandle your superiors this way?"

Tyler chuckled. "There was a fair amount of roughhousing on base, yeah. But not like we do. I'm serious though."

"Okay. Explain it to me." Donovan wrapped a hand around the back of his neck.

"The Army teaches you how to take orders. They tear you down and build you up, so you have as singular of a focus as possible: do what it takes to protect your nation and your fellow soldier."

Donovan nodded.

"This isn't so different. It's just on a different scale. I do what you tell me to because I believe you have the best knowledge and training to complete the mission."

Donovan tilted his head, his expression curious but open. "And what's our mission?"

"I guess we still have to figure that out," Tyler said, licking his lips. "But I think it involves me getting what I need and you getting what you need. And being happy together while we do it."

A little smile played at the corners of Donovan's mouth. "Sounds like a pretty important mission to me."

"The most important," Tyler said, surprised by the sudden lump in his throat.

"We still need to talk about expectations," Donovan said and there was a note of warning in his voice. "How much of our daily lives will be spent in this dynamic. What being submissive means to both of us."

"I know." Tyler played with the hair at the base of Donovan's skull. "I just wanted you to know that something finally clicked for me. It makes sense in my head now. All I have to do is trust you and do what you want. Like any good soldier, if I see something happening that I know is wrong, I need to speak up, but otherwise, I have to trust that you know what's best for me. That your orders are there for a reason. I can stop fighting it because it makes sense now."

"Huh. I guess that was a hell of a nap you just took." Donovan's tone was dry now but there was a warm light in his eyes that Tyler could see even in the ghastly yellow glare of the parking ramp.

"I guess so. I just wanted to let you know before we do anything else."

"I'm glad you did." Donovan cupped his cheek. "And you're right. I will look out for you. Always. Without question."

Tyler swallowed hard. "Thank you, Sir."

"You don't know how it feels to hear you say that to me." The husky note in Donovan's voice sent heat through Tyler's whole body.

"It feels pretty good to say it. I *get* it now. Why you wanted this." He tugged Donovan closer. "Kiss me before we go in and check on Eddie?"

"With pleasure."

Tyler closed his eyes and slid a hand up Donovan's arms as their lips met. The soft prickle of Donovan's beard was familiar and right. His skin was warm and his tongue even warmer as it teased between Tyler's lips in a heated, claiming kiss that Tyler felt down to his toes.

And while it made blood rush to his cock, it also filled him with a sense of peace and rightness he hadn't felt in well … ever.

"God, I love you, Tyler," Donovan whispered as he sat back.

Tyler let his eyes open, staring at Donovan with a feeling of punch-drunk happiness that he realized was real, deep, committed love. He'd never felt anything even close to it before. "I love you too."

But the worry over Eddie and Andrea—who was probably all alone and worried sick right now—tugged at him, reminding him he was needed elsewhere.

"We better get in there," he added with a reluctant little sigh as he drew back.

"Yes." Donovan opened the driver's side door, flooding the cab of the truck with light.

Tyler got out with a groan. It felt good to stretch his legs as they walked toward the entrance to the ER, even as anxiety over Eddie built within him again. His knuckles brushed Donovan's and he reached for his hand out of instinct.

Donovan paused, turning to look him in the eye. "Are you sure you want to do this? We don't have to. Not tonight."

"What if I need it?" Tyler asked. He meant it. Fears about his friend were crowding in again and his heart hammered. He needed Donovan's touch to anchor him.

"Then I'm behind you one hundred percent."

"Thank you." Tyler turned and rested his forehead against Donovan's shoulder for a moment. "Thank you, *Sir.*"

Donovan pressed a kiss to the top of his head, squeezed his hand, and together, they walked into the ER.

It took time to hunt down Andrea and when Tyler found her, she was pacing the waiting area.

"Ty!" When she spotted him, her voice rose above of the murmur of hushed and anxious voices and she ran into his arms, burying her head against his chest. "Oh, thank God. I'm glad you're here."

"I'm sorry it took so long." He kissed the top of her head. "How's he doing?"

She wiped her eyes. "He's in surgery now."

Tyler froze. "I thought it wasn't that bad … just some broken bones or whatever."

"He took a turn for the worse. They think his spleen ruptured."

"Fuck. That's serious, right?"

"It depends on how soon they catch it. They said he can live without one."

"That's good." He gently stroked a hand up and down her back. "The kids are with your parents?"

"Yeah." She let out a heavy sigh and pulled away, hugging herself. "I told them their dad had been hurt but that he was going to be okay. That has to be true. I can't lose him, Ty."

"You won't," he promised her, though it wasn't something he had any control over. He swallowed hard, his throat thick with emotion. "He'll pull through this, I promise."

"Is it selfish of me to think that maybe he'll finally be able to get help now?"

"No." Tyler touched her arm, guiding her back to one of the chairs in the waiting area. "I had the same thought."

"Do you think he did it on purpose?"

Tyler sighed and draped an arm over her shoulder. "I don't know. He might have."

"But was he trying to hurt himself or get help?"

“I think maybe they’re the same thing.”

“Yeah, maybe.” She wiped her eyes again. “I just … I feel so helpless.”

“I know. I do too.” Tyler reached for Donovan’s hand again and he squeezed tightly in response.

Andrea’s glance skipped over their joined hands but her expression didn’t change. “Huh. I wondered who you meant when you said, ‘We’ll be there.’”

Tyler gave her a small smile. “Uh, this isn’t how I wanted to do it but … I’d like you to meet my boyfriend, Donovan.”

“We’ve met. At the tavern, remember?”

“Oh, that’s right. Well, we weren’t dating then.”

“Welcome to the family, Donovan,” she said with a tired smile. “Be glad you met Ty after he was out of the service. It’s hell on a relationship.”

“I am,” Donovan said. “But we’d have made it work.”

“I’m glad Ty has someone. It’s so hard to go through this alone.” Tears spilled down Andrea’s cheeks. “God, I did it for so many years when Eddie was overseas, but this …”

Tyler pulled her in to rest her head on his shoulder. “Hey, you’re not alone. I’m here for you. Donovan is too. You’ve got your parents. The kids.”

“I just don’t want to tell them their dad made it home from Iraq and Afghanistan to die from suicide.” Her voice broke.

“Hey, no,” Tyler said, squeezing her closer. “We’re not going there. We don’t know why he crashed. Maybe the roads were slick or there was a deer. We shouldn’t assume *anything*. I mean, it’s bad that he was drinking, but we shouldn’t assume he did this intentionally. And he isn't dying. The surgeons will fix him up and we'll get him the help he needs," he said firmly. "If the VA won't do it or whatever, there's an option for the private facility."

Andrea let out an exhausted sigh and leaned a head on his shoulder. "You know we don't have that kind of money."

"I can get it for you," Tyler said firmly.

"I can't let you—"

"We're not there yet. But I want you to know it's an option if we need to go that route," he said. "I figured out a way."

He couldn't look at Donovan. Could barely believe he was even considering begging Donovan to ask his parents for money like that, but Tyler would swallow every last bit of pride he'd ever had if it meant helping Eddie. And based on what Donovan had said about his family, this was no small gesture of how much he cared for Ty.

"God, I love you, Ty," Andrea said with a little sigh.

"I love you too." He kissed her head again. "Can you nap?"

"Not a chance."

"Would you like anything to eat or drink?" Donovan said, leaning over Tyler with a concerned frown in Andrea's direction. "I'm sure anything from the cafeteria won't be that great, but I'd be happy to grab you anything you'd like."

"Thank you." She sat up and fished a tissue out of her purse to dab at her eyes. "A water, maybe? That's all I can stomach right now. I'm so tired and worried I feel like I might throw up."

"Sure. Tyler?"

"Coffee, please."

"Okay." Donovan stood but Tyler didn't let go of his hand. He raised an eyebrow at Tyler who tugged him in.

After a brief brush of their lips, Tyler let Donovan leave the waiting area. After he'd disappeared through the door, he turned to Andrea, who stared at him with a speculative expression.

She nudged him with her elbow. "So that's new, huh?"

"Ish. Started seeing each other this past summer."

"I have to admit, I didn't expect it."

"The being-with-a-guy thing?"

"Yeah." She laid a hand on his arm. "I'm happy for you. Just surprised is all."

"I know. I wasn't ready to talk about it before now. Honestly, I surprised myself."

"I get it. Does Eddie know?"

"Yeah, I asked him to keep it quiet until I was sure about stuff. I hope you—"

"I understand," she said. "I've always known there were secrets you guys had. It's why I never asked if he was faithful while he was over there."

"He was," Tyler said firmly. "I swear."

"You weren't there for all of it."

"I wish I had been. Maybe if I had, he wouldn't …" But Eddie would have seen and done the same things. It just felt like if Tyler had been there, it would have been different. "He could have talked more to me about it at least," he said bleakly.

"Hayes was there, but Eddie won't talk to him about it either. Believe me, he's tried."

"I know."

"Or maybe you would have ended up *here* too." Tyler knew she meant more than in a hospital waiting room.

"God, maybe." He sighed. "I hate this."

"Me too." She closed her eyes and shook her head. "Tell me something good, Ty."

"Something good, huh?" Tyler thought back. They'd played this game a lot when Eddie was deployed and Ty was home. He'd texted Andrea regularly and she'd asked him for good news. Sometimes it was little things, like his favorite team winning a game. Other times it was about work, like when he'd started at the tavern and when he'd been promoted. When he bought his house. But there was only one big piece of good news he could think of now.

"I'm in love with Donovan."

She smiled at him and though it was exhausted and fear-tinged, it was genuine. "I had already worked that out." She sobered. "Word of warning, Gordo should be here shortly, and Jackson and Hayes are on their way up from Indiana. So, if you aren't ready for that conversation …"

"I'm ready," he said firmly. "It's time."

"Sleeping on the job, private?"

Tyler was on his feet before his eyes were fully open, snapping to attention. His shoulders sagged and he lightly punched Gordo in the chest. "Fuck you. I was a staff sergeant, you asshole."

"Is that any way to greet your best friend?"

Tyler dragged him in for a hug, shaking a head at his ridiculousness. "You're not my best friend, you fucker. That's Eddie."

Gordo sobered; his narrow face filled with worry. "How's he doing?"

"I don't know. I apparently fell asleep." With his head on Donovan's shoulder. He glanced back at him to see Donovan deep in conversation with Andrea. She sipped the ginger ale Donovan had brought her in addition to the water. He'd said it would help settle her stomach. It appeared he'd been right because she'd also been nibbling on a sandwich.

Gordo gave Tyler a speculative look. "Yeah. I saw that. Interesting choice of pillow. I wouldn't think twice cause you used to fall asleep on me all the damn time except he doesn't exactly look ex-military." He narrowed his eyes.

"He's not," Tyler admitted, his pulse beating double-time. "He's my boyfriend."

"For fuck's sake," Gordo said with a groan. "It's a butt-fucking epidemic around here."

Donovan looked up, a frown creasing his forehead. He was on alert, ready to go into protective mode. He might not have been a soldier, but there was more of that energy to him than Tyler had ever realized. He shook his head softly, trying to reassure Donovan that he was fine. He and Gordo would be fine. He sounded like an asshole sometimes, but his caustic words weren't said with malice. If he'd actually been upset, he would have ignored Tyler. Being an asshole meant he was fine with it.

Donovan subsided.

"Protective, that one," Gordo said with a raised eyebrow. Apparently, he'd noticed too.

"He is," Tyler said.

"Good. You need that." Gordo clapped him on the shoulder. "You do know I don't give a shit, right?"

"I wasn't sure," Tyler said with a grimace. "I know things were weird back when Jackson and Hayes got together."

"Yeah, that was weird as fuck. I don't know, it just … it felt so fucking strange then. Like they had this secret life none of us knew about, you know? I was pissed because I never saw it coming. And I felt like they'd lied to me. It wasn't about them being into dudes. It was about the trust."

"I know."

"At least I knew Frenchie used to suck you off, so it's not like this was totally out of the blue."

"Oh my God." Tyler looked up at the ceiling. "That was like … twice."

"Honestly, I thought at the time that it was desperation. But maybe not so much."

"I really don't know anymore." Tyler went to tug on his ball cap and realized he wasn't wearing it. He ran a hand over his head instead. "I … it didn't mean anything then. I mean, I loved Frenchie but not *that* way. I honestly thought it was desperation too. But this guy … Donovan … he's something else, man."

"Good." Gordo squeezed his shoulder. "Good. I'm glad. You need someone to look after you."

"What the fuck is that supposed to mean?" Tyler sputtered, but the sight of two more familiar faces coming in the door stopped any argument he was about to start with Gordo. They greeted Andrea first, giving her warm hugs and checking to see if there was anything she needed. After she took a seat next to Donovan again, they gave him curious looks as they walked over to Tyler and Gordo.

"Bout time you fuckers showed up," Tyler teased.

"First of all, fuck you," Jackson said. He clasped Tyler's hand and pulled him in for a hard, back-pounding hug. "And second, we made it here in half an hour less than the GPS estimated."

Tyler snorted. "You always did have a lead foot."

"Hey, I kept our Bradley out of harm's way, didn't I?"

"You did, you did." Jackson was a damn good driver, even when he was wrestling a twenty-seven-ton tank into submission. He'd been terrifying in a Humvee.

Hayes moved a little slower than his husband, thanks to a prosthetic leg. Of all of them, he was the only one who had stayed in the service as long as Eddie had. He'd been injured in the same engagement that had cost Frenchie his life.

But he had weathered it differently, going grim and distant for a while before slowly bouncing back with the same enthusiasm that had always been a part of who he was. He was in a much better place than he'd been just a year before, and Tyler was damn grateful. He gave Hayes a hug, glad to see him.

After their greetings, Jackson slipped a hand around Hayes' back and rubbed it.

"Just so you know, Hewitt's gone over to the queer side too." Gordo jerked a thumb toward Donovan. "He's shacked up with a dude now."

"For fuck's sake," Tyler said with a laugh. "I don't even know where to start with you. We're not living together"—*yet*, Tyler's brain helpfully added—"and how about letting a guy come out when he's ready, maybe?"

Gordo shrugged. "You were drooling on his shoulder in plain sight when I walked in. What do you want? Us to throw you a coming-out party?"

"I'd like you to not be an asshole, but I guess that's too much to ask for," Tyler said with a roll of his eyes.

Jackson nodded. "Seriously. He's a lost cause."

"Hey, Donovan?" Tyler called softly. Donovan looked up from his phone. "Want to meet the guys?"

"Of course." He rose to his feet and joined them.

Tyler did the introductions, and they all shook Donovan's hand.

"So, a chef, huh?" Hayes said with a speculative look. "Good. Maybe you can teach this useless piece of crap how to boil water without burning it." He nodded at Tyler.

"Jesus. With friends like these …" Tyler shook his head with a rueful smile.

Donovan smirked. "Oh, we've been working on his cooking skills for a while."

Tyler's skin heated as he thought about their last cooking scene. They hadn't done any recently, but Jesus, it had been hot.

"Chef or not"—Jackson looked Donovan up and down—"you better be good to Hewitt. We give him a lot of shit but he's ours to fuck with. Anyone else hurts him, they're a dead man. You understand?"

Donovan nodded gravely. "I understand."

Tyler wanted to sink into the floor. "You're all an embarrassment. I don't know why I'm still friends with you."

"Cause no one else would have you," Jackson said.

Gordo put him in a headlock and gave him a noogie. "Besides. You love it."

Tyler shoved him away. Donovan caught his eyes and grinned, clearly amused by their interactions.

They bantered for a while longer until Hayes cleared his throat.

"Hey, guys?" he said with a little grimace. "Can we take a seat? It's been a long day and my stump is starting to bug me."

"Yeah, of course." Tyler gestured for them to go ahead.

The mood quieted after that. They spoke quietly, catching up a little as they waited for news. Every time Tyler glanced at the clock, the hands seemed to move slower and slower.

Laughing and joking around with the guys had relieved some of the tension, but now, it began to creep in again.

What if something had gone wrong in surgery?

What if they were losing Eddie?

TWENTY-THREE

Tyler was half-dozing on Donovan's shoulder again when a woman in scrubs appeared in the doorway. "Family for Eduardo Silva?"

They rose to their feet as a unit as the woman approached Andrea. "Please, follow me to the surgical waiting area. Someone was supposed to come get you and take you there earlier, but it's been chaos tonight. There was a big pile up on I-96 and we're a little short-staffed."

"It's okay," Andrea said quietly. "Just … tell me one thing. Is he out of surgery?"

"Not quite yet. The surgeon is closing up now, but he wanted you to know that it went well, and they'll be sending your husband to recovery soon. The doctor can give you more details once he's done."

"Oh, thank God." Andrea sagged against Tyler, and he hugged her close. Donovan stepped back to give them some space. "Can we all go?"

"Yes, of course. We'll put you in a private waiting area. We have several we use for large families."

They quietly followed her through a maze of hallways until they reached the waiting room. She pointed out the bathrooms and a small area with vending machines before ushering them into the private area.

"Please, have a seat. The surgeon will be with you as soon as he's able."

They were all silent a while. Donovan noticed the tension thrumming through Tyler's body again as he sat, leaning forward with his elbows on his knees, staring at the floor. Donovan made slow, sweeping strokes up and down his back, hoping the soothing gesture would help.

Hayes, who sat next to Tyler, glanced over at the two of them. "So, how'd that happen?"

Tyler lifted his head. "We work together."

"Oh, wait, is this the guy who was pissing you off?"

Donovan let out a little snort, pausing his strokes to squeeze the back of Tyler's neck. "Yeah, that was probably me. Unless Tyler has a beef with more chefs than I'm aware of."

Tyler nudged him with his knee. "It was you."

"Ahh yeah. Well, hate sex is fun." Hayes grinned at them.

"Who did you have hate sex with?" Jackson asked, his expression curious.

"You never met him," Hayes said with a dismissive wave. "We were stationed together at Fort Hood when I was in Texas. Well before we were … anything."

"Ahh."

"We were constantly getting on each other's nerves," Hayes continued. "It was hot though."

"Not hotter than sex with your husband, I hope." Jackson's voice was deep, and he glowered as if jealous, but there was amusement in his eyes.

"Never." Hayes leaned into him.

"How is it that every dude I know has a fucking boyfriend or husband and I can't find a girl to save my life?" Gordo groused. "Statistically there's fewer of you. It makes no fucking sense."

Tyler snorted. "Maybe if you were less of an asshole, you'd have better luck."

"Fuck you."

"Thought you weren't into that." Jackson smirked at him. "But if you're having no luck with girls, you could come over to this side." He waggled his eyebrows.

Gordo snorted. "Not a chance man. You do you, but … no."

"Poor, sad, lonely man," Hayes teased. "Nothing but his hand and tears for lube."

Gordo crossed his arms over his chest. "I fucking hate you all."

Donovan, who had been observing their banter with amusement, asked the question that had been lurking on the edge of his brain all night. "Is this some sort of military thing? Just giving one another shit constantly?"

"Ugh, yes," Andrea said with a roll of her eyes. "It's how they cope with stress. It's funny for the most part but sometimes I just want to throw things at their heads."

Jackson leaned forward, frowning at her. "Hey, if we're bugging you now—"

"No." She waved it off. "I get it. It's fine. Honestly. It just took me a while to get used to it."

Jackson slipped an arm over her shoulder. "Hey, show me some pics of the kids. It's been a while since I've seen any and I bet they're getting big."

"Sure." She shot him a little smile and reached for her phone.

Jackson bent his head over Andrea's phone as he looked at pictures while Tyler flipped through a men's magazine. Donovan resumed rubbing Tyler's back as he scrolled through his phone, not really seeing the words on the screen.

He liked Tyler's friends. They were a bit loud and caustic, clearly not worried about being overly PC. But there was real warmth and affection there and no denying they would do anything for one another. He understood the laughter and joking now. He could only imagine what it was like as a soldier, knowingly stepping into danger. He imagined you had to laugh, or the fear would become crippling.

Half an hour later, when the surgeon walked into the room, Tyler stood up straight. Donovan stood too and he reached out, settling his hand on the back of Tyler's neck again, reminding him he was never alone.

The surgeon raked a hand through his graying hair. "Eddie Silva's family, yes?"

"Yes." Andrea stepped closer. "That's us."

The surgeon glanced at them, then back at her. "Would you like to speak privately or …"

She shook her head. "These are his brothers. Maybe not by blood but they were in the service together and …"

He nodded. "I understand. I just had to check because of HIPPA laws."

"How is he, Dr. Doyle?" Andrea twisted her hands together, clearly not willing to wait another moment. "Please, just tell me. Whatever it is."

The doctor appeared calm, but Donovan assumed after years of this, he was used to delivering bad news. Donovan desperately hoped the surgeon had good news for them tonight. He couldn't imagine what it would be like for Andrea and all these guys if the surgery hadn't gone well. But mostly his heart ached at the thought of what it would do to Tyler.

Donovan held his breath as the doctor cleared his throat.

"Eddie's surgery went well. We were able to remove the spleen and stop the bleeding in his liver. He will likely need further surgery on his leg, but he'll need to see an orthopedist about that. He made it through the procedure, and he's stable now. He's in recovery and it will be a little while before you're able to go in, Mrs. Silva. After he's woken and settled in a room, the rest of you can visit. That probably won't be until morning, so I suggest the rest of you go home and get some rest."

"He'll be okay though?" Andrea asked anxiously.

The doctor gave her a serious look. "The spleen removal was textbook perfect, and I have every reason to believe his bones will heal with proper treatment. However, as we discussed earlier with the police, your husband had a rather high blood alcohol content when he was brought in. In the course of removing his spleen, we discovered his drinking has caused some liver damage. It's not critical at this stage but it is something that will need to be monitored closely. And if it isn't addressed, I'm afraid he'll be in for a very rough road. Alcohol abuse is one of the leading causes for liver failure and he does not want to be dealing with a transplant on top of his other struggles. I'm not trying to pass judgment. I simply want to be sure you understand the gravity of his current situation."

"I know." She sagged against Gordo who'd had his arm around her. "I know it's bad. We're trying to get him help."

Tyler had also slumped against Donovan, and he rubbed his shoulders for a moment.

"He'll pull through this accident, Mrs. Silva," the doctor said in a kind tone. "He's at a point where his life can go one of two directions, and neither will be an easy road. But for now, he's out of the woods. You can take solace in that."

"God I'm fucking beat." Tyler dropped onto the bed with a sigh.

After long hugs and plans to meet the others in the morning, they had left the hospital, driven straight to the nearest hotel, and checked in.

They had nothing with them, not even a toothbrush or a change of underwear, because they'd left the tavern and driven straight through to the hospital. But they'd gotten a few toiletries from the check-in desk, and they'd make do.

Donovan held out a hand to Tyler who looked half-asleep already. "Come on. Into the shower with you. Then we can sleep."

Tyler let out a little grumble, but he took Donovan's hand and let him drag him upright. "Fine, fine," he muttered. "Could've passed out right there though."

"You seem to be able to pass out anywhere," Donovan said drily. Not that he minded.

"Hazard of being in the military. You snatch sleep whenever you can."

"I get it." Donovan led him into the bathroom and closed the door. "Strip. I'll get the shower going."

Tyler let out a jaw-cracking yawn. "So bossy tonight."

"That's 'so bossy tonight, *Sir*' to you."

A small smile played on Tyler's lips as he lifted his shirt off. "Oh, right."

Donovan chuckled as he cranked the shower handle to the on position. "Did you forget already?"

"No. It kinda got crowded out by everything else though."

"I know. I'm not going to push tonight. You're in no shape for it."

"No?" Tyler dragged a hand over his abs with a tired little smirk before he reached for the button of his jeans.

"Mentally," Donovan amended. He stripped off his clothes as quickly and efficiently as possible.

"Yeah, that was fucking stressful," Tyler said with a sigh.

"Hey, Eddie is out of the worst of it," Donovan reminded him. "There's hope."

"There is."

They stepped into the shower together and Donovan made a little circle in the air with his finger. "Turn around. I'll wash your back."

"Yes, Sir." Tyler shot him a cheeky look before he did what he was told.

"Just can't resist, can you?" Donovan asked with a smile. He put some of the hotel-provided body wash in one palm then rubbed them both together. He used his soapy hands to wash Tyler's back, digging his thumbs in to the spots that were tightly knotted.

"Fuck. That's … unnnghhh."

Donovan pressed a kiss to the back of his neck. "I'm proud of you, you know?"

"For what?"

"For coming out tonight."

"Oh." Tyler leaned forward, letting his head hang, so Donovan moved up, using his thumbs to dig into the muscles along his spine. "It wasn't as bad as I expected actually."

"Good."

"It's not like I thought they'd all stop speaking to me or something. I mean, maybe it was dumb to worry at all. Andrea was fine with it when Jackson and Hayes got together, and Gordo was a dick at first but he came around with them too, so it feels stupid now. But …"

"It was a valid fear," Donovan acknowledged. "Sometimes, you just don't know how people will react and it's incredibly stressful to think that you could be rejected. I understand your reluctance. I guess you were right when you said you always go big though."

"Guess they all suspected anyway. I thought I was being all stealthy with the blowjobs but apparently not. I almost wish they'd said something then."

"Would you have believed them?" Donovan dropped his hands, then stepped forward, encircling Tyler's waist with his arms, and hooking his chin on his shoulder.

Tyler was silent a moment. "Probably not. I had to meet you to *get* it."

"I'm glad you were open to it then."

"I am too." Tyler turned in his arms and pressed a hand to his cheek before leaning in to kiss him deeply.

The rest of their shower was done in silence. There were long, lingering kisses as they soaped each other's bodies, and they were both hard by the time they were done.

"Will you fuck me, Sir?" Tyler's voice was ragged as he turned off the water.

Donovan shuddered, as much from the heated words as from the blast of cooler air as he pulled back the shower curtain. "I'd love to. But we don't have supplies."

"Damn it. We should have stopped somewhere." Tyler let out an annoyed grumble as he toweled off. Donovan hastily dragged a towel over his body as well. "We don't have to use condoms anymore, you know. I told you that a few weeks ago."

"You did," Donovan acknowledged. He just hadn't been ready then. But given the steps forward they'd taken tonight, maybe it was the right time now.

Tyler looked at him imploringly. "I don't have much more in me but after the night we had I just want … I need …" He swallowed hard. "I need you."

"I know." Donovan dragged a thumb down his cheek. "I do too. We'll just have to be creative." He reached for the lotion on the bathroom sink. It was unscented. Good.

"I trust you, Sir," Tyler said. There was nothing but open, honest submission in his eyes. Donovan still wasn't entirely sure how that switch had flipped for him but clearly it had. Tyler was in.

One hundred percent. It appeared that was just how he operated. Questioning everything up until the moment he decided to take the leap. Donovan found it a little frustrating but mostly endearing. He could work with it.

"Come here." Donovan dragged him to the bedroom, shivering in the cool air. He tossed the lotion on the bed. "Kneel."

Tyler tipped his head back as he sank to his knees and Donovan felt a catch in his throat. The look in his eyes was powerful, tugging at Donovan's heart with its intensity. The gesture was without hesitation. Whereas before Tyler had been struggling with an internal battle of accepting this role, there was a calm sureness in his expression now.

"You are so beautiful like that." Donovan's voice was husky as he brushed a thumb across Tyler's lower lip. "So perfect. You're everything I've ever wanted."

"I didn't know I wanted you, but I did." A strangled little sob left Tyler's throat. "I needed *this*, and I had no idea. I just knew I was searching for something."

Tears glittered on Tyler's lashes and Donovan pulled him to his feet, then tumbled him onto the bed, pressing him down against the white sheets. There were no words, just heated kisses and their bodies reconnecting. He swept his hands across Tyler's muscular frame, letting the touch become possessive and needy.

He ravaged Tyler's mouth, pressing his arms up over his head, feeling the needy little movements of Tyler's hips as he rubbed his cock against Donovan's hip.

Donovan fumbled for the bottle of lotion and poured some into his palm, barely able to stop kissing and touching Tyler long enough to do it. He slicked both their cocks, stroking them together for a few minutes. Tyler's whole body was strung tight with tension, his breath short and rasping against Donovan's mouth.

Tyler reached for Donovan, but he shook his head. "On your stomach."

Tyler rolled over and Donovan groaned at the sight of him stretched out, arms over his head. There was nothing for him to grip onto on the headboard, so Donovan pressed his palms against the sheet. "Don't move from this position."

Donovan smoothed his hands over the muscular swell of Tyler's ass, parting his cheeks to stare at his hole. God, he desperately wanted to bury himself inside Tyler's tight, clenching heat. He used the lotion to slick himself again and settled over Tyler's body, sliding his cock along the groove of his ass.

"*Mmm.*" Tyler let out a helpless groan.

Donovan covered Tyler's body, surrounding him, boxing him in. He nipped and licked at Tyler's neck and shoulder as he fucked between his cheeks. Heat built between their bodies, slicking their skin with sweat.

He let the fear that he might lose Tyler flow out of him and drift away, secure in the knowledge that Tyler was his. He slipped a hand under Tyler's chest and settled his palm against Tyler's throat, pressing in just enough to let him feel his presence.

"Is that what a collar will feel like?" Tyler whispered.

"Yes." Donovan's voice was hushed too. "It'll be a reminder that I'm with you. We can find you something discreet for every day. Maybe just a necklace to wear under your shirt. But I want you to carry me with you every day."

Tyler let out a groan, fucking back against him. "I want that too."

"I want something heavy for play though." Donovan pressed harder as he imagined it. "Something thick and sturdy to remind you you're owned."

The helpless jerk of Tyler's body made Donovan grin. "Oh, you like that, do you?" he whispered roughly.

He liked it too. It did something to him, feeling this strong man submit to him. Feeling him soften and settle into his role. He was awed by Tyler's strength, his willingness to embrace a whole new side of himself.

He dragged the head of his cock over Tyler's entrance, making him tremble.

Tyler let out a needy little whimper and pushed back, encouraging him. Donovan rose on his knees to get a better angle and sank forward, pushing into Tyler's body. The lotion was slick but he hadn't prepped Tyler otherwise so he took it slow, knowing it would burn.

Tyler's breathing was harsh, but he was pliant in Donovan's hands as he rocked slowly in and out.

"Do you have any idea how amazing I think you are?" Donovan whispered.

Tyler shook his head and Donovan pressed against his throat a little tighter, rocking his hips a little harder and faster. "You are. The most amazing man I've ever met." Donovan crouched over him, knees on the outside of Tyler's thighs as he nipped at his ear, licking his way down the side of Tyler's throat. He let up on the pressure at his throat and drove into him again. Over and over, until his head swam and the pressure inside him built.

"I love you, Sir," Tyler rasped and the helpless need in his voice made Donovan's cock jerk. He'd never felt anything like this, buried to the root inside Tyler, slowly claiming him. For all their combativeness at first, this sweetness was equally intense, piercing into Donovan's heart. He'd wanted this for so long and to have it now was almost more than he could take.

"I love you too," he said roughly. He drove his cock deeper into Tyler, dragging a strangled sound from his throat. "I love you so much it aches."

He pressed tightly to Tyler's throat again, feeling him begin to shake.

"And I'm going to make you mine."

With one last savage thrust, Donovan came, spilling into Tyler's body, his whole body shaking with helpless shudders as he emptied himself like he could mark Tyler as his from the inside out.

He'd barely reached underneath Tyler to stroke his cock when he erupted, coming with a desperate roar that he muffled against the pillows. Releasing his neck, Donovan jerked him through the release until he whimpered and shook.

After, Donovan rolled them onto their sides, still joined, as he finally eased up on Tyler's dick.

"Love you," he whispered, because now that he could say it, he wasn't going to let the opportunity pass him by. "So much."

Tyler let out a little murmur of agreement. They lay there a while, their ragged breaths smoothing out as Donovan held him close, their bodies still joined. Eventually, he'd have to get up, but for now, he simply wrapped his arms around Tyler's chest and held him close.

Mine and only mine.

TWENTY-FOUR

"You look weirdly happy for a guy whose best friend is in the hospital."

Tyler let out a little laugh and blinked back tears as he walked farther into Eddie's room. He was stretched out on the hospital bed, still hooked up to an IV, but otherwise he looked better than he had any right to. He had some scratches and bruises on his face and arms, and his left leg was in a cast, but he was alive and in one piece. And for now, at least, he was safe.

"How're you feeling?" Tyler asked. He took a seat beside the bed and studied his face.

"Like I got hit by a tree."

Tyler shook his head. "Pretty sure you were the one who hit the tree, not the other way around."

"Really? I would have sworn it jumped out at me," he joked.

Tyler sobered. The happiness he'd felt since he'd woken up in Donovan's arms this morning faded and worry rose to the surface again. "Seriously, what the fuck happened?"

Eddie grimaced. "Honestly, I'm not entirely sure. I think I misjudged the corner and lost control."

"No deer or slick roads or anything?"

"I don't think so." He sighed. "That would make it better, wouldn't it?"

"You were drunk. There's no undoing that."

"I know." Eddie picked at the thin hospital blanket.

"You could have died."

"I know that too." He closed his eyes.

"How much legal trouble are you in?"

"I'm not sure. There will be charges though."

"I was afraid of that."

Eddie shook his head. "I deserve it. I know that. I fucked up."

"You did. What if the kids had been with you?"

He blanched. "I wouldn't …"

"Six months ago, did you think you'd have driven drunk?"

"No." Eddie's voice was a rough whisper.

"I'm fucking glad you're okay but goddamn it, I'm pissed at you," Tyler said. He hadn't even realized it. He'd been so worried that this had been all that had filled his head. But now that he could see with his own two eyes that Eddie was okay physically, the anger bubbled up, spilling out in a torrent he could barely control.

"You could have *died*, you idiot. I could have lost you. Andrea could have lost you. The kids. You can't do that to us, man."

Tyler realized his cheeks were wet and he wiped at his face angrily.

"I know that! What do you want me to say?" Eddie's voice was pained.

"That you're going to get *help*," Tyler said. "Inpatient rehab. Whatever it takes. And I don't give a flying fuck if you can't afford it. I have a plan." That plan relied on Donovan's family being very generous, but fuck it. He'd sell his house to pay them back if he had to.

Eddie sighed. "Hayes has been raising holy hell with the VA all morning. Pretty sure by the time he's done, I'll have a spot."

"Good." Tyler glared at him. "But if you need anything, you come to me. You hear that? I don't care how fucking proud you are. You come to me or Hayes or Jackson. Or Gordo. Doesn't matter. But you don't do this alone."

"Thought you were usually the one taking orders?" Eddie joked. "You're sounding pretty bossy there, dude."

Tyler crossed his arms over his chest. "It's been a while, but I was a staff sergeant, remember?"

"Yeah well, you never outranked me."

Tyler let out a heavy sigh. "Not the fucking point, dude."

"I know."

Tyler took a seat on the edge of the hospital bed. He reached out and took Eddie's hand. "Seriously. I love you, man. You're too important for me to lose. The broken bones will heal and you'll figure out the legal shit. But if you don't stop drinking, your liver is going to be shot. Do you want to end up too sick to play with your kids because your organ is failing, and you can't find a match for a transplant?"

"You wouldn't give me part of yours?" Eddie joked.

Tyler scoffed. "I would in a heartbeat, but I think the odds of us being a match is pretty damn low."

They both looked down at their clasped hands, Tyler's much paler skin contrasting with Eddie's rich brown tones.

"Huh, you mean you're not *actually* my brother?"

Tyler gave him a wry smile. "Not when it comes to blood types and tissue markers. Pretty sure that's all livers care about."

"Damn. Assholes."

"Tell me about it." Tyler had spent a good chunk of the morning googling organ transplant facts and it had been pretty clear that matches were more likely to be found among members of the same ethnicity. It wasn't impossible that he could help Eddie that way, but the odds were much lower than if Tyler were Latino too. He sobered, swallowing hard. "But I mean it. What do I have to say to get through to you?"

"Nothing."

Worry flickered over Tyler but Eddie shook his head.

"No, I don't mean that nothing will get through to me. I mean I woke up from surgery and I realized I can't keep going on like this." He let out a heavy sigh. "Because you're right, if I do, I'm going to leave my kids without a dad and my wife without a husband."

Tyler nodded.

"And I don't want to leave *any* of you. I fought so fucking hard to not come home in a body bag. I just need to keep fighting now."

"Exactly."

"And I know how fucking hard it was for all of us to lose Rafe and Frenchie. I won't do that to you too."

"Good." Tyler squeezed tightly. "Because if you do, I'll kick your ass."

"The others already threatened me." Eddie let out a tired sigh.

Tyler chuckled. "I'm serious. I'll sic Donovan on you too if that's what it takes."

"Pretty sure Andrea's scarier than all of you."

"Pretty sure she is," Tyler agreed. "So don't let us down. *Any* of us."

Eddie nodded, his expression grim and determined. "I won't."

Tyler leaned in, carefully wrapping his arms around Eddie. "Thank you."

"Thanks for having my back." Eddie patted him awkwardly.

"Hey, can we get in on this?" Hayes asked.

Tyler turned his head to see him, Jackson, and Gordo in the doorway, looking hesitant and hopeful.

"Hell yeah," Eddie said, gesturing with one arm. "C'mon."

They piled on, as carefully as three large fully-grown men could manage, and the last of the tension slip from Tyler as the five of them clung to one another like they hadn't done since Frenchie's funeral.

Tyler let out the heavy breath he'd been holding Eddie pressed their temples together.

Eddie had a ways to go but Tyler had to believe that he'd get through this.

For the first time in years, he had hope again.

"There's one thing I want to do before we head home," Tyler said. After returning from Grand Rapids, they'd swung by Donovan's place for a few belongings and were heading over to Tyler's.

Tyler was so tired he felt like he'd been hit by a truck but he had one last thing to take care of before he crashed for the next twelve hours or so.

"What's that?"

"I want you to stop by my parents' place. I want to tell them about us."

Donovan's mouth opened and Tyler was grateful they were stopped at a red light because Donovan wasn't looking at the road. "You sure you want to do that now?"

"Yes," Tyler said firmly. "I want to tell them. Unless you don't want me to, Sir."

Donovan blinked. "Of course I do. If you're ready, we'll do it now."

Less than ten minutes later, Donovan pulled the truck up in front of Tyler's parents' home. "Do you want me to come in?"

Tyler hesitated. "Actually, maybe let me talk to them alone first. If that's okay?"

"Whatever you think is best." Donovan squeezed his fingers. "I'm here if you need me."

Tyler was almost too tired to be nervous as he hopped out of the truck and walked up the sidewalk. His dad looked confused when he opened the door.

"Sue, Ty's here," he called out. "Did you know he was stopping by?"

"No." Tyler's mom came out of the living room. "What are you doing here, honey?"

Tyler licked his lips. "Just want to talk to you for a few minutes."

"Sure. You want anything to drink?"

"No thanks."

A few minutes later, they were seated in the living room. From Tyler's spot on the couch, he could see the cab of his truck. He couldn't see Donovan clearly but knowing he was close helped. "I have something I want to tell you. I'm … I'm dating someone. The chef at the tavern. Donovan Ryan. He's … he's a man."

There. Bandage off in one quick rip.

"A man?" His father gave Tyler a puzzled look. "I don't understand. Where did that come from?"

Tyler shrugged. "I don't know, to be honest."

"So you've never dated a man before?"

"No," Tyler said honestly. "But once I got to know Donovan, I realized we were really good together." That was an extremely brief version of their relationship but it would have to do. "We've been seeing each other for almost six months now."

"So, you're gay?" His mother asked. A concerned frown crossed her face. "Why didn't you tell us before now, honey?"

"No." Tyler rubbed his head. "I'm not gay. I'm dating a man. I'm bisexual, I think. And I didn't tell you before now because I only figured it out myself."

"But you said you've been seeing this Donovan guy since June," she said. She pursed her lips.

"Oh." Tyler let out a relieved little laugh. "Well, I wanted to be sure it would work out before I made a big deal out of it."

"But it's a big deal?" His father asked.

"I love him, yes." Tyler swallowed hard. "And I can see a future with him."

"Oh, honey, that's wonderful." His mom rested a hand on his. "I am so happy for you."

His dad frowned. "I still don't understand where this came from. One day you're straight and now …"

Tyler sighed. His dad wasn't trying to be a dick, but this was the exact sort of thing Tyler had feared. "I wish I could make it easier to understand. I just … It seemed pretty fucking stupid to tell someone who was great for me no because … well, because I've always been one thing in the past. So, yeah, I was straight before. And now I'm something else. But it doesn't really matter, you know?" Tyler swallowed. "I know this is an adjustment for you, but I really am happier than I've ever been. I hope you can accept that, Dad."

His dad sighed. "You always did want to go your own way. If I had anything to say about it, you'd have been a plumber like me with a wife and kids, but I know I don't get any say in it."

"Well, I think it's turned out okay," Tyler said. "I don't regret my military service and I love my work at the tavern and being with Donovan. Kids are something we'll talk about eventually so that could maybe still happen. But either way, I'm happier than I've ever been."

"Good." His mom squeezed his arm. "That's all I want for you. Honestly. Your dad too."

His dad let out an unimpressed 'hmmph' but he nodded. "I guess we better meet him then."

A little of the worry slipped from Tyler's shoulders. "I'd like that. How about you come have dinner with us next week? We'll cook."

"You cook now?" His mom sounded so surprised that Tyler laughed aloud.

"A little bit. I'm getting better at it."

"Well, how 'bout that?" his dad said, a smile beginning to creep across his face. "Maybe he is good for you."

Tyler smiled. "He is. He really, really is."

EPILOGUE

"Just so you know, the party is winding down," Donovan said gently.

His grandmother turned to him with a guilty start and set down the wooden paddle she'd been inspecting. "Oh, I'm sorry. I was being nosy again, wasn't I?"

He grinned at her. His parents had driven her to his birthday party but when they were ready to leave, they discovered Grandma June had wandered off. Thankfully this time she was only in the kitchen.

He and Tyler had moved in together recently and Donovan had taken over the space. Tyler hadn't argued. It was now filled to the brim with his cooking tools and they'd already done a scene to christen it. He knew their family and friends were surprised they'd taken that step so quickly but when it was right, it was right. Neither of them wanted to waste any time. Life was far too short for that.

"A little bit nosy," Donovan agreed.

His grandmother pointed to the crêpe spatula. "Another Joseph Lynch piece?"

"Yes. I just bought that," he admitted. "Well, one identical to that. I don't store the new one in the kitchen though." He gave her a little wink.

He'd broken his original bedroom toy on Tyler's ass last week. Tyler had looked rather proud of himself after that. It happened sometimes, especially with wooden toys. It was less of a testament to how hard Donovan had been using it than how often he'd used it. Sometimes wooden tools had stress points that weakened over time.

Still, Tyler had threatened to frame it to prove how firm his ass was and how hard of a beating he could take. Donovan had rolled his eyes.

Fucking masochistic veterans.

His grandmother's smile widened. "I wondered why there were crêpes on the menu tonight."

He shook his head at her. "By the way, Mom and Dad want to leave soon, if you can tear yourself away from my cooking tools."

She laughed too. "Oh, I suppose I should go. It is late, and I have a breakfast date tomorrow."

"With friends or a date-date?"

"A date-date," she said. "I'm not getting any younger. Figure I might as well meet men for breakfast. Who knows, I could die by dinnertime."

"You're not going to die by dinnertime. But enjoy your date."

She grimaced. "I've been underwhelmed by most of them so far. None of them have much stamina. Nothing like your grandfather"

Donovan rubbed his forehead. "That's bound to happen when you're in your seventies."

"Oh, no, he was only sixty-three," she said. "He just couldn't keep up with me."

Donovan felt a sudden flash of sympathy for the men of Pendleton. "I hope tomorrow's date is better."

"Thank you." She tucked the spatula back in the white pottery crock where he usually stored it. "I do wish I could figure out who Joseph Lynch really is."

"Oh? What do you mean?"

"He's a bit of a mystery. Rumor has it he lives in Pendleton, but no one actually knows who he is. He designs and makes all of these tools, but he hires someone else to sell them at the farmers markets and festivals."

"Huh," Donovan said as he slipped his arm through his grandma's, steering her toward the front door. "Interesting."

As they approached, Donovan could hear Tyler talking to both sets of parents. Their friends were still in the living room. They'd kept the party dry, out of deference to Eddie, but he and Andrea had headed home with the kids a few hours ago, so Donovan suspected a few drinks would come out now. As long as everyone was safe about getting home, he and Tyler didn't mind.

"You really are so much happier now that you've found someone," his grandmother said with a pleased sigh. "I'm glad you finally found the right guy."

Donovan smiled, resting a hand on the back of Tyler's neck, and squeezed once. "Me too."

"Tyler Hewitt!" Donovan's voice thundered down the hall and Tyler grinned to himself. Oh yes, this had gone exactly as he'd planned.

Donovan pushed open the door of Tyler's office and glared at him. "Where are my strawberries?"

Tyler shrugged. "Needed them. We had a ton of daiquiri orders tonight."

"Oh, you did, huh?" Donovan crossed his arms over his chest and glared at him. "Well, you know what that means, don't you?"

Tyler shrugged as he stepped forward, waving a clipboard. "I have to fill out the form."

Donovan sputtered. "That is the least of it." He closed the distance between them until they were almost nose-to-nose. "Thirty minutes in the humbler."

Tyler squirmed, grateful the tavern was closed, and he and Donovan were the last two people there. "I thought we'd agreed on twenty."

"Thirty," Donovan said with a low growl. "And if you sass me again, I'll make it forty."

"I wouldn't dream of it." Tyler smirked.

Donovan narrowed his eyes. "Finish your work. I want you naked, bound, and begging me within the hour."

"Yes, Sir," Tyler said. "Anything you say, Chef."

"Anything I say, huh?" Donovan purred in Tyler's ear an hour or so later as he pressed him down onto the bench. He was still breathing hard from the grappling he'd had to do to get Tyler subdued tonight.

He'd been fired up. Pushy and mouthy and … Donovan let out a satisfied little growl as he secured Tyler's hands to the bench straps. Sexy as hell. Donovan loved this. He loved Tyler's easy submission. The way he looked to Donovan to lead. The way he surrendered and seemed grateful for the structure and guidance Donovan gave him. But he loved nights like this as much or maybe a little bit more. When Tyler challenged Donovan to be his very best.

They had lost none of the heat and unpredictability of their earliest scenes, only gained a sweetness that was so good it sometimes made it difficult for Donovan to speak past the lump in his throat.

Tonight, with Tyler stretched out over the bench, squirming as Donovan reached for the humbler and slipped his nuts through the hole in it, Donovan felt a sense of awe that he'd found someone like Tyler.

Someone so strong, he was more than Donovan's equal. Someone who had shown Donovan how to be a better Dom. He'd longed for something he thought he'd never find, only to discover that he could have more than he had ever dreamed.

He strapped Tyler's thighs to the bench and stood, grinning down at him. "Let's begin."

The first smack and subsequent howl made Donovan let out a deep sigh of contentment. "Oh, is it hurting already?" he teased. He smacked Tyler's thigh again, causing him to squirm and cry out as the movement made the torture to his balls that much more painful. "Just gotta warm you up, and then I'll break out the dragon's tail."

Tyler let out a low keening noise of desperation and Donovan laughed.

He spanked Tyler for a while, dragging the torture out. Now that he'd told him what he intended to do, it was worse to make him wait for it.

By the time Donovan stopped, Tyler's body shone with sweat and he panted hard.

"How are you feeling?" Donovan asked softly and ran a hand across Tyler's balls, cupping the abused flesh.

Tyler let out a tormented groan. "How the fuck do you think I'm feeling?"

"I think you're feeling very lucky to have a Dom like me."

Tyler stilled. "I am, Sir."

"I'm the lucky one." Donovan stroked down Tyler's back from his neck to the base of his spine, before reaching for the dragon's tail.

A quick flick of his wrist sent it zinging across Tyler's ass, leaving a red line in its wake. Donovan beamed at the unholy noise Tyler let out. Thank God they were in a well-insulated house, because Tyler was vocal as hell when he really let go.

Donovan did it again, striping Tyler's ass with hit after hit, as quickly as he dared, knowing just how much Tyler could take, delighting in his desperate cries of agony. When he was done, he knelt between Tyler's thighs and grabbed both cheeks, parting them, He dove between, licking and teasing at Tyler's hole, gripping the sore flesh of his ass and kneading it as he quickly worked him open with his tongue.

A slick of lube and he pushed inside, hearing Tyler's needy, panting breaths. Their balls slapped together, Tyler's still in the grip of the humbler, undoubtedly aching. That thought only made Donovan fuck him harder, trusting with absolute certainty that if Tyler needed him to stop, he'd let it be known.

But Tyler only panted and shoved back, body tensed as Donovan drove into him with a ferocity and desperation that took him by surprise every time.

"I love you," Donovan gasped, and he emptied inside Tyler, hands gripping, body shuddering, whole world going fuzzy and white.

"You too," Tyler slurred, his own body jerking helplessly with his release.

It took much too long for Donovan to release him from his bindings and free his balls but when he did, he drew Tyler down to the floor, cradling his head on his shoulder. Donovan stared up at the ceiling, sucking in lungsful of air as he stroked Tyler's damp hair and guided him into a kiss.

Tyler looked at him, his gray eyes unfathomably deep and glazed with contentment.

Donovan didn't have words but he could see everything he felt reflected back in Tyler's gaze, so he merely nuzzled closer and held him tight.

The following day, Tyler stared at himself in the mirror as he folded back the sleeve of his dark blue shirt. "Does this look okay?"

Donovan scrutinized him, then nodded. "Yes. You look perfect."

Tyler swallowed. He hadn't been sure what to wear tonight but he knew Donovan liked the way his best pair of jeans hugged his ass and the look of his midnight blue button-down on him so he'd gone with that.

Donovan slipped his arms around Tyler's waist and Tyler smiled.

They looked good together. Donovan's red hair and lean build contrasted with Tyler's dark hair and wider frame. He had a sudden thought that he'd like to see what they looked like when they played together. What he looked like on his knees as he took everything Donovan gave him.

"What are you smiling about?"

"Oh, just thinking about how good we look together. And how good for me you are, Sir." That word fell from Tyler's lips so easily these days he had to be careful not to let it slip out at work.

"I try." Donovan reached up to touch Tyler's day collar. It was simple, a dark metal chain that hooked onto an O-ring. It lay flat against his chest and tucked discreetly under the collar of his shirts. Even if it slipped out, it looked more decorative than kinky.

But Tyler loved it, nonetheless. No matter how chaotic or crazy his day got, Tyler always had the reminder that Donovan was with him.

"Ready for this one?" Donovan held up the thick leather band Tyler wore during scenes.

"Yes." Tyler had to take a deep breath. Because as much as he loved wearing it in private, this would be the first time he'd worn it in public.

"Kneel."

Tyler turned away from the mirror to face his Dom and sank to his knees, the gesture as easy as breathing now.

"You belong to me, Tyler Hewitt," Donovan said as he wrapped the collar firmly around his neck and secured it. He tugged on the silver D ring and smiled.

Tyler smiled up at him. "I'm yours, Sir."

The ritual and routine of the familiar exchange was soothing, allowing Tyler to slip into a different state of being. The world around them faded until he had tunnel vision and all he could see was Donovan.

Every day, when he walked into the tavern, everyone knew him as Tyler Hewitt, bar manager.

But tonight, he'd walk in as Donovan Ryan's submissive.

"It's okay to be nervous," Donovan said as Tyler pulled up to the tavern and put his truck in park.

"I know." Tyler licked his lips.

"We don't have to go in."

Tyler shook his head. "I want to go."

"Well, if you change your mind at any point, we can leave. Just tell me."

Tyler turned in his seat to look at him. "I don't think I'll want to but thank you, Sir."

"I'm always looking out for you, "Donovan said, running a hand across the back of his head with a smile.

Tyler nodded. *That* he was sure of.

Still, his heart beat double-time as they walked into the tavern. A few of the staff gave them curious glances as they passed, and Tyler kept his coat and scarf on until he was inside the private room. Like they'd discussed earlier.

He breathed a little easier once the door shut behind him. The room was half full, the munch already underway.

Tyler unwound the scarf. He shrugged off his jacket and felt like everyone must be watching him but when he glanced around, he only caught a glimpse of someone he didn't recognize who gave him a small, distracted smile before turning back to the person they were chatting with. Tyler hung the clothing over the back of a chair and turned to Donovan. "May I get you a drink, Sir?"

"Please. That Traverse City IPA if it's available."

"It should be," Tyler said with a little smile. "I made sure we had it on hand for tonight."

Donovan nodded, taking a seat in the chair next to Tyler's. "You're allowed one this evening."

"Yes, Sir. Thank you."

Tyler walked toward the small bar area, his heart still racing as he waited in line.

Not capable of submission. *Ha.* Look at him now.

Lacey was working the event tonight and there were a few people ahead of Tyler. Ordinarily, he'd have been tempted to slip behind the bar and help out but tonight he was at Donovan's beck and call. Subtly, of course. This was just a munch. But they'd talked about going to a play party someday. The thought made Tyler nervous but excited.

They didn't usually go this far with their dynamic. Where Tyler had to ask permission to have a beer, where Donovan made all the choices for Tyler. That wasn't something that worked for them on a day-to-day basis and Tyler was perfectly content with what they did have.

But tonight was something new, something they'd never tried before. A test of sorts, an opportunity to show how willing he was, when he'd been nothing but bratty and mouthy the night before. He shifted restlessly, his balls still aching faintly from the scene they'd done.

When Tyler reached the front of the line, Lacey greeted him with a confused smile. "Hey, I thought you had the day off."

"I do." Tyler tried not to fidget, wondering when she'd put the pieces together. "I'm not here to work."

"What are you doing here then …" Her words trailed off and her eyes went wide as her gaze landed on Tyler's throat where the black leather and silver ring were on display. "*Oh.* Never mind."

Tyler managed a faint smile. "Yeah."

"So, you and Donovan are …"

"Yep."

They'd come out as a couple to their co-workers shortly after Thanksgiving but clearly no one had picked up on the rest of it.

"Cool. Is this your first munch then?"

Tyler nodded. They'd talked about coming sooner but between the chaos of the holidays and finding a night when the munch was held that they could both get time off work it had taken a while. And some understanding from Rachael.

"Well, your secret's safe with me," Lacey said with a bright smile.

Tyler cleared his throat. "I appreciate that. It's not a huge secret, I just don't necessarily need all the bartenders and servers knowing what I'm up to in my personal life, you know? Not really work appropriate."

"I understand." Her smile was reassuring, and she made a little zipping motion over her lips. "So, what I can I get you?"

"Two of the Traverse City IPAs, please."

After Tyler paid for the beer and tipped her, he carried the cold bottles back to the table, setting one in front of Donovan. "Sir."

He looked up with a smile. "Thank you."

Tyler slipped into the seat beside him.

The woman across the table—the one he'd recognized from the gallery downtown at the mixer a few months ago—smiled at Tyler. "Hi. I'm Annette. This is my wife, Lydia."

Tyler shook both their hands.

"So, your Dom was telling me all about the scene you did last night. Sounds amazing."

Tyler's body heated. They'd discussed this ahead of time but it still made him squirm to think about people knowing exactly what Donovan did to him. But he liked that squirmy feeling so he nodded. "It was."

Annette gave them a curious look. "How long have you two been together?"

"Dating, since June. I collared him in November." Donovan draped an arm across the back of Tyler's chair.

"Aww you're still new," she cooed. "It's been ages for me and my wife, so I always love to see new couples."

Tyler smiled and the anxiety slipped away. Sitting beside Donovan, wearing his collar, he'd never felt more right.

This time last year, he'd never have dreamed he could tolerate spending time with Donovan, much less be here at a munch like this as his collared submissive. But there was no question that he was finally where he belonged.

A while later, Tyler pressed his shoulder against Donovan's to whisper in his ear. "Is that who I think it is?"

Donovan followed Tyler's gaze and caught sight of Jude standing in the doorway, a hesitant expression on his face. A handsome older man with silvery hair and a beard stood on one side of Jude, one hand on his shoulder. A younger guy, big and dark haired, hung back a bit behind them both.

Jude turned back to smile reassuringly at the younger guy, guiding him into the room with a possessive hand on his back.

Huh.

Donovan shook his head and leaned in to speak in Tyler's ear. "Well, more power to them if they can make a three-way relationship work," he said softly.

"You sure you haven't changed your mind on wanting one?"

Donovan glared and hooked a finger through Tyler's collar at the back, making it press against his throat, not enough to restrict his breathing, just a warning.

"I'm sure. You're more than enough work for me," he teased.

Tyler let out a little noise of disagreement. "Excuse you. I'm very well behaved, Sir."

"You weren't last night."

Tyler's expression turned to one of outrage. "You told me to act up!"

It had been such a hot scene. It had been a while since they'd had the time to do longer, more intense play and Donovan had taken his time planning it. They'd talked it out ahead of time and he'd encouraged Tyler to get bratty, to push his buttons and argue until Donovan wrestled him to the ground and cuffed him. He'd tied him up after that, Tyler struggling the whole time, until he'd gotten him fully immobile. He'd had his wicked way with him then and left them both gloriously wrecked and happy.

Donovan reached out, squeezing a spot on Tyler's thigh that he knew he'd left tender, and Tyler shot him a glance that was both a warning and filled with heat.

Donovan just grinned. Winding each other up was definitely still a part of their dynamic and Donovan wouldn't have it any other way.

Tyler froze, then patted his pocket. "I have a message, Sir. May I check it?"

"Of course."

Tyler still worried about calls from Eddie, but he had been doing well. Shortly after being released from the hospital, he'd been admitted to an inpatient program. It had been a slow recovery and Donovan knew it chafed at Tyler that he couldn't talk to him for most of it, but the program had appeared to do Eddie good.

The last time Donovan and Tyler had gone up to Grand Rapids to see him, he was back home. He'd gained some weight and his face looked much healthier.

He'd taken Donovan up on his offer to have Kate Ryan defend him in court and she'd arranged for a plea deal. Eddie had been charged with a relatively minor count of reckless driving. Her impassioned speech about his military history, mental health struggles, and willingness to enter rehab had left Eddie with a suspended license and probation. Probably the best he could hope for under the circumstances.

It would be a long while before Andrea, Tyler, and the rest of the guys could fully relax and trust that Eddie was on the road to recovery, and there was always the possibility of him backsliding. Donovan had reminded Tyler it wasn't a linear path. But Donovan was hopeful for all of them.

Now, he was relieved to see Tyler roll his eyes and shake his head at his screen before he typed out a quick message. When he was done, he tucked his phone back in his pocket.

"Good news?" Donovan asked.

"Just the guys being idiots." He looked at Donovan. "That reminds me. I'm supposed to ask if you want to go on our next camping trip."

"I appreciate the offer," Donovan said. He dragged his fingertips down Tyler's spine, enjoying the way he quivered in response. "But no. This will be the first one since Eddie got back and I think the five of you should just enjoy your time together. Tell them thank you, though. I'll come another time."

"Okay." Tyler's smile was easy. "I'll pass that along."

Donovan tuned back into the conversation across the table.

"I was disappointed by the selection at KinkCon this year," Annette said with a frown. "Very few good vendors." The group around them been talking for a while about implements and who to buy from. Donovan had asked them to send him the links to several sites.

"Oh, I got this great paddle recently," Donovan said to Annette. "Let me show you."

He reached for his phone but was surprised to find his pocket empty. He checked his jacket but didn't find it there either. He remembered setting it on the console in the truck on the drive there and suspected he'd been too focused on Tyler and making sure he was okay to remember to grab it.

He rose to his feet and Tyler shot him a questioning look. "Just need to run out to the truck. Keys?" Tyler fished them out of his pocket and handed them over. "I'll be back in a minute."

Donovan passed by Jude's table as he left the room and he acknowledged Donovan with a nod. The silver fox looked up too and Donovan felt a flicker of recognition. God, he looked familiar, but Donovan couldn't place him. Maybe he recognized him from around town or perhaps he'd dined at the tavern before.

Donovan had retrieved his phone and was halfway back to the building before he spotted Jude striding toward him. "Wait up a sec."

Donovan raised an eyebrow at his ex. "What do you want, Jude?" he asked warily. He hadn't been surprised to see him at the munch tonight, though he'd been hoping to avoid him.

"To apologize." He jogged toward Donovan and stopped a few feet from him. His hair flopped over his forehead, and he pushed it back with an annoyed little flick of his hand.

"Oh. For what?"

"For being a pushy asshole before." He grimaced. "Once I got over being hurt, I realized you were right. I was way out of line."

"Okay."

"I was feeling really shitty about where I was at."

"You aren't now?"

Jude shrugged. "Things are looking up for me. It's given me a slightly different perspective."

"Huh. Does this have anything to do with the two guys you were talking to pretty intently earlier?"

Jude gave him a half-smile. "It might."

"The silver fox looked familiar, and it just hit me who he is. Isn't he a friend of the family? I swear I remember seeing him at parties your parents held, and I know we spoke a few times."

"Yeah." Jude dragged a hand through his hair. "He is. My dad's best friend actually."

Donovan winced. "Wow. And he's … kinky?"

"Logan? Yes. I mean, I'd never have guessed it, but it turns out he very much is."

"Didn't he have a wife?" Donovan had a vague memory of a blonde woman on his arm.

"*Did* being the operative word," Jude said. "They've been divorced quite a while."

"Still. Getting involved with your dad's friend … that's not going to be easy."

"I know."

"What about the other guy?"

"It's complicated too."

Donovan coughed. "You don't say." Combining any three people would be.

"You were the one who told me to give it a shot." His tone turned a little defensive.

"How's that?"

"You said, 'if you want a triad with a Dom, go find it'."

"Ahh." Donovan considered the idea. "I had no idea you intended to follow my advice to the letter but good for you. I hope you're happy." He meant that with all sincerity. "I genuinely wish you the best."

Jude smiled faintly. "Thanks. Looks like things are working out with you and Tyler. You sure didn't waste any time claiming him."

"Why should I? Life is short. You never know what's going to happen."

"When did you get so philosophical?"

Donovan shrugged.

"You're happy though? He's what you wanted?"

"He is." Donovan smiled, his heart light in a way he'd never experienced before. "He's everything I've ever dreamed of."

"I'm glad." For the first time in years, there was peace on Jude's face. "I want you to be happy."

"I am," Donovan said with a smile. "I truly am."

"There you are, Sir." Tyler smiled at Donovan as he took a seat beside him again. "Thought you got lost."

"No." Donovan chuckled. "Just ran into Jude."

"I noticed he slipped out and wondered if he'd ambushed you. Everything okay?" He rested a hand on Donovan's thigh.

"Yes." Donovan smiled. "He's happy, I'm happy. It's all good, I promise."

"I'm glad. Did you find your phone?"

"I did." Donovan pulled it out and scrolled through until he found the picture of the paddle he'd bought Tyler for Christmas. He held his phone out to Annette. "This is the piece I bought."

"Ooh that's gorgeous. Look, Lydia."

"Oh God that looks painful," Lydia said but she sounded delighted. "Please, can we get it, Mistress?"

They all laughed, and Donovan glanced over at Tyler to see a smile stretched wide across his face. It hit him square in the chest.

"I love you," he said roughly.

"Love you too," Tyler whispered softly. He reached out and touched Donovan's cheek, eyes alight with happiness and wonder. "Yours and only yours," Tyler whispered.

Donovan had to blink hard for a moment because he was so happy the feelings were almost too much to contain.

Contentment filled him at the sight of Tyler beside him, wearing his collar.

Right where he belonged.

THE END

Looking for more books in the Naughty in Pendleton Series? check out *Flipping the Switch*!

The next book in the series features Jude, a feisty, irreverent switch. Tony, a sweet submissive with a secret. And Logan, the silver fox Dom who just happens to be Jude's father's best friend. Could three be the perfect number for true love?

Grab it now!

***

If you loved Donovan and Tyler together, check out *Showing His Strength*, a FREE dirty and sweet outtake that offers another glimpse of their future together.

Read it here!

BRIGHAM'S BOOKS

Pendleton Bay Books

Visit the fictional small town of Pendleton Bay on the shores of Lake Michigan. All books set in this universe can be read as standalones but characters from other books/series may appear from time to time.

There are three series set within the Pendleton Bay Universe.

Naughty in Pendleton Series

An ongoing m/m romance series set in the town of Pendleton Bay with characters exploring the kinkier side of romance. BDSM elements will appear in all books.

Date in a Pinch: When chemistry teacher Neil gets an unexpected delivery at the high school where he works, he's mortified when his crush, Alexander, sees the contents. Curious but inexperienced with kink, Neil has no idea how to live out his fantasies until the hot lit teacher offers a helping hand

***Embracing His Shame*:** Forrest, the town's accountant, may look uptight but he's anything but. When he offers local mechanic, Jarod, an indecent proposal to fulfill his shameful fantasies, Forrest will have to decide if he's willing to give Jarod a chance to show him that he can have love *and* the kink he longs for.

Made to Order: Donovan, head chef at the Hawk Point Tavern, loves to be in charge in the kitchen *and* in the bedroom. Tyler, a former solider, is pretty sure he's straight and definitely only into kink if he's the one dishing it out. Until he and Donovan start butting heads about who is calling the shots …

Flipping the Switch: Jude is a feisty, irreverent switch, longing for the perfect relationship that will allow him to be himself. Tony is a sweet submissive with a stressful home life and secret career. And Logan, the silver fox Dom who has a bag full of toys and no one to play with. Oh, and he just happens to be Jude's father's best friend. Could three be the perfect number for true love?

Flirty in Pendleton Series

An ongoing m/m romance series set in the town of Pendleton Bay.

***Geeks, Nerds, and Cuddles*:** Re-release 2021

***Doc Brodie and the Big, Purple Cat Toy*:** Re-release 2021

Poly in Pendleton Series

An ongoing m/m/f romance series set in the town of Pendleton Bay.

Three Shots: Reeve, a local musician, and Grant, a computer designer, have fun in bed together but pursuing a relationship never feels quite right until they meet tavern owner Rachael and try to figure out how to be poly in the small town of Pendleton Bay.

Between the Studs: Re-release 2021

Peachtree Books

Visit the real life city of Atlanta, Georgia. All books in this universe can be read as standalone but characters from both series do crossover.

There are two series set with the Peachtree Universe.

The Peachtree Series

Complete, continuous m/m series featuring an age gap, light kink, and found family

Off-Balance: Coworkers Russ & Stephen meet over a spilled cup of coffee and navigate the complexities of a nineteen-year age gap, a big difference in income, and the death of Stephen's estranged father.

Love in the Balance: Their story continues as Russ introduces Stephen to his family, searches for his absent mother, and asks Stephen to marry him.

Full Balance: They navigate new challenges as they take in a teenage foster boy named Austin and decide to make him a permanent part of their family.

Peachtree Place

Standalone m/m books in the same universe as The Peachtree Series

Trust the Connection: Evan & Jeremy find a love that will heal both their scars in this slow-burn, age-gap romance about living with a disability, believing in yourself, and building the family you always wanted.

The Midwest Series

Complete m/m series featuring four couples. Stories intertwine but can be read as standalones. Opposites attract m/m sports romance with numerous bisexual characters.

Bully & Exit: Drama geek Caleb is sure he'll never forgive Nathan, the hockey player who dumped him in high school, until he learns the real reason why in this slow-burn, second-chance new adult romance. ALSO AVAILABLE IN AUDIO.

Push & Pull: Lowell & Brent have nothing in common when they leave on a summer road trip, but by the end, the makeup-wearing fashionista and the macho hockey player will realize they're perfect for each other in this enemies to lovers, slow-burn story about acceptance.

Touch & Go: Micah, a closeted pro pitcher, and Justin, a laid-back physical therapist, have nothing in common but when Micah blows out his shoulder, he'll have to choose which he wants more: baseball or love? An enemies to lovers, out for you romance.

Advance & Retreat: When fate brings Ian and Ricky together, a college swimmer will have to figure out how to reached for the gold without losing the sweet hotel manager who lights up the stage as sizzling drag queen Rosie Riveting. An age gap sports romance with a gender fluid character.

The West Hills

Standalone m/m series featuring three different couples

The Ghosts Between Us: Losing his brother in a devastating accident sends Chris spiraling into grief. The last person he expects to find comfort in is his brother's secret boyfriend, Elliot, in this slow burn, hurt/comfort romance.

Tidal Series – Co-authored with K Evan Coles

A complete, continuous m/m duology that takes Riley & Carter from best friends to lovers in this slow-burn romance featuring the sons of two wealthy Manhattan families.

Wake: After a decade and a half of lying to himself and everyone around him, Riley slowly come to terms with his sexuality and his feelings for his best friend, Carter, shattering their friendship.

Calm: Carter reaches his own realization and they slowly build the relationship they've been denying for so long.

Speakeasy Series – Co-authored with K Evan Coles

Complete, standalone m/m series featuring characters from the Tidal universe

With a Twist: After Will learns of his estranged father's cancer diagnosis, he returns home and slowly mends fences with him and falls in love with his father's colleague, David. Enemies to lovers, opposites attract, interracial romance.

Extra Dirty: Wealthy, pansexual businessman Jesse is perfectly happy living his life to the fullest with no strings attached, but when he meets Cam, a music teacher and DJ, he'll find that some strings are worth hanging onto in this age-gap, opposites-attract romance.

Behind the Stick: Speakeasy owner and bartender Kyle has taken a break from dating when he's rescued by Harlem firefighter Luka. Interracial romance and hurt/comfort.

Straight Up: When hot, tattooed biker chef Stuart meets quiet and serious Malcolm, they both have secrets they're hiding. Gray ace, bisexual awakening, lingerie kink.

The Williamsville Inn

Standalone m/m holiday romances in a shared universe with Hank Edwards

Snowstorms and Second Chances: Erik and Seth don't hit it off at first, but when a snowstorm leads to them sharing a room at a hotel, Erik discovers a whole new side of himself and his feelings about the holidays. A forced-proximity, bisexual-awakening romance with a second chance at happiness.

The Cupcake Conundrum: Adrian comes face to face with the biggest mistake of his past, Ajay, a hookup who he ghosted on. He'll have to make amends and win Jay's heart back in this single dad, second-chance interracial romance.

Colors Series

A continuous f/f series featuring a bisexual character and opposites attract trope

A Brighter Palette: When Annie, a struggling American freelance writer, meets Siobhán, a successful Irish painter living in Boston, the heat between them is undeniable, but is it enough to build something that will last?

***The Greenest Isle**:* After Siobhán's father has a heart attack, she and Annie travel to Ireland to care for him. Their relationship is tested as they navigate living in a new place and healing old wounds.

Standalone Books

Baby, It's Cold Inside: Meeting Nate's parents doesn't go at all like Emerson planned. But there might be a Christmas miracle for the two of them before the visit is through in this sweet and funny m/m holiday romance.

Bromantic Getaway: Spencer is sure he's straight. But when an off-hand comment sends him tumbling into the realization he's in love with his best friend Devin, he'll have to turn a romantic vacation meant for his ex into the perfect opportunity to grab the love that's always been right in front of them in this best friends to lovers bi awakening m/m romance.

Cabin Fever: Kevin's best friend's dad is definitely off-limits. But he and Drew about to spend a week alone in a cabin the week before Christmas. And Kevin's never been any good at resisting temptation. An age gap, best friend's father m/m holiday romance.

Corked: A sommelier and a wine distributor clash in this enemies to lovers, age-gap m/m romance that takes Sean &

Lucas from a restaurant in Chicago to owning a winery in Traverse City.

***Inked in Blood:* Co-Authored with K Evan Coles** An unexpected event changes the life and death of a sexy, tattooed vampire named Jeff and Santiago, a tattoo artist with a secret. A paranormal, age-gap m/m romance.

Love in the Produce Aisle: Tyler's a disaster when it comes to cooking, but when Michael swoops in to rescue him, it's more than just the kitchen that's hot in this m/m opposites-attract short story.

Seeking Warmth: When Benny gets out of juvie, he's lost all hope for a future for him or his sister, but the help of his ex-boyfriend Scott will show him that hope and love still exist in this m/m YA novel about second chances.

The French Toast Emergencies: A series of grocery story mishaps leads to Arthur and Samuel sharing more than a loaf of bread during a sudden snowstorm in this forced-proximity m/m short story.

The Soldier Next Door: When Travis agrees to keep an eye on the guy next door for a few weeks while his parents are out of town, he never expects to fall in love with a soldier heading off to war. An age-gap m/m novella.

ABOUT THE AUTHOR

Brigham Vaughn is on the adventure of a lifetime as a full-time author. She devours books at an alarming rate and hasn't let her short arms and long torso stop her from doing yoga. She makes a killer key lime pie, hates green peppers, and loves wine tasting tours. A collector of vintage Nancy Drew books and green glassware, she enjoys poking around in antique shops and refinishing thrift store furniture. An avid photographer, she dreams of traveling the world and she can't wait to discover everything else life has to offer her.

Her books range from short stories to novellas to novels. They explore gay, bisexual, lesbian, and polyamorous romance in contemporary settings.

Want to read more of her work? Check it out on BookBub!

For news of new releases and sales, join her newsletter or follow on BookBub!

If you'd like to become an ARC reader, take part in giveaways, and get all of the latest news, please join her reader group, Brigham's Book Nerds. She'd love to have you there!

Made in the USA
Monee, IL
17 July 2021

73796452R00229